REALM
—OF THE—
SKYBORNE

REALM OF THE SKYBORNE
Copyright © 2022 by Jennifer M. Waldrop

Cover Design and Interior Formatting: Damonza.com
Editing: Roxana Coumans, Roth Notions
Proofreading: Belle Manuel
www.jennifermwaldrop.com
July House Publishing | Your story, your way

www.julyhousepublishing.com

REALM
OF THE
SKYBORNE

SKYBORNE SERIES BOOK TWO

JENNIFER M. WALDROP

JULY HOUSE PUBLISHING

The Far Isle
North Settlement
Western Settlement
Leeward Isle
Adrina
Banished Arrival Location
Observatory Town
Southern Settlement
Idia

Characters from REALM OF THE BANISHED

Eastdow

Regent Ephrem Kalederan —— Renia (SHAL) Kalederan

Carina Kalederan   Balene Kalederan   Judith Kalederan   Nayla Shal

Drakestone

Regent Karish Dsiban —— Ovia Dsiban

Malik Dsiban   Darius Dsiban

Seabrook

Regent Femi Temmar —— Alrun Temmar

Seeley Temmar

Arborvale

Regent Torin Tiernach —— *Elain Tiernach*

Vera Tiernach   *Conall Tiernach*

Monterra

Regius Kymar Shal —— *Salene Shal*   Anya Shal

Renia (SHAL) Kalederan   Berith Shal   Regius Emerson (Unknown)

Sundale

Parents Deceased

Asha Chander   Regent Ian Chander

Other Characters:
Uden, Master of the Swath
Meethra, Godfly
A1, Emerson's Pet

Felicia, Nayla's attendant
Bara, Seeley's messenger
Becca, battlefield healer

Characters from REALM OF THE SKYBORNE

Idia

Chancellor Vitis Innar —— Ex-Wife

Rhijn Innar

Other Characters:
Everly, Healer, Rhijn's Cousin
Kelvin, Energy Systems Director
Kellis, Political Strategist
Leah, Council Member
Rhea, Council Member
Pollux, Council Member

PROLOGUE

"I HOPE YOU'RE ENJOYING your stay, though it is *dank* down here," a silky, feline-like voice echoed from down the corridor.

Moisture dripped from the damp stones, plopping into a small puddle, mimicking the tempo of the boot impatiently tapping, the only other sound in the cavern.

The prisoner didn't answer. He stood with his arms crossed over his chest and his lips pressed into a hard line as a svelte female figure sauntered into view.

"What's this about, Emerson?" Darius demanded. "Please tell me this isn't to satisfy another one of your creepy location fantasies. You know I'd do anything for you, but this is extreme, not to mention dirty. As in filth." He gestured to a stinking pile of hay rotting in the corner.

"Funny, this particular cell has been inhabited by both of my lovers now." A half-crazed giggle escaped Emerson's lips as she changed the subject.

Darius exhaled loudly, tilting his head back and running his fingers through his long charcoal hair in exasperation.

"So that's what this is about?" he asked. "I promise, I was only doing what I had to do."

"You're lying," Emerson bit back, not letting the pouty glint in his dark eyes or his boyish features hiding under his neat facial hair sway her.

Darius shook his head, opening his mouth to protest.

"Aren't you curious how I know you're lying?" she asked.

"Emerson, please. It's you and me. She meant nothing to me. Please don't lose focus."

"It seems you're the one who lost focus. Not me. And I asked you a question." The slim fingers Emerson had wrapped around the bars of Darius's cell were turning white at the knuckles. "You weren't only doing what you had to do. You enjoyed it, craved it, even. Craved *her*."

"How are you so certain?" he obliged.

"Because, I had her too." Emerson tilted her head to the side, blushing. "And now she's all I can think about. Think of it, we could have made quite the threesome."

"She's my half-sister," Darius said, wrinkling his nose. "Had I known…"

"I figured that'd make *you* want her even more. It's depraved. I'm not sure I can be with you after that."

Darius reached through the bars and tugged on Emerson's waist, bringing their bodies as close as they could be with rusted steel between them. "Let me out of this cell, and I promise I'll make it up to you. You can still want me. Let me show you," he said, running calloused hands across the thick skirting that staved off the bite of the crisp mountain air covering her backside.

"She told me what you said to her, Darius," Emerson hissed, pulling away. "That you *loved* her."

Darius froze. "I only told her what I thought she wanted to hear," he spelled out carefully.

"You've been playing me for a fool, my love." Emerson stroked a burgundy nail across Darius's stubble. He reached for her hand as she pulled it back through the rusted bars of his entrapment.

"I'd never do such a thing, Emerson. I—"

"It's *Regius* now. And not only did you make me look a fool, you lost my favorite new toy. I sent my most valuable asset to save your ass from that prison in Seabrook, and you not only failed to recover the ember, but our hero as well. I should kill you."

"I'll make it up to you." The male's usually smooth voice trembled.

"Emer—Regius, at your side, we'd be unstoppable. Please let me give you what you need."

She glared at him. She knew how he was now. *Disloyal.* Still, she couldn't help but remember the way his supple lips felt between her thighs.

Darius ran his tongue across his upper lip, reading her thoughts. "Regius," he purred. "Let me make it up to you."

"How do you plan to do that, Darius? Nayla and her friends aren't even in this realm anymore." Emerson threw her hands into the air, spinning to walk down the corridor.

"But she'll come back. She has to," Darius yelled down the hallway. "And when she does, we can…"

&

Darius's voice faded as Emerson stormed out of the prison deep in the mines. Whatever he was saying didn't matter. Apparently, she was on her own now, and she had work to do.

The mines, which served as her laboratory, were in disarray since Nayla had used her power to collapse the entrance. Fortunately, only the outer rooms and the facade had taken damage, she thought, stopping to look back across the wooden slat bridge which was strung across the chasm from the keep to the mine's entrance.

Having the hanging bridge constructed had been the first thing she'd done after Nayla escaped, so she could access the most important area in all of the frigid northern territory, Monterra. And she had only lost a few workers during the bridge's perilous construction. None of her children had been killed. That might have changed things.

It seemed amusing *at the time* to allow her to flee.

"I thought we could have had fun, her running, me chasing," she mused to no one in particular as she made her way across the other half of the hanging bridge. She sighed and clasped the temporary rope handrail as the bridge swayed on a draft coming from the long, narrow slit in the structure's roof, which hid the mines and provided a convenient passageway for A1 and her babies to fly from.

"Mother," A1 chirped as it flew up and perched on her shoulder.

"Ouch," she swatted her creature away. "Lovely. You made me bleed," she said, looking at the tears in the shoulder of her emerald frock and the bright red blood spreading across the fabric.

"I told you not to do that." Emerson huffed as she ran her fingers across the wounds, using her healing power to stitch the skin back together. "And don't think I don't hold you partially responsible." She poked A1's belly with her pointed red nail.

"Mother," the creature chirped in apology, flapping its peach fleshy wings to keep up with her.

"We should have been able to stop her before she made it to the pass. But it seems she gained some sort of immunity to your influence, pet."

Emerson blew past keep workers and guards barking orders, demanding an audience with her advisors as she made her way to the main meeting chamber where a large intricately carved mahogany desk stood as the focal point in the room. A large tapestry hung behind it, depicting the jagged mountain range that surrounded the territory seat of Monterra. All other seating, side tables and ornamentation was sparse, but each piece was crafted with the same detail and in the Monterra colors of carmine and black.

She snapped her fingers as she strode in and a head guard and messenger followed her, along with several creatures who'd been perched on squat pedestals placed right outside the single door for them.

Standing behind the imposing desk, which only made her look more delicate, Emerson clicked her nails across the surface, waiting as her stepfather's advisors filed into the room.

Levi, a particularly absent-minded advisor, shuffled in last, pulling the door closed behind him, muttering something to himself. The insubstantial male was a progressive mess. Today was no different. His dull mud-colored robes sagged around his thin frame and stick-straight white hair sprang from his head in every direction.

Emerson huffed in agitation, smoothing her burgundy-streaked chestnut locks back from her face. "What, Levi? I'm losing patience."

"Well, I picked up your coronet from the jeweler, Regius, and I'm afraid it may not fit." Levi set the black box down and lifted the lid, worrying his hands as he surveyed the contents. "I'm afraid they've crafted it to the measurements of a male's head."

This was just one of the many slights delivered to her after Regius Kymar's death, seemingly in protest to her ruling instead of her younger stepbrother and the rightful heir, Berith.

Oh, Berith, if you only knew, Emerson thought. She'd immediately buried him in paperwork, so he hardly had time to question the circumstances of his father's death or her lineage. To the knowledge of everyone outside of the late Regius and his second wife, her mother Anya, Emerson was the rightful heir as Kymar's second full blooded daughter.

His first daughter, who he had with his previous wife, had gone missing almost thirty years prior. That didn't stop them from questioning Emerson's right to rule, however, as many of the territories had converted to a patriarchal lineage and more than a few of the elder males in Monterra seemed inclined to do the same, favoring Berith over her.

"I told you I don't care about such things," she said, slamming the lid on the box. "As if a ring of metal with a chunk of decaying Cerisium affixed to it could possibly interest me."

The insignificant male appeared shaken at her dismissal, taking the closed box and hiding it behind his back, as if he hadn't been the one to bring it.

"I have some items that demand immediate action," she continued, ignoring him. "I've learned quite a few things from our prisoner. Here is what I need."

The messenger took furious notes, and occasionally asked Emerson to slow down so he could catch up.

She paused, grabbing a sheet of paper from a stack of blank pages, and began scribbling something down. "What's Seabrook's Regent's name?" she asked.

"Femi Temmar, I believe," an advisor spoke up.

"Right." She swept her hand across the page, finishing her note with a flourishing signature. She briskly folded the paper into thirds and handed the document to the messenger to seal. "That should go to Karish immediately. And tell your carrier to convey to Karish he complies or I will end his son."

"But Emerson, Regius Kymar wouldn't—"

"Do I look like Kymar?" Emerson snapped. "Kymar is dead. His murderer has escaped to a different realm. There is a possible antidote to my creature's dusting, which I've worked tirelessly for years to create. And the ember is missing!" she screamed. "Do you think I give a shit about how Kymar would have handled this or a silly metal band showing my position. In case I'm being unclear, Kymar never had to deal with anything like this. He was content to sit on his hands while Karish kept the ember at Drakestone and periodically got their seerers killed off by their ridiculous prophecies trying to use it. At least Torin had the guts to send a spy in to steal it. And now a female whose origin is unclear, is presumably in Idia, with the *ember*, without *me!*"

She slammed her fists onto the desk. An ink bottle tipped over and ink spilled onto the stack of blank papers sitting at the corner. Emerson grimaced and picked the vessel up, chunking it across the room. Black ink splattered on the wall where it struck.

All six advisors slowly turned to the dark mess, then back to their Regius.

The messenger fumbled back through the door after sending her letter and over to the spilled ink, making more of a mess trying to clean the stain off the wall with sheets of paper.

"Levi, I want you and the rest of my advisors to discover how Nayla was able to resist my creature's dust. Was it her connection to the ember or has someone developed an antidote?"

"They would have to have a highly skilled healer and access to a source of Cerisium to craft an antidote," Levi said, shifting from foot to foot. "And the only source of Cerisium on this continent is our mines, Regius."

"That would imply a leak," another advisor inserted.

"I know what it would imply," Emerson barked. "I expect you imbeciles to figure out who that is and bring them to me."

She turned to A1 who was hovering over her shoulder. "And you my pet will send your B level brothers and sisters to locate the godflies. It is very important that you don't alert them to your presence. I just need to know where they've gone, *for now*."

Emerson glanced at the small square window near the ink spill that she had cut into the wall in the meeting chamber, large enough for her creatures to slip through. The Light Star was setting when she began her meeting and had now sunk below the horizon. She walked over and leaned against the ledge, staring at the first of the three moons now visible, and sighed.

"You're dismissed," she said without turning. Eight pairs of boots clopped across the room and toward the door.

"Wait," she called, smiling as eight males immediately halted at her command. *That* was power, she thought, as the heady sensation flowed across her awareness. "Not you all, just A1," Emerson instructed, and they continued on, leaving her alone with her favorite creature.

"Pet, bring my prisoner to my room. I have something he can help me with."

∾

A knock at the door alerted Emerson to her lover's presence. He was so predictable. She'd known the first thing he'd do was come to her the moment he thought he was free. It was sweet. *Almost.*

"Do you think I'll ever forgive you?" she asked, as Darius let himself in. Four of her A-level creatures hovered in a square perimeter around him, taloned fingers at the ready.

"I hope you can." Darius walked over to her as she sat at a vanity in front of a smokey mirror. He looked at her in it, pressing her to answer the question, as he bent forward, sliding the neckline of her emerald velvet robe aside and pressed a kiss to her exposed collarbone.

"Makers, you smell. Go bathe," she coughed, brushing him away.

"If I've been released, then why are these things following me around?" Darius asked as he emerged from the bathroom a while later, gesturing to the flapping creatures circling him.

"Who said I released you?" Emerson asked in mocking sweetness, raising an eyebrow at him.

He blinked as understanding sunk in. "Well, I suppose your bed is better than that cell."

Darius's swift hands caught the hairbrush she sent sailing toward him. He set it down on the desk. His exposed flesh rippled and flexed as he laughed. Damn the selfish bastard for being so good looking, she thought, her eyes dipping to the V leading below his hips. Only a few short steps, and he slammed his tall body into hers. Her legs instinctively wrapped around his waist as he roughly crushed her against the wall, showing no care for her lithe form.

"I guess I'll have to work off my penance then, Regius," Darius growled into her ear.

Emerson's mouth was swollen by the time she lay back on her bed, propping herself up on a pile of plush red pillows. He wasn't Nayla, but she didn't care. She had needs, and he was available, so she spread her knees and slowly opened the velvet robe, teasing her prisoner.

"Are you ready to make it up to me, Darius? Even though you're only my second choice?" she taunted, voice radiating heat and power.

Darius smiled coquettishly and crawled up from the foot of the bed and stopped between her open legs. "I think it will only take a couple thrusts to get from second to first." Cocky as ever, he reached down and untucked the towel which had been wrapped around his waist, exposing his thick arousal.

Emerson emitted a throaty laugh. "Not so fast," she said, and pointed between his full lips and the apex of her thighs. A wicked grin grew across her face as Darius's mouth dipped between her legs. "You have some work to do first."

CHAPTER ONE

I THREW UP A hand to shield my eyes. They sluggishly adjusted between the dim room at the traveler's inn in Seabrook's territory and this new bright world my companions and I successfully landed in. I dropped into a crouch this time, thankfully, instead of hitting my ass like I'd done before in the Swath. Heat radiated off the soft sand beneath my boots, causing sweat to bead on my chest and neck. Squinting, I lowered my palm hiding the midday Light Star, and attempted to assess our new surroundings.

An imposing figure stepped into view, blocking the light star which created a halo around their shadowed frame. I lurched back as I realized the figure brandished a long pole which they'd extended the pointed end downward to meet my throat.

Shit.

An immediate ambush was not at all what I was expecting. I threw up a shield around me and my companion's forms, seeking them in the energy tapestry surrounding us. I accounted for each of their essences, breathing a sigh of relief.

I turned back to the threat. The Skyborne above me poked at the hard line of air vibrating in front of his pole and chuckled as my eyes focused. I got my first good look at him. Gasping, I fell backward, letting the shield waver. Nothing might have prepared me for the Idian who stood above me. I scrambled back to my feet, but a distinct whimper sounded inside my shield.

"Nayla," Conall cried, his voice rough and panicked. Was he hurt?

I couldn't tear my eyes away from the Skyborne who'd haunted and tantalized my dreams for months now. It couldn't be him. Our gazes were locked and in that moment the sensation of recognition crawled across my skin, though he quickly hid his expression behind a serene facade. *How was this possible?* My breath caught, heart hammering in my chest. His elevated stature, sharp angular features, pale hair and piercing blue eyes were the same as they'd been in my dreams. He stood tall, slender, yet unmistakably fit. Sinewy muscle tensed beneath his garments as he assessed me withdrawing the weapon.

"*No,*" he breathed, blond eyebrows coming together, creating a deep crease between them.

"Nayla, come quick. It's Conall," Malik demanded. "His leg, there's too much blood. I think he's broken his femur and tore an artery."

Conall was hurt. That snapped me out of the stunned state of inaction fixing me in place. I whipped around, scrambling over to where Conall lay. Malik was desperately trying to staunch the bleeding, pressing his hands down heavily over the wound.

"Nayla, this can't be happening," Conall said, regret and pain coating his quivering voice. His soft brown eyes blinked up at me from his wan face, pleading.

"She'll heal you, Conall," Malik reassured. "Stay with us."

Time stilled, and I filtered through the sounds in our vicinity. I moved past the roaring thud of my own frantic heartbeat, searching for his, following it to its source, begging it to slow. To stop pumping so much of Conall's blood from his body. Kneeling, I reached my hands down to his wound. I sifted through the pulsing energy, propelled by his heart to where the blood was escaping in a torrent. Conall was trembling, going ashen with shock. He had seconds before it would be too late.

I felt the separation of the flesh and his frayed blood vessels drifting in the escaping flow of blood, like disjointed threads of spider's silk from a ruined web dancing in the breeze. I searched deeper, sensing the location of the tear in the femoral artery. The jagged bone had practically ripped it in two. I just had to reconnect that shredded tissue without touching it.

Oh makers, please help me do this.

I had one chance. Energy coursed from my fingers into his leg, following the exploratory feelers I'd sent first. Sweat beaded on my brow as I urged them to find order, to reestablish the pattern they'd held moments earlier. Like a broken vessel, the pieces found their way, rough edges connecting—fitting tightly once again. Their altered state shifting as the energy I directed vibrated from my own awareness into Conall's body. I waited for what seemed like an eternity, but must have been only seconds. I wasn't sure at first if I had accomplished healing the artery, but the flow of blood from the wound slowed to a trickle. Slumping to the side, I shook the cloudiness from my head. I wiped my trembling hands, which were covered in Conall's sticky blood, on my pants. The red streaked handprints down my thighs echoed the gravity of the moment.

"You need to finish the rest of the smaller veins and the jagged bone needs healing so it doesn't re-tear the artery. And he's still bleeding too much; he needs his blood replenished." I turned in the voice's direction. It was him. The Skyborne who'd prodded me with the pole was kneeling eye-level with me. His rich voice was calm, yet insistent.

I reached into my power, urging that channel to stay open, to give me more. Bringing my companions to Idia, which I assumed was where we'd landed, had taken almost everything. Holding the shield was shaky, and repairing the artery had pushed me closer to my limit than I was comfortable with. My grip on reality was escaping me, evidenced by the hazy halo around the male kneeling in the dune in front of me.

I knew I shouldn't use more. Especially after what had happened with Malik. I cringed as the vision of my sword pressed into the soft tissue of his stomach, and the betrayal which showed in his eyes, right as Asha had the excellent sense to knock me out before I could do any more damage. My hands trembled involuntarily, and I glanced at Malik who winced, sensing my thought path.

"I can't. Everything… it's too much." My voice cracked as I stifled a sob, leaning forward, placing my hands on the hot sand to steady myself. The world was becoming distant as I struggled to keep it together. "I'll hurt him."

"Lower your shield and we will help him," the Skyborne persuaded.

I jerked my head back in his direction. We were speaking the same language, but I had to strain to understand his smooth, melodic accent, so different from the many dialects I'd studied as I'd trained to carry out Vera's task to steal the ember.

"You just had a weapon at my throat. You expect me to trust you?" I demanded, my fighting instinct kicking in.

"Please. Your friend is going to die if you don't accept our help."

Conall's large body, now unconscious, lay limp on the blood saturated dune. *No!* He couldn't die now. Icy panic rolled through me. A deep umber hand grabbed my arm. *Seeley.*

"Lower them, Nayla. *Now,*" Seeley implored, squeezing, his tawny eyes worried-streaked.

I turned back to the Skyborne. "I will kill you if you can't save him or if you hurt any of my friends." I whipped my head around to the others who I just now realized were surrounding us. "I will *kill* you all," I seethed.

I probably seemed like a wild animal to them, my dark, unruly hair blown out around my shoulders. My petite figure crouched on the dune over my injured friend, gnashing my teeth with threats of violence. I didn't care. They needed to know how viciously I'd defend my own.

The male's wide mouth curled up slightly before he pressed his lips tight. "Seems like good enough motivation to me. You have our word." He kneeled, waiting, drilling me with that piercing gaze.

I released the shield and felt Malik drag me back away from Conall as several Idian Skyborne rushed forward to Conall's side. As they worked, Malik stroked my back soothingly. Seeley paused, a hand rested absently on his paunch and his other went to his temple, eyes glazing for a split second before refocusing.

"They will save him, Nayla. You did the right thing." Seeley spoke the truth. It was his sight, a vision, I knew. A shudder of relief coursed through me. I was thankful to him for being able to reach me at that moment. Coming here had been a risk, but we'd had no other choice.

The male Skyborne from my dreams appeared to be assisting a female whose nimble hands were hovering above Conall's slack form. Her blonde hair, a few shades darker than Rhijn's, was pulled back into a practical knot at the base of her skull, which only made her delicate features appear more severe. Her lean form was clad in a nondescript, loose-fitting white uniform of straight legged trousers and a pullover with cropped sleeves. It looked cool, comfortable and easy to work in.

"She must be a healer," Asha observed. "They brought her in case something like this happened. Smart. I'll be damned." Asha had apparently gathered her bearings already.

I glanced at her. "What do you mean?"

"Look around us, Nayla. We're in the middle of nowhere. They had to have expected us."

I scanned my periphery. Asha was right. There had to be nothing for miles. Just endless undulating sand dunes as far as I could see.

The soft terrain had cushioned the rest of our falls, but Conall's leg must have landed on a large sandstone mound jutting out of the dune nearby, causing the break. Beyond the other Skyborne who were observing the healing, there were enough horses for all of us and a small carriage. Or what kind of appeared to be a carriage. The horses were normal enough, but the carriage was constructed with a shiny, whitish and grey metal-like substance. There were no wheels, and it seemed to hover just off the ground. Cylinders of aqua liquid were attached to what I thought was the rear of the thing, and I perceived an undulating thrum of energy coming from them.

My pulse quickened as I studied the contraption. I recognized my bodies' response as unease, and not just about Conall. It stemmed from the otherness or being confronted with the unknown. I squared my shoulders and cut that nagging judgement off before it unfairly influenced my perception of these Skyborne and how they lived. I had a role to play here. I would put the ten years of training I'd undergone to steal the ember to use.

I glanced back to where Conall lay. He was still alive. That was good. I wouldn't have to kill the first Idian Skyborne I'd met. The one, *Rhijn*, kept stealing glances up at me as he aided the healer. It was *him*; I was sure of it then. I thought of my dreams, and my face went bright red. I leaned my face into Malik's bony chest so the male wouldn't see it. I'd hoped I'd been quick enough.

Long moments later, footsteps shuffled across the sand in our direction. Rhijn approached where Seeley, Malik and I kneeled, waiting. Asha, I noticed, was busy inspecting the carriage, bravely running her hands across its smooth seams.

"Hey, my name is Rhijn," the Skyborne said as he approached us. "You're the leader?" He aimed his question at me.

I know your name, I wanted to say. He didn't need to know that yet. Maybe never.

"I… no. It isn't like that," I stammered. Just like in the first dreams, pure and utter fear gripped me. It didn't make sense. They had helped stabilize Conall, so I knew I should be more open. But it was pure instinct. No matter how hard I fought it, the prickle at the back of my neck was there.

He eyed me suspiciously, as if he didn't believe me, and addressed me again, reinforcing that. "We need to move your friend back to the capital as quickly as possible. He is stable now, but he needs a transfusion of blood. That transport over there can get him there within the hour. The horses are for the rest of us."

No one responded. I glanced from Malik to Seeley for help.

"We mean you no harm. I know this all must seem very strange to you, but we're here to welcome you. And Kellis—" He pointed at a male hovering over the healer. "—figured you'd be more comfortable with the horses. He made the assumption some of our ways might startle you at first. Your friend, though, cannot afford the luxury. I need your permission to send him with our healer in that transport."

"I want to go with him," I blurted out. "I need to."

Rhijn furrowed his brow in concern. "Is he your bonded male?"

"What?" I asked.

"He means your husband or boyfriend," Seeley clarified.

"Oh, no, he's my brother."

I could have sworn tension dissipated from Rhijn's face at my answer. *Damn ember.* I was still trying to will the cloudiness in my head to clear and the perky vibrating almond of darkness I'd quickly stashed in my breast pocket wasn't helping.

"There isn't enough room in the transport. Your brother, Everly, our healer, and Kelvin to operate the controls will already be a tight fit. I'm sorry. He will be in the best hands in Idia within the hour."

Everly huffed up at Rhijn. "So, what does that make me?" she said, putting her fists on her hips, clearly annoyed.

Rhijn laughed. It was a deep, magnetic sound. "No offense, Everly. Your excellence is why we wanted you to come with us. You know no one exceeds your skill."

He looked at her with fondness, and a strange twinge of jealousy hit me. *No way.* I was losing my mind.

"Conall. His name is Conall. Take him," I heard myself say.

I was lost in my own head, chastising my ridiculous thoughts when Rhijn reached down from where he stood to grab my hand to help me up. His hand came at me in slow motion and I panicked, stumbling back across the dune before he could touch me. I glanced back at him with wide eyes. A brief flash of hurt darted across his face before an expression that appeared a lot like resolve took hold.

"Seems our primitive kin have a lower level of manners than we expected," he scoffed under his breath, smirking at the male he'd identified as Kellis.

Seeley shot a scolding furrow of his brow in my direction, then offered his hand to Rhijn, showing gratitude for the help. Malik followed suit, and the males clasped forearms, formally introducing themselves.

Asha walked over and pulled me up off the dune. "Don't you worry about this one," she said to Rhijn and his company, dragging me toward them. "She is just experiencing a little bit of shock right now. It happens when Nayla uses too much of her power… Doesn't act totally right. Last time I had to knock her out. She'll snap out of it."

I glared at her as she was making circles with her finger pointing to her head.

Asha laughed, nudging me forward as she turned to survey the horses. "So, which one is mine?"

Rhijn walked away from us and as he did, I swore I heard him whisper my name. It was official. Somewhere between our realm and this one, I'd lost my mind. After what had happened with Darius and then Emerson, I was officially done with lovers for a good long while, despite the direction my dreams had taken. Those thoughts would get me nowhere. I had a job to do here. That was all. I didn't know if I was scolding myself or the ember, but either way, any thoughts in that vicinity would be staunchly repressed, ignored, and definitely not acted upon.

One of the other males walked up to us, introducing himself. "I'm Kelvin. I oversee the energy systems. This is Kellis, our political strategist. The twins—" He motioned to two stocky, identical looking females outfitted in matching grey unembellished uniforms. "—Leah and Rhea, are grunts. Don't pay them any mind." They chuckled about some apparent inside joke. "As you may have guessed, we were expecting you. Welcome to the Realm of the Skyborne, *Idia*. It is our job to escort you back to the capital, where you will stay until we can relocate you to the settlements. Chancellor Vitis will be overjoyed to welcome you home. It's been a long time coming."

He handed me and Malik moist towels he'd pulled from Everly's pack. I accepted it with thanks and scrubbed the dried blood from my hands.

Wow. That was all I could think. This was all moving so fast my head was spinning. There was no way to know what we might have encountered upon arrival, but a welcoming party would have been at the bottom of the list of guesses.

I studied Kelvin. The male's countenance was warm, yet reserved. He was mid-height and of average build, with skin a lighter brown than the deep hue of Seeley's, but his curly hair was cropped close to his head in a similar fashion. He shifted his hazel eyes between the members of our group, expecting a response.

"So, I can pick?" Asha interjected.

"Excuse me?" Kelvin asked.

"My horse, you didn't answer my question."

Kelvin laughed. I think the Skyborne had decided they liked Asha already. Everyone did, it seemed. It was a quality I envied.

"I think this one will do just fine for you." He guided her over to a white mare with ruddy patches speckled across its body. The animal tossed its head back, playfully shaking out its red and white streaked mane. Its feisty temperament and wild, fiery locks mirrored its rider perfectly. Asha stroked the horse, and it nuzzled her approvingly before she launched a long leg up and over the saddle, getting comfortable. A breeze caught her red waves and she nudged the animal with her heels.

"If days are anything like they are back home, time's wasting. Let's get moving," Asha demanded as she surveyed the cresting light star, her gray-green eyes squinting before she turned to us to see what the holdup was.

Everly and Kelvin loaded a limp Conall into the carriage, and within moments it lifted a higher over the sand and took off toward the horizon, across the endless desert terrain, leaving a trail of dust in its wake.

Leah and Rhea showed Seeley and Malik to their mounts. My stomach dropped as I turned to find Rhijn guiding an obsidian stallion over toward me. Rhijn walked like a stalking wolf, I thought as he approached, long-limbed, broad shouldered and in total control of himself. Fear prickled up my spine, and my hands became cold and clammy. Rhijn held out the reins for me. I stared at his light yet sun-kissed and well-veined forearms, still lost. *How could he be here?*

"I feel like Samson and you will get along stupendously." I just stood there as the gelding flicked his head to the side, trying to jerk the reins out of Rhijn's hand. "You can ride, can't you, *primitive one*? Or did the Makers not even give you horses when they banished you?"

That shocked me out of my stupor. Was he trying to joke with me? *Damn it, pull yourself together.*

I snatched the reins from him, giving a nice glare, careful not to come in contact with his excruciatingly beautiful skin, and deftly mounted the sleek beast. *No*, his completely normal, unappealing skin. I guessed he was just a part of the welcoming party and when we got delivered to their Chancellor, he'd depart our company. The male put me on edge. I was looking forward to the moment I'd be rid of the distraction. Since we'd made it here, I knew what we needed to do.

CHAPTER TWO

WO HOURS LATER, we were riding in pairs. Rhijn and Kelvin up front, Malik and Seeley next, then the twins. Asha and I brought up the rear, a position I specifically filtered back to on purpose.

"I see somebody has a crush on a certain striking Idian." Asha looked over teasing.

"Makers, Asha, *shut up*," I hissed. I wasn't in the mood to joke, my thoughts bouncing between worry for Conall, unease about the Idians, and exhaustion from using the ember.

"If you haven't already claimed him, might I go after him?" She looked at me, raising an eyebrow, ribbing me.

"He's all yours," I huffed through gritted teeth, trying to keep awake and focused. The rhythm of Samson's gentle canter kept causing my head to lull into a light slumber, only to jerk awake on a sharp inhale. I hoped Asha was the only one who noticed.

"Oh, I'm kidding," she conceded, rolling her eyes at my seriousness. "I'm sworn off males for a while."

I caught the brief sorrow on her face before she plastered a smile across it, looking up toward the flaming sphere in the sky. "This kind of reminds me of home," she said, referring to Sundale, the only one of our home territories with desert and always bathed in rays from the light star.

I watched her, suspecting she was thinking about what Berith, Emerson's stepbrother, had done to her during her time in the Monterra prison.

"Did you hear him call us Banished?" I asked, attempting to distract her.

"I did. I mean, that's sort of what we are, if you think about it. I also heard him call you *primitive one*. If that isn't flirting, I don't know what is." Asha gave a playful growl and raised her hands and pawed the air like a cat in my direction.

"Seriously, I'm going to quit talking to you if you don't stop. And for your information, I've sworn off males too."

"And females?" Asha raised an eyebrow at me.

I glared at her. My ears were burning and I glanced up to the head of the party. Rhijn had turned to look at me. I could almost sense what he was thinking. I was *primitive*. And not in the flirty way Asha suggested.

⌇

We rode all day. It would have been the middle of the night back home. Droopy eyelids and weary lines etching tired skin revealed the fatigue on my companion's faces, but none of us were about to insult our hosts after they'd been so welcoming thus far. Outside of the whole pointy pole to the throat thing, I mused. Either that or they were happily leading us to our doom.

We stopped occasionally to take a ration of the preserved cakes of fruit and grain, and slices of cheese the Idians passed out. They were similar in shape and texture to the food from our home realm, but the flavors burst across my palate, different from anything I had before. I caught my nose wrinkling at first because of the intensity, but I was already gaining a taste for them.

When we paused for a break, Seeley approached me. "You doing okay, Nayla?" he asked, smiling warmly.

"I am, thanks. I know we're all tired. And I'm worried about Conall."

"Malik and I are, too, but he will be fine. I *know*. These Skyborne will be our allies. You need to find a way to accept their friendship."

I knew he was referring to how I treated Rhijn. But I couldn't help it. It had to be some sort of automatic reaction from seeing a figment of one's imagination come to life before their eyes.

"You did notice he had a weapon at my throat, right? I'm pretty confident I wasn't hallucinating."

"It seems perfectly reasonable. They needed to make sure we weren't a threat."

"Did any of the rest of you arrive at a deadly sharp point at your neck?" I raised my eyebrows at him.

"We weren't the one using the ember. He probably sensed it on you."

I almost resented his reasonableness. I rolled my eyes. "Oh, I'll accept them. I, well, that was just *him*. There is something about him I don't like."

"Really? He appears nice enough to me. Is it something specific?" Seeley asked, tilting his head to the side curiously.

"He's the male from my dreams," I whispered before my cheeks could warm.

"What?" Seeley grunted under his breath, and gave me an incredulous look out the side of his eye.

"Nothing. I'll tell you later," I murmured, wishing I hadn't said anything.

I turned to Kellis, who nudged his mount and was trotting over to me, still treating me as the de facto leader. Kellis was a short stocky male, his russet hair cut close on the sides and spiked aggressively atop his squarish head. A smattering of freckles were dusted across his nose and cheeks which were pink, like Asha's, from the sun.

"It's only another two hours," Kellis explained. "We'll be there by nightfall. I'd like to ride with you if you wouldn't mind and learn about what your home is like. And prepare you for what to expect when we get to the capital; the shining city of Adrina."

A wide grin overtook Kellis' face exposing two perfectly square rows of teeth as he spoke of the city with pride. I remembered from the introductions he was a political strategist, which must be an important position. It relieved me that he was who wanted to speak with me, which meant he must be their leader on this excursion.

"That would be nice," I said, keeping my voice light, trying to be amiable. "We are all very much looking forward to seeing Adrina and learning about the Idians."

As we rode, I told Kellis about what our realm was like, how the six territories worked, and the Regents who oversaw them. I explained our struggles with rationing resources and described the Swath, the central forest on our continent, which was warded by an invisible boundary which kept Uden and his creatures and the Skyborne separated. A boundary which was encroaching into the territories at an undetermined speed. He was probably taking careful mental notes to relay back to his ruling council and the male they referred to as the Chancellor.

I left out the parts about what Karish and the late Kymar, now Emerson, were planning until I got to know my hosts better. I also suspected my alliance with Uden, should wait as well, along with the fact that few of the Sol Ros had anything more than the common power to speak of. Few of which I was one. I wanted to meet this Chancellor of theirs to get a gauge on him before I shared too much. I looked at my companions and they'd each paired off with an Idian Skyborne, and were presumably carrying on similarly guarded conversations.

Asha rode beside Rhijn, two groups ahead of us. His eyes went wide before I saw his broad shoulders shake with a chuckle. This seemed to encourage Asha to become more animated with whatever tale she was spinning, her hands gesturing expansively in the air, eliciting a deep rumble from the pale-haired Skyborne.

"Nayla," Kellis interrupted my thoughts, "you were saying?"

"Oh, I think that's about all. I've talked about us long enough. The *Banished* was how you referred to us." He winced, but I pressed on. "I want to hear about Idians. You alluded to things about how you live that would startle us."

"Very well. But please don't let Rhijn's Banished comment offend you. Our understanding is that your sect, the Sol Ros, was exiled from Idia by the Makers. We expected the banishment to end well before now. You are long past when we would have thought you'd be back, and we have been waiting to welcome you home. Banishments rarely last that long, from what our seers can ascertain. But the Makers have been silent." He could tell what he was saying to me was shocking. "We will have plenty of time to discuss this later."

"There are a few things you will need to learn about how we live," he continued. "Each Idian believes it's their duty to use their power to benefit the whole. You said your subjects use their own power, the common power was the term you used, to heat their homes, and provide security and other such things for themselves."

"They're not my subjects," I interjected.

"Then you are the emissary?"

I almost laughed. "It's kind of a long story as to how the five of us ended up here. It is true we are, or were, all future Regents, or a part of ruling families." I paused, realizing what it would suggest if I finished my thought. "Please tell me the Dar Kepler drink wine, right?"

Kellis nodded with a wry grin. "So, a conversation best had over wine then?"

I truly laughed then. I liked him. Without looking, I knew Rhijn had glanced back at me, drawn by my laugh. Just a peek to confirm. Sure enough, I caught a second of eye contact before we both looked away.

"Who is he?" I dared to ask Kellis.

"Who, Rhijn? He's no one important," Kellis said, chuckling.

That was a relief. "So, you are saying how you use your power is different?" I urged him to continue.

"Yes, that appears to be true. Maybe the biggest difference between those of us who were left on Idia, and the factor which enables us to live so differently than the Skyborne from your realm, from what you've described. To give you the best description, I'll defer to Kelvin since the power systems are his domain, but a layman's explanation would be that we use our power to draw energy into community wells for storage. Each Idian Skyborne visits a power well once a week. We teach our youth, as soon as their power blossoms, how to channel the surrounding energy into a concentrated area and feed the collected energy into the wells. When they are young, it's a small contribution, but we find it easier for them to learn during the malleable phase of youth."

"That sounds kind of scary, to have all that concentrated power in one place," I said.

"Well, there are wells around the capital, surrounding towns, and even in the settlements. We think we can even train some of your people to fill them."

His excitement was contagious. I didn't want to think about how limited our access was to the energy around us. And little did Kerris and the Idian Skyborne know, their lofty goal of training us to feed the wells was most likely out of reach.

"Here is where the process gets fun," he continued. "All of that power gets distributed throughout our population to power everything. You'll understand why we call Adrina the shining city. Brilliant lights positioned in homes and along the streets illuminate the city. The power well can fill cells for the transports, carriages, I think you called them. Every home has warm running water, self-powered cooking devices, and temperature controls. Kelvin tells me he and Rhijn are working on a piece of equipment that can preserve food which can be used in each home. The advances we've made are nothing short of incredible since…" Kellis trailed off.

"That's okay, you can say it. Since the Sol Ros were banished."

We held each other's eye for a moment of understanding.

"I think you and Chancellor Vitis will like each other," Kellis said decidedly.

We chatted over lighter topics as we finished our ride and I asked him a litany of questions about what to expect when we got there. The more I was prepared for, the better. Their light star was setting quickly, and soon we were riding in the dark when a faint glow on the horizon appeared.

"You have two light stars?" I asked, mouth gaping.

Kellis laughed. "That, Nayla, is the shining city. Adrina."

Soon the city came into a closer view and I'd seen nothing like it. I swung my head around to my companions, and their faces showed the same slack-jawed awe as my own. The white stone arches of Eastdow always amazed me, but this blew Eastdow out of the water. What seemed like a million tiny lights came into view and reflected off the shiny canvas of the surrounding sand creating a mirage effect.

Kellis trotted ahead, and the twins and Asha followed. Malik and Seeley were sharing their reverence together, so I didn't intrude. I found myself riding beside Rhijn, who seemed to find the wonder on my face entertaining.

"Beautiful, isn't it?" he asked gently.

"Breathtakingly so."

"There's only one thing I've ever seen that's eclipsed it."

"What's that, Rhijn?" I asked, honestly curious.

"Maybe one day I'll tell you." He gave me a wicked grin, nudging his horse into a run, yelling behind him, "Catch up if you can."

I nudged the stallion. "All right, Samson, I'm counting on you, boy."

❧

I was flushed as we rode through the gates of the capital. Rhijn was waiting for Seeley, Malik and I.

"You only won because you had a head start." I patted Samson, "It's not your fault he cheated, boy."

Rhijn raised an eyebrow at me.

We rode around to the stables on the outskirts of the city and left our horses with the unusually tidy stable hands. When I slid off of Samson, I stumbled from fatigue and Rhijn reached out to steady me. "I've got it," I said, before he touched me.

"Sorry," he answered, brows furrowing.

My behavior was clearly confusing the male. What he didn't know was what I feared would happen if our skin collided. My skin heated at the thought and I turned away.

"Kellis told you about the transports? They are perfectly safe and the easiest way to get up to the terrace of the Chancellor's estate where the rooms you will be staying in are. Chancellor Vitis is waiting on us."

I slung the small traveling satchel over my shoulder and the stable hand unloaded Samson's pack laying down my assortment of weapons I'd carried through the realms.

Rhijn stared down at them and whistled. "I don't know if I should be frightened or impressed."

"She can defend herself if that helps you decide," Seeley chimed in, giving me back-up based on my earlier comments.

"I can imagine," Rhijn replied. "You two can take that one." He pointed to the second transport behind the one that had pulled in front of us. "Asha's gone ahead with the others. Like I said before, two is the comfortable number for these things. We've tried larger ones, but they consume too much energy. The ride through the city is about thirty minutes, then up the big hill to the landing area on the covered terrace at the Chancellor's estate." He held out his hand to the carriage's door, which had slid open. "After you."

I eyed the strange machine, then began inspecting it in earnest. Of course, Asha had just jumped in hers without a second thought. I glanced forward to where Malik was walking around the one they'd been assigned. Seeley apparently had already gotten in, and was poking his head out searching for his partner. Malik shot me an *are you sure we can trust these things* look.

I shrugged, and tapped a nail against the cylinder attached to the back which I was studying. "Who is operating the controls on theirs?" I asked Rhijn, who was watching me.

"In the city, you can program them to where you want to go and they'll take you. Theirs has already been done and see…" He gestured for me to see inside and he moved his structured yet nimble hands over the illuminated controls and the carriage came to life.

I gave the machine a shove and it rocked back and forth before coming to a stationary position once again. I noticed Malik had gotten in theirs and the door had sealed. Sighing, I resigned myself to the experience, handing Rhijn my gathered weapons that would have been awkward on my body in such close quarters, and crawled in. I had a feeling this wasn't going to be the only new and strange contraption we'd encounter, so I'd better brace myself.

"Sit back. The transport will jolt forward at first." It did, and I steadied myself against a wall. Rhijn didn't budge as I jerked forward, catching myself. His pursed lips and wary squint suggested he was more than capable of keeping his hands to himself. I supposed that was a point in his favor.

As we traveled through the city, he told me about the different buildings and structures, pointing out power wells as we passed them. I couldn't really make out any details at the speed we were going, but it was an interesting ride nonetheless and it was clear Rhijn, like Kellis, was quite proud of his city.

"The Sol Ros call your sect the Dar Kepler, but I haven't heard any of you mention that name." Rhijn regarded me and I continued, "We were taught you were the sole source of our demise and evil incarnate."

"What do you think?"

"I haven't decided what I think yet, but so far I can say I've seen worse evil."

"Is that how the rest of the Banished feel about us?" he asked.

"I think they are becoming increasingly desperate, and the Regents of the most well-off territories aren't doing much to reassure them of their future. They just feed the Skyborne a bunch of empty prophecies. Coming here and taking back what they believe is theirs consumes them. They forget to consider the basic needs of their subjects." We were quiet for a moment.

"Is that what you're here for, Nayla?" He forced the eye contact, attempting to sniff out a deception in my answer.

"No, it is not. It is a long story about why we are here. I plan to tell the Chancellor and his advisors when the time is right."

"I see. I'm sure *they* will be eager to hear your tale."

"Is it like this, how it is here in Adrina the same elsewhere in Idia? Like what Kellis described about using your power for the common good?" Out the window opposite Rhijn, neat rows of houses and businesses lined the streets we passed through. Only a few Skyborne were out on the streets at this late hour, but they went about their business in a relaxed, natural way. They probably didn't realize the two carriages passing by them were carrying the Banished, the first to arrive since the Crossover.

"There are certainly worse off areas, but I think our basic needs are met across the board. That is each Idian's most Skyborne right. The Dar Kepler are a peaceful people historically. And that is a very ancient phrase. I wouldn't advise throwing the name around casually. Do you understand what it means?"

"I only know it alluded to your sects' use of dark power." I shivered.

Rhijn huffed a laugh under his breath. "It alludes to the power that lives in the space in between. The void, if you will. There is nothing inherently dark or evil about it. And you should be aware, when the armies of the Sol Ros disappeared from that battlefield, we quickly began plans to integrate those who'd been left, mostly the young and vulnerable, into our society. Today, we live as one, almost completely merged, and the social stratification no longer exists. That doesn't mean everything is perfect politically, but we don't have conflicts like we did back then."

A light flashed and a message came through the black stone tablet on the console and Rhijn read it. "Your brother has taken the blood transfusion successfully, and the healers do not detect any lasting damage to his brain or nerves. He should make a full recovery."

Seeley had confirmed the truth, but I slumped back on the bench across from Rhijn, tears of relief welling up in my eyes. He looked concerned and dug around in a small compartment and pulled out a small cloth and handed it to me.

"What is this?"

"It's called a tissue. A small disposable handkerchief."

"Oh, thanks," I said, snatching the tissue from his extended hand and dabbing my eyes. "Thank you. Tell the healer, Everly, she has my gratitude. When can I see him?"

"We're almost there. They are keeping him unconscious while they complete the final healing. We can take you to him if you need proof, but they won't allow him to wake until tomorrow."

I just stared at the front of the carriage. The lights on the black panels, below the glass windows blinked on and off and on a larger central black marble-like tablet a map showed our track through the city between two waypoints, as Rhijn had explained.

He watched me studying it. "Are you okay?" His deep voice was brimming with concern.

I closed my eyes. "We have carriages too. They're just drawn by horses." Guilt niggled at the edges of my mind for how rude I'd been. "Look, I'm sorry for—"

"You don't need to apologize. You've clearly been through a lot. And I can imagine this must not be easy."

Running my hands across my face, I fought the tears welling up. How could I ever explain to the male sitting next to me that he was the entire reason I'd been able to escape the Monterra prison, help free the godflies, and walk between realms. Everything he'd taught me in those dreams was how we were here and not dead by Darius and Emerson's creature's hands. I wondered if Rhijn even knew. And now the male's understanding was threatening to crumble the tough exterior I was clinging to. I squeezed my eyes closed trying not to think of everything that had happened in the last few weeks and how exhausted I was. Not to mention the odd sensation of closeness I had to him from the dreams—how embarrassing.

But none of that mattered. This was just another mission which I had been trained for. I steeled myself and bit back the tears, transforming myself into the character I needed to be so we could discover what us Banished had waiting for us when we returned. "I appreciate your understanding. I just need a good night's sleep."

After a jarring jump three stories upward, our carriages settled on a large open terrace on a stone pad where they settled and went still. Rhijn pushed a button, and the door slid open. He stepped out first and started to offer me his hand, but hesitated pulling it back and resting it at his side. "I'd offer you help, but I've noticed you don't appreciate the physical contact."

"Great," I said, surprised.

The terrace was immense, going for yards in both directions. Exterior doors and windows lined a covered passageway supported by sleek square columns of a homogeneous tan stone-like material and was polished to a shine. Over the top was what looked like a shield, similar to that which surrounded the Swath. Rhijn noticed me staring at it.

"It protects the terrace from sand storms. It can get pretty windy up this high."

"Oh." I nodded, absorbing my surroundings.

The grounds on the terrace were lined with hedges and trapezoid shaped floral gardens, with walkways crossing manicured lawns every so often. They were similar to the intricate gardens surrounding the royal training yards at Drakestone, but somehow more luxurious and simpler at the same time. I looked to my right and in the distance, I saw a conical shaped statue spraying water into a small Skyborne made pool.

"Is there a spring beneath this place?" I asked Rhijn.

"Energy from the estate's power wells propels the water in the fountains," he answered.

"Rhijn, my boy, you return!" boomed the larger-than-life voice of a tall, broad chested male making great strides in our direction. He reached us and clapped Rhijn on the back as he turned to me with a warm and open smile.

"Nayla, meet our realm's esteemed guardian, Chancellor Vitis Innar. This is Nayla Shal, the apparent leader of the first group of travelers from the Realm of the Banished."

After the introduction, Rhijn turned around to grab my satchel and his items out of the carriage, and hoisted them onto his shoulders.

Chancellor Vitis brushed a lock of his dark blond mid-length hair from his eye and clasped his thick hands behind his back. He leaned down toward me. "How was your journey, Nayla? I hope my son made every accommodation for you and your companions."

"Your son?" I almost choked on the words.

"Rhijn? Yes, my son. Did they not mention that?"

Oh, I was so going to have words with Kellis. No one special, my ass. And right when I was beginning to think Rhijn wasn't so bad. I flicked my eyes between the two males. I could see the resemblance immediately. The chancellor's coloring was overall a bit darker than Rhijn's, eyes the color of the summer sky instead of an icy shade, and so on.

"Is something wrong, dear?" Chancellor Vitis asked.

"Oh, no, umm... your highness. It's been a long day. It was night when we left."

"Well, that explains the dark circles under your eyes."

"Father, that is not a proper thing to say to a female," Rhijn chided.

I glared at him. "*A primitive* you mean?"

The Chancellor burst into a jovial laughter. "I'm glad to see you two have hit it off. Sounds like you've had enough for one day. Let's take you all to your rooms. I'll have some food sent up and you can get situated and take your rest." He looked over at my satchel. "Is that bag all you brought?" I nodded. "I'll send a tailor first thing to arrange for some suitable clothing for you and your companions. And we'll make sure you can visit your brother first thing in the morning. I've been to see him. When he first arrived, he was so pale. The color is returning to his face nicely now. He will feel much better in the morning."

This male, this Chancellor, had more energy than I knew what to do with, reminding me of the fiery red-head in our party. "Yes, your highness." I repeated, not knowing what to say.

"You can call me Vitis in casual settings such as this. In the council meetings, Chancellor Vitis will do. No, your highness, or any of that other nonsense. Go now." Chancellor Vitis spun to affront Seeley and Malik, and I gave them a sympathetic shrug as Rhijn and an attendant led me away.

A part of me wanted to demand we stay up and get answers, but my exhaustion was winning the fight toward the offer of a comfortable bed. I could be Nayla the Emissary tomorrow. We walked through the covered walkway and through one of the exterior glass doors into a spacious bedroom suite. A large four-poster bed sat facing the windows next to a sitting area with a sofa and a small table. Two chairs and a taller table were positioned in an alcove close to an interior door. The furniture was simple and lacked any sort of ornateness. Utilitarian even, and I thought I liked the pieces as I ran my hand over the glossy surface of the bedpost.

The attendant was emptying my satchel and looked bemused at the pitiful items she retrieved from it. Still, she dutifully shook out the few clothing items and hung them in a small closet. Conall and Seeley had the presence of mind to bring them to the traveler's inn where we'd met them in Seabrook. Right before Darius and his fighters, with A1 in tow, had busted the door down and we fled to Idia using the ember. If not for that, I'd only have the clothes on my back.

Unbidden, thoughts about my last week came flooding in. Traveling to Monterra with Malik, how he'd been captured and tortured, the whole *thing* with Emerson, discovering the monstrosities she was creating intent on sending them here to overthrow these Skyborne who'd been nothing but kind to us so far. How she'd killed her step-father, the Regius of the territory, blamed it on me, then saved my life. How I'd almost killed my own half-brother, Malik in a power induced haze. I'd thought we'd have a moment's respite, but when we'd gotten the bird from Bara that Darius was near and we'd been surrounded, we'd had no choice but to flee.

I turned around to notice Rhijn was still here, watching me.

"Why are you still here? *Your Highness.*"

An annoyed grimace crossed his face. "Children of the officials don't carry titles, and we certainly aren't royalty. Kellis told you about the running water, right?" He asked, diverting the subject. I nodded. "I just wanted to show you this one thing." He looked excited and mischievous.

Good makers, this male. "Okay, if you promise you'll leave after."

He stopped short and considered me. "I'm not sure what I've done to make you so aggressive toward me," he stated suddenly. "You seemed perfectly amiable in the conversation with Kellis."

I was taken aback. "Why am I the only one who finds it off-putting that I opened my eyes in a completely new realm to a weapon pointed at my throat?" I motioned my hand for him to get on with it. "Show me if you must."

"I thought we had moved past that in the transport. You have the void stone and I was being cautious. Do you require an apology?"

I stood there with my arms crossed, watching him. I was too tired to have this conversation, much less think of this Skyborne standing before me for a moment longer. "Please just show me."

"Your friends have much gentler manners than you," he said as he led me into a bathing chamber. I tensed as we entered the smaller space, and he must have seen it.

"I'm not going to hurt you," Rhijn emphasized, startled by my reaction. "I would never hurt you. I just wanted to show you how the shower works."

"Can't the attendant show me that? *Your Highness,*" I asked, yawning, but secretly enjoying his irritation the misuse of the title caused him. Served him right for calling us primitive and banished. And I was doing good to be on my feet much less minding my tongue.

Rhijn practically stomped over to the knobs on the wall and wrenched one on. Water burst out of a fixture in the ceiling. He punched another button and three streams came out of small squares in the wall.

"Touch it."

"Touch what?" I asked.

"The water. Feel it," he demanded.

I reached my hand at the rain shower coming from the ceiling. "It's warm," I sighed, surprised despite myself.

"See this handle, it controls the temperature. These buttons open the fixtures in the wall." I barely heard him as I was mesmerized, waving my hand through the downpour of warm water before me. Rhijn shut the shower off abruptly.

"Anyway, that is what we do instead of a bath. You might enjoy it after your travels. I find it helps me sleep better." He hastened toward the door, leaving me standing in the bathroom with my hand still dripping.

He didn't turn back to look at me, but he muttered, "I wanted to show you because it was my invention." That caught my attention, but before I could respond, he'd left through the interior door that I imagined led to the inside of the Chancellor's estate.

CHAPTER THREE

I SHOULD HAVE BEEN paying better attention when Rhijn showed me the shower. I turned the first of the four knobs. Nothing happened. I twisted a larger one with two levers and water streamed down from the ceiling. Smiling, I stepped underneath. Gooseflesh sprouted immediately, and I jumped back, trying not to slip on the wet floor. I shimmied around the waterfall and twisted the knob I'd turned before. Freezing water burst from the wall and hit my shoulder. I wrenched it off, glaring at the annoying yet potentially wonderful contraption.

Squaring my shoulders, I moved the outside lever on the large handle, bracing for a burst of water to hit me from some hidden spout. Nothing happened, but then steam started coming from the stream from the ceiling. Gingerly, I put a toe into the water.

"Makers," I sighed, stepping further into the deliciously warm water. The moment I stepped into it, I realized what a glorious invention it was and understood why Rhijn had been eager to show it off. I'd have to figure out how to adjust the spouts on the wall some other time. And maybe I'd make a point to be a nicer to the shower's inventor.

Closing my eyes, I tilted my head up to the source of the stream, letting the warm heat pour over my body. After long moments, I pressed my palms into my face scrubbing away the anxiety and my worry for Conall.

He was safe, I reminded myself. I exhaled a deep breath and reached for the shelf where the scrubs and creams were located.

"I guess I can't stay here forever, can I?" I glanced over to my pile of clothes where I'd placed the ember on top. "I'm not talking to myself if I'm talking to you, right?"

It did not respond. "Thanks," I said.

⁘

Rhijn had been right. I slept like I hadn't slept in months that night, thankfully in a deep dreamless sleep, the ember resting dormant in the pocket of the sleeping gown I'd found in the wardrobe. I guessed it was tired too.

The next morning, after breakfast was delivered, the tailor arrived as promised. I would have preferred to skip it and went straight to Conall to appease my churning stomach, but my manners were already in question thanks to Rhijn. Part of gaining an understanding of these Skyborne was accepting their hospitality, so I swallowed my restlessness and sifted through the assortment of garments he brought. Each piece was constructed with simple lines and neutral colors. Whoever had sent him had apparently gauged my size correctly and only a few pieces had to be tailored. I was grateful for the generosity of the Idians, as we'd arrived with the minimal supplies.

I selected a simple white dress that cinched at the waist, which I thought would be cool in the balmy weather of Adrina. Unsure of what to do next, I peeked out into the hallway. I'd been considering shifting into the tailor and wandering around, but I figured his position wouldn't warrant that kind of behavior. The attendant from breakfast maybe? Until I learned their patterns, it probably wasn't wise—no matter how eager I was to see what these Idians were all about.

Everly came practically skipping around a corner, and pulled her hands from the pockets of her uniform holding them out in my direction. "Nayla," she exclaimed, voice soft, but eager. "I'm Everly. We didn't properly meet yesterday. I'm here to take you to your brother. And before you ask, he's doing well. Asking about you, so I promised I'd bring you once he'd eaten his breakfast."

Relief flooded through me as I assessed the healer, who's blonde hair was down today in loose waves that were clipped back at her temples. Her crisp tan uniform, like the one she wore the first time I'd seen her, appeared freshly laundered and seemed to go with her clean minimal makeup look.

"Thanks," I said, allowing her to take me into her embrace. I didn't squeeze too hard for fear of breaking the female who gave the term petite a whole new meaning. She pulled back and ran her sky-blue eyes across my freshly washed face.

"I don't know what Rhijn was talking about. You seem perfectly pleasant to me." She winked and her thin lips teased up at the edges as if she knew something I didn't. "Come."

I grimaced at whatever awful things Rhijn might have said about me and followed her down the different hallways and stairwells, and across an open expanse of cut chartreuse grass to a separate hexagonal shaped building. Rows of translucent windows which seemed to glow from within were evenly placed across its many stories. "This is the infirmary where I work."

I nodded, taking in the unique structure and the strange materials the Idians used.

"Conall tells me you're able to do some healing too. More than what you did on the dune yesterday. I understand your power was exhausted."

"It was." If I'd have been at full strength, I wouldn't have needed their help. But this was probably better. Accepting their help would encourage a connection to form between us and the Idians and that connection would allow us to find out if they were a threat. It's what I'd done with Darius—albeit a little too well. A chill of dread shivered across my shoulders as I thought of the intimate moments that I'd shared with the male I'd later come to find out was my half-brother. The male who'd tried to assault or kill me on more than one occasion because I'd slighted him and stolen the ember from their territory, Drakestone. My relationship with him allowed me to get closer to the ruling family and their secrets than I would have otherwise. I flinched the sordid memory away hoping Everly wouldn't notice.

We entered through its glass doors which slid open as we passed through. She stepped into a sort of mini transport that took us up through the atrium to what I assumed was the top floor. It attached to the wall then the door slipped open.

"Well, what you were able to do saved his life. I can see how important you are to each other." Everly reached over and squeezed my forearm as she led me out of the transport, noticing my interest in the hovering machine. "There are many different kinds of transports for different needs. He's through here."

My stomach dropped as we entered the room. Rhijn was standing with his back to us, posture stiff and formal, speaking to Conall who was in some sort of elevated rectangular basin covered with metal which looked very similar to that of the transports. Above his head, a cylinder was plugged into the back of the contraption and was glowing as the liquid inside vibrated. Four clear pipes came out of the wall going down and connecting on either side of the basin, and water was flowing through them.

"Conall?" I asked, stepping up to the basin and running my fingers along the impossibly smooth metal.

Conall's ash brown hair was wet and slicked back against his skull as if he'd dipped into the substance which I assumed was water filling the basin. His chestnut eyes were bright and two dimples were dotting his radiant rosy cheeks. He looked healthier than he had only a day earlier before his injury.

Rhijn turned, letting his eyes hunt across me like he couldn't stop himself. I got the feeling if I'd had my eyes closed, I would have felt their cool trace all the same.

I tried to ignore him as I approached his side and looked down at my brother, who was apparently naked in the tub. The metal panels covered most of his muscular body so only the tan skin of his chest and above was visible.

"Nayla, I've missed you." Conall pulled an arm from the water and wrapped it around me pulling me against the edge of the metal basin. Water sloshed up and soaked the front of my white dress. I didn't stop him though, allowing him to keep his big wet arms around me for a moment more.

"What is this thing?" I asked, and took the towel Everly handed me.

I should have felt more relieved to see Conall alive and well, but the odd environment and all of the unfamiliar contraptions in it had me on edge.

"A healing pod, but it would be easier to let Rhijn explain. He's the inventor."

"You invented this too?" I asked, turning to Rhijn feeling my eyebrows crawl up my forehead.

"No, she means since I invent things, I could explain it better, but you go ahead, Everly. You're great at talking." Laughter danced in Rhijn's eyes as he razzed the healer and I couldn't help but gawk at them.

Everly shook her head, trying to keep her face drawn into a serious expression, but I could see their chemistry and that this must be a joke between them. It almost reminded me of how Conall and I were, but maybe there was something more to their relationship. How uncomfortable would it be to be having steamy dreams about a male that was committed to someone else? Especially when she was responsible for saving my best friend.

"We call these healing pods." Everly cleared her through to draw my drifting attention. "Essentially it uses power like the one in the wells, which you'll see later. But depending on how a healer alters the energy flowing through the water which is pumped in and out by these tubes, it has a different effect. Using these, we can treat three times as many patients as we would be able to versus working with each patient directly. But it's only good once the acute injury has been dealt with. Like with Conall, we're using it to reduce the swelling, and for micro healing."

"Micro healing?" I asked.

"Encouraging the most delicate fibers in the muscles and the finest blood vessels to regenerate," she answered.

"Everly says when I'm done with my soak, my legs will feel springier than before. Can you imagine if we'd had these while we'd been training?" Conall asked.

"That's pretty incredible." I walked over to the window in the room, looking out over the Chancellor's estate needing a minute to process. From here I could see it was no mere manor, but an orderly complex of which this building was just a small section of.

"Your rooms are over there." Rhijn tapped a finger to the glass pointing in the direction of the long terrace we'd arrived on.

"Where are yours?" I asked in a low whisper.

Rhijn looked down at me as if reading my thoughts, and his eyes darted to my lips, then back out the window so fast that if I weren't tracking every small movement of his, I'd have missed it. "I live on the Leeward Isle. I moved over there as soon as I finished my education, and take the ferry here when I need to use the labs in the city. After I got my own house, my father had the section of the estate where my childhood room was converted into offices which had been needed for a while. If I need to stay overnight, I have a room that I use in the same line of guest suites you all are staying in, but at the far end."

"Oh," I said. So, he was close. The sound of metal shifting drew my attention and Everly was punching some buttons on a metal box with a face similar to that of the stone tablet in the transport.

"Control panel," Rhijn explained.

The metal panels covering Conall's body lifted, then slid on top of each other out of the way. He shifted and Everly reached out a hand to help him. "Rhijn?" she beckoned.

Rhijn went over and offered Conall support so he wouldn't slip as he exited the tub. Or at least I assumed that's what happened because when I finally turned around Conall had the towel wrapped around his waist and Everly was pulling a curtain forward.

"We'll be down the hall in the breakroom when you're ready, Conall. Feel free to linger." Everly eyed Rhijn and grabbed my arm, ushering me out of the room and down the hallway into another smaller space. She punched some buttons on a machine sitting on a shelf and it sputtered before dripping out some clear steaming amber liquid. "Tea?" she asked to which I nodded.

We took our tea and sat on a grey 'L' shaped couch which lined two of the four walls. She tucked her legs underneath her, then took a sip from the steaming cup and eyed me like she was trying to decide what to say.

"Go ahead," I urged her, knowing the feeling.

Everly curled her fingers around the cup. "I have about a million questions for you, but Rhijn says I shouldn't badger you and offer instead to let you ask the question so you'll become comfortable with us."

"He did, did he?" I raised an eyebrow. So, he was scheming too. *Interesting.* "How about we swap questions then?"

"I knew I liked you!" Her face brightened. "Okay, you go first."

What did I want to know? Rhijn's calculated approach was wise, I had to admit. This female was obviously close to the ruling family. She'd be someone worth befriending. "What made you want to become a healer?"

"Oh, I didn't expect you to ask that," Everly murmured.

"What did you expect?"

"Maybe something about Idia, or Adrina. *Rhijn?*" Her mouth twitched and I narrowed my eyes. "I was good at it at a very early age. Rhijn and I got into some trouble when we were kids and I had to heal him before Vitis saw the injury so he wouldn't ask questions. We were somewhere we shouldn't have been as usual. Anyway, I found I enjoyed it. My parents went to live with Rhijn's mother in the north when I was a teenager. Our mothers are close and she'd lived in the city apart from her while I'd been growing up. When they moved, I chose to stay and study the art of healing. Okay, my turn. Why did it take you all so long to come back?"

I set the tea on the table and ran a hand through my hair, eyeing the door trying to decide how much to share. "Our way back was blocked for many years. The Makers had abandoned us. Something I did was able to reopen that channel."

Everly hesitated, waiting to see if I'd continue, her thin lips turned down at the edges. When she understood I was finished she huffed tapping her cup impatiently. "That was incredibly vague. I hardly think it is fair, but since you're the guest, I suppose it is your turn."

We swapped questions until I had the sense of what made Everly tick. Though she was more reserved than me, if we'd grown up together, we'd probably have been friends. I got the distinct impression it was Rhijn doing the trouble causing in her stories too, which wasn't what I'd expect of the somewhat formal male. And Everly was the one keeping him from getting caught. They were an odd duo. Conall and I were more equally matched comparatively.

Overall, I was satisfied with the encounter. I'd always been good at getting people to share, without over divulging myself. I looked up at the ceiling, thinking. What else did I need to know that the Chancellor might be unwilling to share? I started to open my mouth to ask the question formulating in my mind.

"I can sense your trauma," Everly blurted out. Her eyes widened as if she'd surprised herself.

I snapped my head across the couch to look at her. "You what?"

"You feel frayed around the edges. It's a part of how I heal, I sense things with people, among my other gifts which help. I don't mean to pry, but your vague answers, and the way you seem to craft everything you say… isn't usual. I don't know what you've been through or what your intentions are here, but if you ever need to talk…"

"Talk about what?" Conall's voice drifted into the room, followed by Rhijn who stood half a foot over Conall with his arms crossed over his more compact chest.

I felt exposed. Like Everly's observations and comments had stripped me of a shift like Emerson's powder. I blinked at her, trying to understand how it was possible she was seeing past my finely tuned veneer. I plastered on a fake smile and turned toward the door. "Nothing. We were just…" Words failed me. I couldn't come up with a clever lie which was a problem I never had.

Rhijn squinted at Everly, a mini glare almost. I jumped to my feet stepping between them practically puffing out my chest, which was strange. Maybe I wasn't as good as I once was if I'd gotten to know her enough to feel protective. Or maybe she was right and my emotions were frayed. She was just so kind, and forthcoming. Everly was the *unusual* one if you asked me.

Rhijn froze, his eyes affixing themselves to my form and his nostrils flared, even as his head quickly turned away. "Sorry," he said, the lump in his throat bobbing. "Your dress."

I looked down at my damp dress which, thanks to Conall, was clinging to my figure and somewhat see-through. "Thanks," I murmured to Everly who only shrugged, though I supposed her nonchalant attitude was realistic. A body was a body and I'd never been particularly modest. It was Rhijn's reaction that caught me off guard.

I glanced back up and Rhijn had turned and was headed out the door. "Council meeting in an hour. Everly will take you to the tailor then show you to your room to get situated, Conall."

I held my hands out by my sides. "I guess that gives me time to change."

CHAPTER FOUR

FTER I'D SLIPPED into a new, nearly identical white dress, an escort brought me to a large council room where the rest of my companions were awaiting me. Simple dark leather chairs were tucked underneath a long grey table which sat in the middle of the room. The walls were adorned with framed landscape scenes, and images of Skyborne, who I assumed must have been former Chancellors, as the last in the line was Chancellor Vitis. The fact that around half were female didn't escape my notice.

As soon as I saw Conall who was lingering inside the door, I wrapped my arms around his waist.

"Oh, Conall, I'm so glad you didn't die," I confessed into his *dry* and alive chest. He squeezed me back and kissed the top of my head.

"You saw me like half an hour ago," he said, smirking.

"Well, you were in a strange machine, naked, and soaking wet. Did you get settled in your room?" I asked, patting his bicep.

He nodded then turned me to face a full room watching us, including Chancellor Vitis, Kellis, the twins, a few faces I didn't recognize, the rest of my companions and, of course, Rhijn. I stuffed my hands into the pockets of the dress I'd changed into and shuffled over to an empty seat at the large oval table in the center of the room. Unlike the meeting chamber in Eastdow that was warded to keep secrets in, this room was open to an exterior terrace, giving the impression that the Idians might come and go as they pleased.

"Good afternoon, Nayla," the Chancellor addressed me. "This is my council. You have met most everyone here." He introduced the two females and a male I hadn't seen before as different advisors. "Kellis has relayed to us what you shared with him yesterday, so there is no need to repeat yourself. I will get straight to it; do you carry the void stone?"

Everyone turned to me. "The what?" I asked. I looked around the room, having no idea what they were talking about.

An insistent mental nudge from Malik opened the connection we shared. *I think they mean the ember.*

What do I tell them?

The truth, I suppose. I don't see any reason to hide that since they seem to already know. You have it still?

I picked it up as soon as we landed before my eyes were fully adjusted and slipped it back into my pocket.

"Nayla?" the chancellor pressed. "I'm making the assumption it is what has given you the ability to walk between realms."

Realm Walker. My chest tingled as the entire room waited for me to respond. I looked to Seeley, who nodded encouragingly.

I released a breath. "I think what you are referring to is what we call the ember. It was the only remnant that was left after our ancestors made the crossover. That's how it got its name."

"I don't want to be pushy or make you feel threatened, but I would love to see it," the Chancellor said warmly, leaning forward in his seat.

I immediately tensed, distrust clouding every other thought I had. I glanced at Seeley. He nodded again.

"Nayla, the first thing you need to know about us is we would never take something from you by force. Especially something that doesn't belong to us." The Chancellor's blue eyes were alight with interest.

"It's not that I don't trust you," I lied. It went against everything we'd been taught. I still wasn't convinced and I looked between the Idians, ready to bolt. But where would that leave my friends? Hostages. I wouldn't make it half a mile unless I used the ember. No, no, that was a bad idea. Allies, these Skyborne were all but presenting themselves as allies to us.

Rhijn had said they were peaceful. I needed to go with it. "You all have been very generous." I shifted in my chair. "It's just that—"

"I think we have something that would make you feel more trusting." Vitis cut me off. He wasn't buying it. He waved a thick hand at his son. "Rhijn, you may show them."

Rhijn? Of anyone in the room… Still, he walked around to my chair and kneeled beside me, impressively coming up to my eye level. I couldn't tell if the trembling I was feeling inside was showing on the outside, but I prayed to the makers it wasn't.

"Don't worry, I'm not going to touch you," he whispered so only I heard, his voice had a light teasing melody to it. *Did he know what it would do to me? Oh makers.* Warmth crept up my neck, and I ran my hands along my loose hair, hoping my dark locks would cover the red flush on my neck I knew was there.

He pulled a white velvet cloth out of his breast pocket and set the cloth in his left palm, unfolding it. Inside, hovering above the cloth, was the exact mirror of the ember. My jaw unhinged. "After the banishment happened, on that great battlefield, our *sect*, the Dar Kepler, found this. We know it as a void stone." He studied me as my breath caught as I stared at the glowing almond shaped object hovering in his palm. I jerked my head toward Chancellor Vitis, then my friends, to see if they were seeing what I was.

"Nayla, I don't think you should…" but Conall trailed off as I pulled out the dark cloth I kept in my breast pocket, unfolding it.

"I have the other half. The other void stone." I held the cloth next to Rhijn's palm to compare the two specimens. Mine animated, a pulsing rhythm mirroring my heartbeat thrummed through my palm. The white luminescent stone in Rhijn's outstretched hand was beating in a similar tempo. My head floated up and our contrasting eyes, similar to our contrasting stones, locked. I couldn't tear my gaze away as I wondered at the implication of this. It was as it had been in my dream and only reinforced the contrast of my simultaneous reluctance and draw toward this male.

Leather creaked as the chancellor rose from his seat to come around to have a closer look. The large male towered over me and Rhijn as he peered down at the *stones.*

"Uncanny, how alike they are, yet perfectly opposite. Much like their bearers it seems," he said, looking between Rhijn and I. "You can put them away now, children. I wanted to confirm what I suspected. Now it will be up to us to figure out what they are and what to do with them."

I breathed a sigh of relief as the tension dissipated in the room and I stuffed the ember back into my pocket, slumping back in my chair. I looked over at Conall and mouthed the word, *sorry*.

He gave me a half-hearted smile and turned to Vitis. "You mean you don't know?" His tone was a bit too confrontational, but he had a point considering all of their technology and even I'd expected more than *we'll figure it out*.

"Well, that was exciting," Asha exclaimed, drawing our attention. "So, we think these two things are connected and somehow going to help us fix this giant mess we are all in?"

"I do," replied the Chancellor solemnly. "But we need to understand where they came from."

"The ember, our void stone, was found on the plain where our ancestors landed in the new realm. They didn't know what it was. Only that it radiated power and killed anyone who tried to use it." Seeley recited the history, addressing each council member as he spoke. "It wasn't until Nayla came into possession of it that it seemed to have changed. Animated. Is that what happened with Rhijn?"

"Yes, but we didn't lose many Idians to the stone before we understood it hadn't found a bearer yet," Vitis explained. "And believe me, the day Rhijn touched it for the first time was the scariest day of my life."

"But that still doesn't tell us where they came from," Conall observed.

Vitis looked from Everly to Seeley. "Perhaps in the coming weeks some light will be shed upon it. Until then we'll have to do our best to understand."

A hush settled over the room as the weight of our situation set in.

"We've been here just over a full day and I feel like we've already made a breakthrough. What's next?" Asha said, practically vibrating the table with her foot tapping. Her eagerness effectively lightened the atmosphere of the room.

Vitis chuckled, giving Asha a once over, a grin lingering on his lips.

He sat back in his chair, which his broad frame filled. Chancellor Vitis had a commanding presence. Not only was he larger than most Skyborne, including his son, he had the effective quality of leadership to sense and control the energy in a room. I glanced at his hands, which were splayed across the smooth arms of his chair. They too were large and strong like the rest of him.

He nodded to Kelvin, who stood tentatively. Kelvin wrung his hands before him and cleared his breath. "Chancellor Vitis has requested I give our guests a tour of the power wells. It is the technology most central to who we are as Idians, the reason we live as comfortably as we do. Learning about it will give you a better understanding of us for when you return. Of course, if you're recovered from your journey that is."

My companions rapidly nodded their heads.

"Very well. Transports are waiting outside. We'll go to the well in the city center. I've scheduled an hour for a demonstration. When we arrive, citizens should be finishing up with their dispersions." Kelvin gestured toward a set of double doors which attendants opened to reveal the long terrace where we were dropped off the day before. Four transports waited outside.

"They've already been programmed. Once you close the door, they will take you to the central well. Pair off in twos, please. See you there," Kelvin said, shoulders relaxing, seemingly resigned to the fact he was doing this.

Before I got cornered by an Idian, I grabbed Conall's free arm and dragged him to the first transport. Once inside the privacy of the vehicle, I breathed a sigh of relief. The contraption was still strange to me, but I was just happy to steal my best friend away for a moment of privacy.

"Makers, Conall, I can't believe you tried to die on me." His chest rumbled as he leaned back on the bench seat we shared. "And not even heroically befitting your level of prowess!" I pressed the back of my hand over my forehead and sighed dramatically.

"Oh, Nayla, it's going to take a lot more than that to be rid of me." His head leaned against the glass, which filled each of the windows in the carriage as he blinked down at me. "It is so different here, like a sensory overload. How are you coping?" he asked, reaching out a firm hand to massage the base of my neck.

I fiddled with the end of my braid, which I knew had become my tell in my time as Vera. He noticed the lie I was preparing to deliver, to which I gave a meek smile.

"Remember on our hikes, how we would speculate about what Idia was like now?"

"Sure," he said.

"Well, what they've been able to do, all of their inventions—they're incredible. I mean, have you taken a *shower* yet?"

"I have," he grinned. "Showers are pretty incredible."

"I think they may be better off without us."

A weight hung heavy in the air at my statement, and I leaned my head against Conall's solid shoulder, trying to ignore the jittery nerves flitting around in my stomach. Our trip was another whirlwind ride through the city. The Light Star was still climbing in the sky and Idians were out and about, other transports zipping by ours on the opposite side of the street. Outside of how advanced and orderly their society appeared, they intrinsically seemed similar to us. Nothing outwardly denoted they were a different, darker sect of our kind like we'd been taught.

At the central well, Idians were finishing up their dispersions. Kelvin ushered us inside an open-air room where a large pool covered with glass was positioned in the center. All around it were pedestals, similar to the one in my dream. Each pedestal had a bowl formed at the top which held water. A citizen's hands broke the surface of the nearest one, his eyes closed in concentration. A slight vibration rippled across the water and the male's hands faintly glowed.

The dispersion kept us enthralled, until finally the male released a breath and relaxed, opening his eyes. He smiled then as he pulled his hands from the water, wiping them on a cloth that was draped over his shoulder. Kelvin walked up to the male and clapped his shoulder.

"How do you feel?" he asked the male in a loud, clear voice.

The male wrinkled his brow, then twisted to the five of us standing around him, waiting to hear his response. His eyes widened in alarm as he realized who we were. His chin raised, pride overwhelming his features.

"I feel good, strong," he said, looking at his hands. "I feel a sense of community, like my dispersion contributes something valuable to our society. I think all Idians experience something similar, a sense of civic pride, when they gather power to the wells."

He looked at Kelvin to gauge if what he'd said had been the right answer. Kelvin nodded, releasing the male to go on his way. Other Idians passed us as well, having finished their dispersions, until the room only held our party.

"Without delving too deep into the technical theory, I'll explain how our power systems work. Depending on the size of each well, they have a range of pedestals surrounding them. Water, which serves to insulate the energy delivered into the system, fills each basin. In the very center, there's a small hole sealed by a special piece of metal which connects to the line of salinized water which feeds the main basin. Capturing and pulling the energy from the void, the space in between where matter flashes in and out of existence and bits of energy are fleeting, is relatively safe and seemingly endless."

"This captured energy then transfers through the saline filled cylinders to the main basin where it is stored. Do you sense that low humming vibration?"

I glanced at Conall, then my other friends. Malik had his eyes closed and began slowly nodding his head. His power licked out from him in waves trying to assess the make-up of the well.

It seemed only he and I were able to sense it. I felt it as soon as we entered the room. I hadn't known what to make of it.

"Come closer," Kelvin requested. We surrounded the pedestal he stood beside. Kelvin placed his hand into the water and pointed at the metal seal. "See," he instructed. I picked up on the vibration before I saw it. His finger glowed as I sensed energy seeping down into the channels below. "The faint light is a bi-product of the energy transfer. It is harmless. Come." Kelvin pulled his hand from the water and brought us to the edge of the pool. I leaned over. Beneath the shallow surface of the water was a large sheet of glass making up the floor of the pool. Underneath was another large body of water with the same special metal standing vertical creating a maze within the large basin.

"That is where the energy is stored and released to meet the needs of the citizens. The smaller cylinders you see attached to the transports are made in the same concept. They can be plugged into conduits and recharged from these larger wells. In theory they could be charged directly, but it is too risky, and not efficient, since the energy in them is so much more concentrated."

"How do you pull the energy out of the void?" Conall asked.

"When you see an object, can you sense it as well? Sense its makeup?"

I nodded. To my surprise, Conall did, too.

"Objects are made up of different units. Inside each unit's smallest part there is an intense force that holds it together. If you can compel one of the particles in the void the very moment it blinks into existence to divide, the energy produced is exponential. That energy can be coaxed into the conduits that begin in the pedestals and flow down to the larger basins. The humming is the localized vibrations, or energy signature coming off the stored energy. From here, conduits of the insulating saline solution run underground to each home and business."

"It's incredible," Malik said, mirroring Conall and I's sentiment from earlier.

"Can I try?" I asked, before I thought better of it.

Kelvin looked at Rhijn, who considered for a moment, then nodded.

I stepped forward, but Conall grabbed my arm, trying to pull me back. "Nayla, no," he warned. "You know what they're doing. It's not allowed."

Rhijn looked between Conall and I, raising his brow in question.

"Our sect, the Sol Ros, believed, based on the decree by the Makers and outlined in the Ukarid, that using the power of the void is strictly prohibited from our kind. It is why we went to war with your sect, the Dar Kepler," Seeley explained our history. "Just a difference of opinion. Of course, we aren't married to those ideas, right, Conall?"

Conall grimaced, nodded, and released my arm.

"Ah yes, that ancient document. We have it still should you like to see it. It is quite the piece of history. The language is archaic, principles defunct as far as we're concerned here on Idia. Our sect, as you say, haven't esteemed the Makers for a long time. Since long before they went dormant one-thousand years ago. We did not buy that it was their divine right to exclusively use this power. My ancestors saw fit to use it to benefit all Skyborne. You disagree?" Rhijn asked, giving a pointed look to Conall.

Conall clenched his jaw, his athletic body tensing.

Rhijn ignored him, and turned to me. "Nayla, you sense what we're doing. The choice is yours."

I looked at Conall, knowing he wouldn't approve, but I couldn't resist. Somewhere deep down I knew the void was the power I'd been tapping into. "Conall, it's fine. This won't be the first time I've used it and I didn't become corrupted then. I'll be fine now."

Malik cleared his throat and smirked at me sideways. His chuckle was audible through our mental connection.

You sure you know what you're doing? he asked incredulously. Malik stood with his arms crossed, head angled in my direction. His sharp eyes betrayed nothing.

I do, I thought.

"No power crazy this time, okay?" Asha inserted, saying what I knew Malik was thinking. "Remember, keep your head grounded. Don't overdo it."

Kelvin waved me forward. I placed my hands in the basin like the male Skyborne we'd observed.

"Okay, now focus on the space in between. Once you have that, try to track the vibration of the tiniest spaces filling and emptying."

"I feel it." And I did. I felt innumerous bits of energy and matter flickering in and out of existence.

"Okay, now grab one of the particles and compel them apart," Kelvin instructed. "As soon as you do, you'll need to harness that energy down onto the metal plate. Once it is there, it will naturally gravitate toward the energy well."

I smiled. This was going to be easy after how I'd used the void in Monterra, and walking between realms with my friends. I nodded, grabbing hold of a few dozen particles with my mind as soon as they flashed into existence. They shook precariously in my mind's grip, their essence desperately trying to depart. It was similar to lifting an object where I'd compel the makeup of the object against the surface it rested upon. But instead, I felt an ability to compel it against itself. As each particle popped apart, a glowing light enveloped my hands. I swished them triumphantly in the water toward the metal plate sending the energy I'd collected into the conduit. A satisfying warm radiated from my chest—I'd done it.

There was a fluorescent blue, blinding light. Water from the bowl exploded outward, emptying completely. I looked down and an uncontrolled glowing light still pulsed off my hands onto the plate, which was now bright as the hottest forged metal. Shouts came from all directions. Kelvin yelled for back-up right as a final, larger burst of energy sprang forth from my palms in a tidal wave, zapping into the plate, leaving a raw hollowness sprouting from my arms to my core. A deafening pop shook the space and the metal cracked in half. The rest of the pedestal followed suit, rumbling as it crumbled inward.

I looked around, my body threatening to double over. Everything was still for a moment.

"Get back!" Rhijn shouted. I lurched backward, but it was too late. The collapsed pedestal erupted outward in a burst of light and debris. The expanding pressure released from the explosion hit me lifting my feet off the ground and I sailed into a column holding up the roof. A starburst of agony shot from my back across my body as I slid down to the floor, slumping motionless on my side. My cheek rested on the cool stones and directly in front of me charged salinized water was gurgling up from a hole in the ground where the pedestal once stood.

"Makers," Rhijn swore, as he ran toward the spring. Power from his hands pushed the water back, desperately attempting to seal the hole. It worked except for the streams that meandered through the cracks between the stone tiles. One crawled nearer and nearer to my face.

Strong arms behind me dragged me upright as I was pulled away from the trickle. I grimaced as Conall deposited me on the steps outside the building and kneeled to assess my condition. The sun was so searing. "I—"

CHAPTER FIVE

"I TOLD VITIS I thought this was premature. Citizens will be without power now for days best-case scenario, weeks at the worst." Kelvin's gentle voice did not disguise his frustration.

"It's sealed. The worst damage is mitigated. We can divert the power from the estate's wells until this can be fixed. There is enough stored to cover the lost time from this well."

I peeked my eyes open to see Rhijn, who spoke with Kelvin, tracking the latter's pacing. Rhijn was taking a methodical approach to the problem, but Kelvin stopped and pinched the space between his eyes. He didn't seem convinced.

"Hey there, you okay?" Seeley asked. "She's awake," he called to the others.

"I'm fine." I waved him off, though my whole body ached like I'd tumbled down a rocky hill, but I couldn't feel any serious damage. Maybe they'd let me have a soak in one of those healing pods.

"Well, that was one way to do it," Asha announced. "Maybe that's why the Makers didn't want us using the void." Asha gave a pointed look to Rhijn, and nudged me with her boot. "*Showoff.*"

I rolled my eyes at her, grinning.

"It's our fault." We all jerked our heads toward Rhijn's resonant voice. "To be honest, we were afraid you wouldn't be able to feed the wells, much less pull that much power from the void. Had we known, we would have cautioned you on the amount," he continued. "Aside from the damage, this is a positive thing. My father will be overjoyed."

Rhijn kneeled down to where I was seated on the steps. His voice was quiet as he spoke. "It's my fault. I should have guided you. Forgive me?" The softness in his usually astute eyes startled me.

My eyes shot to Seeley, who smiled knowingly.

"Not your fault. There's nothing to forgive. I tend to get a little over-zealous. That's all." Brushing off whatever connection Rhijn was trying to make, I scooted backwards and scrambled to my feet. "What can I do to help fix this?" I asked, turning to Kelvin. I glanced back over my shoulder to see Rhijn giving Seeley *a what the hell?* look.

It took a full week to fix the central well. Fortunately, Rhijn's plan had worked and Adrina's residents only experienced a lapse of the few hours it took to make the transfer connections to the chancellor's estate well.

During that time, Vitis taught us more about Idian society. It wasn't a utopia, but it was much more effectively structured than in our realm. Rhijn even took Malik and Seeley to an outlying well in a low populated area so Malik could try to do a dispersion. He came very close to succeeding, and they suspected he would probably be the first with another few tries.

Also, since the well incident, Rhijn seemed to be avoiding my presence and his father had eased off encouraging us to form a friendship. Unfortunately, this only had the opposite effect, increasing my curiosity about them. Not to mention that I was now feeling like an outsider. As if I was being ostracized because of the accident I caused.

Before I knew it, I caught myself stalking around the estate. It was wrong, but the temptation got to me. No one was as good and kind as Chancellor Vitis. There had to be some ulterior motive, and I was determined to discover it. My increased suspicion was precisely why I was traipsing through the estate wearing the facades of various attendants and groundskeepers at every opportunity.

Fresh ocean air came in on a breeze off the channel between Adrina and the Leeward Isle. I stood under an awning of the loggia, appreciating the open-air layout of the estate. It made the spying I was engaged in so much easier, I thought as I leaned down to manicure some hedges near the smaller council room on one of the lower levels currently occupied by the Chancellor and Rhijn. I heightened my senses so I could hear what they were saying.

Shuffling footsteps came closer to the opening, then a chair was dragged across the floor. A heavy body thudded into it followed by hands plopping down on the small desk which sat right inside the entryway.

"We've been through this. I've been overly welcoming to her. She doesn't want anything to do with me. What's the point?" I peeked around the column I kneeled in front of. Rhijn threw his hands into the air as he paced back-and-forth in front of his father.

"I think you've been avoiding her too. That's what I think. Calling her and her friends primitive doesn't help."

"I was teasing. She isn't like us. She thinks we are the origin of all evil. Or she is undecided about that, anyway. Why wouldn't I want to avoid her? You must have seen how she's different around me. She has no problem hugging her friends and I've seen Kelvin and even you pat her on the back or rest your hand on her shoulder. She treats me as if I have some sort of disease. If I walk around a corner, she spins the other way."

"I think you are misjudging her, son. She is conflicted, yes, but there is goodness in her. And power. What she did with that well is nothing short of a miracle. I don't think *she* even knows what she is capable of. You are well matched in that." Vitis paused for a moment, studying his son. "Maybe she is afraid of you. Did you ever think of that? And maybe you are afraid of her?"

"She's not afraid, she's avoidant. Honestly, I don't know if I should be telling you this, but I'm not sure if I want to strangle her or kiss her and I'm afraid I might snap and try both," Rhijn grumbled.

Hot shame flooded through me from the tips of my ears down to my toes. I suppressed the urge to shake it away. I was spying on them. I was no better than what Rhijn thought of me. And the male who was such an honorable Chancellor and father to his son thought I was full of goodness. This was not the conversation I was hoping to hear.

And Rhijn wanted to kiss me? Holy crap. I'd store that away in a vault to investigate later. The truth was I'd been hoping to hear them conspiring against us. How messed up was that? I turned around and tried to shuffle on my hands and knees back into the shelter of the column. I bumped headfirst into a pair of legs attached to a particularly annoying female friend of mine.

"Excuse me, gardener?" Asha cleared her throat. "What type of hedge is this?" She pointed down at the hedge to my right, then crossed her arms.

Shit. I looked up at her, glaring.

"It's a dwarf boxwood, miss," I snarled back at her, grateful for my knowledge of plants and what I'd been secretly studying about the plant life here in Idia.

"Maybe you can come over here and tell me what type of flower is blooming in this adjacent garden?" She sauntered down the outdoor hallway, swishing her hips haughtily as she went.

I begrudgingly got up and followed her. Rhijn looked out in our direction and squinted suspiciously at us. *Double shit.*

"Nayla, what in the hell are you doing except trying to ruin this alliance?" Asha scolded.

"Quiet," I said as I shifted back into myself.

"Don't tell me to be quiet when you're the one doing… Makers only know what you're doing." She shook her fiery locks at me tossing her hands in the air. "What *are* you doing?"

Rhijn came stomping around the corner. "Where is the gardener?" he asked, eyeing me.

"Oh, he went off to find some fertilizer, I think. Something about there should be more blooms from those flowers this time of year. And funny, I bumped into Nayla. She's always been a plant lover, you know. I'm sure she'd love a tour of the greenhouses. Or some flowers? Those yellow roses are her favorites. Myself, I prefer red," she said loudly and sweetly smiled, pointing at a rose bush flush with flowers. "Oh, I just remembered the tailor is expecting me. I'm needing a few things adjusted." Asha blushed. She'd filled out since we'd been here. Her wan frame, which was a consequence of her time in the cells of Monterra, was recovering. I straightened as Asha slipped away. "I'll come with you," I called after her.

"I'm good, thanks!" she chirped brightly, shutting me down.

Damn her. I rolled my eyes, stuck now in the presence of the Sky-borne who'd just confirmed to the Chancellor we'd been avoiding each other among other things.

"My father thinks we are avoiding each other," Rhijn stated matter-of-factly.

Well, that was bold. He stood with his feet spread and back straight as if I were about to push him over. I ignored the way his fully erect stance made the fabric of his shirt stretch taut across his shoulders, the vee at the top widening so a glimpse of his smooth skin showed.

"Is that weighing on your conscience, *your highness*?"

"No, but he feels I'm being a poor host."

I learned from my eavesdropping that our avoiding each other was not *all* Chancellor Vitis thought.

"Listen, I'm not particularly keen on being your plus one, and you don't appear to want me tagging along with you either, the primitive Ban-ished Skyborne and all. I get it, really, I do. The feeling is mutual. But if it makes your father feel more comfortable with this alliance, we can play nice in front of him. Satisfied?"

He crossed his arms across his chest and smirked down at me. Eyes twinkling, he pointed to the hedge Asha had asked me about. "I think that's actually a dwarf holly. Their leaves are very similar, so they are often mistaken for one another. I've just seen these develop red berries in the winter months."

Oh, my Makers, shit. "I don't know what you're talking about," I said, turning on my heel and charging away.

"I think your rooms are the other way," he called out to me. A low self-satisfied rumble vibrated down the corridor.

"I'm going somewhere else," I curtly replied.

CHAPTER SIX

R HIJN STEPPED BACK into the room only to fall under the scrutiny of his father's discerning gaze. Ignoring him, he reseated himself at his desk in an attempt to focus on what they were meant to be working on.

"What was that about?" Vitis was still eyeing him.

"Nothing." Rhijn flipped through a stack of papers, taking one from the pile. "I've figured the cost for the upgrades you asked us to make on the wells. I think if we purify the metal, maybe increase the thickness and use a different material for the pedestals... maybe a synthetic stone..." Rhijn's eyes drifted toward the terrace, his attention following his stare. "If we converted them to—"

"Rhijn, you're distracted." Vitis came to stand in front of him, taking the paper he'd been turning over in his hands to study it for himself.

"Sorry."

"Thinking about the female?" The Chancellor gave Rhijn a knowing smile.

Rhijn shook his head, slumping forward over the desk. He couldn't tell his father about Nayla's shifting. Her *spying*. He'd confront her about it at some point. For now, it was better for the council to think their intentions were honest. That trust between the Idians and the Banished was blossoming.

"It's not even her," he lied to both his father and himself. "It's like the stone's pull toward each other is relentless. I think she feels it too, but her resolve seems to be much stronger than mine. Or she's not even chancing it, so she's limiting her interactions with me."

Somehow that excuse stung less than what he suspected the reality was. He had been trapped in her gravity the moment she gnashed her teeth at him on that dune. *What a divine creature*, he'd thought. Fierce, protective, beautiful, capable. His blood had heated as she'd stared up at him even as recognition flitted across her gaze before she concealed it. Because she couldn't recognize him. It was impossible. She must have seen that he was Skyborne like her, Rhijn rationalized. Still, the thought of her even now, the prowess he could see she possessed, did more than pique his interest.

She, on the other hand, seemed repulsed by him. Maybe she preferred males more like Conall, the one who she called her brother, but who she shared no traceable biological relation with. The male was built like a warrior, wrapped in rippling muscle which emitted strength making Rhijn feel tall and lanky by comparison. Or perhaps she preferred females. Or it was because he was Dar Kepler, that ancient, outdated name. The Banished may initiate platonic relationships with the Idians, but Prejudices ran deep. He'd read that's how it had been in the early days after the banishment.

His mind was reeling. Why was he even considering her romantically anyway? They had too much to accomplish without this side-plot distracting them. Rhijn's brow furrowed as he tried to reason out why he was so transfixed by this female when a thought occurred to him. Since the dreams had started almost a year ago, he hadn't taken a lover. Rhijn had seen a few females, but there hadn't been any chemistry there worth exploring. That must be what was going on. He'd been denying himself for too long for some clearly unattainable fantasy. He was a male in his prime and his hormones were causing his brain to misfire. Relief flooded through him. Now that he'd identified the problem, he could deal with it accordingly.

"Son, I asked you a question." Vitis's stern voice interrupted his trailing thoughts.

Rhijn blinked, regarding the stout male trying to ascertain whether he was in father or Chancellor mode. *Chancellor... great.* That meant whatever he was about to say wasn't a suggestion. It was a directive.

"I think you need to spend more time around each other. To explore whatever this pull you describe is directing you toward. There are still things we need to understand about the void stones and the Banished."

Rhijn felt his face blanch. He'd just decided that less time with her, and more time with some other female would be the cure to whatever was ailing him. He gritted his teeth. "Actually, I was thinking—"

"So," the Chancellor cut him off. "You and Kellis will take them to the Leeward Isle. Tour the museum, gauge their reactions. See if you can gain some insight. Bringing hundreds of foreign Skyborne here is going to be quite disruptive and we would be wise to have as much of an understanding of their character as possible. The fact that a small group showed up here first has been a greater stroke of luck than I think any of us realize. So, think of this mission I'm sending you on as an opportunity."

Rhijn's chair scraped across the stones louder than he'd anticipated as he shoved it back to stand. "Fine. I'll do it."

"Rhijn, it's critical that we get this right. I understand everyone is anxious to take action and not everyone here is in support of our plan, but this extra diligence is my duty to the Idians."

"What's to stop her from going back to their realm and bringing Makers knows what back with her? You didn't see her on that dune. She was ready to fight in a way that suggested that violence is still very common in their society. Even an acceptable way to achieve their ends. I'm afraid if we drag this out too long, she'll do something brash and the Idians will pay for it."

"Then I guess it is up to you to make sure she doesn't." The Chancellor gave him a final fatherly stare before Rhijn nodded and left the room.

CHAPTER SEVEN

"I THINK HE KNOWS I can shift my appearance." I told my friends what had happened out in the walkway after Asha had abandoned me with Rhijn. "Do you think he's told the Chancellor?"

"I think if he did, we'd already know about it by now," Conall suggested.

Asha tapped her freshly manicured nails on the sleek table we were gathered around in Malik and Seeley's much larger room. "I think there's a reason he's not ratted you out."

I rolled my eyes, the *kiss her* comment sparking in my mind trying to release itself from the vault.

"She's right, Nayla. He's going to hold it over your head to get something he wants. You need to be careful around him," Conall warned.

"Conall, you are so dramatic. These Idians saved your life and have asked for nothing in return. Believe me, I know an evil male when I see one. That is not what these Skyborne are," Asha said.

"I tend to be one for snooping around, so typically, I would agree with Nayla's tactics, but I think somehow Rhijn can sense her. The connection between the void stones is likely why." Malik looked at me then. "You need to be more careful if you plan to keep this up. Or at least let me know so I can help hide you in shadows."

"You all need to slow down. No more spying. No snooping. Am I not your seer? Have I not told you time and time again these Idians are the path?" Seeley asked.

"If we knew a few more details, that might give us a little more reassurance," Conall pushed.

"Conall, you are fully aware Seeley's sight doesn't work like that. Pressuring him isn't helpful either." Malik placed a loving hand on Seeley's knee, squeezing it softly. Malik's defense of his partner was… well, sweet.

"I'm with Seeley. I wish I would have grown up here," Asha said, admiring her freshly manicured nails. "The shower alone would be worth it."

"Asha, you abandoned me. What were you thinking?" I was still mad at her.

"What was *I* thinking? What were *you* thinking, spying on the Chancellor and his gorgeous son? I mean, if it was for the view, I totally get that. I'd be more than willing to comfort either of those Skyborne if that's what it took to secure this alliance. Just putting that out there. What title do you think the Chancellor's partner has? Lady Chancellor?"

Malik and Seeley exchanged a glance, and Conall huffed and looked away. I couldn't help but giggle at Asha's humor. "Asha, you are too much. Besides, I thought you'd sworn off males?"

"Well, I did. That's until I saw that mountain of a male. I'd climb that hill. I'd hike his peak. I'd traverse—"

"Makers, Asha. You're worse than Nayla." Conall reprimanded, cutting her off.

Asha and I fell into a fit of laughter at her antics.

When we'd contained ourselves and wiped the tears from our eyes, Seeley cleared his throat. "No more spying, Nayla, promise me?" Seeley urged.

"Okay, Seeley, I relent, I relent." I held my hands in the air to them in supplication.

"Promise?" Seeley pushed.

"Promise," I forced out begrudgingly.

The image of Emerson, her creatures and what might be going on at home was a flashing beat in my mind dampening the mood. Surely after Darius had left the inn empty handed, Emerson wasn't doing anything crazy. But I couldn't deny the way she'd revolved between emotions like a flipping coin. As if sensing my thoughts, the ember vibrated in my pocket.

"When should we go back?" Malik asked, thumbing his goatee.

"We'll need Rhijn's void stone," Seeley said.

"You think we can take it?" Conall asked, leaning forward.

Seeley rolled his eyes. "No, Conall. We need him to use it to help us. Nayla, do you think he will?"

I shrugged my shoulders wondering why everyone was looking at me. "I suppose if that is what Vitis orders him to do he will." Standing, I walked toward the door. We were due for the next council meeting on the hour. "Come on. There's only one way to find out."

This council meeting had been one of the longest yet. Both sides were becoming increasingly enlightened with each meeting, and we were building a trust that I never would have expected before meeting the Dar Kepler. Especially considering my spying, which I was pretty sure Rhijn was onto. But curbing that seemed to have helped ease my suspicions about them, along with the hard truth I forced myself to face. That I had almost wanted there to be something wrong with them. I was trying to be much more receptive now. Except to Rhijn, obviously. Every time I saw him, my mind still threatened to recall a dream, and not the scary ones anymore. *Stop, stop,* I chided myself.

Daydreaming, I see. Anything worth sharing? Malik teased through our mental connection.

Shut up, I thought, tossing my hair over my shoulder.

My gaze darted around the room. Everyone was looking at me. Oh wait, had I said that out loud? I shifted uneasily in my chair, glancing at the door. "I can see we all are in need of some fresh air and to stretch our legs," I announced to the room, ready to bail on this council meeting.

"Nayla," Chancellor Vitis addressed me, smiling patiently. "I think you and your companions will be prepared enough to visit the settlements very soon."

I'd heard the term settlements mentioned several times, but with no clear explanation as to what they were referring to.

"And what are the settlements?" Asha asked on our behalf, prompting him.

"Oh, yes." Vitis gave her a warm grin. "As you've learned, most Idians in this area live either here in the capital of Adrina, or across the channel on the Leeward Isle. Adrina is centrally and strategically located to provide the best access to the resources the different regions provide. Smaller clusters of Skyborne live in rural or mountain towns across the continent. But outside of that, there are three other sites, the settlements, which are primarily inhabited by the stewards. One on the southernmost tip of this continent, in the old Dar Kepler lands, then two to the north on the twin peninsulas." He gestured to a map rolled out across the table. "These are fully functioning cities of which we have been the stewards. Successive generations of Skyborne here have managed and upgraded these cities in preparation for your return. Many of them believe their work is their calling, a life's mission so to speak."

Vitis paused, waiting for this to sink in.

"You mean you have designated valuable resources in anticipation of the Sol Ros coming back? You have created homes for your enemies?" Conall asked, incredulous. He looked over at me with eye-brows raised. I suspected he'd be back on team *let's keep spying* after this.

"I know it may seem far-fetched, but it is true. With the way we can harness power, a little goes a long way here in Idia," Vitis explained.

It had been time to come back home to Idia due to the worsening conditions in our realm, but I hadn't thought of how we would live. If we had come back as conquers, we'd have taken the lands and homes from the Skyborne who'd lived in them. If we could've convinced the Sol Ros to come in peace, we might have hoped for some sort of camp for refugees. But Vitis and his subjects, the citizens of Idia, had orchestrated something so much better. It was so incredible gooseflesh sprouted down my arms.

"What's the catch?" Conall, ever the military strategist asked, zeroing in on Vitis.

"Good question, Conall, and right of you to ask. We take the peaceful and productive society we've built very seriously. You won't come back only as refugees. We expect the Skyborne of your realm to contribute. That is why it was important for us to show you the wells. I know you are eager to get back and get the process started, but we can't let you come back until we know that you'll be able to draw the power from the void and feed it to the well. With so many new bodies to care for, our population won't be enough to sustain us for long. It is my number one priority to protect the Skyborne who live here and their way of life. I'm sure you understand. And, after Nayla's demonstration, we have great confidence you'll succeed."

This information had us all dumbstruck. "Stop gaping, Nayla." Asha smirked. Apparently unphased, she encouraged Vitis, tapping his hand. "Go on."

I squinted in her direction. She was acting as if she'd heard this before. She wiggled her eyebrows at me in return. *She couldn't have.* I looked from her to the Chancellor, who continued at her behest.

"You will be broken up into teams to go tour the sites. Leah and Rhea can take Seeley and Malik to the settlement on the northeast peninsula. The land is covered in old mountains and tall sparse pines. The area is quite majestic and peaceful. Asha and Conall can go with Kelvin and Kerris to the one on the northwest peninsula. It is the quickest journey, and lively brooks and streams run throughout the long stretches of prairie and farm-land which is surrounded by a densely wooded forest." My stomach curled into knots at what was coming. "Rhijn, Everly, you will make the trek south to show Nayla the southernmost settlement. There are sloping hills with jutting limestone karsts dotting the terrain, and a fascinating cave system that sinks into the ground running underneath the hills. They were histori-cally used as hideouts during the more tumultuous times in our history."

"I believe the museum has an exhibit," Kellis interjected.

"Yes, Nayla, I think you would find a series of tunnels concealed underground quite inspiring." A shit-eating grin spread across Rhijn's face as if he couldn't help himself and I scowled at him. He definitely knew I'd been spying.

Vitis coughed. "Nayla, the power wells at the old Dar Kepler royal estates are quite the sight, rustic, yet serene in their natural beauty. You should feel very much at home."

Did the chancellor just refer to my natural beauty by comparing me to a power well? I blinked.

"Nayla can come with me to the northwest peninsula. I think Asha would like to visit the natural wells in the south, right, Asha?" Conall edged closer to the front of his seat.

"Oh, I don't think so," she grinned. "I believe Chancellor Vitis has read us all rather correctly in our interests, don't you Nayla?"

Corner, meet me. I wiped my palms down the white linen covering my thighs. "Umm, yes, I would love to see the royal power. I mean the old well." Oh wow, what was I saying? I was definitely going to throttle Asha.

"Excellent, then it's settled," Vitis declared before I could embarrass myself further. "First, we believe it's important you learn more about what it's been like here in Idia for the last thousand years since your banishment and witness the history we've kept since the Makers changed us. This education will be a standard practice for the Banished who return, to ease their transition. We keep a record and collection of artifacts across the channel on the Leeward Isle in a facility called the Museum of Skyborne History. Kellis will be your docent, but Rhijn will accompany you as well. Being my son, he has of course learned the histories as well and even spent a few years working and studying at the museum, which houses an extensive library."

Seeley cleared his throat and leaned forward in his seat. "I understand the need to educate us, but I've been thinking of when we should plan to get back. If something were to happen while we're gone…"

"Right. If we are touring the settlements and the museum, how can we prove that we'll be able to feed the wells?" Conall demanded, acting like the leader everyone expected me to be.

"Or won't collapse them," Kelvin observed, eyeing me.

I widened my eyes at him, and huffed under my breath. At least I'd been able to do it. Vitis was glancing between me and Seeley, wheels clearly turning. Somehow, I knew what he was thinking, but we'd agreed that we wouldn't share how tumultuous things were back home until we knew we could trust them. And as much as that pained me, trust took time. At least a little.

"What are you afraid might happen while you're gone?" Vitis looked between me and Seeley, and I nudged Seeley under the table.

"It's just, as we've explained, the realm is changing at an accelerated pace. I'm sure it's fine for another week or so. Right, Seeley?"

Seeley sighed, nodding his acquiescence. It wasn't that I didn't feel the urgency he did. I was just being prudent with my intention to discover what we'd be bringing these Skyborne back to. It was our responsibility to do some reconnaissance while we were here, a plan which was still evolving in my mind since we'd arrived. They had their own parameters as well as we'd just learned.

"You're sure?" Vitis waited for any of us to protest. When no one spoke, he continued. "I don't think it is wise for you to begin bringing Skyborne back until you know more about us and you'll be able to practice on the wells at the settlements. Unless there is some other reason for urgency?"

Vitis paused again and guilt nagged at the back of my mind, but if I told them a mad healer had an army of power blocking monsters poised to release upon them, I didn't think they'd be as welcoming. And there were the innocents it was our duty to protect. I supposed I could just start bringing the Banished back—it's not like they could stop me. But if we didn't force it, our transition could go so much smoother. War could be avoided. They'd even help us coordinate, educate our people and give them shelter. Sounded like a hell of a deal for some patience.

When none of us spoke up, Vitis continued. "After you take a trip to the Leeward Isle, you may meet with your respective groups to discuss the details of your trips to the settlements. A ferry leaves for the Leeward Isle at mid-day. Plan to meet at the terrace where the transports park, ready for an overnight or two on the Isle, then you can plan your journeys to the settlements the morning after next. You're dismissed."

I stood, stretching my stiff limbs. My muscles itched to spring into action, or at least do something physical. Between the meetings and the transport rides, it seemed Idians spent more time stationary than we did in our realm. As the room cleared, I glanced between my companions. Conall's large hands clapped down on my shoulders, kneading.

"We need to spar later or something. I'm going to lose my edge with all this sitting," I said, leaning into his hands.

"Sounds like we're going to have a full afternoon of walking around this museum," Seeley said. A grin stretched across his face. "Do you think that is where they keep the Ukarid?" he asked, shifting excitedly between feet.

"I bet," Asha said. "Vitis told me they have an actual human skeleton at the museum, too. It's not on display, but he said if I told the keepers he suggested I ask, they might let us see it."

Malik glanced at her sideways. "That's demented, don't you think?"

"No way," she replied.

"I'm with Asha. I say we ask to see it." Seeley's bright eyes focused on his partner, pleading.

Malik sighed. "Fine."

Seeley, who was an avid history lover, clapped his hands together triumphantly and practically skipped from the room, chattering with Asha about the Museum.

You are so under his thumb, I poked at Malik.

He glared at me.

Is there anything Seeley wants you won't do? I teased.

One day you'll understand, he thought, shrugging, and picked up his pace to jog up beside Rhijn who was halfway down the hall. That was strange, I thought and used my power to enhance my hearing.

"Hey, Rhijn, I wanted to ask you about a possible favor while we're on the isle…" Malik's voice faded beyond the edge of my range. What favor could Rhijn be helping him with? Strange indeed.

⸕

Conall caught up to me in the hallway. "You don't have to go with him if he makes you uncomfortable. I'll go try to reason with the chancellor."

"You don't understand, Conall. They've decided I'm the leader and if I reject all interactions with the Chancellor's son, it doesn't look good. He has the other half of the ember too, so it makes sense that I'll have to work with him at some point. I'll be fine. I just don't like him. I don't fear him." That wasn't the total truth. I did fear him, but not entirely for a reason Conall needed to know about. "And besides, Everly will be with us as a buffer. When it's time, you need to go with Asha and have fun.

Please don't worry about me. You know I can take care of myself, okay?" I put my hand on his shoulder, squeezing.

"Be careful, my primitive one," Conall teased.

I wasn't sure when Conall had decided to call me that, but I supposed it was an attempt at mocking Rhijn. I still cringed. "Don't say that. And I get that I have a problem with him, but he isn't that bad. You might like him if you gave him a chance."

"Nayla, if you don't like him, then I don't. I trust your gut instinct."

But it wasn't my gut instinct about Rhijn. It was an instinct that resided just a little lower than my gut.

CHAPTER EIGHT

HE SAME STYLE of cylinders which powered the transports also powered the ferry. It was a slow steady ride across the channel, then a long uphill walk through the narrow streets from the dock to the steps of the museum. Bright colored buildings leaned into each other with an occasional narrow alley between them. My heart was thumping as we entered the building, face flushed and I was feeling much more alive than I had sitting in that meeting room.

"Feel better?" Conall asked, jogging up beside me.

"I don't think I would have survived being the Regent of Arborvale. I would have gone crazy," I answered.

"What do you think we'll do once we're here?" he asked, nudging me playfully.

"I don't know. I haven't given it that much thought," I said, staring up at the imposing building. Everything in Adrina had a minimalist look, all clean lines and calming colors, but on the Leeward Isle the aesthetic was livelier. The museum was a pale yellow with a few long narrow windows framed with white across the front. A pair of towering white doors stood ajar at the top of the steps and opened into a large atrium. Through them, and a sort of protective vibrating wall of energy they explained was for security, and past a large central desk was a courtyard with more flowering plants and small trees.

"I like the idea of helping integrate the Skyborne from Sundale into Idia once we get them here. My brother Ian and I have built a great relationship with them, and I know we'd be able to help the transition go as smoothly as possible," Asha added.

"I guess I'll help Asha and Ian," I said, smiling at Conall. "What about you?"

"I don't know. All I've ever done is military training, fighting and stuff related to that. Training with my father to be Regent one day to run Eastdow. Maybe I can help run a settlement," he said, wiping sweat off his brow. "Kellis, are there any settlements in more temperate locations?"

"The two northern ones tend to have milder climates, with the furthest north being rather chilly most of the year," Kellis replied, leading us into the Museum. He grabbed a stack of documents and passed them out to each of us. "Hi Jess, this is the group of visitors who I arranged the private tour for today. If you don't need anything from us, we'll be off."

"You're all set, Kellis. Welcome, and enjoy," the young female behind the counter offered, eagerness dancing off her broad smile as she overtly took us in. Kellis nodded to her, then led us out of the entry into the first exhibition wing.

"It seems like over the centuries the Makers had been a lot more involved in the daily lives of the Skyborne," Seeley observed as we walked through a hallway with images hung every few feet along the wall with placards detailing what each exhibit represented.

Seeley cocked his head to the side, then scribbled something down on a leather-bound journal Vitis had gifted him. He'd take a few steps, then another few notes.

"Curious!" his voice rang.

Malik hovered by his side, nodding occasionally and running his fingers across his distinct facial hair. They were having a private conversation through their mental connection, I realized.

I approached and grabbed Seeley's arm, giving it a light shake. "What's curious?"

"Oh, nothing. Malik doesn't think it makes sense. I'm going to keep looking."

"For what?" I asked.

"As soon as I figure it out, I'll tell you." Seeley squeezed my hand. "Promise."

I decided not to press and went to look at what Kellis and Conall were heatedly debating about. It was an artist's depiction of an expansive battlefield on a flat surface twice as wide as I was tall and easily Conall's height. Conall was apparently unconvinced at Kellis' claim that the Dar Kepler weren't the ones to send the Sol Ros to their banishment.

"There's no way the Makers would have banished over half of their favorite species. It was your sect." Conall's lips were pressed into a firm line and he crossed his arms, studying the painting.

"It wasn't the Dar Kepler. The records clearly show they were just as confused when they survived that day. It had to have been the Makers. There's no other explanation. The Sol Ros were going to annihilate us and the Makers stopped it. And then completely abandoned us, it seems." Kellis clasped his hands behind his back and watched Conall, who was grimacing.

I squinted to make out the individuals. Large groups of Skyborne were lined up in orderly rows and wearing uniforms in colors I recognized of the six houses that were stewards of the six territories of the Sol Ros in our realm. Slate grey for Drakestone, the elegant navy of Eastdow, the rich hunter of Arborvale, the bright yellow-gold of Sundale, the silky ocean blue of Seabrook, and finally the color that reminded me of dried blood from my own true lineage of Monterra. Maybe it was more maroon, I thought, studying the image. I wasn't as well versed in military strategy as Conall, but Monterra's troops were clearly in the most advantageous position of the six. I supposed that was a perk of being the Regius's army.

Across from them was another, much smaller force of Skyborne, presumably the Dar Kepler, in all black. *Of course, all black*, I chuckled.

"What?" Kellis stopped arguing with Conall to ask.

I waved my hand at the painting. "Oh, the black. It's just so typical. The bad guy always wears black in the stories. You guys should have picked a different color."

Rhijn laughed behind his hand as he approached. "I think I look pretty good in all black."

Rhijn always looked good. It was simply a fact. He had forgone his more casual loose linen attire for a fitted black shirt, tucked into equally fitted black trousers that emphasized his towering height and fit looking physique.

I wrinkled my nose at him, overtly glancing up and down his lean form. I shrugged, as if he wasn't all that impressive. "You look fine enough, but I think I wear it better. You just haven't had the pleasure to see me in it yet." A half-embarrassed grin crept across my face as I quickly pivoted and slipped off to find something else to look at. *Did I actually just flirt with him?*

The next image was of the near-empty battlefield. The black clad Dar Kepler stood in apparent confusion that their adversary had completely disappeared off the battlefield. A group of male territory heads representing all six colors stood on a high plain above the enemy armies, who displayed equal confusion.

"What happened to them?" I asked Rhijn, who'd followed me over to the image.

"Those who eventually accepted what had happened surrendered. My people were lucky. They would have been obliterated. They didn't want any more bloodshed though, so they allowed the surrendered to work off their debt to our society. While it was offered, they never integrated with us. Prejudices ran too deep for too many years."

"And what of those who didn't surrender," I asked, bracing for that penalty.

"They were imprisoned, in a sort of exile situation. But as the generations went on, the elders died off and the younger generations let go of the old ideas and began to integrate. Now, as you've seen, we have no sects or different groups like we did then."

A sick oily sensation rooted in my gut as I imagined what bringing back the citizens of my collapsing realm would be like. Nodding, I turned away and walked over toward an archway leading to the next section of the museum.

I held up the shiny map Kellis had given us when we'd entered the large rectangular building which was laid out in corridors with anterooms snaking around a square interior courtyard. I oriented it so the section we'd just exited about early life in Idia was behind us.

"Not sure if I'm being sensitive, but some of those displays in that last room called things that are still commonly a part of my life in Sundale *crude* and *primitive*, and I find that a touch insulting." Asha looked at me, eyebrows raised as she sauntered ahead. "Tell me I'm not the only one?"

"You'd rather have servants haul up your bathwater, then waste energy heating it? And that's not to mention draining it or the basic toilet facilities," Rhijn said, catching up with her and poking her shoulder teasingly.

"That doesn't sound much like an apology to me," Asha replied, stopping to put her hands on her hips and stared him down.

Rhijn slapped his stomach and burst into laughter. "You can't tell me you don't love the shower. You just can't." He shook off the laughter. "Okay, you're going to love this next wing." Rhijn's wide smile was pure, almost childlike. When we entered the next room, I understood why.

The wing we approached contained early experiments that had led to the invention of the power cells, transports and other modern conveniences the Idians enjoyed.

I came to the first pedestal in the center of the space and bent down to inspect the object on it. "What's this?" I asked.

"This was created by Kelvin's mentor Tad. He was in Kelvin's position before he retired. Those two are responsible for a lot of the progress you see here, like this prototype," Rhijn said, his elegant hands keeping a rhythm with his animated words. "What we use now is far more efficient, but this early cell was the first of a new generation that changed everything. Look at this coil system here," he pointed to a diagram of the power cell which showed a sectional view of the object and the metal chambers inside it. "It was this innovation that helped us move from the heavier previous generation to the current models, which enable us to travel further with the transports and even carry a second Skyborne."

He led us over to an image of a transport that looked barely large enough to hold a single Skyborne.

"We still used horses to travel longer distances until about fifty years ago. Long before I was born," Rhijn said, eying me.

I looked away intently, studying a different diagram on a nearby wall. Sometimes it was hard to judge the age of Skyborne in early adulthood, which lasted from twenty to fifty. I assumed Rhijn and I were around the same age, but I hadn't been sure.

Further down the corridor, there was a full-size model of the image.

The metal of the exterior wasn't as smooth as the transports they used now. I reached my finger out and ran it along the door toward the handle.

Smooth fingers gently closed over my wrist and I jerked back.

"I'm sorry. I should have told you," Kellis apologized. "I'm afraid we can't touch the artifacts. Only the curators may do so, and they do it using incredibly strict protocols. And gloves. The items here are very old. This transport is almost two hundred years old itself. We find the less we handle them and the more pristine and controlled we keep their environment, the easier they are to preserve."

"Oh, I'm sorry. I didn't know," I said, wringing my hands as heat crawled up my neck.

"Nothing to apologize for. I forget you wouldn't have known. I'm told Vitis has let it slip that we have a human skeleton here. I think after the Ukarid, we'll ask if we can see it. Sound good?"

I nodded, craning my neck to look at the object hung overhead.

"You have flying transports?" I asked, trying to change the subject and bumping into Conall, who steadied me before I tripped into a display.

"Not yet," Rhijn replied. He ran his fingers through his pale hair and wistfully looked up at the suspended model. "It's a dream. Maybe one day." He pointedly glanced at Kellis.

"Between you and Kelvin, you might achieve the impossible." Kellis grinned, shaking his head. "As you've noticed from your maps, the next space we approach is the documents room. The highlight is, of course, the Ukarid."

Seeley was practically vibrating as he moved to Kellis' side. A rare smile was plastered across Malik's face as he looked lovingly at Seeley.

We passed through several rooms featuring different books and papers. Finally, we came to the viewing area in the center of the wing. It was a dark room with black walls. Several metal sterile looking benches were lined up down the center of the room and under glass on a center counter was a large, pristine document.

Seeley approached and touched his fingers to his mouth, then glanced at Malik. For my friend who was so interested in books and history, especially thinking about his sight, this must be incredibly awe inspiring. I walked up beside him, and he smiled when our eyes met.

"I had no idea we'd be standing here looking at such an important piece of our history a few short months ago. Just think of what this document means. It was the catalyst for us becoming who we are as a species, but imagine all the humans who died for it to happen. A sacrifice they weren't even aware they were making, all to give us a glimpse of the power the Makers held." Seeley shook his head in disbelief.

"It's unthinkable," I said, putting my hand on his shoulder. My throat constricted, and I stepped away giving Asha space to see it.

"I wish we knew more about them. Was there truly no record left?" Malik asked Kellis.

"Unfortunately, we only have some ancient preserved bones, a few images, and what information the Makers were willing to let us retain, which isn't much. This document itself is over five thousand years old."

"How hasn't it disintegrated into dust? It looks brand new," Conall observed.

"It is a living document. An extension of the Maker's power. And as you saw in that first exhibit, when the Makers left us here in Idia, we were practically starting from scratch."

"Like we did after the crossover," Conall said in a hushed tone. He leaned in to get a closer view, keeping his hands stuffed in his pockets.

"So, it seems," Kellis replied. "I imagine the humans who made the change weren't expecting to be quite so unprepared. They were left here with their new power and little else. It appears to have taken generations and many conflicts to organize into the tribe like *houses* that seem to have continued on in your realm."

"Vitis's father wasn't the previous Chancellor?" Malik asked.

"No. I've mentioned before that isn't how it works here. And trust me—I have no interest in being the next one," Rhijn scoffed. "We have many old political families here that are represented, as well as many new names who have come into prominence. Innar is an old lineage, but the previous Chancellor, Kellis' Grandmother Chancellor Ireena, was a relative newcomer to the political scene. Whoever is Chancellor is determined by who is judged best fit to lead after the previous Chancellor has decided to step down. I think there is a document in the library detailing the process in more detail if you are interested?"

Seeley started to accept Rhijn's offer, but Asha huffed loudly.

"This old piece of paper and your history is very interesting and all, but my feet are aching and I am *dying* to lay my eyes on this skeleton." Asha shifted around on her feet, stretching them and looking at Kellis intently. "*Dying,* get it?"

"Makers, Asha. You're incorrigible," I said. "All right, Kellis, you'd better lead the way."

⁓

Kellis got clearance to show us the Human skeleton display from the head curator and we were soon traversing a maze of hallways which began at a doorway behind the large desk at the main entrance.

"The reason this is kept away from all of the other exhibits is because the specimen's organic material is so sensitive, and precisely monitored, any slight change in air quality, light or temperature may trigger an increased rate of decay," Kellis explained as he led us through a final set of glass doors. Controls lined a desk near one wall and a tablet like the one in the infirmary displayed information. Kellis opened the metal door on the other side of the room. The air was dry and smelled a little too clean, like antiseptic. Boots clacked across the smooth floor, echoing in the small room as we approached the display.

Seeley sniffed, breaking the silence after long tense moments.

"They look exactly like us," Malik said. His hands trembled slightly, and a subtle shadow unfurled around him. Seeley threaded his hand through Malik's and leaned his head against his shoulder. Malik's shadows retracted as he absorbed the comfort of his partner as they took in the image before them.

Asha stood frozen, a hand over her open mouth.

Conall tilted his head to the side, furrowing his brow. "It's unsettling," he said, studying the image.

The five of us stood in front of an illustration mounted on the wall of a human family. A couple was sitting on a bench in a wooded area where flowers grew in an organized fashion, like the gardens in Arbordale. The man had his arm around the woman while a girl was bent down scratching behind the upright ears of a small, very friendly looking wolf. The wolf reminded me of the semi-domesticated cats that lurked around in the Eastdow gardens—friendly to Skyborne if they were getting something they wanted, like food or attention, assuming you could coax them into trusting you.

The family was perfectly lifelike and exactly our duplicate. Beside the image was a glass cube with a skeleton labeled "HUMAN." Next to it was another nearly identical one labeled "SKYBORNE." A diagram with circles illustrating the slight differences and explaining theories on the causes was installed between them. Mostly minor improvements were noted, like slightly wider eye sockets, which likely led to Skyborne's improved visual capability, pelvis alterations that eased childbirth, and added flexibility in the knee and ankle joints. Interestingly, the skull size was the same, indicating the adequate processing capacity of the human brain.

"If you directly study the differences between their skeletons and ours, you'll notice slight differences—"

Rhijn had raised a hand to stop Kellis from his memorized explanation, seeing us and how strong our collective reaction was to the display before us. Unease followed by shame made me shift uncomfortably, and I caught myself twirling a piece of my hair. I looked up and Conall was watching me. He nodded at my fidgeting fingers and I abruptly put my hand to my side.

"I've always wanted a pet wolf," Conall said, shrugging while seeming to have read my thoughts. His boyish smile spread to me, then Asha. Seeley and Malik grinned as well, though Malik was trying to repress his.

"You don't have dogs in your realm?" Rhijn asked, inclining his head, waiting for a reply. He pointed to the friendly wolf. "That's a dog. Humans had them and they are one of the best things the Makers let us keep. I'll have to introduce you all to Galaxy. She's at my house here on the island. That dog is my pride and joy!"

"You have a wolf—I mean dog?" Makers, I really didn't want to like him, but what would that say about me?

"I do. You'll love her too. Just wait. I'm supposed to take you all around the island tomorrow, so we'll go by and meet her." His grin was so wide his teeth were showing.

Seeley sniffed and wiped his eyelids as he giggled. "This place is too much. I think we all could use a drink."

CHAPTER NINE

T HE LIGHT STAR was setting as we met in the foyer of the pink boutique inn where Kellis had arranged rooms for us before he'd gone back to Adrina. Asha and I were sharing one, Seeley and Malik were together, which left Conall and Rhijn. I would have spared Conall and roomed with him, but that would have left Asha with Rhijn and though she sometimes deserved it, I figured she'd only find a way to make me pay for it later.

"Wow, look at you!" Seeley said, grabbing my hand and spinning me. The above the knee black dress I was wearing spun as I twirled.

Rhijn was staring. "I told you," I gloated, to which he swallowed.

Conall stepped in front of him and reached up and fingered the braid that was woven around my head like a crown. The other half of my dark locks flowed in soft waves down my back. "What's going on here?" he asked.

"Asha braided it. What, you don't like it?" Asha had been begging me to let her play with my hair. "Asha finally convinced me she was quite adept at braiding and not to judge her own hair as the example of her quality work."

"No, I like it. It's just… different," Conall replied. "Feminine."

"Okay, thanks, I guess," I said.

Rhijn cleared his throat. "You're… breathtaking." His smooth voice didn't show an ounce of insincerity. I was hoping Malik would stomp down the stairs right about now.

"What about me?!" Asha blurted, nudging past me. She held out her hand to Seeley for a spin. Seeley laughed, obliging. Asha's similarly cut green dress spun like mine had. When she stopped spinning, she brushed her flame-colored locks out of her face. "No need to shower me with compliments. I know I look good."

We were all giggling at her when Malik walked in the front door and shook off his coat. "I almost made it before the rain started."

"And where exactly were you for the last hour? I came out of the shower and you were gone." Seeley tapped his foot, eyeing Malik. I wondered if his tapping had more to do with his anxiousness to get back to our realm than his suspicion of his partner's activities. We really hadn't been here long and before we brought Skyborne back, it was reasonable to do our due diligence. Wining and dining however felt excessive, and guilt clouded the otherwise happy evening.

Malik patted his breast pocket, smirking. "I saw something I had to go back and pick up."

We passed numerous storefronts on the way from the museum back to the inn. I had no idea what the mysterious item could be and why Malik was being so secretive about it. I guess that was his way, though.

"You aren't going to demand he tell you what he had to sneak off and pick up?" Asha exclaimed, throwing her hands to the sky. "Makers, you two."

"I've learned when Malik wants to keep a secret, there is no forcing his hand." Seeley turned, crossing his arms and peered out the window. "The rain has already stopped. Shall we?" Seeley threw open the door to the inn and sauntered out into the night.

Rhijn rushed to catch up and took the lead. He'd promised us there was a cafe a few blocks from the inn which served the best Idian food on the Isle. I looped my arm through Conall's on one side and Asha's on the other, and we followed along.

There was a small space in between buildings that came into view. "Through here," Rhijn said. The street turned from stone to wooden planks and the walls narrowed into an alley. At the end, twinkling lights came into view, and the alley eventually opened up into a hidden courtyard. Vines flowering with papery pink blossoms were growing up trellises and white cloth covered tables were positioned throughout with canopies to protect them from the frequent showers. Globes of light were strung zig zagging throughout the space. In the center was a bigger table, and a server came and led us over to it.

Malik squeezed Rhijn's shoulder. "It's perfect. Thanks, buddy."

Buddy? Since when do you call people, *buddy?* I thought to Malik, raising an eyebrow in his direction.

When they help me orchestrate elaborate surprises, Malik thought back, and reached forward to pull Seeley's chair out for him. I narrowed my eyes at him, trying to figure out what he was up to.

"This place is beautiful," I complimented Rhijn's selection.

"You like it?" Hopefulness laced his voice.

I nodded.

"I'm glad," he said. "I come here a lot. The food is as superb as the ambiance. This place serves many of the dishes in elaborate sauces which have stewed for hours to develop the intensity of the flavors."

The server handed out paper menus, which I turned over in my hands as he began pouring the house wine in each of our glasses.

"We don't have restaurants like this in our realm. Most of what is served is the daily special and not cooked to order like this where we each can make an individual selection."

Rhijn leaned across the table, indicating to the menu. I lowered it and he tapped the third item down. "Based on what I've seen you eat, I think you'll like this one."

I read his recommendation of marinated whitefish in a lemon curry sauce over baked yams. "That sounds lovely."

"I'd suggest you get a side of the chili oil too, if you like it *spicy*," he suggested. "You can drizzle the oil over the top and it really elevates the experience."

Asha leaned forward as if to say something conspiratorially which caused dread to roil in my belly. "From what I understand, Nayla definitely prefers things spicy—Ouch!" she cried, glaring at me.

"What?" I batted my eyelashes at her innocently.

"If you've bruised my shin, I'm going to double your payback."

"Ladies," Conall chided.

Since when had he become the mature one, I scoffed inwardly.

Conall shifted his attention toward our host. "Rhijn, if I was craving a *meatier* dish, do you have a suggestion?"

I raised an eyebrow at Conall, and he shrugged, cocking his head to the side. He was attempting to be civil to Rhijn as I'd requested, though I had caught the slight flexing of his chest at the vee of his shirt. I could forgive a little showing off, so I smiled at him approvingly.

Rhijn was thoughtful for a moment, appearing not to have caught Conall's flaunting, and then suggested a braised lamb in a mint curry served over white rice.

After we'd placed our orders with the server, I picked up my wine, and the ruby liquid sloshed in the glass as I raised it for a toast.

"To our new friends, to the future and to what life will be like for all the Banished when we finally bring them home. Cheers," I said, clinking my glass with my friends.

A round of cheers went up, and I relaxed as I let the smooth oaky liquid play across my tongue before warming the back of my throat. Rhijn was watching me. *Yum*, I mouthed so as not to interrupt the conversation which had sprung to life at the table.

After we'd eaten the meal that was even better than Rhijn had promised, a quartet that had come out of nowhere began playing. Malik cleared his throat, looking uncharacteristically nervous. "Seeley, would you dance with me?"

Seeley glanced at me but I could only shake my head because I had no idea what had come over my usually cynical half-brother. Seeley put one hand to his chest, then gave Malik his other to be led to the dance floor.

Malik pulled Seeley close, and they chatted softly as they swayed back and forth to the gentle music.

"Nayla, do you want to go dance, too?" Conall smiled at me encouragingly.

Rhijn raised a hand to stop Conall, who was standing up from his chair. "Let them have their moment," he whispered.

Conall's eyes widened, and I glanced at Asha, whose hands were shaking her napkin as she picked up on what was happening.

My heart was fluttering in my chest, so nervous and excited for my friends. The song changed into a slower, more romantic sound.

All eyes were on the dancing pair as Malik stepped back from his partner and reached into his pocket. Seeley's eyes widened and his breath caught as he focused intently on Malik, who dropped to his knees.

"Don't listen—"

"Shhhhh," I hissed at Conall. Asha was leaning an ear in their direction, and I heightened my senses to do the same.

"Seeley, so much has changed since you came into my life. You showed me how to laugh. That this world could be a better place. That I could be a better male. Every day I get to spend with you keeps getting better and better. Will you do me the greatest honor of my life in becoming my husband?"

Seeley murmured something which I took for a yes, because Malik slipped the ring he'd evidently been shopping for on Seeley's finger.

Seeley pulled Malik to his feet and grabbed his face, placing a loving kiss on him.

We were a romantic species, and Asha and I were cheering and whistling the loudest among the other dinner guests. I looked over and surprisingly Rhijn, who'd helped orchestrate this proposal and just winked at me, was right there with us being as loud as possible. Conall didn't seem quite to the same level of excitement as we were, but he was clapping none-the-less with a dumbfounded look on his face.

Malik and Seeley walked over hand in hand, and showed us his newly adorned finger, which Asha and I fawned over. The ring was silver with a turquoise braided inlay through it, and the design suited Seeley perfectly.

He had turned and was busy being congratulated by the onlookers, so I grabbed Malik and threw my arms around him, sniffing into his chest. Malik pulled away and held me at arm's length. "What's wrong?" he asked, eyebrows raised in concern.

"Nothing. I'm just so damn happy for you guys," I replied, in between sniffs.

"I hope one day I find a love like that," Asha said, sighing dreamily.

I wiped my eyes with a napkin. "Makers, Malik, I didn't know you had it in you."

Seeley's grin appeared painful. "Is it the wine, or was that just the best? Malik, I've never been so surprised. He truly didn't tell any of you?" Seeley asked, incredulous.

We collectively shook our heads. "No, apparently Rhijn was the only one special enough to receive a warning," I said, sticking my tongue out at Malik.

"Very mature, Nayla," he said, huffing a laugh, then nodded at Rhijn. "I needed Rhijn's help. And he totally came through for me. I owe you big time."

"Well, thank you Rhijn for helping my *fiancé*. I couldn't have imagined a more romantic proposal, in a more beautiful location, surrounded by the best of friends. Tonight was perfect and I'll never forget it." Seeley beamed, not able to keep his hands off Malik. "Now, when can we get the check?"

CHAPTER TEN

"Hey lovebird, what are you doing up so late?" I called to Malik, who walked over to the breakfast bar at the inn and faced his back toward us a little too intentionally.

His hair was a tousled mess, and he looked like he'd hardly slept, yet I swore he was faintly glowing.

"Rough night?" Asha blurted, and I giggled behind my hand.

"You two should learn to mind your own business," he said, scowling back at us.

"Malik, you're practically beaming." I slapped the table and Conall shook his head at Asha and I, who were now in a full-fledged laughing fit. "I'm sorry Conall. I mean, can you imagine, Seeley has turned our dear stoic Malik into a lovesick fool. It's perhaps the greatest thing I've ever seen."

The innkeeper handed him a tray stacked full of breakfast delicacies and he turned to us. "You're just jealous," he smirked under his distinct facial hair, keeping his tone flat.

"Ignore these two lunatics." Rhijn flicked his hand in my direction. "You guys up for some exploring today? There's some fantastic hiking right outside the village."

A blush crawled across Malik's cheeks, and he cleared his throat. "Seeley asked if we could stay in today, perhaps another night at the inn, just the two of us. So, that's what we're doing."

"Oh, that's right. You guys got the Regal Suite. I wouldn't want to leave that decadence either. Seeley said there is a bathtub where bubbles shoot out the sides." Asha leaned toward me as if she were sharing a secret. "Well, I think I'm going to cut this visit a day short too and catch the mid-day ferry. Enjoy your hike." She stood, dusting off her hands, and headed for the stairwell before I could think of a taunt to call out after her. Malik turned with his tray and followed her up.

"I guess that leaves us three then." Rhijn looked between Conall and me uneasily.

"Oh, yay…" Conall replied.

⁓

We repacked the backpacks Vitis gifted us and hoisted them onto our shoulders. Rhijn was waiting outside when Conall and I came down to meet him. Conall had pressed me to cut today short too, but I liked the Isle and wanted to see more of it. Even if it was with Rhijn as a guide. And after what he'd done for Seeley and Malik, that was yet another point in his favor. At some point I was going to have to acknowledge he wasn't so terrible.

Conall reluctantly agreed to come, but only so he wouldn't be leaving me alone with Rhijn.

"You guys ready?" Rhijn asked, and we took off down a street that he explained led outside the city. As we walked, he pointed out unique buildings and waved to people he knew on the street, stopping occasionally to introduce us. Everyone seemed to have a great affection for him. Like how the Skyborne of Eastdow adored Conall.

"Ohhhh," I cried, peering in the window of a shop we passed. The scent of cinnamon and baked bread wafted through the air and the corners of my mouth puckered and began salivating. "What's in there?" I asked, pointing to the door.

"You're hungry after all that food you ate for breakfast?" Rhijn raised a brow, stopping to look down at me. His lips quirked downward in what I knew was a repressed smile.

At that moment, I was willing to whine and grovel if that is what it took for whatever smelled so delicious in that shop with the words *Ma's*

Baked Goodness written in a swirling script over a painting of a braided bun on the glass pane set into its door.

"She does have an impressive appetite," Conall said and clapped me on the back.

I squirmed out from under his arm. "Eww, Conall. It makes me sound weird when you put it like that." I shuddered to think of how Rhijn would take Conall's description of my appetite.

Rhijn ignored the comment and tapped on the glass, and I saw movement in the back of the shop. "They're closed for the day, but let me see what I can do."

An elderly Skyborne opened the door and her weathered face brightened when she recognized Rhijn. "Oh, you handsome thing, what do I owe this surprise?" She reached up on the tips of her toes to pat his cheek with her flour covered hand.

"Oh my, look what I've done," the baker giggled. "Come in, come in."

Conall and I followed her in, and Rhijn shut the door behind us, dusting the flour off his face.

"It's so lovely to see you on this sunny afternoon, Ma. My friends couldn't help but be drawn in by the aroma of your shop, but as they are newcomers to this realm, they didn't know you closed early today. I thought, maybe if you had anything leftover you might be willing to sell it to us so they could sample your delights?"

He was laying it on thick, but the elderly baker's cheeks had turned bright pink and her eyes were wide open, transfixed on his every word. She reached out a hand to pat his cheek again, then looked at it, remembering the flour, and pulled her hand back, wiping it on her apron. "For you dear, anything."

She scuttled to the back of the shop, and I flashed Rhijn a look. He shrugged his shoulders and gave me a sly smile, to which I rolled my eyes.

Ma came out with a paper sack and held it out to Rhijn. "Free, so long as you come back sooner between your visits?"

The crafty old female didn't let the package go until he'd agreed to her terms. We exited the shop and Rhijn rifled through the package as we traipsed down the street back on our exploration mission. He handed me a long skinny tube of bread that was covered in cinnamon and sugar. Greedily, I took it and sunk my teeth into it, tearing the top off and pushing it into my mouth with the fingers of my other hand. Warm vanilla curd which filled the center set my tastebuds alight, and I wiped the excess that had gotten on the side of my mouth with my hand.

"Mmm… So yummy," I said as I chewed. Both Conall and Rhijn had stopped to stare at me. I finished chewing and swallowed. "What?" I asked, shoving another bite into my mouth. "Come on," I eked out over the pastry, and walked around them, leading the way down the street.

I smiled as I heard their footsteps eventually pick up behind me.

❧

"This is the trailhead?" Conall asked, wrinkling his nose. He surveyed the overgrowth, toeing a vine that was in our path.

"Yeah, it doesn't get used often enough. Just step on the branches or push them out of the way." Rhijn's long legs had no trouble stepping over the scattered brush that occasionally crept across the trail.

I shrugged and hopped across a branch in the path, chasing after Rhijn, who was already a distance down the trail.

Conall grumbled, following us. He eventually passed me and caught up with Rhijn and the two of them led the way up the path, seeming to make a game of who could jump further or higher. Conall grunted as he stumbled, but righted himself just as fast before he fell.

"I'm not healing either of you if you twist your ankle," I called ahead. Jumping between the stones across the branches was addictive, though. I'd jog the smooth stretch of worn path that was more sand and dirt, then hopped across the rocks enjoying the careful foot placement it required. I'd much rather be doing this than sitting through a council meeting any day.

Sweat was glistening off my brow and dripping between my breasts when we came upon the view of the ocean. We'd been climbing and as we crested the last hill, we came to a high cliff that plummeted down to waves which lapped against the rock face below. Every so often, a larger wave would come in and crash, sending a fine mist of salty water up into the air. I held my outstretched arms toward it and felt the mist on my fingers which were swollen from the rigorous hike. It was breathtaking, and I felt alive.

Seabreeze whipped the loose tendrils of hair around my face, and I undid the braid which had come loose and re-wove the three long strands.

Rhijn walked up to the outcropping I was standing on and tilted his head to the side, studying me. "What do you think?"

"It's… I don't know. It's everything. Does that make sense?" I wiped the sweat on my forehead onto the outer shirt I'd peeled off, which left me in a cropped sleeveless top. I was glad he'd suggested I'd worn pants, however, because my legs would have taken quite the beating had I not.

"It makes perfect sense," Rhijn agreed, flicking his gaze between Conall and I.

Conall, who'd taken his linen shirt off too, not being used to the heat here and probably something dumb and male influencing his action.

He walked up to Rhijn, who still wore his light tunic, and their contrast struck me. Conall was tall and built like a warrior, thick bulging muscle which emanated physical strength, but crowned with the charming face of a kind male. Warm chestnut eyes and cool brown hair, and two cute dimples. Devastatingly handsome, but approachable.

Rhijn was all hard angles and tight lean muscle and stood half a foot taller, which made his height that much more impressive. His blond hair hung straight down to his shoulders on either side of his stone-hewn face and his cool toned eyes made him appear like an entirely otherworldly creature standing on that jagged cliff side in the sun—striking. But the Skyborne here seemed to find him as approachable as Conall. I peeled my stare away from them and looked back out at the ocean.

"Don't you think we need to head back? I know I haven't been here that long, but I'm fairly certain it's going to be dark soon," Conall said, tugging at his backpack straps, which made his pecs flex. He gave me a lopsided grin. *Definitely showing off.*

"Oh, I forgot to tell you. That is our destination." Rhijn pointed at a cute building sitting on a cliff overlooking the crashing waves below. "I thought we could give Seeley and Malik some privacy."

"What's that building?" Conall asked, weariness of Rhijn lacing his voice.

"My house." Rhijn hopped over a rock and jogged to where the trail picked back up, and turned around to gauge our reaction.

"Really," I gasped. "You live there?" *On this breathtaking cliff?* I didn't add.

Rhijn nodded, and I grabbed Conall's hand to pull him forward. Okay, that was cool. Even I had to admit that.

Conall rolled his eyes, but let me pull him into motion.

My grin hurt by the time that we walked up to the wooden gate of Rhijn's home and I pinched my cheeks to massage them. I loved the jagged cliffs, the balmy air, and the deep aqua and bright turquoise of the sea on this isle. The colorful houses and shops. *How could one feel melancholy surrounded by so much energy?*

Rhijn moved his hand, and a lock clicked. The gate swung open on a whine. A booming *RUFF* echoed across the yard, and an enormous creature bounded into view.

The thing had wiry black and grey hair, was almost the size of a foal, and a sizable set of jaws that a long, wet tongue was lolling out of. The animal raced over to Rhijn and bowed down with his front two legs. His furry tail beat back and forth on his rump, which was sticking up in the air.

Rhijn patted his chest, and the animal jumped and put its front legs on either side of his shoulders so it was standing as tall as him. Rhijn ran his hands up and down the dog's sides, and the dog rubbed the side of Rhijn's neck with his nose before giving his cheek a lick.

"I know, girl. I've missed you too. Now go say hi to my new friends." Rhijn directed her to acknowledge us. "This is Galaxy." He hooked his thumbs in the straps of his pack and watched Galaxy assess us.

I swallowed the breath lodged in my throat. "Hi Galaxy," I croaked out. The furry beast started beating her tail even more furiously and ran around me, poking her snout around sniffing, probably assessing what was different about me from the normal Skyborne here on Idia she was used to. She stopped in front of me, then jumped up and landed her furry paws on my shoulders like she had Rhijn. I lost balance and both Galaxy and I went tumbling backwards.

"Humph." My backpack cushioned my fall and the beast was standing over me, licking my face and pawing at my hands. I started trying to bat the thing away, but the dog became more intent, as if this was some sort of game. Of course, I gave in, tittering at every ticklish lick and shoving my hands into its thick fur. "Stop it, you silly dog," I said between giggles.

"Galaxy, here," Rhijn commanded in a stern voice.

The dog jumped back, but looked at me as if to say, "awe, please. Can I keep playing with her?" Galaxy sat obediently at Rhijn's side, coming up to the tall male's hip.

"Sorry, she usually has better manners than that. She's only allowed to do that if she's invited." Rhijn tussled the hair between the dog's ears.

"Not to mention she's making me feel left out." Conall held his hand out to Galaxy like Rhijn had instructed, trying to get the dog's attention. She gave it two sniffs and let him scratch under her chin. Her ears flopped as she pranced back over to me, nudging with her wet nose, urging me to get up.

Conall walked over and reached his hand down to pull me to my feet. I stood, dusting myself off.

Galaxy brought a small stick over to Rhijn and gave a whimper. "Play later," he said. The dog dropped the stick and I'm pretty sure she sulked as she trotted away.

"Come, I'll show you where you can put your things. I had a friend of mine stock a few food items, so we should be covered for tonight and in the morning." Rhijn opened the door with a glass panel and ushered us in.

The main room had a fluffy looking couch and two matching chairs facing a set of floor-to-ceiling windows that faced out to the sea. The room was a modest, comfortable size, and even included a kitchen and dining area. I walked over and ran my hand down the smooth handle of the piece of equipment I'd learned was a prototype for keeping food cold called a chiller. I looked at Rhijn for permission. He nodded.

I opened the door and a cool blast of air hit me. I smiled and closed it, shaking my head. "I'm sorry, I still can't believe you can make air this cold and one day I might have one of these where I live." I turned, inspecting the space. "Ohh, what's this?" I pulled on the handle and a door flipped open. It was a dark open space lined with metal racks. A few controls sat at the top on a long skinny panel. I glanced at Rhijn, who was watching me explore.

"Oven," he said. "It cooks food. You program what you're cooking and what shelf it is on and it does the rest, even scanning the particles in the dish, sensing when it is done and keeping it warm until you're ready to eat it. How do you cook food in your realm?"

"We have ovens. But not this fancy, so I wasn't sure. We use our power or fire to heat them. And they're made with stone most often." I closed the oven.

"Here, I'll show you to your room," Rhijn said.

I still had my backpack on, and Conall was inspecting the windows.

"There's only two. Mine and the one for a guest." He opened a white wooden door for me, and I entered. A comfortable-looking bed covered in simple white bedding sat in the middle of the room, and a chest and mirror was positioned against a wall. There was another window on the outside wall, and a door adjacent to it.

"That's a small bathroom with a shower," he said, raising an eyebrow at me.

"Perfect." I silently clapped my hands.

Conall peeked in the room, and Rhijn turned to him. "Conall, you can have the couch. It's comfortable, and you'll have a stunning view of the light star's rise."

Conall shook his head. "I can stay in here with Nayla. This bed is plenty big." He set his pack on the chest. "Nayla, is that fine with you?"

"Yeah," I shrugged, "of course." I started unpacking my bag into the drawers of the chest. "I think I'd like to take a shower before dinner. Then I can help cook."

Conall burst out laughing. "*You're* going to help cook food? No way."

"I can help, as long as the directions are thorough and my instructor is patient." I put my hands on my hips and smirked at both males, who were looking at me incredulously.

"You can't cook?" Rhijn asked, raising a brow.

"I'm our realm's Chosen One. Why would I have ever needed to learn?"

Oops.

"*Chosen one?*" Rhijn eyed me curiously, but I raised my hand to stop him.

"Forget I said that. Not important. What is important is I have plenty of other skill sets. For example, I can hunt and cook meat over an open flame, so I'd consider that sufficient. And I can use a knife, so point me to whatever needs chopping." I gave him a haughty grin, and shooed them out of the room, eager to wash off my salty skin and the dust that I knew was coating my feet from our hike.

An hour later, we'd all showered and changed into clean, loose-fitting clothing. Conall was outside throwing the stick to Galaxy and she was running it back to him excitedly.

Rhijn, who was standing in the kitchen pulling things out of the chiller, noticed me watching him. "Conall wanted to make friends. She loves playing fetch, so they'll be fast friends after this."

Warmth flooded my chest. "Here, let me help." I held out my hands, and he placed onions and mini onion in them.

"You said you were proficient with a knife, go ahead and cut those up."

I started off to my room to grab one of my knives.

"Where are you going?" He opened a drawer and gestured at the knives in it. "Wait, you have knives in there?" Rhijn glanced at the guest-room and his jaw fell open.

"What?" I huffed and selected an appropriately sized blade from the drawer and set it down on the wooden board he'd set out for me.

I tackled the big one first, chopping it into tiny pieces. Sniffing, I raised my hand to wipe the tears spilling down my cheeks. Rhijn reached out a hand to stop me and we both froze.

"Oh, no. Don't do that," he said. "The juices from the onion will burn your eyes. Here, let me."

I stood stiller than I ever had. My heart froze, then started thundering in my chest. At least if it happened here, it was only him who would witness the shuddering mess I'd become. Rhijn picked up a cloth and brought it to my cheek, which prickled with the sensation of his nearness. An early warning sign of what I knew would happen if he touched me. I swallowed, clamping down on the images that were flooding my mind.

"I'm not going to hurt you," he said, misunderstanding. His voice had an edge to it and I repressed a shiver.

"Go ahead." My eyes tracked his movement.

His lips turned down into a deep frown. "I don't get you." He dabbed the cloth on my face, soaking up the tears caused by this horrible vegetable. It was an oddly intimate thing to do, and his eyes softened as he worked, though our skin never touched. I was kind of… disappointed, though that didn't make any sense.

He finished, placing the cloth on the counter and held up the other smaller onion, looking away. "This one isn't so bad. Peal the little bulbs apart and cut the pieces up as fine as you can."

Rhijn and I worked in silence. He got out pots and pans, and took the onions and cooked them on a heated dish on top of the oven. He added cream and spices, and in another pan, he cooked a curled-up type of seafood. In a third pot, he cooked a fine grain I wasn't familiar with.

Conall came in through the door, and made his way over to the kitchen. Galaxy eagerly tracked at his heel. "That smells amazing. What can I do?"

"Grab out a bottle of wine from the chiller, and three glasses," Rhijn instructed, and brought a spoon covered in the sauce up to his lips. He stuck his tongue out to test the heat of the liquid before putting the spoon into his mouth. My eyes were transfixed by the action. He pulled the spoon out clean. "Perfect."

Conall did as Rhijn asked, opening the chiller. "There isn't any wine, only a bottle of this pink stuff."

"Actually, that is a type of wine. You'll like it. Nayla, here," he handed me three bowls. "Put a scoop of the grains in the bottom of the bowl, then give it to me."

I obeyed. Rhijn put a scoop of the seafood sauce he'd made on top and I took it over to the table. We finished dishing out the food and seated ourselves around the small circular table.

I picked up the pink wine placed in front of me and swirled it in the glass, then took a sniff. A hint of green, mint maybe, and citrus with a touch of sweetness glided up from the glass. I took a tentative sip, letting the liquid play across my tongue. "S'good," I said and swallowed.

Conall moaned, and I flicked my gaze from my plate up to him, raising my eyebrows. "Yeah?"

He gave a satisfied groan and swallowed the bite. "The food here is unbelievable. I can't believe you're this good of a cook, Rhijn."

Rhijn beamed. "I'm glad you like it. It means a lot."

This was the nicest Conall had been to Rhijn, and I was afraid to say anything to break their tentative treaty.

"There is something I've been meaning to bring up." Rhijn shifted in his chair.

I sighed. *Great, that didn't last long.* "Yes?"

"You should be aware we don't shift here. It isn't illegal, but we consider it an abuse of power. In case you were wondering." Rhijn eyed me pointedly.

"I'm not using my ability," I blurted out defensively. *Anymore.*

Conall reached a protective hand over to me.

"I'm not accusing you… well, actually, maybe I am. We both know it was you posing as the gardener. I don't see why we need to pretend otherwise. I'm not sure if that was a one time thing, or if you've been doing it since you got here. I'm simply wanting to make you aware of our ways. Do with that information what you will."

"Nayla would never—"

"It's fine, Conall. Rhijn is right."

"But—"

"But nothing. I got caught." I worried my bottom lip, trying to decide how to move forward. "You haven't told anyone else?"

Rhijn shook his head, watching me.

I nodded. "Listen, I'm not going to apologize for being who I was trained to be. You don't know the complete story. I've spent the last ten years learning how to play a certain role, being taught to trust no one. I am not built to trust easily, okay? All to get the stupid ember." I patted my breast pocket where the offended stone vibrated in discordance.

"That makes sense. I'd like to hear the story if you'd be willing to share it." Rhijn leaned forward and rested his elbows on the table. A serene expression crossed his features and seemed to welcome me to continue.

I tossed my napkin on the table. "Why do you always have to be so damn perfect? You should try getting mad or something. It's no wonder I'm having a hard time believing you all are authentic. Real Skyborne have complicated emotions. Life isn't so simple. Even your father seems to take everything in stride. It's so frustrating." I wanted to pull at my hair or throw things.

"You want me to get mad at you?" he asked, cocking his head.

I huffed a breathy laugh. "Never mind. Thank you for bringing it up away from the others. I won't do it again." I downed the rest of my glass and stood from the table. "On that note, I'm going to bed."

At some point later, the bed shifted and Conall's weight moved on the mattress and beneath the covers.

"You awake?" he whispered.

"I am now," I hissed back, turning over, wrenching the covers with me.

"Hey, no reason to get testy with me." He reached a hand over and rubbed my shoulder. "I'm glad you stood up for yourself, but I wish you'd let me do it for you."

"Why?" I groaned.

"Because I care for you, Nayla."

"Conall, just go to sleep okay."

"Nayla?" he insisted.

"I care for you too, Conall. I mean, I love you. You're my brother." I flopped onto my stomach. "Now can we go back to sleep?"

Conall sighed, and I felt him ease back onto his pillow. A few moments later, his breathing became even, and I closed my eyes to join him in slumber.

CHAPTER ELEVEN

Emerson shifted her weight, bending and stretching out her saddle weary legs. "This would be a whole lot easier if you hadn't let Nayla slip away with the ember. We could have been here days ago."

"But then we wouldn't have gotten to make love in that stream. The way your skin pebbled as the chilly water trickled over your breasts is a sight I'll not soon forget, *Regius,*" Darius purred as he wrapped an arm around her waist, pulling her to him, groping her chest with his free hand.

Emerson batted him a way. "Don't. I'm not in the mood." She gave him a sharp look laced with expectation.

"Yes, Regius," he grumbled, obliging.

A defeated, powerless pout flashed across his features; the expression Emerson savored. Manipulating his emotions was becoming too easy. So much so that it wasn't fun anymore. A lively, somewhat antagonistic energy ricocheted through her senses demanding to be funneled somewhere. She knew it was eagerness for the havoc she was about to unleash on Seabrook, but unless she channeled it, siphoned off a little, they'd take over. And she wanted this victory for herself.

Eyeing Darius, she unfurled her healing power toward him, curious to see what she could do. Focusing, she sent his blood pacing faster through his veins, sending a warm coaxing energy to a certain piece of his anatomy. A featherlight whisp chased up his chest, to his neck which reddened in response. Sweat beaded on his upper lip and she saw his pupils dilate. The power was intoxicating as she urged his sensations along, observing the gratifying strain at his crotch.

He moaned, before his eyes peeled open, flicking to her. "Makers, Emerson. What are you doing?" he panted.

She giggled, clutching him through his trousers. Taunting, teasing him.

"You know why I like you, Darius?" Emerson asked, as she stroked him.

He moaned in question, his head lulling to the side as he stared down at her.

"You're like me. An afterthought, second to the chosen heir, who no one believed was capable of anything. Today we're going to prove them all wrong." The intensity in her eyes ratcheted up like the pulse she felt throbbing through his erection as she squeezed.

"Stop it, or I'm going to take you right here in front of the entire damn army," he growled.

Right, she thought. She had been getting carried away with her experiment. Emerson sent a douse of cold, pulse-slowing energy through him and his olive skin paled. Darius gave her a pained look as he dropped to his knees catching himself from faceplanting with an outstretched hand. He threw a pleading look in her direction. That had been too strong, she noted as she motioned for him to get to his feet, nodding back toward the approaching force.

Hundreds of soldiers clad in the dusky grey of Drakestone marched at their back. Karish, down to the spare heir, had been all too eager to allow Emerson the might of his army. She'd wanted the full count of soldiers, pointing out that after she took Seabrook, he'd be sandwiched between allies. She'd even considered sending him one of Darius's adept fingers for encouragement, but Karish, after he'd seen her creations, had relented. At least someone on this Maker's forsaken continent understood who they ought to ally with.

She'd sent her Monterra force further south to Sundale, knowing she could trust her generals to claim the desert cities which stood like mirages shimmering between the edge of the desert and the coast. Scanning the sky she assessed her wall of creatures, *her children*. General Orien Standish had looked too relieved when she'd informed him that none of them would be accompanying him south. Emerson was pained to part from her babies and eager to see what they could do—what she'd bred them for. And the army her late step father had been secretly building for decades was more than capable of crushing any opposition to the takeover of the southernmost territory.

Emerson regarded the monumental sandstone walls of Seabrook proper. Femi had refused to surrender. The stubborn female expected and likely prepared for a siege, having plenty of time to do so as Emerson's formidable army had traveled. What the Seabrook Regent didn't know was Emerson wasn't patient enough for a siege. She'd take Seabrook before the light star set. With her creature's ability, it was only a matter of a few hours, then the first territory would be hers.

Before the week was over, she'd have control of over half the continent. An anticipatory shiver jutted down her spine. Once Sundale and Seabrook were secure, she'd set her sights on Arborvale and its newly elevated female steward, leaving Eastdow and its fickle Regent Torin Tiernach for last. Then when Nayla came back, she'd have no choice but to bow to Emerson's will.

CHAPTER TWELVE

A BALL OF DREAD had seated itself in my stomach while we'd ridden the ferry back across to Adrina the next morning. We'd be leaving this afternoon for the settlements and it would be the first time I'd be apart from my friends since we'd arrived here. I was curious though of what we'd see of our future homes.

I walked into the office Vitis kept in the non-residential section of the estate reserved for conducting the Chancellor's and his advisor's duties. I'd gotten his summons shortly after we'd gotten back. "You asked to see me?"

Vitis turned slowly toward me. He leaned back in his economical chair, elbows on its arms and fingers pressed into a steeple in front of his chest, the picture of an ever in control ruler.

"You and your companions seem to be adjusting to life here in Idia well."

"Thank you?" I said, unsure.

Vitis's chest rumbled in silent laughter.

"To your credit, you have been very welcoming to us. We had no idea what to expect. The way you have slowly introduced us to different aspects of your way of life here has made it easy, though I admit it takes effort to accept what is so different from what is common for us," I said, eyeing the chair across from him, hoping he wasn't going to ask me to sit.

"The five of you are not representative of how everyone in your realm will be, are you?" Vitis asked, getting to the point.

"What makes you say that?" Shrugging, I bit my lower lip.

"When you came here, you had little to no supplies on you, except weapons, and Rhijn said you were in a panicked state—like you were running from something. But you all are clearly in the political leadership of your various territories, so I can tell something doesn't add up. I feel the enormity of the task we are faced with. I sense that you know very well and you are afraid to tell us what we'll be up against when the Sol Ros return."

I narrowed my eyes at the usually in control ruler, noticing the circles newly darkening underneath his eyes, and the pad of paper with illegible scribbles as if he were making mindless scratches on the pad while deep in thought. Chancellor Vitis was worried.

I was torn between my desire to keep learning about the Skyborne here to continue building my trust with them, and empathy for the disruption and challenge Vitis would be expected to lead the Idians through when we returned.

"I understand your position, and I will tell you not all of us Banished are as receptive as we are, but you'll forgive me if I want to continue learning about you before we have this conversation. We are weeks, if not more, from bringing anyone back to Idia. And I think—"

There was a knock at the door.

"Come in," Vitis said.

The door cracked open, and red hair appeared first.

"Oh, I—am I interrupting? I'm early." A deep blush formed as Asha poked her head into the room.

"Of course not. Please come in. I was trying to encourage Nayla to open up about what we'd be dealing with when the Banished returned," Vitis explained as Asha walked in, right past me, and leaned casually on the edge of the Chancellor's sleek desk.

"I told him I'd fill him in as best as I could, but you were the one to ask if he wanted the whole story," Asha explained, looking between us.

"Well, it appears Nayla needs more time with us, and for that, I have an idea." He smiled, knowing whatever he was about to say would be unwelcome.

"Nayla, Rhijn can swing by your chambers to take you on another tour before lunch. Perhaps to the estate's power well. It is a favorite place of his and it's a comfortable walk from your room." Chancellor Vitis gave me a knowing smile. "Maybe you can try to feed the well again before you leave for the settlements this afternoon."

I wasn't eager to give it another try yet and itching to escape this conversation. What if I caused more damage? I had a feeling Malik would succeed on our behalf. The damnable male held my stare just long enough to drive me well into madness. It seemed his son and I had found a comfortable arrangement, despite the fact that he'd confronted me about the shifting. We were amiable and content to keep each other at arm's length. But here Vitis was, trying to encourage our connection again. I still hadn't confirmed that he planned to help us in transporting the Banished over. I supposed I could use this as an opportunity, though I'd likely have plenty of those in the coming days.

Coming to a decision, I folded my arms over my chest. "Actually, I would prefer—"

"Asha, would you care for a tour of the gardens?" he asked her, voice notably deepening as he cut me off.

"Again, Chancellor, you know what's best." She grinned and placed her small hand in the much larger palm he extended, and he led her from the room, leaving me standing, mouth agape.

⁂

"Makers! Rhijn, you startled me." He caught me as I was stepping out of my door to wait for him. I'd figure I'd just wait in the hallway. Better than to be in a space with beds considering my dreams.

"Conall isn't actually your brother, is he? Another long story, I'm guessing?" he asked, leaning against the wall outside my room.

"No, not exactly, but why do you ask?"

"I don't get the sense that he likes me very much. Less than you even."

"Your appeal *is* debatable." I smirked. "And I thought you two were starting to get along? He even complimented your cooking."

"That was before I asked you about the shifting. He is awfully protective of you."

"Yeah, he is," I replied matter of fact.

"Why were you waiting for me outside your room?"

I didn't answer.

"Fine. You ready?"

"I am whenever you are."

He led us down the hallway, away from the council rooms and the common area. "Tell me the story. I'd like to hear it. *Truly.*" He was so earnest.

"Fine, but if we're going to be partners, you're going to have to stop being so formal, okay? Relax a little. Unless that's just your personality." I mock-groaned.

"Friends with the *Chosen One?*" Rhijn raised an eyebrow down toward me as he walked by my side. "Lucky me."

I couldn't help but chuckle as I said, "*Incredibly.*" As we walked, I told him of how I'd been traded *or sold* by the male I believe to be my father, Arbordale Regent Ephram Kalederan, to Conall's father and the Eastdow High Priest to take the place of his dying daughter. Of course, Conall hadn't known, though sometimes he'd suspected. I confessed about the shifting, telling him how I'd taken her appearance for ten years during the training and used it to sneak into Drakestone to steal the ember on behalf of Eastdow, but also for all the other territories, really. How I'd been dubbed the Chosen One. Also, about how, in an odd turn of events, I'd discovered Malik was actually my real half-brother.

There, it was all out now. Well... almost. The fact that I was of the Shal lineage from the paintings, my Regius ancestor the main driving force who'd been against the Dar Kepler, wasn't something they needed to know now—if ever. They knew my name, but I didn't think the connection had been made.

"So Conall didn't know you weren't his sister until just under a year ago?"

"I think he knew. He told me as much, but as far as I am concerned, he is still my brother." I shrugged as if it were no big deal.

"And you've discussed this with him?"

"What?" I looked up at Rhijn, who was peering down at me sideways. "Well, not in so many words, but essentially." I shook my head, annoyed.

"It seems you both were lucky to have each other. Your strength is impressive. Few could hold it together for that long without cracking. Especially after the way your family treated you. You must have really believed in the mission?" he asked.

"No, I'm not much for the prophecies. It was a means to an end. I didn't have a choice, either. You're right, though. I'm lucky to have Conall. He got me through it. I wish you two would become friends because the angst between you is getting on my nerves. And I don't need your praise or sympathy… *friend.*"

The trickling of water was coming nearer.

"I have a theory," Rhijn said, ignoring my rebuff.

"Great. Let's hear it."

"I think you destroyed that pedestal because of your connection to the void stone. I don't think you realize the depth of the power it is giving you."

"Is it the same with you and the one you hold?" I asked.

"Yes, but I've had years to learn to control it. Back where you're from, the Skyborne aren't able to use much power, are they?" He didn't seem to have an ulterior motive. "That is why the others are struggling so much to feed the wells. Only Malik has come close to succeeding."

I nodded, then he continued. "You weren't going to tell us until you learned if you could trust us. I understand that. But this is something we suspected. Everly has some sight. So does my father. Not as profound as your friend Seeley, but it has still been helpful to gain insight into your realm."

"That is how you knew we'd arrive on the dunes?"

"My father or Everly didn't see that."

"Then how did you know?"

Rhijn took a deep breath and held it for a while before he exhaled.

"Ah, here we are," he said, dodging my question.

The hallway opened out into a wide-open area. There was a large open-air stage or platform made of the same smooth stone the rest of the estate was constructed from, and a grassy, perfectly manicured knoll surrounding it. Pavers dotted the lawn in a decorative pattern and orderly hedges lined clean walkways leading to the center. I saw the well positioned well behind the platform. I started down the trail, then froze. The space was the setting of many of my dreams. My skin prickled and Rhijn came up behind me. I jumped.

"Everything okay?" he asked, reaching out a hand, then thinking better of it, pulled it back.

"Can you get into that pool?" I asked him, thinking of one dream in particular where I'd been lying in the pool and he'd stepped up out of its depths, shirtless, water trickling—no, nope. Not going there.

He gave me a strange look. "Missing baths that much?"

Makers, I must sound odd to him.

"No," I said. "This area just reminded me of something. What were you saying?"

"Oh, your connection to the void stone and your friend's power. Well, I've spoken with my father and Everly, and we believe your youth should be able to learn and grow into their power once they are here. Many of you, like Malik, should be able to learn to feed the wells too, but doing so may take more time here and practice. You did it so easily because when you use the stone, it opens your channels so you can see things others can't."

"Then how do your people use their power then? Without the stones?"

"They learned to feel the void. To seek it out. We aren't as closed off to it, so it develops deeper and quicker. Youth here sense the space in between very early on."

"I told you they teach us it's a dark power. Evil. Even if the Sol Ros are able to use the power of the void, I'm not sure they will. It goes against everything we've been taught. The belief is deeply ingrained in most of us."

"You used the power in the void willingly," he observed. "Malik did too."

"I'm a skeptic. But the first time, it was more a matter of life or death, which helped," I grinned. "Malik, well, he's his own creature." I thought of Malik's shadows, how they made me think of the in-between. Maybe he's been seeking the void all along and that is why he'd come the closest to feeding the wells.

"What are you thinking?" he asked.

"Oh, of Malik." I explained my theory to him.

"You're likely right. The rest of the Banished will have to learn that the energy isn't good or evil. It just is. It's how we use it that taints the one constant in this vast multiverse. I think they'll see that once they are here."

That was overly optimistic as far as I was concerned, and I thought Chancellor Vitis felt the same. I walked over to the ledge of the terrace behind the pool and its pedestals. From this vantage point, sprawling Adrina stretched across to where the rolling dunes of the desert began. In the other direction, the city reached towards the sea. If I enhanced my vision, I could faintly see all the way across the channel to the Leeward Isle and the now familiar colorful structures that dotted its coast. It was expansive, and awe-inspiring from this vantage point. I sighed deeply and turned toward Rhijn, who'd taken a spot on one of the pavers on the knoll. He sat cross-legged with his eyes closed, taking deep concentrated breaths.

We'd agreed in a roundabout way that we were partners now. He'd help us, and Seeley would be happy I'd established that. Now either me or Malik would need to successfully feed the wells. Then we could start bringing the Banished back.

Rhijn didn't budge as I approached him, so I sat on an adjacent paver. A calm, steady energy lapped off him. At the edge of my vision, I caught the corner of his broad mouth twitch up. I shook my head, tossing my hair back, my closed eyes to the heavens. Heat from the mid-day rays of the light star washed my skin in warmth, radiating from my upturned forehead to the very core of my being. As I sat there absorbing the energy, I had the oddest calming sensation. Despite the obstacles we were bound to face, there was a chance, a small one, that everything might work out.

Later that afternoon Conall and I walked together to the designated meeting area. He was quiet, concerned. The Idians had advised us on what to pack. Stewards were assigned to each settlement, tasked with keeping up with repairs and maintenance. We were advised there'd be plenty of food and miscellaneous supplies there, only to bring clothing and food for the ride, and an extra power cell to fuel the transport for the return trip.

Two transports would carry each group to their destination. I was nervous to part from my friends, but excited to see the old Dar Kepler city. We'd been here almost a week and a half already, and I was slowly becoming comfortable with our hosts—even the painfully beautiful Skyborne who'd invaded my dreams.

Members from each group trickled in to the parking area. Malik walked behind Seeley, peppering the twins with questions. Seeley caught my eye, and I gave him a sympathetic wince.

"You going to survive the trip?" I asked him.

"Oh, I have a feeling these three are going to be a basket of fun," Seeley quipped back. "They haven't stopped discussing the finer points of effective espionage since we were assigned to their care. I've packed mostly books," he patted his bulging duffle.

Asha bounded up to us, eager to explore. Vitis followed closely behind her, leaning to whisper into her ear. She gave him a skeptical smirk and boldly patted his chest.

"This guy." She jerked a thumb in the Chancellor's direction as she sauntered over to Conall and I.

"Hey," Conall said. "Travel buddy." He attempted a smile.

"Makers, Conall, I'm not that bad to get paired with. You're not going to be glum this whole trip, are you? Nayla, do something..." Asha pleaded.

"I don't know what to tell you. He'll quit pouting, eventually. That's what usually happens anyway."

That perked him up. "Hey! That's not fair," Conall grabbed my waist, tickling my sides until I was squirming and batting him away.

"Stop, Conall. I relent, I relent. You never pout," I begged. He stopped, and I jumped away. "Except for when you do."

Asha and I were cackling as he started to chase me. It took me back ten years to when we were so much closer to our youth. Seeing his lighter side was exactly what I needed. I let him catch up then adeptly ducked under his reaching arm, swinging up behind him, delivering a playful jab to his side as I swung my other arm around him. He captured my hand, and we stood there, me hugging him from behind, enjoying his strength and warmth.

A cool gaze fluttered across my skin, and I stiffened. When I opened my eyes, they locked on Rhijn, who stood eerily still watching our display. The muscle of his jaw ticked before he pivoted on his heel and put his bag in the furthest transport.

Conall pulled me around to his front, craning his neck down to me as he kissed my cheek. I couldn't help but notice the gloating edge to him and catch the flick of his eyes in Rhijn's direction. Before I could chastise him, he grabbed my face in his hands. "Be careful, okay? Everly," he called out. "Take care of my girl."

My girl? It was so bizarre; I shook my head. "Conall, stop. I'll be fine, okay? You be careful, too."

Asha, probably sensing my discomfort, grabbed Conall and dragged him away.

I was grateful when Everly ushered me into the transport in front of Rhijn's and climbed in. She punched a couple of buttons on the control pad, and the transport lifted before zooming off. The other transports followed suit. When we reached a fork in the main road, I saw the other four take the opposite direction in the rear window.

I faced forward, breathing a sigh.

"So, you going to tell me what that was about with your *brother*?" Everly asked.

"If I only knew," I answered her, not wanting to confront the looming oddness with Conall that even Rhijn had seemed to pick up on. And had that been jealousy I'd seen dart across his angular face? No, he was just interested in me because I had the other void stone. If it had been Asha, he'd be trying to buddy up to her.

It was almost two full days' ride at high speed before we'd make it to the southern settlement. A long time in the cramped quarters of the transport as far as I was concerned.

We both napped leaning against opposite walls for the first quarter of the ride. When I awoke, we were passing through the dunes, light star rising, and Everly was scribbling in a notebook she'd pulled from her pack.

She looked up and grinned. I felt cornered suddenly. "What?" I asked her, dreading that eerie sense she had about things.

"So… what's your deal with Rhijn?" she asked, wiggling her eyebrows.

I swallowed. "Are all Idians so direct? And this early in the morning?"

"Well, I figured since we have the female code of secrecy between us and a long ride, you can confess whatever seems to be the problem to me. I'll tell you if it's justified or not, then you can quit acting weird. Sound like a plan?"

"The female code of secrecy?" I asked. I could tell she'd been dying to ask me this question, making me skeptical about this *code* she'd formulated.

"Yeah, you know the one where we swap stories about our lovers, among other things and don't tell a soul. It's a real code, kind of like our question swap, but better," she assured me.

"Oh, I wasn't aware of that particular code." I thought of Asha who seemed to relish in getting me in trouble and making me reveal my secrets. But I thought back to my younger sisters, Carina, Balene and Jude. We used the 'female code,' I supposed, with all the secret huddles we shared.

I raised an eyebrow at Everly. I hadn't had a chance to tell Seeley that Rhijn was the male of my dreams. *From* my dreams, I corrected myself. I was actually avoiding that conversation if I was being honest with myself. I had thought I'd bear it on my own. Besides, I didn't want them to think I was even more of a rake than I already was.

Everly waited patiently as I concluded the internal debate I'd been having. "So…" she prodded.

I rolled my eyes. Her and Rhijn were obviously close, but I didn't get the impression she'd gossiped about any of our earlier conversations. It just didn't seem like something she'd do, not that I was a great judge of character. "Okay, but you swear not to tell?"

"Of course," she said, beaming eagerly, knowing she'd won and the information was about to spill from me.

"It all started when I gained possession of the ember, the void stone," I clarified. "I started having these dreams, which were terrifying at first, but then became something else entirely."

"And what does that have to do with Rhijn?" she asked.

"How well do you know him?" The last thing I wanted to do was confess this to a lover of his. That would be the height of embarrassment.

"He's my cousin. I've known him since I was born, I guess. I'm thirty-three. Which makes him thirty-four until I catch up next month. We grew up together. So, the dreams," she urged me to continue.

"He was in them. All of them."

"Makers," she swore under her breath. "I suspected you had a connection to him, but I didn't realize it was like that. They told you I have some sight, right?"

"They did. Did you see me?"

"No, not you specifically. But I saw the other void stone. It was no longer dormant, and I figured it was only a matter of time before the first of you would return. But it makes sense now. How he led us to where you'd arrive."

"That was him?" I asked, a chill lancing up my spine. I stared off, unfocused, as I added up my interactions with him. "He said it wasn't you or the chancellor, but when I asked him, he dodged the question."

She laughed. "Yes, I suppose he would. You were already bolting from him at every turn. He probably was trying not to spook you any worse. He is a good male. He'll respect your boundaries, if you give him a chance."

"I wasn't bolting from him," I grumbled. "Besides, we have a truce now. We're partners."

She raised an eyebrow at me, shooting an incredulous expression across the transport. "So, about these dreams. Some were scary, which explains why you were avoiding him, but you said there were others?"

My face flamed, and I had to look away.

"I see," she said, and burst into laughter.

"Shouldn't this be some part of the female code? Not to laugh at the expense of the secret sharer?" I demanded. "Anyway, those are unimportant. I haven't had any dreams since I've been here, and in the most significant ones I had, he taught me how to access the void and helped me understand how to reach Idia."

"Whoa, really? That's heavy. Does he know?"

"Makers, I hope not. Can you imagine how mortifying that would be?"

She snorted. "Terribly. So that's why you've been treating him as if he were some sort of contaminate. The creepy, sexy male from your dreams live in the flesh. Makes sense." She looked off into the distance for a moment and came to a sudden determination. "I think you should tell him."

"No way. Absolutely not."

"What if he's been having dreams about you too? Did you think of that?" she speculated, shrugging her shoulders.

"I hadn't thought of that. But he hasn't. It's only the connection between our void stones. Maybe something subconscious. But I think the stones have wanted to be joined. I feel it when I'm near him. I can't determine if it would be a good thing or not though."

Everly sat thoughtfully for a moment. "Both Chancellor Vitis and I have had varying sights about them being joined, so you are probably correct. They are doing what they need to do to draw back together. I feel like they are some sort of essence that was unexpectedly split in half. Rhijn thinks his has a personality."

"Mine does too!" The ember vibrated in my pocket in agreement.

"See, if you two would figure out how to be open with each other, think of the things we could all learn." Everly's rebuke shut me up. "Anyway, consider it. Only another day's travel."

Everly told me more stories about adventures she and Rhijn had in their youths, about the scenery we passed and details of the city we were approaching.

The Light Star was trekking upward in the sky the next morning as we finally approached the city. It formed a large glowing gold semicircle behind dark buildings which were stacked on top of each other. The details of the rough-hewn stone came into view as we approached. It was rudimentary construction, even by the standards of my home realm.

Everly noticed my skeptical assessment. "Don't worry. On the inside, it is much nicer. These are historical buildings and we've worked hard to preserve them."

We pulled up to a newer set of buildings on the outskirts of the city. The transports parked themselves next to each other, and the doors unsealed and opened.

CHAPTER THIRTEEN

I SHOOK OUT MY numb legs, which were cramped from sitting for two days during the trip to the settlement. We'd only had short breaks to attend to our personal needs, so I eagerly jumped out the open door. My boot slipped as I stepped across the uneven cobbled stones that were slick with age and busted my butt.

"Everly. Nayla. Did you have a pleasant ride?" Rhijn greeted, crawling out of his own transport. He surveyed me on the ground, not making a move to help me up. Just giving me a *suit yourself* smirk.

"Oh, yes. It was very enlightening," Everly replied coyly, grinning and lent me a hand which I took almost pulling her off her feet onto me.

I squeezed her hand for an extra moment infusing as much threat into my mock glare as possible.

Rhijn flicked his gaze between us and shrugged, probably thinking I was being difficult.

"Everly told me all of your most embarrassing stories from youth," I said, trying to deflect.

He raised a brow. "Well, since you now know my darkest secrets, maybe you can defrost in my company?"

I stuttered back, as if he'd struck me. I don't think he realized how cutting his words were. Especially since I'd thought we'd formed a tentative friendship. "I—"

"Let's go. Grab your pack. The transports won't travel further into the city. The streets are narrower and winding the further we go. They can't make the turns, they're too tight." Everly said and swung her pack up onto her shoulders, grunting under its weight, and headed up the road.

Rhijn gave me a long hard smirk before we fell in line with Everly, making our way through the settlement. Silence hovered eerily around us and our soft steps made up the only sounds. They'd said stewards lived here, taking care of the place, but it seemed vacant. Each building we passed looked like it might house a business. Bakeries, storefronts, and clothes makers would fill these shops one day. It took little vision.

"Where do the Stewards live?" I asked.

"See up there?" Rhijn pointed to a space between the buildings that allowed a view further up the hill as we climbed. There was a much larger structure, like a castle. Old though. Weather had eroded the hewn limestone which had been quarried from the karsts which dotted the surrounding landscape. Lichen and moss covered the structure which sagged on the peak the city was built upon.

"Nicer on the inside," Everly huffed, as we gained in elevation.

I smiled. Though in a practically abandoned city, this trek was right up my alley. It energized me after sitting for so long in the transport. I glanced at Rhijn and he appeared to be enjoying it as well. Many twists and turns later, we approached the castle grounds.

"This building will be the equivalent to the Chancellor's estate back in Adrina. It should be the settlement's governor's building. It is strange though." Rhijn paced around the open courtyard in front of the main entrance hurriedly, clenching and unclenching his fists. "Stewards should greet us. I suppose we are early though."

He strode up to the large wooden doors, pressing them open. We followed and I squinted to make out the layout of the dark space. Dank air hit me as soon as I entered. Rhijn stepped further into the chamber, lifting a hand, lighting fires in a few braziers.

"I thought you said they had the same type of lights like in Adrina?" I asked.

"The braziers are supposed to be ornamental. An homage to the history of this building. The power appears to be turned off," he explained calmly, but his brow had furrowed.

I watched him survey the room that was likely used as a reception hall. Nothing appeared out of place. And it was, as Everly said, modern, like the interiors in Adrina. The walls were a smooth white, and paintings were hung over staged sitting areas. Several doors lined each side of the room, with shiny round handles. Rhijn grabbed one and turned it, opening the door.

"Come on. Stay close," he said and took off briskly into a corridor, which had open air windows along its length. It led up a staircase onto a second level, following the natural rise. A gentle breeze filtered between the columns holding up the ceiling. I shivered, considering pulling another layer from my pack.

I peered down to a lower veranda which was carved from the slope below. It was the distinctive rows of a vegetable garden. I would have recognized that in any realm. Fruit trees lined the edge of the gardens. A bench sat in the center and a figure sat—

Everly screamed in my ear as I realized what we both had laid our eyes on. The sound echoed ominously across the stone city. She fell into me and I threw my arms around her to hold her steady. For a healer, she seemed oddly squeamish.

Enhancing my vision, I saw the body of a mid-aged male. He was bloated and cracking. Dried blood caked his skin around lacerations on his face, neck and hands. A brown cloak was in tatters and he was missing his legs from the knees down. Gore oozed from the stumps. Everly gagged and buried her face in my shoulder.

The dark fluid of decay had seeped from the mouth and nose, and maggots and other creatures who'd taken up residence wiggled in the red flesh which had burst open in places. This corpse wasn't fresh. It had to be a week, no more than two based on its stage of decay, another delightful thing I'd learned while I'd trained as my realms Chosen One.

"Are you seeing this?" I asked Rhijn.

"Makers." I glanced over. His face was pale. Had he never seen a dead body? Was I going to be the only one not to panic? *Figures.*

"I'd say he's been dead for around eight to ten days. I'm surprised none of the other stewards haven't noticed a dead body, or a missing worker."

"Shh," Rhijn clipped, silencing me. "Listen," he whispered.

I did, but I didn't hear anything. I shook my head at him.

"What could have done that to him?" I asked Rhijn.

Everly sobbed into my chest. "There's more of them."

"More of what?" I asked, apprehensively.

"We don't want to hang around to find out. This way, there's a passageway out the back. We can't go back how we came. They could be on our scent already." Rhijn charged forward. I glanced to the floor as I pulled Everly along. Dried blood dotted the walkway.

"Rhijn, the floor!" I jumped, almost stumbling across the discarded limb of a deceased female. "I think all your stewards are dead."

"Quiet, they'll hear you." He assessed Everly and came over to take her off my hands. He grabbed her cheeks. "Everly, pull yourself together. We'll make it out of here, but I need you to carry yourself. Here, stay between me and Nayla."

Reluctantly, Everly fell into place in-between us. "Your father said they'd all been vanquished back to their realm or killed," she sobbed.

"What did?!" I demanded. "What is probably hunting us?"

Rhijn stopped, spinning around abruptly. The intensity of his eyes alarmed me. "Creatures. We don't know what they're called, but the first time they came, they showed up out of nowhere. A few months under a year ago. They decimated the stewards here. They showed up at the observatory months later. We thought we got them all. No, I am certain we got them all. These—"

"Arrived when we did," I interrupted. It was too close to lining up with every time I'd used the ember. That was when the Swath had started expanding too, I was almost sure. "We don't know if they're the same ones, but where was their weak spot?" I asked, thinking of Emerson's creatures. I'd been thinking of how to immobilize them.

Rhijn tilted his head at me, as if surprised at my line of thinking. "I really hope we make it out of this, because I'm dying to pick your brain." He smiled, the first truly unguarded smile he'd given me. I fought the mirrored grin that was creeping across my face. *Focus*, I reminded myself.

"They're intelligent. They'll try to outwit you. They work in teams. Hard exoskeleton, insect-like wings are a vulnerability. Also, a soft patch at the neck joint. If you can pierce them with something sharp there, they'll go down." Everly was panting as she rattled off facts she remembered. "Don't let them team up. Did I say that already?" Her gaze nervously darted back and forth between me and Rhijn.

"We'll make it if we can get back to the transports. But we need to go. We'll figure out how to send them back to their realm when we can come back with reinforcements." Rhijn took off, doubling his pace.

More bodies littered the halls we ran through. Everly kept pace, but barely. She was struggling, heavily puffing, and we were still in the castle. When she lagged, I'd offer an encouraging word.

A searing pain lanced across my back and I called out. "Incoming, behind us!" I spun. There were two of them, but different from the creatures Everly had described. "They're from a different realm!" I shouted. Rhijn dashed back. We had our backs to Everly, who we were keeping sheltered against the wall between us.

I thrust my hands toward my boots and pushed my energy down. My two blades ejected from the sheaths hidden along the lengths of my calves right into my awaiting hands. I looked at Rhijn, who was weaponless and astonished. Without thinking, I tossed him one handle first.

"You're beginning to scare me," he said as he caught the blade out of the air. We raised them against the hovering creatures in unison.

They were lithe and quick, with segmented furry bodies, the size of a small mountain cat. They flew on hornet-like wings, similar to the godflies, but so much less elegant, and more deadly. Bred for speed and maneuverability. When they weren't flying, they landed on the balcony rail, and sticky feet attached to the surface easily. One skittered up a wall and another onto the ceiling.

Everly cried out, her hand going to her mouth as she stared at the creature, studying her from its inverted position above her. Pinchers clicked. They'd determined she was the weak link. At least they weren't a more humanoid hybrid, like Uden and his ilk. They'll be easier to kill this way.

I swiped my knife toward the nearest one. My other hand shot up toward the one hovering above Everly. It took a few seconds longer than I preferred, but I wrapped my head around its make-up. *There*, I thought, sending my energy into its weakest spot. The creature's body split in half at the lowest segment. What had appeared to be the head was in fact its opposite. A clever camouflage. The other creatures hissed, closing in as their brethren's thinking half crashed to the floor at our feet, the rest of its body still attached to the ceiling by its sticky feet.

Rhijn was a quick learner. He swung toward one as it approached him, feinting, using his power with his left hand and taking the creature with the knife in his right. Only two down. Rhijn sent a blast of power toward them, throwing them backward off the balcony.

"Run!" he yelled. We took off down the corridor.

The slice on my back stung as we ran, but thankfully I didn't feel any effects of a poison. The creatures weren't venomous. Everly slowed in front of me. "Go, Everly, you can do it," I cried to her.

Rhijn doubled back. He handed me my knife and scooped her up in his arms. I shook my head. That was going to slow us down, but he was still faster than Everly would have been. She knew it, too.

"Leave me," she said. "The realms need you two more than me." She struggled, trying to force him to release her.

"Stop it," he shook her. "We're all getting out of here. This way." We ran through an open door and I shut and barricaded it behind me. Creature's insect-like feet clicked over the door and pinchers clipped underneath. We made it up a level, then down two before we reached another open-air balcony.

"This is the most dangerous part. We need to make it to there." He pointed to a rusted gate all the way on the other side of the yard. "Then we'll be back in the streets. We can lose them as we wind through the narrow passageways and reach the building with the transports from the back. Everly, you need to run for your life."

He set her down. My ears rang as buzzing in the distance rapidly approached.

"They're coming. Now!" I cried. Everly shuddered, but found her footing.

I flew across the grounds, crushing the soft grass underneath my boots. To make it to the back gateway, it was an open expanse with no shelter. A whoosh of power passed me as the buzzing got louder. I turned to see Rhijn had sent the creatures who'd rushed him and Everly tumbling backward in the air, but they were quickly recovering.

Damn it, they were only halfway, when I'd almost reached the gate. They wouldn't make it. I patted the gate, wishing I was opening it to flee through. Steeling myself, I turned, digging my boots into the soft ground, and sprinted toward them. A creature dove toward Everly. Rhijn was fighting off two. I sent my knife flying. It struck true. As the creature fell, I met it, yanking my knife from its head segment, and spun on another. It darted, but I attempted Rhijn's fake. It worked! My blood was humming and everything was coming into sharper focus.

Rhijn cried out, then growled. A creature had sliced across his stomach. The wound appeared shallow. He'd jumped back in time. The creature dove toward him again, but my knife got to it first.

"Thanks," Rhijn called.

This time Everly screamed. We both spun. Three creatures had surrounded her and were zipping, dragging shallow gashes along her exposed limbs.

My stomach clenched as horror reverberated through my body. I threw out both hands, two collapsed in front of her. She was trying to block the third, who darted forward, attaching its pincers to her neck.

"No!" Rhijn called out. He whipped a quick burst of power the creature's way, but it held tight. Panic flooded Everly's eyes.

I raised a hand to the four creatures who flew toward her. They fell. I was using too much power. I knew my limits now. But I couldn't let Everly die.

The other creatures who'd seen how easily I'd taken the others out hesitated. They'd edge closer, but I'd raise my hand and they back off. No telling how long my bluff would hold.

We gingerly approached Everly in the creature's death-grip. Its head tilted back and forth, considering. It hadn't severed her carotid artery yet, but it was too close. Blood trickled down her neck in a steady stream. I reached out, sensing. The artery had a slight tear.

If I could just touch the ember, I'd be able to access more power and disintegrate the creature at her throat before it could move. Still, I reached out, trying to grab onto the miniscule vibrating particles which were the creature.

Everly coughed, and blood trickled out the side of her mouth. "Take care of my cousin, Nayla," she said. She'd assessed this no-win situation and decided. Or she'd seen it.

Makers, seeing your own death. I shuttered and refocused.

The other creatures clicked and hummed. I was wildly swinging my hands, warding them off as I worked on the particles making up the creature who was seconds away from killing Everly. The creature pinched harder, as if sensing what I was doing, finishing her artery cutting well into her throat. At the slight motion, Rhijn jumped, grabbing it and ripped the thing in half with his bare hands. When he'd finished with it, he slumped to the ground beside his cousin, drawing her into his arms.

"I'm sorry," she mouthed, looking at me.

"What?" I yelled, as a creature bravely dipped. I sliced toward it with my blade and it retreated.

"Dreams," Everly whispered between gurgles, more blood bubbling from the gash in her neck. "Ask her." She was speaking to Rhijn. What a traitorous bitch, I thought of the dying woman. So much for the female code.

"Don't you die on me," Rhijn demanded of his cousin.

Everly grasped at her throat in a last-ditch effort to heal herself. For Rhijn, I realized. His eyes were squinted in a grimace as if he were experiencing her pain. Rhijn turned to me. "Help me heal her," he begged.

I shook my head. "It's too late. The wound is too complex." Much worse than Conall's had been, I thought. "I'm doing all I can do to keep them off so she can die in peace."

"Rhijn—" Everly spoke her last word.

A deep sob sounded across the yard. Rhijn laid her body down and stood, his pale hair whipping back as he turned to me and the creatures I was fending off.

"Easy, Rhijn. We need the rest of our power to get out of here." He wasn't hearing me, though. "Rhijn, I—we need you. They need us." His arms raised into the air, his pulse a palpable thrum of energy bleeding off him. It was like he was in a trance, his desire to fight the creatures he was stalking towards. "Please. Don't let Everly have died in vain. We need to go."

His grief paused and for a second, he focused on me, eyes narrowing. "You need me?"

"Makers, Rhijn, out of all that, that's what you heard?" I asked, still swinging my arms frantically.

His glassy eyes betrayed his resolve but still he looked over his shoulder at me, the vulnerability of his expression seizing my heart. *Did he need to be needed?*

"Fine, yes. If knowing I need you snaps you out of it, then yes, I do. I can't do this alone. Please, Rhijn."

He sniffed back the tears that were trailing down his face. "Okay." His voice was low and broken causing my heart to pinch. "Ready to run?"

I nodded. He took one last look at his cousin, who we couldn't save. His chin trembled. I could see leaving her like this was making him sick. He clamped his jaw tight and shot a large blast of power at the hovering creatures. They tumbled back.

"NOW!" he yelled. We took off. Rhijn matched my pace, taking the lead. We reached the gate and burst through into the streets. He was right. We were much quicker at navigating them and gaining speed. We ran for minutes or hours, I wasn't sure.

Finally, I recognized the backside of the building where we'd parked the transports. Rhijn climbed and flipped himself over the surrounding fence in a swift motion. That was a fancy maneuver. I mimicked him, not landing quite as gracefully. We spun around the corner, coming up short.

My heart plummeted. Our transports were ransacked. One was lying on its side and stones surrounded it. The windows were busted, but still in place, unlike the power cylinders. Of the four, only one was intact, and it was empty.

I was out of ideas and starting to panic. I looked at Rhijn, eyes pleading.

A creature came out of nowhere. Rhijn grabbed my bare forearm and flung me out of the way, toward the transport just in time. The place where he'd touched my skin still tingled, and for a moment, the world slowed down. I waited for some otherworldly force to take over my body and bring me to my quaking knees, but nothing happened.

"What are you waiting for? Get in!" he demanded.

I reached for the door, pressing the button. It opened and Rhijn practically shoved me inside, crawling on top of me, furiously pressing buttons. I used my power once more to split a creature who was dangerously close to slipping inside the closing door. Rhijn pressed a button, and the transport lifted off the ground.

It petered out, floating back down to its resting position.

"Shit," he muttered.

"Wait, Kelvin said you could power the cylinder from the transport."

"In theory. But it's too risky."

"Look around us, Rhijn."

The creatures were bashing their bodies into the transport, which was rocking precariously back and forth.

"Show me how. I'm not afraid." I showed him my hands, ready. This was just another challenge in a long line of them.

"These cylinders take more than one Skyborne's dispersion to fill. Actually, quite a few. It might require all we have left, or even more than we have."

"Do you have the void stone?" I asked him.

"We can't use them. You see the consequences." He gestured to the creatures surrounding us.

"We don't know if that is true or just a coincidence, and it's not going to stop us from using them. Please, Rhijn." We were eye to eye. I put my hands on either side of his neck, savoring the smooth texture of his warm skin. "Please. I don't want to die here."

He nodded. "Okay, let's do it." He pulled up a program on the screen which had a handprint outline.

Rhijn and I took out the void stones. The transport lurched, and the ember fell from the cloth I kept it in. I searched the floor for it. When I found the ember, I immediately reached for it. It touched my fingers, and the depthless dark crawled up my forearm. I watched Rhijn. The ember's glowing opposite shroud his own forearm.

He stared at mine. "Incredible."

He grabbed my elbow and urged my hand toward the pad. "Don't do *anything*," he commanded.

"What? Why?" I asked.

"I don't want you to blow the transport to pieces."

As soon as my hand hit the panel, aligning with the outline, his body came up behind me. We were kneeling on the transport's floorboard, my chest to his back in the cramped space as he placed his hand over mine, threading our fingers against the panel. I gasped as his power surged through me, drawing mine out. He exhaled, his chin dipping beside my face.

"I thought that might kill us," he confessed, his breath warm on the skin below my ear. The transport rattled again and a crack echoed in the small space as the glass of the front window splintered. More power flowed through our joined hands into the panel.

"Makers, Rhijn," I exclaimed, jerking back at the impact of the increased energy flowing through me, but he looped one of his sinewy arms around my waist, holding me in place against his chest. Our breaths were coming in shallow gasps as we fought to keep control.

The transport's lights and systems came on. I glimpsed back over our shoulders and the cylinder was glowing, refilling. I leaned my face into the crook between his neck and chin, closing my eyes to bear the undulating energy ripping through me.

Angry shrieking sounded and I craned my neck around Rhijn's broad shoulders again to see the creatures assaulting the filling cylinder.

"We need to go now," I told him.

"It's not full."

"Rhijn, now!" I jerked our hands back, leaving him no choice but to punch the sequence to take us away from here.

The transport lurched upward, then forward. I wasn't sure what buttons he'd pushed, but I hadn't seen it go this fast yet.

As I steadied myself in the bench seat next to Rhijn, I felt my heart thudding relentlessly in my chest and I realized how hazy I was as the fight-or-flight feeling dissipated seeping out of my pores only to be replaced with a hazy exhaustion. We'd made it. The city became blurry behind us and I lost sight of the last tailing creatures.

I regarded Rhijn, this time willing to let him see my unguarded smile, but he was out cold. *Of course.* The one time when I was willing to be truly nice to him and allow a connection to form between us.

I started laughing—cackling, really. It had to be the overuse of power, and I was quickly becoming hysterical. I reached up and ran a finger along his pretty tear-stained face, then across his wide, supple mouth. Why had I been so afraid of him? I shook my head, ignoring the blood seeping from the wound at his stomach, and curled up against him. That felt right. I moved his arm to accommodate me and nestled in closer to his large, warm body. Yes, this was where I was supposed to be.

CHAPTER FOURTEEN

I AWOKE TO RHIJN gently shaking me. The transport had stopped, and I had no idea how long we'd been out.

"I figured we'd powered the cylinder enough to make it to the observatory town," he said as he reached a tentative hand down to help me out of the transport. He was testing the waters.

Fine. I reached up and took his hand. Heat flared up my neck as the contact reminded me I'd snuggled up next to him in the transport, making him my own personal pillow. At least I prayed that's all I had done.

The front of his shirt was soaked with blood.

"Makers, Nayla, are you hurt?" he exclaimed, spinning me around.

"This?" I gestured to the blood on the hemline of my tunic. "I think it's yours." I pointed to his stomach and the angry red wound. He only then seemed to notice.

"Your back," he said, wincing as he moved the serrated fabric covering my upper shoulders.

Now that my consciousness had been directed toward the wound, the ache I'd been ignoring welled to the surface.

"Oh, yeah. That." Considering we'd lost our healer, and I didn't think I'd be able to heal myself at that angle, my cut would have to wait until we made it back to Adrina to be healed properly. "What is this building?" I asked. There was one enormous building made of nondescript grey stones, with a domed roof with no windows and only a single metal door. The structure had one large rectangular opening at the top and did not appear like a dwelling.

"This is the observatory. The building houses a telescope and other equipment that allows us to see the stars. This location was the closest place to the settlement I thought we could make it to. There is a town further down the way." He pointed in the distance, where I faintly made out a gathering of square buildings.

I glanced over at the transport. The cylinder had mere drops of energy remaining.

"This is the other site you said creatures arrived?" I asked.

"Yes, but we rounded them up and sent them back to their realm. We'll have to do the same at the settlement. The Skyborne who lived here were evacuated, and no one has moved back since. A few Skyborne have returned to the town."

"Okay, well let's go inside and I can try to heal you."

"Are you sure you're ready?" he asked, referring to my power.

"Yes, I was able to heal Malik after—" I cut myself off.

Rhijn didn't probe, allowing me to process whether or not I wanted to continue my thought.

"I lost control once before," I said as we approached the building. "Malik, Asha and I were fleeing Monterra, and I got disoriented from the overuse of power. There was someone there I thought we needed to go back for. Emerson. Anyway, she wasn't what I'd thought she was. Malik tried to stop me and I misunderstood his intention because of the haze I was in. Before I knew it, I'd punched a blade into his gut. Asha had the good sense to knock me out before I did any more damage. When I woke up, I was horrified at what I'd done. I healed Malik, but he would barely speak to me. Only Malik and Asha know," I confessed.

"The female Emerson, she was someone special to you once?" he asked. I didn't sense any judgement.

"Oh, not exactly." My cheeks heated as I turned away. "It was kind of a one time thing before I confirmed what a terrible female she is. I got lost in the moment. I haven't always made the greatest choices when it comes to lovers."

Rhijn opened his mouth as if to say something then closed it, his eyes trailing off into the distance momentarily before turning back to the door. He pushed it open and guided me through, his fingers absently drifting across the small of my back leaving little flares behind them. We stepped into a large open space, the ceiling towering over us over two stories above. A large device sat in the center of the room on an elevated platform reached by a set of metal stairs. A long tube extended up and through the roof and a series of straps, pulleys and crank handles were attached to it.

On the ground level, tables and chairs lined the walls. Papers and equipment I didn't recognize littered every surface. There was a modest space with a minimal kitchen. Another raised platform extended around the perimeter of the room. I followed Rhijn up a set of stairs. They led to an open loft containing a bed with a chair and a writing desk next to it, and one door, which presumably led to a bathroom.

He looked back at me and shrugged. Having only one bed was not ideal after what I'd confessed, and he seemed to gather that. I had trained to deal with all sorts of situations though and I'd treat this as such.

"We need to remove your shirt before I can heal you," I said. I walked down to the kitchen and opened a cabinet, searching for a bowl. When I'd filled it with hot water and found a soft cloth, I returned upstairs, setting the bowl down on the desk. He was struggling to detach his shirt from the dried blood sticking to his skin.

"Sit," I instructed. "I need you to lean back so your stomach is stretched flat." He complied. I kneeled between his knees and reached my hand gingerly under his shirt. I gave a gentle pull on the fabric, and he winced. It was slow going, but I wrung out the water of the cloth and dabbed the dried blood until the fabric finally detached from his skin. I looked up from my work. He wasn't watching my hands—his eyes were on my face.

"Maybe I should get sliced in the abdomen more often," he gave me a half-hearted grin, assessing my position between his long, taut thighs. "Had I known this was all it took to get close to you…"

"I see you're still power crazy." I glared at him, ignoring the suggestive tilt of his pelvis making me think he might be aware of how cuddly I had gotten in the transport and taken that as some sort of hint. "I'm going to make sure this leaves a nasty scar," I grumbled, and I got to my feet. He sat up and I helped him ease the fabric over his head. A trickle of blood seeped out of the wound as he shifted.

"Go lay on the bed."

"Why? I liked this position fine," he teased. "You said you wanted me to be less formal."

"Do you want me to heal you or not?" I asked, hands going to my hips suspecting his playfulness was him trying to mask the pain he felt over Everly's death—a distraction. I made a mental note to try to get him to talk about it soon.

Rhijn flopped down on the mattress, scooting over enough so I could sit next to him. I cleaned the wound with the cloth, removing any linen filaments and other debris. He closed his eyes and took deep, steady breaths as I worked.

"Okay, I'm ready to seal it. The wound is deep enough, I'll need to make two passes, which will hurt, unless you want your pretty physique disfigured." Makers, I was flirting with him back.

"*We* wouldn't want that."

"*We* don't care. I'm only concerned for your sake."

I pressed my finger across the seam of the gash. I didn't have to go as deep as I would have before the ember had given me greater access to my power. I still wanted to get close to ensure that I worked in layers and his skin and muscle were stitched together evenly.

Out of the corner of my eye, his left hand gripped the comforter and his right grabbed the wrist I was leaning on, squeezing. I glanced up at him. He gritted his teeth as his intense stare bored into me. It stole my breath—the way he was looking at me.

I finished the last pass. His grip on my wrist relaxed, and the tension in his body followed. I ran my fingers across his defined abs, inspecting my work. Gooseflesh followed my fingers, and he squirmed beneath them. He snatched my hand before it traced another path across his now unmarred skin.

"You should be careful doing that. It might have unintended consequences." His voice was low, gravelly.

I smirked. "I think you're all talk, Rhijn. Besides, considering my recent track-record, whatever you are referring to is not on my agenda. Understand?"

"Suit yourself. I guess I should offer to heal your back now to return the favor."

My jaw dropped. "You mean you could have healed yourself this whole time?" I stammered.

He nodded, grinning.

"Unbelievable," I said.

Rhijn sat up, his demeanor becoming more serious. "I'll try to cut away the fabric of your shirt so I can work, and I'm not very good. Truthfully, I only have gained the ability recently and you'll probably need real healers to look at it when we're back in Adrina. But it will do for now."

I rolled my eyes and tugged my shirt up over my head, hissing as the sticky blood and skin peeled apart. Rhijn looked at me, wide eyed.

"What? It was part of my training. Enduring pain in case they caught me. I think they were using me as an experiment to see if the pain would force my channels to open more as some sort of instinct, though. Let's get this over with." I lay down on my stomach, giving him access to my back. My cut was much shallower than his, and healing would only take moments if he were more experienced.

"You are kind of making me feel like a wimp," he said as he finished.

I sat up, stretching my back. His work wasn't as bad as he made it seem, but there was still some stiffness.

Rhijn's eyes met mine, then went to the bralette, a fantastic Idian invention Asha had gifted me, then to the ceiling.

"You can take a shower first. I'll try to find us some supplies." He found a wall to stare at as he continued. "Tomorrow I'll go to town and see if they have any full power cylinders for the transport. If not, it may take a few days to have this one filled in town. I don't think we should use our power again."

For once, I agreed.

I walked over to the door of the bathroom, but turned, when a gentle touch of calloused fingers landed on my shoulder. I glanced back at him. Healing each other had been so intimate, and the space between us seemed to vibrate with electricity. It had to be the void stones reaching for each other, I thought, as I stood in the doorway, shifting between feet, not knowing what to make of his gesture.

"Thank you," he said, squeezing.

I cleared my throat. "You're welcome." I slipped into the bathroom and leaned against the cool tile wall. Taking deep, steady breaths, I attempted to calm my flopping stomach and my traitorous body, which was responding to his mere existence.

"Do you think each one of those tiny dots of light have a realm like ours?" I asked, as I pressed my eye to the eyepiece of the telescope like Rhijn showed me.

"They say there are untold realms, so probably many of them do," he replied. He looked through the lens and made some adjustments, the piece of equipment rotating slightly in response. He turned a knob, moving aside so I could look.

"Do you see the swirling arms?" he asked, and I nodded. "That is a universe. There may be numerous realms inside each one. That is what makes the most sense to me, but it isn't necessarily the case. Your realm may be in our universe, or another one entirely. At night you can see one of the arms of the universe Idia is located within."

"This isn't the first time you've shown me this," I told him.

He looked at me bewildered, narrowing his eyes, before clarity struck.

"Everly." He said, pain flashed across his features and his eyes went glassy. "How could I have forgotten her final request was to ask you about dreams."

I'd figured he'd remember eventually, and I'd rather have that conversation way out here in the middle of nowhere. And it seemed we'd been avoiding discussing her death.

"Are you going to continue?" he prodded.

"She was your cousin. From what she said, you two were close. I'm truly sorry, Rhijn." I put my hand on his forearm and squeezed.

"Thanks," he said, and turned so I wouldn't see the tears I knew were crawling over his sharp cheekbones.

"Do you want to talk about it?" I asked tugging him toward me.

He shrugged as I wiped the tears off his cheeks. "I don't really know how. I've never lost anyone before. Have you?"

"Not like what Everly was to you. I know when things that have happened that hurt me in the past, being held by someone who cares about me helped." I opened my arms and Rhijn grabbed my wrist and pulled me into his embrace, leaning his chin down onto the top of my head. We stood there holding each other for long moments and I felt the salty drops land on my hair as I released my own tears onto the soft fabric of his shirt.

After a while, Rhijn's long arms gave me a final squeeze and I pushed myself back from his chest. "I'm okay," he said looking down at me, eyes tracing the details of my face. He coughed. "So, about these dreams?"

He clearly didn't want to elaborate about Everly, but at least he'd released some of his grief. Not wanting to push, I explained the same thing I'd explained to her about the dreams, but in even less detail.

"So, this is the reason you've been afraid of me?" he groaned, exasperated, rubbing his eyebrows with the heels of his palms.

"I'm *not* afraid of you. And it's not a big deal. They were only a few dreams. And honestly, I don't know if we'd be here if you hadn't intruded on them."

He stepped back, huffing. "Don't blame your wild, *primitive*, imagination on me, Chosen One."

I rolled my eyes.

He stretched out an arm leaning on the railing, muscles flexing, which his fitted shirt only accentuated. He was doing it on purpose. "So, you were saying something about one where I had my shirt off?"

I snapped my head in his direction. If he didn't know before, he definitely knew now. And he was trying to shock me. My cheeks flushed. I tamped it down, determined not to lose control. "I never kiss and tell, *your highness*," I crooned.

He let out a deep, throaty laugh. I'd won that point. A wide grin crept across my face before I turned back to the telescope, studying the night sky.

"What is that dark spot at the top right?" I asked him. He leaned in and took a look.

"That is a void zone. It's the only one we've been able to identify. We aren't sure what it is, but if you look closely, light seems to bend into it and disappear. It's a most interesting phenomenon."

Rhijn jerked, standing up straight. He stood, extending tall, then twisted his torso.

I sent my energy around him and noticed the swelling in his low back. It was minor, but enough to make him sore. Sleeping in the transport and on the floor as he had the last few nights couldn't be helping. I placed my hand on his low back and encouraged the muscles to relax. He looked at me, wrinkling his brow, then sighed as the discomfort was relieved.

"Better?" I asked.

"Yeah, thanks. I don't know why I never thought to do that."

"You can have half of the bed tonight. Just stick to your side."

He chuckled. "Deal."

We'd been interacting peacefully for several days. He'd officially touched my bare skin, and I didn't fall to my knees in a trembling mess, thank the Makers. I supposed I officially liked him. We'd shared the bed last night, and he'd not even hinted at crossing any boundaries.

The more I got to know him, the more I questioned how glad I was about his restraint. Especially as he climbed on his side in only his sleeping pants. He leaned back, putting his hands behind his head, his torso constricting, lean muscles rippling as he did. His shoulder-length pale hair was tucked behind one ear, and had slipped down alluringly, brushing his defined cheekbone. It made me itch to trace my fingers along the smooth lines, and weave them through that silky hair. He was easily the most attractive male I'd ever seen.

Spending all this one-on-one time with him wasn't helping either. It was easy to forget the rest of the world existed in this secluded town, staying at this even more secluded observatory. He was slowly chipping away at my resistance, whether or not he realized it, and I knew it was only a matter of time before I caved to my baser instinct. Maybe I truly was a primitive being, after all. Needless to say, I was eager to get back to Adrina.

"What is this?" I asked from the bathroom after I'd taken an excessively long shower. I was wrapped in a towel and peeked out the door, holding up a black lacy ensemble that I had pulled out of the package of clothing Rhijn had procured from town. He'd found a female who'd pilfered through her own belongings to find some unworn items to send for me. Most everything she'd sent had been practical and fit well, more or less, until this.

"A nightgown?" he said from the other room. "How am I supposed to know? The female just handed me a bag of clothes."

I stuck my head out of the door, scowling. He stared at me from across the room. Challenging me.

"Fine," I said. I had no idea what this female who'd included this outfit had interpreted my relationship with Rhijn to be. I couldn't see my image in the steam clouded mirror, but I knew it was indecent as I slipped into it. It reminded me of Emerson's attire that night, but all black. If that dress I'd worn on the isle made Rhijn stagger, this thing might stop his heart.

The straps that held up the top were lace with a satin ribbon woven through them. Two silk triangles trimmed in a delicate lace made up the top, which was held together by a silk band below the bust. A ribbon tied into a bow sat in the middle, and the fabric which fell to mid-hip had a slit that ran down the center to the hem, putting my navel on full display. A pair of matching silk shorts, also trimmed in black lace, sat low on my hips and barely covered my ass. I shrugged as I assessed myself. The nightwear would technically be comfortable to sleep in. Breezy even, which would be better than the heavy blouse I'd worn last night.

We'd been going back and forth with this game of who could shock the other more for the last few days. I'd told him about Darius, the Swath and other adventures Conall and I had. He told me a few stories of his own which Everly had failed to share, that confirmed the rowdy picture of the reserved male lying on the bed right outside this door. His invention stories were my favorite, though. He'd have these ideas, and wake in the middle of the night and start sketching or go to the laboratories and begin tinkering.

I stepped outside the bathroom.

Rhijn choked on the water he'd been sipping, spraying it to the side of the bed. "I think I should have picked you up a little more decent nightwear." He still struggled to recover.

"Am I making you uncomfortable?" I fingered the black lace at the top.

"That's not the exact word I would use."

"Then what word would it be?" I asked, coyly, knowing nothing would come of this.

"I don't think you are prepared to hear it." He swallowed.

"I'll be the judge of what I'm prepared to hear."

"Aroused," he bit out.

My eyes flew open. Makers, Rhijn was aroused. Now? He was less than a few feet away on the bed we were sharing. Stupidly sharing because my sympathy got me in this situation. And this stupid outfit.

I followed his eyes as they trailed from my neck, across my collarbone to the delicate lace strap holding the slip up. He unabashedly followed it down to the curve of my breast and the interested nipple I suspected the delicate fabric wasn't hiding. And smiled, owning his trailing gaze.

Aroused Rhijn was bold, and hot. This wasn't the first time I'd responded to his utter masculinity either, I thought, gawking at the planes and hollows of his bare chest in return. Heat was building deep between my thighs as I clenched them. I dared a glance down at the crotch of his sleeping pants. Yes, he wasn't lying. His smile broadened at my movement. My ratcheting pulse thrummed in my ear. This was just another game.

"Fine, you want to fuck me now, Rhijn?" I threw the vulgar word at him, trying to stun him and reclaim the upper hand. "You *want* this primitive female now?"

Instead of being shocked, his eyes turned molten. He nodded decisively. "Very much," he growled.

I froze. *What do I do? What do I do?*

While my mind was entirely unclear on the answer, leaning toward a really bad idea, except for the strong affirmative that was radiating through my body. I teetered on that precipice for what dragged on for an eternity.

Oh, to hell with it. I was done fighting the relentless draw that gripped me every time I was around him. I was over the months I'd spent with those leg quaking dreams about him, my self-pleasure, and the damnable tension between us every time I made eye contact with this Maker's blasted Skyborne. Maybe if I satisfied the need, this magnetism would go away.

Besides, what's another mistake?

If I had fangs or claws, they would have been out. His eyes tracked my every movement, letting on that he sensed the palpable desire swirling inside me. I'd give him the primitive being he saw me as, and I'd take what I needed from him in return. I didn't care what others thought, either. There would be plenty of time to regret my decisions when I was dead, and I refused to deny myself this pleasure. I was in control of my destiny now, I thought, lifting my chin as I stared unabashed at him.

"Nayla," his voice was guttural as he said my name, and I loved how desperate it sounded on his tongue. His nostrils flared, and I caught the shock in his eyes as I crawled across the bed toward him.

For a moment, I couldn't tell if we were bluffing. We were an inch apart, impossibly still. I looked from his lips to his icy blue eyes.

"You're afraid," he said, watching me. Giving me space to choose.

Terrified. I lifted my hand to touch his cheek, but it was trembling too hard. I dropped it before he noticed, and I huffed a laugh at myself. So much for the predator.

Rhijn started to back away, thinking I didn't want this—I didn't want him, I supposed. But I did. Makers, I did.

I panicked and tipped forward before he retreated. The moment our lips touched, a bolt of energy coursed through me. I sucked in a quick breath, then eased forward once more. I gently brushed our lips, then ran my nose along his, before connecting with his mouth again in a soft, exploratory kiss. I couldn't believe this was happening, and he wasn't moving. A chill spread from my chest and I opened my eyes to his stunned blue staring back at me.

Rhijn hesitated momentarily. I felt something snap in him. His hand slid around the back of my neck and he pressed his mouth to mine, groaning as he did. *Thank the Makers*, I thought as he sucked at my lower lip and I opened for him. His tongue slid against mine as he pulled our bodies together.

Hands roamed my body greedily, covering every inch of me. "*You're real,*" he moaned into my mouth, and goosebumps tickled across my flesh. He kissed and tasted my exposed skin, grinding his erection in between my thighs.

"May I," he whispered into my neck, tugging at the hem of the top piece of the frilly nightwear. I nodded, and he pulled it up and over my head, tossing it aside.

"I don't know what to say." He took in my bare skin as I sat before him. "You are so much better than in my dreams."

I flinched. Rhijn had been relentlessly teasing me about my dreams, after I'd finally confessed them in a moment of weakness. He'd never mentioned *his dreams*. I'd never thought he'd been having dreams about *me*, though Everly had suggested it. I was melting into him, losing control. I was not about to lose control.

"Take these off," I demanded, kneeling over him as I impatiently pulled at the waistband of his pants.

He sighed, and he jerked his sleeping pants down. "I feel like we're going to regret this in the morning."

"I'm beyond caring," I said, wiggling free of my silky shorts and taking the full length of him in my hand. He was more glorious than in any of the dreams, too. I threw my leg over him so I was straddling his hips and stroked him lazily. We were actually going to do this. My breath caught for a moment as his fingers caressed across my opening.

"I'm taking a preventative, but we can still stop," he whispered, seeing my reaction and moving his hand away.

"Is that what you want, Rhijn?" I asked him, holding the almost painful eye contact.

He smiled, revealing his perfect teeth. Looking up at me he said, "Only if you don't think you can handle me."

Unformal, flirty, *cocky*, Rhijn was something other and made me yearn to explore all of the other facets of his personality. Not only did I think I could handle the challenge of him, I longed to do it. Rolling my eyes, I lowered myself down onto him. He grabbed my hips, halting me as

I struggled against him. The bastard was taunting me. He laughed low as he eased his grip and let me slip down on top of him. His breath caught as I started moving, but he put his hands behind his head and watched me.

"I don't think you understand how infuriating you are," I said, my voice breathy.

"I don't think *you* understand how sexy you are," he said, biting his lower lip, taking me in. "The first time I saw you drink wine, the way you savored it, letting it slide across your tongue. I imagined you were tasting me inside your mouth, *me* warming the back of your throat."

Makers, he was hot, this was hot. *I didn't expect to come this quickly*, I thought as I edged closer to the release I was looking for.

Suddenly he flipped me on my back, and there was an abrupt and terrible vacancy between my thighs. "Don't worry, I'm close too, but the first time we go together—"

His hands slid underneath my shoulders, arching my back up toward him. His hands tangled in my hair, cupping my head, and he planted soft kisses across my throat, licking and sucking. My senses were electric as I arched into him. He was so in control, like he knew what every kiss, every touch was doing to me.

"You'd better enjoy it, because this is a one-time thing," I said, looking away.

His hands guided my head back so our eyes connected. His grin was feral. "You enjoy being wrong, don't you?"

I started to rebuttal, when he claimed my lips again. It was more intense than before, causing me to ache, desperate to get him back inside me. After torturously long moments, he pushed back in. He teased slowly, gently thrusting until I was begging him to go faster.

"I'm really glad you like sex as much as I do," he rumbled against my lips, picking up a rhythm that met the need we were both feeling.

My hands were in his hair, coursing down the rippled muscles of his back, searching for the grooves at the V of his abdomen, and all over his perfect ass. I think I might have been trying to consume him. He pulled our mouths apart as I shattered beneath him. He went rigid above me, hammering in the final strokes of the mess we were making.

After the last wave of pleasure subsided, I realized he had stilled and was resting his forehead on mine. My eyelids fluttered open. His cool blue eyes were piercing into mine as we breathed the same air. I wanted to pause the world at that moment. *Please don't say anything.* It seemed like he was on board with my plan until he opened his damn mouth.

"You know this changes things, don't you?" His voice was husky and satisfied.

Ugh, I thought as I pushed him off me and turned over, already missing his presence inside me. "We'll see how we feel in the morning."

His deep laugh rumbled into my hair as he wrapped his arm around my waist and pulled me into him threading his legs through mine.

Softly, I heard him murmur into my ear, "I'm not your latest mistake, Nayla. I think you know that. I think you would be less afraid if I was."

I was so exhausted from the pleasure I fell asleep in his arms before I could argue.

CHAPTER FIFTEEN

I HATED ADMITTING RHIJN was right, but the first thought I had the moment I woke up the next morning tangled with him was *oh, shit. What have I done?* Gently, I slipped out of his arms. He stirred momentarily, but stilled into sleep quickly. It was a blessing the bathroom door didn't creak as I closed it. I turned on the shower, still amazed by the concept of the warm rain coming from the fixture in the ceiling. I wrapped my arms around myself as the water poured over me. I wasn't sure how long I'd been standing there with my eyes closed, chastising myself, when footsteps entered the bathroom.

I turned to see a naked and perfectly chiseled Rhijn standing before me, raking his hand through his tousled hair, grinning. He would be pale if it weren't for the planes of smooth skin the light star kissed which only enhanced the look of the toned muscle.

"I don't know about you, but I think I'd like to do that again."

Oh makers, I thought, staring at the evidence saluting me. "I don't think so, *buddy*." I said, turning my back to him. The Skyborne had the audacity to step in the shower with me. Our bodies brushed as he leaned in front of me to grab the bar of soap. Rhijn lathered up and began scrubbing himself as I stood there and watched as if this was no big deal he was intruding on my shower. I couldn't look away as the rivulets of water streamed down the ridges of his chest and abdomen. My eyes followed them to where his hand was *cleaning* his still firm erection.

"What are you doing?"

"I've got to deal with this thing somehow, and since you don't seem to want to help." He paused, lifting an eyebrow. "Unless you do?"

My mouth went dry. I was speechless, but I couldn't drag my eyes away as his hand moved up and down. The familiar heat built between my thighs.

"Fine, just watch then," he said, as his breathing kicked up a notch. Veins in his neck bulged to the surface as he groaned.

He glanced down at my piqued nipples. "You know I can tell that's not what you want to do, right?"

My heart was thundering in my chest as I met his eyes. "This—" I gestured between us. "—doesn't leave this town. Doesn't leave this room. What we have done and will do, does not follow us back to Adrina. Understand?"

"If that's the deal, then I guess we'll have to stay here forever," he said as he picked me up and guided my legs around his waist, pressing me against the cold tile wall.

I jerked, grinding against his heat. He pressed another button on the wall and a warm stream of water shot out, soaking our flush bodies. His teeth grazed my jaw as he slid into me. Though I knew we both had the same need, his thrusts were lazy and his kiss tempting and languid this time.

I wanted him to go faster and bring the release, but he was in no hurry. Rhijn leaned back to get a better view of us, and with my upper back still against the cool wall I followed his gaze down to where he slid in and out of me.

"Nayla, you don't know what you do to me. In my dreams, when you landed on that dune, I've been aching for this. For you," he breathed, still watching us. "Touch yourself."

"What?" I said, peeking up at him, blushing. I found it hard to believe he'd been thinking of me like I'd thought of him. He was too perfect.

He grabbed my hand, interrupting my thoughts, and placed it on the bundle of nerves between my legs. "I would, but I'm holding you up." A sly grin slid across his face, seeing my fingers unable to resist the circular motions, increasing my pleasure. When he looked his fill, his eyes tracked up to mine which had been watching him watch us. His gaze was a challenge as he picked up the pace. The corner of his lip hitched up in a snarl.

Our breathing became shallow as we stared at each other, the eye contact becoming a battle of wills. I refused to turn away first. I was getting close as I leaned my head back on the shower wall, still not breaking the gaze. I could tell his experience was the mirror of mine when it hit. I cried out as acute bliss sparked through my body. The utter maleness in his face struck me as we came together. In that moment, his crystalline blue stare was so intense it felt like it somehow became a part of me. As the surges ebbed, I caught a brief flash of emotion dash across his eyes. Fear, maybe. But then it was gone.

He pressed his forehead into the shower wall over my shoulder as I ran my fingers through his hair. I felt so warm and satisfied. "I wouldn't mind a few more days of that," I confessed, giggling, and ran my teeth across his neck. Everything he did felt so good. The type of good that you wanted to escape into or that would lull you to sleep.

He eased me down, and we finished bathing. After he shut the shower off, he held open a fluffy towel before he'd even gotten one for himself. I walked into it and he wrapped it around my shoulders, then leaned down to place a tender kiss on my temple.

"Did you feel that?" he breathed as he nudged and nipped at my ear.

Makers, if he was ready to go again, who was I to complain? "Umm yes, were my moans of pleasure not loud enough for you to hear?" I tried to bat him away but he grabbed my hand, and placed a soft kiss on my knuckles.

He flicked his gaze up to the mirror and our eyes connected. "No, not that. The *other* thing that just happened?"

A ruddy flush danced faintly across Rhijn's cheeks like he was embarrassed. I couldn't understand why after what had just transpired between us.

"What are you talking about?" I narrowed my stare at him and slipped out of his embrace. A nervous energy filtered through me as realization dawned. I could see where this was headed if I didn't deal with it swiftly.

"Look, Rhijn, I like you. I really do and that was amazing." Hands down the best I'd ever had but if I admitted that it would only encourage him. "See, the thing is I'm not trying to get involved. I told you before this started this was a one-time thing."

Rhijn stepped back. The joy that had been etched into his features moments earlier melted and was replaced with a tension that looked an awful lot like horror.

"But I thought…" he trailed off running hands down his face as if he could smudge away whatever he was feeling. "You implied you cared about me."

I turned to him, a guilting twang making my stomach churn. "I'm really sorry. I do care, it's just—I wouldn't have allowed that to happen if I thought you'd…" I hesitated. "*Develop feelings.* I just thought we both needed a release to relieve some stress. You know, a distraction, after everything that happened," I threw in for good measure.

The horror was replaced with color draining dread.

"You okay?" I reached for him, but he flinched away.

He screwed up his features and walked out of the bathroom. "I just need a minute." His voice was a hollow thing trailing behind him.

I let it go and took my time finishing up, drying my hair and applying a minimal amount of make-up gifted to me from the female in town. I put on the clothes I'd set out and gave myself a once over in the mirror before I left the bathroom.

Rhijn was sitting in one of the chairs by the desk at the window with a blank stare on his face.

"Rhijn, what are you doing?" I asked.

He sat completely still and didn't look at me. "Go on and grab breakfast. I'll be down soon."

I narrowed my eyes in his direction. "Fine." I headed downstairs, not looking back.

⁓

I was almost finished with my breakfast when he walked down the stairs and out the door of the observatory not even glancing my way. He was acting so strangely. Solemn almost.

"Rhijn, what's going on?" I asked when he walked back inside a while later.

He jolted to a standstill and angled his head in my direction. "I just don't understand how you could experience that and just pretend like nothing happened."

My hands were quivering on their own accord under the table. I was so confused. "It's just complicated, okay? This isn't just about us."

"There's someone else?" he said, his jaw tightening and his light eyes narrowing interrogatively. Everything about his stiff posture radiated defensiveness. "If there is, I'm astonished. Impressed even."

His reaction caught me off guard. "No, there's no one else," I whispered, wrinkling my brow with concern. That's not what I'd meant. I was thinking of what we'd have to do over the coming months. Of bringing the Banished home and dealing with Emerson and whatever chaos she was likely inflicting upon the realm with her monsters. We didn't have time for a romance. "Rhijn…"

"Don't," he said, "just don't." He grabbed the book I'd been reading while I enjoyed my breakfast and thumbed through it. "What's this about?"

"Oh, you know, the usual—fairy lands, males who can turn into wolves, and virgin maids," I said, an embarrassed grin slipping out.

"Well, I don't think you'll have time to finish it unless you're an exceptionally fast reader. The power cell is full and we should leave soon."

I looked up at him, surprised. "I thought last night you said it'd be at least another day or two."

"I lied." He didn't make eye contact again before he walked to the stairs. He paused halfway up and turned to me slowly. I stopped chewing, his stare stopping me short.

"You shouldn't read fairy tales. They'll set you up for unattainable expectations. In the wild, do you think a wolf feels remorse over the hare in his maw? No, he eats the rabbit alive."

It was a chilling thought, and suddenly I was no longer hungry.

⁓

We spent the next day of the passage not speaking. Not really, anyway. He wouldn't look at me and we took turns monitoring the controls and resting. I'd tried to strike up a conversation with him several times, missing the annoying but entertaining banter we'd developed. I flipped through the book I'd been unable to finish, and it thankfully was a distraction, but not enough that I could completely lose the focus which inevitably returned to Rhijn.

It was after sundown when Rhijn finally broke his silence.

"We'll get to Adrina tomorrow. You don't have to worry; I'll keep my promise."

I knew exactly the promise he was referring to.

"But you technically didn't promise."

He bored into me then. "If I didn't know any better, I'd think you almost sounded glad." He shook his head. "Go to sleep Nayla, we'll be there when you wake."

"Rhijn?" I said, ashamed at the pleading in my voice.

"What?" He paused. His words were so aggressive. "Huh, what do you want from me? Oh wait, I know the answer. *Nothing.*"

His words struck like a slap. We barely had a connection, so it confused me why it pierced so deep. That wasn't exactly true, though. I'd known him for months now if you counted the dreams. And he'd been having them too, though he hadn't shared their contents with me. Rhijn reached over and pulled a curtain he'd rigged up closed, so he didn't have to see me.

I lay on the bench, unable to sleep. I couldn't get comfortable, even though he'd given me the full thing to stretch out across. It had to be hours since I'd been like this when I heard a shuffle from the floorboard that he'd made his bed. I peeked outside the curtain and Rhijn was lying on the floor looking up blankly at the ceiling.

"You're awake?" I asked him.

He looked over at me. "What does it look like?"

"There is room up here, where it's more comfortable." I couldn't believe I'd said that. Wasn't I the one who had specifically wanted to not get involved with this Skyborne?

He laughed under his breath. "Yeah, thanks, but no."

I shut the curtain and lay back, contemplating what was really going on. For several days, he'd been in my space, joking and flirting. Annoyingly so. Taunting me about the dreams. I didn't understand this shift. I mean, maybe he thought our romp might have turned into something more. But I couldn't help that. I'd been clear and I really didn't think he should be punishing me for it. I needed to deal with this before we got back to Adrina. We could still be friends. We were both adults.

"Are you acting this way because of what we shared?" I asked through the curtain between us.

"*Shared?* Is that what happened, Nayla? We shared that?"

"Yes," I said meekly. It wasn't like me, but I was entirely unprepared to deal with this. Despite all of my training, this Skyborne had gotten into my head. He had said we'd regret this and at the time I had totally agreed, but didn't care. But after the shower, I thought as my cheeks warmed, any semblance of regret I might have felt just wasn't there. He was having the exact opposite reaction.

"You told me you didn't want anything to do with what is between us and I should have listened. Now you want to act like we can just be friendly, like it won't affect me. Like I should just be fine with our obviously one-sided connection." Rhijn's deep voice was pained.

"You regret it I see. You said we would and you do. I'm sorry for that."

"What, and you don't?"

At least he was talking to me. "No, I don't. Do you think I should, Rhijn?"

"You are quite shameless, aren't you? You don't get it at all." He was quiet for a moment. "And for the love of the Makers, stop saying my name like that."

I gasped softly as hot tears pricked my eyes. I turned over on my side, away from him as they trickled down my nose and cheek.

CHAPTER SIXTEEN

I COULDN'T WAIT TO get out of the transport when we arrived at the capitol. It brought us right up to the terrace where the rooms where we Banished were staying. I hadn't slept but a few hours and my emotions were on edge. I knew Conall would be there waiting for me. We'd signaled in yesterday morning and learned Malik and Seeley hadn't returned from their trip to see the other settlement yet. Their trek had been the furthest in the opposite direction of our journey. Conall and Asha had arrived back two days prior.

Rhijn's father was with Conall when we returned. I flung myself out of the carriage, stumbling, fatigue setting in, and Conall was there to sweep me into his arms. It felt so good to be held by someone who loved you unconditionally. Who'd proved they did, time and time again. Rhijn set my bag at my feet and walked over to his father.

Conall lifted my chin, and his eyes widened. "I heard what had happened, the creatures, but you were safe right, you weren't harmed?" he demanded.

"No, I wasn't harmed."

"Then what's wrong, Nayla?" he asked. Damn him for knowing me so well. Rhijn didn't notice, or care, I supposed, that my eyes had a lightly red rim now, the only outward sign that I wasn't fine.

"He didn't do anything to you? Rhijn didn't hurt you, did he?" Conall looked panicked before he stared daggers toward Rhijn.

He'd been looking at us and absorbed Conall's stare full on. The tension was threatening going in both directions, to say the least.

"Conall, no, stop. He didn't do anything wrong. It's Everly," I lied. I was upset we'd lost her, but she wasn't the reason I'd been crying. Conall didn't need to know that though.

"I told them sending you with him was a bad idea. I knew I couldn't trust him," Conall seethed, seeing through the falsehood.

"Conall, please stop." I grabbed his arm before he stormed over to Rhijn and did Maker's only knows what. "Rhijn was a perfect gentleman. I'm the primitive one, remember?" I forced a chuckle at my own joke and Conall shook his head, but Rhijn drew in a sharp breath.

"As long as you are okay, my primitive one, I won't have to kill him," Conall said, his use of the nickname making me cringe and I saw Rhijn bristle and turn away.

"Conall, don't say that," I brushed him off.

Rhijn was ignoring us now. I sensed it as I overheard him telling his father the southern settlement was overrun with monsters again.

"Kelvin assured me the area was safe. I never would have taken her there and put her in that kind of danger if I'd known we could've been attacked like that. And Everly," Rhijn paused, voice cracking. "We couldn't save her."

Vitis embraced his son and Rhijn's shoulders trembled. Eventually, he pulled away, and both male's eyes now matched the pink hue of mine. My heart ached for them.

The Chancellor cleared his throat. "Your message said you'd both used your power together to refill the power cell? Her power didn't hurt you?" He was looking over Rhijn's hands and glanced at me.

I'd overheard this male encourage Rhijn to form a connection or bond or whatever to me, and now he was afraid I'd hurt his son. Oh, no way was that going to fly. My emotions were too frayed already to have anyone lump anymore guilt upon them. I pulled away from Conall and spun to face Vitis and Rhijn.

"I didn't want to use my power with his, but we had to. We would be dead if we hadn't. We knew the risks, but I assure you in the moment, an energy burn or whatever horror you expected to befall your precious son would have been far more pleasant than the fate awaiting us had we not gotten the remaining cell recharged enough to get us out of there."

The chancellor's eyes were wide with intrigue. The surrounding air shimmered with my anger, like the boundary of the Swath.

Rhijn stepped in, "that's not what he meant, Nayla."

"What exactly did he mean then, Rhijn?" I snapped back at him.

"Whoa kids, I feel like I missed something." Asha's candid voice carried over to us as she approached.

Conall wrapped his arm around my shoulder again and pulled me into him, flinching at the static surrounding me.

"I'm sure there is a perfectly reasonable explanation, right Rhijn?" Asha continued.

"Apparently I've been foolish. I thought if you two could learn to get along, form a connection, your powers might be able to be combined. Amplified. It stands to reason that the energy orbiting you two is connected. And if those powers touch, or are used together, I thought it might have gone one of two ways. And I shudder to think of the way it evidently did not go. For *both* of you." The Chancellor had stepped in. "Nayla, you mean as much to Idia and your home realm as Rhijn does. I won't see either of you hurt. We need you both in your full capacity if we are to right the wrongs done to our realms and the countless innocents between them. Go now and rest. You are reasonably exhausted. A week with my son can do that to a person."

Rhijn scowled. There were moments when I thought Chancellor Vitis was what a father would have been like, if I had a normal one. Whatever normal meant. "We can talk more tomorrow," Vitis concluded, sending me away.

I started to resist his command. But I'd gone toe to toe with Chancellor Vitis before and I wasn't up for the challenge today. I broke his authoritative, *fatherly* gaze first and let Conall take me and my things to my room.

I was so tired, I barely managed to shoo him away and crawl between the covers. After a few moments alone, the strangest sense of sorrow consumed me. It was like an out-of-body experience and I could not figure out where it was coming from. The pulsating ache in my chest felt otherworldly as if it wasn't my own, but no less intense than if it was. But that didn't make any sense. I rationalized it was probably because I hadn't known Everly that well, or all of these external forces finally getting the better of me. That had to be it. I lay on my bed with a steady stream of tears flowing onto the pillow before sleep finally found me.

∾

Conall sat across from me as we had breakfast and I told him all about the creatures we'd encountered and how Rhijn and I had to combine our powers to get the transport to start. He peppered me with questions, for details of the creatures, and every third question, something alluding to me being damaged by Rhijn. Ever since I'd told him about what had happened with Darius, he was overly protective and I understood that. It was getting to be a little much though.

"Chancellor Vitis said the creatures haven't always been here. They've shown up in the last year, they think. Do you think it has something to do with the Makers, or the ember... I mean void stones?"

"It has to, Conall. I'm not sure what else to think. They were like nothing I've encountered yet."

He sat back in his chair. "The crazier this all gets, the more I am able to believe it." Conall shook his head, running his fingers through his hair. "You are okay though, Nayla? I'll stop asking if you promise me."

"I'm fine Conall." I wouldn't do my best friend the dishonor of making a false promise, though. He understood I was done talking about it, and he had the sense not to push. "Your eyes tell a different story." A melancholy, which I knew was for me, laced his voice punching at my already tender gut.

"Conall, can you go get Seeley?" I'd heard Malik and Seeley's party had gotten back late yesterday afternoon while I'd been sleeping.

"Sure. Why, what's going on?"

"I just need to talk to him, please," I said.

"You can talk to me. You know that."

"I know, and I appreciate it. I need to ask him about something. Please, go get him." Begrudgingly, he left to do as I asked.

I picked at the food Conall had brought me as I waited for Seeley. He had sight, so maybe he could help me figure out what was going on with the connection I shared with Rhijn through the void stones. That was all I cared about, I told myself.

✍

About a half hour later, I was sipping my tea when Seeley popped through the door, followed by Conall. Seeley took the chair across from me and Conall started to drag one closer. My hesitation must have been easily decipherable, because Seeley placed his hand on Conall's intended chair, stilling it. "Conall, could you give us a moment alone? I'd like to speak with Nayla privately."

Thank the Makers for that Skyborne, I thought. Conall looked at me and I grimaced apologetically before he relented and left us. I knew his feelings would be bruised, but I'd make it up to him later.

"So, what did you want to speak to me about so urgently?" Seeley asked, then sat patiently, waiting.

An uncontrollable smile crossed my face as I tried desperately to shut it down.

"Oh Makers, you did not! You dirty Skyborne," he cried.

"Seeley," I pleaded, horrified, "stop it. That is not what I wanted to talk to you about."

"I see you are not denying it then. How was it? Oh, that male is a fine piece of meat. If my heart weren't so entrenched with Malik and engaged, I might give you competition." Seeley was holding up the ring on his wiggling fingers.

"You would not. And it was amazing. Like nothing I've ever experienced before," I said, blushing the darkest shade of red imaginable. "He regrets it, though. We have hardly spoken since. I shouldn't have crossed that line. Seems to be one of my brilliant character flaws."

"Oh, sweetie, don't go down that road. Tell me what happened."

"About the sex?" I asked, surprised.

Seeley deep belly laughed. "Oh goodness, I would love to hear about that some other time over a nice glass of red, but no, between you two in the before and after parts."

So, I told him everything I thought was meaningful without getting into the boring bits. When I'd finished, he sat for a moment thinking and reached between us for the pot of tea. He turned over a simple white cup and poured, then refilled mine. Holding up a scoop of sugar he gestured to my cup and I nodded a yes. We both stirred the sweet crystals in until they dissolved, then I took the warm cup in my hands, letting it permeate the chill I'd been experiencing since we'd gotten back.

"Why don't you just have a reasonable conversation with him, you know—like adults?"

"I tried, Seeley." And I had tried. I didn't see how I was responsible for fixing whatever had gone wrong between us. It wasn't just about that either. There was more than a budding romance thanks to the void stones. Besides he took everything I said wrong now that he'd put a wall up. "I think you're failing to take several factors into account."

"Which are?" he asked, tapping his full lips.

"First he's from a completely different realm… who knows what their customs regarding this type of thing are. And second, we essentially just met."

"So, you slept with him? Not judging. Just trying to understand your thought process."

I shrugged. "There's nothing wrong with a one-time tryst if both parties are willing. Besides I think we both needed the distraction. He would hardly talk about Everly's death. Like he was trying to be fine but I could tell he wasn't."

"I just don't get why he clammed up immediately afterward. You said the first time he was tender and held you after. Such a large swing is strange. It's like something's got him spooked. Maybe there is something else at play here we aren't seeing."

"He tried to be tender after the second time too, but I shut him down." I buried my head in my hands groaning, intent on ignoring whatever Seeley was hinting at.

Maybe I shouldn't have been so harsh and let things fizzle out on their own. It was just the way that he'd looked at me, his eyes were bright, intoxicating. He'd shut down the second I'd said *develop feelings.*

"Ugh, why do males have to be so frustrating?"

"I saw how he looked last night at the dinner you missed. The Skyborne was dripping with angst and unrequited love. And rejection. I don't think regret is what he is feeling."

"I think you've read too many romance books. Oh, and I forgot he said I didn't need to worry, he'd keep his promise. You know, the shower one."

"But he didn't exactly make that promise from what you said."

"I know, that's what I told him."

"Maybe he thinks you still want to keep the distance between you. Has something changed?"

I thought about it for a long moment. Standing, I walked over to the double glass doors which led out to the long terrace and drew back the sheer curtains covering them. Gardeners were outside tending the perfectly manicured hedges, and sweeping off the clippings into large bins. Seeley came up beside me and stood silently while I pondered his question. "No, I think it is too messy."

"Then what's the problem?"

"I think this sadness I feel isn't only coming from me. Is that crazy?" I turned toward him, studying his face for the answer.

"You think you slept with the guy twice and now he is experiencing earth-shattering sadness radiating through your non-bond?"

I couldn't help but laugh as I walked over and flopped down onto the freshly made bed. "Why do you always have to make everything so silly? What you just said sounds absurd."

"Well, it was your insinuation. And it's probably true."

I went completely still. "No. It can't be."

"You asked for my opinion. There it is," Seeley stated matter-of-factly as he stood over me at the foot of the bed. There was such a calm authority in his open features. A patience I knew I'd never possess.

"What do I do?"

"Well, if you don't want the relationship, then nothing. Sounds like he got the message."

"What makes you think he wants the relationship?" I asked.

"Cue earth-shattering sadness, anyone? He is probably afraid you are even more likely to permanently reject him now, and he's acting defensively. Males are dumb—you know this."

"But what about what the Chancellor said? About if Rhijn and I were to use our power together, it might be what it takes to right the wrongs in our realms."

"It can be done without that." Seeley slumped down onto the bed next to me, and put his hand on my knee, squeezing. We looked at each other.

"Is that your sight or your hypothesis?"

"Both," he said.

"There is a consequence if we don't though?" a rhetorical question. I knew the answer.

"You can't make the decision to be with Rhijn based on that. Can I ask you something you won't enjoy hearing? Well, two things actually."

"If I said no, would you not ask, Seeley?"

"Umm… probably not." He smiled, leaning up on an elbow as he turned to me. "Why do you think you are not allowing yourself this thing you clearly want?"

"But I don't." *Lie.* I grabbed a pillow from over my head and crushed it into my face as if it might hide me from Seeley's ability to read my emotions.

"Maybe the second question will help a bit. What are you going to do about Conall?"

I felt like the wind had been kicked out of me. "Seeley, it's not like that between me and Conall. He is like a brother to me. There was even a moment back in Seabrook where we could have crossed that line and we didn't. And that was the end of that. For both of us."

"I think you are being naïve," he said, and I felt him tap the pillow I was speaking through. "You may not be meant for each other, but I'm not sure that's how he sees it yet. I think he still sees you as something else and that's why he's been acting so strange lately. Rhijn is making him feel like what is between you is threatened."

I set the pillow aside and looked up at the ceiling. I really wanted to hurl the fluffy white rectangle across the room. "Oh makers, if that's true, it makes this even more of a mess." But I didn't need Seeley to confirm the truth I knew. It had ended that day before it ever began, *for me*. Conall was still confused about our relationship now that he knew my true identity and I'd been ignoring it hoping it would just go away on its own.

"You know I love you like a sister, right? Nothing I am about to say comes from anywhere other than love. So, hear me. You need to make some hard decisions, like *now*. We need to get this show on the road. Malik and I are with you one hundred percent. If you choose to be with Rhijn, Conall will not respond positively, but he will come around. Asha is brash and a bit crazy, but she's up for the ride. We don't know what is happening back home, and I am worried if we don't get back soon bad things are going to happen to the people we care about."

Seeley was right. What he said still sparked anger in me. "Why is this my call? Why am I the de facto leader? We're all Skyborne groomed to be regents. All capable of making these decisions together. Just because of the stupid ember. I wish I never would have retrieved the damn thing. I don't know what the right thing is now. If I don't handle this well, Skyborne might die. How am I supposed to live with that?"

"Stop being petulant. There is no one right thing. There are many right things. My relationship with Rhijn will not affect the outcome of how we are going to proceed. If you hadn't slept with him, *no shame*, but maybe it would be different. And now feelings are involved, which complicates things, but keep trying to befriend him. Maybe he will get over it and come around. Or…better yet, maybe you will get over yourself, and see things his way. You will find a way to work together because you need each other. And you are not bearing this alone."

He got up from the bed and gave me a *you know I'm right* look. Seeing Seeley stern was frightening. He bent down and kissed my forehead. "Think on it. I'm here anytime you need me. Always, my friend."

CHAPTER SEVENTEEN

R HIJN RUBBED AT the spot on his chest where Nayla's words had pierced him like a jagged, rusty dagger, entering, then twisting. And it wasn't a dull twinge he could easily ignore either. It was a constant reverberation that only her company could ease. Granted being around her was the last thing he wanted. How coolly she'd rejected him, then expected that he would be completely fine with it.

Caught feelings.

As if it were that simple. Rhijn scoffed and pushed himself harder, tearing across the worn stone sidewalk. He wanted his lungs and legs to burn so much that the ache in his chest was an itch by comparison. He'd already ran what had to be miles as he started yet another lap around the edge of the chancellor's estate. His shirt was drenched and his water bottle almost empty. But he wasn't nearly finished.

Makers, how had he let it happen? He didn't know anything about them or their ways. Yet he was stupid enough to believe something otherworldly might happen between them. And it had. Like how it was supposed to happen when you found the one Skyborne who was supposed to be yours. He'd known she was that for him the moment she'd landed on that dune.

Rhijn gritted his teeth as he charged up one of the many flights of stairs that led through the winding pathways around the different levels of the estate. It was the damn dreams and the stupid void stone trying to draw them together. Had she not been the star of them he'd never have let it happen. He'd just kind of assumed it was fate.

"You look like you need some water—among other things," Asha called, saying that last part from the side of her mouth. She was reclined in a metal outdoor chair sipping a pale-yellow liquid from a delicate stemmed glass outside his father's private offices. A large pitcher of the stuff was set on a tray in the middle of the patio table, a jug of water next to it.

"What are you doing out here?" he grumbled, wiping the sweat from his brow.

"Waiting on Vitis to finish up a few things," she said, gesturing to the empty bottle he carried. He handed it to her and watched her refill it without spilling a drop.

"Another tour?" Rhijn gave Asha an incredulous look. His father's interest in the young female was unusual, but he supposed the female was the odd member of her group so the Chancellor was trying to be welcoming. Asha's brother was one of the Regent's they'd learned so he figured it made sense.

"You know your father." She twirled a red lock and eyed him suspiciously. "Are you *trying* to kill yourself?"

He huffed, crossing his arms.

"Because your face is beet-red and I could have sworn you were falling up the stairs. You know, as opposed to *running*." When he didn't respond, she continued seeming to be unable to help herself. "It doesn't have anything to do with a certain dark-eyed Banished female, does it?" Asha gave him a wide toothy grin.

"I don't want to talk about Nayla."

"Noted." She said, the grin slipping from her face, before she forced it back. "Very touchy though, considering."

"Considering what?" He gave her an exaggerated groan.

The double doors behind them swung open and his father's imposing form stepped through saving him from whatever goading he was about to receive from the brash female before him.

"Ah, hello, son. Out on a run, I see," Vitis beamed, assessing Rhijn.

His father's sandy hair was freshly trimmed and his attire crisper even considering his usual tidy standards. Rhijn caught something woodsy on the breeze. Was that cologne? He shook off the strangeness.

"Yeah, I'm not finished. I'm going to do a few more laps." *I can still feel my legs.*

"Well, Asha and I were about to go tour the estates library. Shall we, Asha?" Vitis grinned down at the blushing female and Rhijn couldn't suppress an eye roll. Asha took the arm that was offered to her and the peculiar pair went off in search of discovery.

"She'll come around," Asha called over her shoulder and he heard the rumble of his father's chuckle.

Rhijn covered his eyes for a moment. Did everyone know? How embarrassing.

He spun and took off in the opposite direction ready to 'fall up' some more stairs, as Asha had put it.

And why was everyone so cheery? Did no one but him, and Seeley he supposed, understand the gravity of the situation they were in? He and the female who'd been content to gut him were expected to transport hundreds of Skyborne between the realms. Convince them their long-lost enemy was now their friend and offer them a place of refuge. Not to mention teach them how to use a power that they were fundamentally against. So much so that his sect had been completely annexed from their early society. It was impossible. He swore the Idians had some type of deep seeded and fool-hardy savior's complex.

No, he chided himself. That was a defeatist attitude. He patted the pocket where he carried the void stone. This situation they were all in was just another puzzle to solve. A problem. And all problems had solutions. He would approach it as such, like his research. It was nothing more than one overwhelming experiment and Rhijn would see it through till the end.

CHAPTER EIGHTEEN

"GUESS WHAT, NAYLA?" Seeley said, catching me in the hallway the next day. He was fluttering his lashes and vibrating with excitement.

"What?" I crinkled my nose at him.

"Malik, my gorgeous, dark and mysterious *bonded* fiancé, succeeded in his first distribution." Seeley's glee was contagious. My face brightened, and I smiled widely at his pride. "Oh, but when he tells you, don't let on that you know."

"That's amazing," I said. "Bonded?"

"Just look at us next time we're in the room together."

"I look at you guys all the time. You're disgusting." I made a vomiting gesture, thinking of how mushy the couple had become since we'd arrived in Idia, and wondering what had changed which had led to their engagement.

Seeley giggled. "No, I mean really look at us. I want to know if you can see it before I tell you what it means."

I promised him I would. Satisfied, he looped his arm through mine as we traipsed down the hallway leading from the wing of the chancellor's estate to the meeting rooms.

"You've been lying low since you got back," he observed.

"That's because she's been avoiding a certain handsome Idian," Asha blurted as she stepped from her room, joining our walk.

"Actually, he's been avoiding *me*. And I've decided it's all for the best. Our tryst was a good thing. He's not bothering me anymore, and I got him out of my system." I haughtily lifted my chin, shrugging off Asha's goading. I had confidence that Rhijn's duty wouldn't let our fling stop him from working with me when the time came. He was too perfect to let that happen. After Seeley had left, I'd thought about what he'd said, but came to a different determination. Regardless of whatever emotions my counterpart was experiencing, he wouldn't let them get in the way of helping Skyborne. And now he was no longer a lingering temptation popping up around every corner.

All and all, my plan had worked perfectly, and I was happy about it. I almost believed myself as I repeated the mantra which helped to tamp down the weird ache in my chest. No one else needed to find out.

Especially Conall, who was still in the dark, and I planned to keep it that way based on Seeley's perception of how he'd react. I had faith that Conall would eventually realize our relationship wasn't like that and I didn't need to confront it. Asha had guessed what had happened between Rhijn and I, though, like she did everything else. I had bribed her with excessive amounts of favors to keep her trap shut.

And Rhijn *had* been avoiding me since we'd gotten back. That and he'd arranged a team to go to the southern settlement and round up the creatures to send them back to their home realm. They were due to leave soon. I had offered to go, to help, but he suggested I stay and learn to feed the wells. To *control myself* is what he'd actually said.

"Besides, Rhijn will be gone soon, so it will make it that much easier," I said.

"Girl, do *you* even believe your lies?" Asha shook her head.

"Ignore her," Seeley said. "And I'm glad you've decided because we need to go home."

∾

I didn't think I would ever get used to how beautiful Adrina was at night. The dry air was perfect, not quite warm enough to sweat, but not cool enough to need a jacket. Apparently, it was like this year-round. I sat at the edge of a fountain on the estate's terrace outside our rooms, which had lights embedded beneath the water. I swished my hand through the cool liquid, watching it ripple, the blue lights beneath the surface refracting with the current my hand created.

Conall had left to go find us a bottle of wine to split. The wine, like the Idians' *dogs*, was another remnant we learned the Makers allowed the Skyborne to keep, which carried over from the human realm. This I was eternally grateful for, and splitting a bottle with Conall was a great comfort I didn't get to enjoy often enough. We had hardly spent any time together since we'd arrived here and I missed him. We were determined to rectify that tonight.

The city lights twinkled as I stared wistfully toward them as I waited on Conall to return. I startled when Chancellor Vitis approached. Loose-fitting tan pants and a white shirt that buttoned up the center made him look more approachable than how the pressed and tucked clothing he normally wore did. He kicked off his sandals next to mine on the stones, before he walked barefoot across the soft grass. It seemed too casual, and I narrowed my eyes at him. He probably strategically planned his outfit to set me at ease, because he clearly wanted something to approach me out here.

"Good evening Nayla," he said in a voice that couldn't help but boom.

"Chancellor," I greeted him.

"I have a favor I'd like to ask of you." He sat down on the lip of the fountain next to me. I'd guessed right. I tried not to squirm beneath his authoritative gaze. "My son needs to teach you how to feed the power wells."

"Why him? And I thought Malik did it already?" I groaned.

"You need to do it since you're the leader. The Skyborne will look to you and since your experience with the void stones mirror each other's, he is likely the only person who can teach you to control your power."

Control yourself, I heard Rhijn's voice in my mind.

"Is this a problem?" he asked.

"No," I said, looking at my hands.

"Once you've been successful, I'll send you and Conall to one of the northern settlements since you didn't really have a real tour of the South-ern one, while Rhijn goes and deals with the creatures. He has to do that before we bring any Skyborne back, though I know the delay is painful. Then you can go back to your realm and we can begin the reintegration."

"I should go and help deal with the creatures," I demanded. I'd been arguing this point to him since we got back.

"That won't be necessary," he replied.

"You know, using my power there would be useful. Especially since I've fought them before."

"Nayla, we've been through this. And frankly, he doesn't want you there. Whatever happened between you two on the trip is none of my business, but I really wish you would stop playing games and open up to each other. Realize you two need each other."

I leaned back at his words; the same things Seeley had told me. Rhijn didn't want me there, and he probably didn't want to teach me to feed the well. "That's not fair—"

"Before you get any further, I've said the exact same thing to him. It seems speaking to either of you is of no use. So maybe you can bond over that? Being completely resistant to reason."

Vitis stared me down until I had to look away. "Nayla, look at me." I obeyed. "Do this as a favor to me? Please?"

His voice was gentler than I'd heard up until now. I knew I didn't have a choice, but I made to consider his request.

"I will, but I have a favor I need in return."

His eyes narrowed.

"I have a feeling you won't mind fulfilling my request. It's related to Asha."

After I'd explained my proposition to him, he was all too eager to oblige.

❧

"What did he want?" Conall asked, as he set two glasses on the edge of the fountain and poured us each a glass of crisp white wine. He'd passed a practically skipping Chancellor on his way back to the terrace.

"He's making Rhijn teach me how to feed the well." I looked off into the distance so Conall wouldn't be able to read anything from my expression. I wasn't sure which of my mixed-up emotions my face would betray.

"Can't someone else teach you? Kelvin? He's the one who's in charge of them."

I sighed. "That's what I asked him too, but he seems to think, because of our connection with the void stones, only Rhijn will be able to do it. But guess what?"

"What?" Conall asked, sourly.

"Once I've learned how to do it, you and me get to go visit the settlement Seeley and Malik went to while Rhijn goes and deals with the creatures. Then we go back home."

He perked up. "That sounds fun. The settlement I went to was a lot like Eastdow, but obviously much more modern and cleaner. Tomorrow, I can go with you if you want. To be a buffer."

"That would be great," I said, to which he nodded, pleased.

Conall and I drank the rest of the wine and he even convinced me to dance with him, though there was no music, but the sounds of the bustling city below.

৯

Conall easily kept stride with Rhijn's relentless pace, but I found myself racing to keep up as we headed toward the landing where the transports were parked the next morning.

"Excuse me children," Vitis caught up with us from behind. I didn't understand why he insisted on calling us that. He wasn't that old, especially by Skyborne standards, and our kind lived even longer on Idia, we'd learned.

"Conall, I have a few questions about the map you drew. Would you mind?" Vitis gestured for Conall to follow him. I groaned, Conall grimaced, and Rhijn ran a hand across his eyes. None of us were fooled by Vitis's carefully timed interjection.

"Go on," I told him. Conall huffed, then left us to go be distracted by the Chancellor.

"Your father is a real meddler." I shot a pointed look at Rhijn.

He didn't respond and kept trudging ahead.

"You realize you're going to have to speak to me in order to teach me to feed the wells, right?"

Nothing.

"Your father asked me to reach out to you," I said. "To try to make peace."

"I wish he wouldn't do that," Rhijn said, raking his hands through his loose hair. I followed the movement, absorbing his aggravation.

A pulsing energy inside me was becoming insistent that I get off of Rhijn's bad side. "He said we should be able to bond over our stubbornness." I smiled and nudged him with my elbow. Again, he ignored me. "Makers, Rhijn. You are making this difficult. Can't you see I'm trying?"

"I can see you are doing something," he said, staring straight ahead as he approached a transport. We got in wordlessly and took a quick ride through the city to a large nondescript building.

We got out, and I followed him through two large metal doors which slid open on long tracks attached to the floor. He walked through the building and then another set of doors until we came to a smaller room, with white unadorned walls, and a miniature power well in the precise center.

"This was the prototype for the wells. What Kelvin based the current designs on. They were done differently several hundred years ago, but with this new option, they operate much more efficiently. Kelvin suggested we use it for you to practice on so you don't blow up the city."

I stood there grinding my teeth.

"Go ahead," he motioned to a pedestal like the one I'd exploded.

"That's it? You are supposed to be teaching me," I reminded him.

"Control yourself," he said, and smirked.

I burst out laughing at his hurtful words. It's all I could do. "You're the worst," I said, shaking my head. I put my hands into the water and searched for the slight units flashing into existence. I sensed them effortlessly. I started to reach for them, but Rhijn jerked my hands out of the water. He was standing behind me with his arms grasping my wrists on either side.

"Why did you do that?" I asked, trying to shake my hands free from his grasp. It was futile.

"You were reaching for too many," he said. "Why can't you understand to just take a little. There's no need to be so intense."

"What exactly are we talking about?" I asked, jerking out of his grip to look at him. He refused to make eye contact with me, staring over my shoulder.

"I'm not going to let you overdo it this time. I'll be right here behind you until you figure it out, so hurry it up so this can be over for both of us."

"You could help by *teaching* me."

"I am teaching you. Now try again." He held out his hands over mine so he could quickly wrench them out of the water.

I exhaled, plunging them in. Once again, he jerked them right back out.

"Again," he said.

We did that eight more times, before I sagged from the exertion and he caught me. "I don't know why I can't get it. It's like they just gravitate toward me and I don't have *control* over it," I complained. "This is worse than when I ran into walls in the channels of my power when I was training to steal the ember."

He raised a questioning eyebrow at me.

"Never mind," I said.

"What does it feel like?" he asked, as he guided me over to a bench.

I slumped onto it. "I don't know. Attraction?"

"Hmm… let's go grab lunch and I'll think about it. We can try again afterward." He walked out of the room, not looking back to see if I followed. I jumped up on wobbly legs and caught up. He took a right out the sliding doors and hurried down the sidewalk.

"What is that place we were just at?" I asked him.

"It is a research facility," he responded, not elaborating.

"Is that where you created the prototype of the chiller?" I asked.

"Yes." I waited for more. Nothing.

"You are the *worst*," I said. "The—fucking—worst."

We came up to a dining establishment, with tables and chairs outside along the sidewalk and in an inner courtyard. There was a counter with a glass window that was propped open where Rhijn said we could order food. A piece of wood was leaned up against the side of the counter with a menu of the fresh items they served.

"What is grouper?" I asked.

"It's a type of fish. It's good," he said.

The female behind the window took pity on me and explained the dish to be a pan-fried flakey whitefish served with a mixed green salad and mashed tubers. They could also make it into a sandwich with the side salad. I told her I'd take it however she preferred it. I'd found while eating in places I wasn't familiar with; it was easiest to go with whatever the locals chose. Rhijn paid with their paper currency and she told us she'd bring the food out whenever it was ready.

I took a glass of water over to a table near the sidewalk. When Rhijn didn't sit down, I turned, scanning for him. He was about to sit at another table closer to the building.

"I swear to the Makers if you sit in that chair I will gut you," I spat between my gritted teeth.

It was the first smile I'd gotten out of him since before we'd been together, though he was clearly trying to repress it. He casually sauntered over and sat across from me.

"I suppose it would appear odd if I didn't sit with our illustrious guest, though threatening me with violence only proves what a primitive creature you are."

I showed him my teeth, glaring, and he chuckled.

Our food came, and I was grateful it gave us something to do besides glare at each other. The fish was so moist and the female produced a spicy dipping sauce I greedily drowned everything in.

"I want to come back here," I said as we walked back toward the research facility. "I love that red sauce. I could drink it."

"You would," Rhijn said, shaking his head.

We went back into the room with the prototype well and got into position.

"I can see how you don't understand the concept of too much, based on how much of that hot sauce you consumed."

I grinned over my shoulder at him, unabashed.

"Let's try to go easier this time around," he said, readying his hands as I submerged mine into the water.

Four more failed attempts. "You don't seem to be improving at all," Rhijn pointed out.

"You don't seem to be teaching me at all, so it's no surprise."

"Fine," he said, grabbing my hands and threading his fingers with mine. He placed our hands in the basin, and moved his body even closer, like we'd been when he'd used our power through me in the transport.

"Okay, don't do anything. Just try to *feel* what I'm doing," he instructed.

His voice lowered to a hushed tone near my ear. My skin electrified, and gooseflesh dotted my exposed forearms. I looked over my shoulder to see if he had noticed, but his eyes were closed. I studied the strong line of his jaw, and the grimace of his supple lips as they opened.

"Are you paying attention?" he asked, annoyed.

I swallowed. "Yes. Trying." Regardless of however I might fight this sensation, it felt good. It had to be the void stones reaching for each other and the twinge in my chest seemed to lessen a bit.

Then I felt how he used his power to slow the energy and keep command of which and how many particles he captured. He only split a few at a time, holding the others at bay, and eased the energy he collected down onto the metal plate, which transferred them into the well. It was incredible.

I was so caught up in the satisfying warmth radiating from his chest and the thrum of energy flowing through us. Instinctively, I leaned into him, wanting to absorb more.

He jerked back. "What are you doing?" he asked. "I told you to control yourself." He stepped away, as if to leave.

"You enjoyed the lack of control I had all too well, if you recall. Twice. I haven't blocked it from my memory even if you have," I said and put my hand back into the water, splashing a little out of the bowl. If he left, I'd figure out how to get back to the Chancellor's estate on my own. *After* I'd successfully fed the well.

I threw my shoulders back and shifted all my focus to the task of feeding the well, filtering the particles as Rhijn had done. I almost had to compel all but a select few particles away, so I'd not accidentally split them and cause another accident. It was like I inexplicably drew them to my energy. I practiced until I felt comfortable, and I could separate a few without mistakenly splitting more than I planned.

"It worked! I did it," I exclaimed. I turned to see if he'd left. He was standing there by the door with his arms crossed over his chest. He frowned, but his eyes betrayed him. Secretly, he was proud.

I walked over to him and grabbed his biceps, joggling him. "This is exciting! You're a decent teacher, after all. I mean, we'd have been done hours ago if you'd tried that first. Anyway, I won't fault you for wanting to spend more time with me." I gave him an exaggerated wink.

He huffed and headed out the door.

"I think this calls for a celebration," I said as we climbed into the transport. "Can you punch some buttons on that panel and have everyone meet us somewhere fun?"

"You're incredibly impulsive," he said.

"You're a killjoy."

CHAPTER NINETEEN

I WHINED RELENTLESSLY UNTIL Rhijn caved and agreed to send a message inviting everyone out for a drink to celebrate Malik and I's success with the power wells. Rhijn and the twins had to leave to deal with the creatures in the morning, but we could have a little fun tonight. He punched a few buttons on the control panel and the transport halted and changed directions, zipping down a side street. We passed by two- and three-story shops, all painted in neutral tones of creams and whites. Occasionally, a shop would have a colored door.

"There are a lot of businesses in this area," I commented.

Rhijn glanced at me, then at the buildings. "The shop owners live in the upper floors and run their businesses down below. That is how all the establishments are in this neighborhood. It is different from how it is on the outskirts of the city."

"Seems convenient."

"Perhaps, but if you sleep right above where you work, you better like what you do because you are tied to it for better or worse." He pressed his lips into a thin line.

"At least they have a choice," I said, thumbing the pocket where I carried the ember.

If Rhijn noticed, he didn't say. Though maybe he didn't feel the same way.

"We're here." He got out of the parked transport and didn't wait for me before he entered the door of an establishment a few yards away. I peeked in one of the two windows and watched him walk up to a long bar and engage the female behind it.

I glanced down the street, hoping I'd see another transport filled with friendly faces, but no such luck. I'd been standing outside for several minutes when I decided I was probably beginning to look weird, so I took a deep breath and slipped inside the forest green door that had the words 'The Library' painted on it in gold gilded letters.

Shelves lined the three walls of the main room, and they were filled to the brim with books and objects which appeared to be artifacts. I glanced over to the long red wooden bar where Rhijn sat. He hadn't acknowledged my presence.

I shifted between feet and bit my lower lip as I quickly searched the rest of the room for a suitable spot to claim for our group. There were several spots open around Rhijn at the bar, and a few other tables open large enough for only four. Another group had pulled two together to accommodate them.

I walked over to Rhijn, who was sipping a pink liquid out of a short glass and squeezed between two chairs to lean against the bar.

"Is that the same wine from the other night?" I asked him.

"No. You wouldn't like this." He smirked down at me.

"I'll have that," I said, holding my head defiantly high, pointing at Rhijn's drink when the bartender looked at me with expectation.

The female poured a few liquids into a glass, gave it a stir and set it down in front of me. I picked it up, studied the liquid, and took a sniff.

"Makers," I coughed, waving my hand in front of my nose. "I hope it tastes better than it smells." I took a sip. Heat crawled down my throat, then spread across my chest. A lingering sweetness played on my tongue as I set the glass down.

Rhijn was looking at me with one eyebrow raised.

"It's terrible. But I like it." I reached up to flag the bartender down before Rhijn could comment. "Can I scoot those two tables together?" I said, pointing to the two tables I picked out. "We have a few more friends coming."

She glanced from me to Rhijn, who nodded begrudgingly.

"Go ahead. I'll wait on you at the table," she answered, waving us off.

I walked over and started rearranging the tables. I looked at Rhijn, who was observing from his barstool and apparently not going to help.

The worst, I mouthed at him. I brought my drink over and sat in a chair that had a perfect view of the door, so when my relief arrived, I'd be able to flag them down. I clicked my fingernails on the smooth surface impatiently. A few Skyborne from the nearest table were staring. They quickly glanced away, but stole a peek right back as if unable to help themselves. I smiled, trying to look friendly.

A groan sounded from behind me. Rhijn was stalking over to where I sat. "What are you doing?"

"Trying to appear non-threatening."

He plopped down next to me right as the door opened and Conall, Seeley, Malik, and the twins, Leah and Rhea, spilled into the room.

Leah made her way over to us and clapped me and Rhijn on the back. "See Rhijn, I told you. It took even less than a full day, now pay up!" She regarded Rhea. "You too."

Rhijn waved a hand at the bartender and she went to work making a drink, presumably his payment to Leah.

"I'll get the next one," Rhea said, accepting her defeat.

"You guys were betting against me?" My eyes darted between Rhijn and Rhea. "Thanks a lot. And that explains why Rhijn didn't even attempt to teach me anything until after lunch. He was trying to rig the bet against you," I told Leah.

"That or he was wanting to spend more time with you," she replied, goading him.

"That is highly unlikely," I said, swirling my glass.

He huffed and crossed his arms as the rest of the group took seats around the two tables.

The bartender came around and we ordered a round of drinks. "So, we haven't gotten to hear of your adventure with the new creatures at the Southern settlement. I heard it was quite the epic story." Rhea inclined her head to Rhijn and I.

"Yeah, I haven't heard it either." Conall cleared his throat.

"Whoa, this is strong," Seeley said, eyes watering as he took a swig of the pink liquid.

Malik chuckled and gave his neck a squeeze. I raised my now half empty glass to Malik. "I believe congratulations are in order first!"

Malik smiled, and he and I clinked glasses. Then the rest of the party joined.

"Bottom's up," Conall said. We all obliged, sucking down our drinks.

It was at least an hour later, and a few drinks in, when Rhea finally convinced us to tell our tale. Rhijn attempted to skim over most of it, but would stop when I would grab his forearm and make a lengthy interjection. My enthusiasm must have been contagious because he finally caught up to my energy level and made animated hand gestures as he explained what happened, tapping my arm back every so often to help him embellish the tale.

Rhijn's smooth voice cracked as he told them about how we lost Everly. About how the last word she'd spoken was his name. A tear trickled down the smooth plane of Rhijn's cheek. I couldn't stop myself. My heart heaved at the weight of the memory and seeing him holding back such grief and guilt. I reached up and wiped the tear with the back of my index finger. He froze momentarily and faced me. I gave him a half smile and squeezed his knee under the table. To my surprise, he returned my smile before he straightened, finishing our story. Everyone sat for long moments, sipping at their drinks.

"So, you guys were at the observatory for several days?" Conall asked, breaking the silence. "What did you do then?"

I had to restrain an eye roll because I knew where this was going. "Where's the bathroom?" I asked, noticing a little slur in my voice. "And water. I need a water."

Rhea pointed in the way of the bathrooms. I walked down the hallway, which got darker the further I went. Nearing the end, hushed voices floated toward me, and I halted on instinct, realizing what a hushed voice usually meant.

"Did you see that female?" A scratchy male voice asked.

"Yeah, why?" Another lower male voice responded.

"I think she's one of the Banished. Did you see she was with the Chancellor's son and the twins?"

I put my hand over my mouth and tried to calm my heartbeat. I knew I shouldn't be eavesdropping, but I couldn't help it.

"Yeah, there's no mistaking Rhijn Innar with that cold stare. Do you think it means they are going to be bringing them back soon?"

"I shudder to think. They were banished for a reason." The first one scratched out.

"They're probably little more than heathens. Does Pollux know about this?"

Pollux, I screwed up my brow, trying to place the name. Was he one of the council members? It seemed familiar, though it could be a misplaced memory.

"Haven't heard. But they've been sending Idians out to the settlements again. First time since Innar sent those creatures back to whatever Maker's forsaken realm they came from. Nothin' good's gonna come from this."

"Well, if anyone can put an end to this, it's Poll—shit, did you hear that?"

I tried to ease my foot back off the board I had shifted my weight on, but it gave a slight whine.

A door creaked, and a short male with dark black hair and pale skin poked his head out. Another taller, but similarly colored male stepped forward. They had to be brothers.

"Eavesdropping isn't polite, heathen." The 'hea' hissed as he said it.

They brushed past me in the hallway, knocking into my shoulder, causing me to reach for the wall to stay on my feet. The liquid in my bladder was urging me toward the bathroom, but the alcohol in my veins was itching to stand up for us *Banished*.

It was my duty, for the sake of all the other Skyborne back home, to make a good impression, so I wrenched down on my wounded pride and turned toward the bathroom.

When I got back to the table, my friends were merrily discussing the power wells and the implications of our successes, but my skin crawled and I could tell we were being watched. I turned to the two men at the table across the room sneering in our direction, assessing Conall, Seeley and Malik. I couldn't make out what they were saying, but I could tell it was about us and it wasn't nice.

I stepped forward because I was about to go let them know my thoughts, but a firm hand wrapped around my wrist and placed a drink in it.

"You heard that somehow, I assume." It wasn't a question. I looked at Rhijn as I downed the rest of my glass and gave a jerky shake of my head. "Maker's, this stuff is effective. You're movey."

He peered down at me, and his brows pinched together. "Movey?"

"You know, spinney. Come on." I tugged his hand which was still gripping my wrist as I tried to move toward the table across the room of Idians who'd gone back to ignoring us.

"Let it go, Nayla," Rhijn's stern voice warned in my ear.

"But it's bullshit," I stammered.

A little loudly, it seemed, because all five males at the table with the two brothers abruptly turned to look at me. My skin itched, and I tried to jerk my hand away from Rhijn's grip.

"Lemme go," I protested.

"We're going to take off," Rhijn told our table, as he pulled out some paper money and set it down. "I think we're more tired than we expected after working with the wells all day."

He means Nayla is getting a bit drunk and about to make a scene, Malik thought, opening our mental connection.

That is so rude, I thought, glaring at him. *I would never make a scene without a good reason.*

Malik laughed, and Seeley glanced between us with understanding.

You okay? He thought.

I'm good, I replied. *You guys stay and… study.* I giggled, looking around at the books finally getting the name of the bar. The last remaining rational thoughts I had were directing me to let it go and not have a confrontation with the males at the opposite table. If I did, it would only show them they were right. I let Rhijn lead me toward the door, but not without throwing a cheesy grin and wave over my shoulder at the males.

In my periphery, I saw Conall catching up to us. "Here, let me—"

Rhijn held up his hand. "I got her, buddy. I need to get back anyway. You stay and enjoy yourself."

He tugged me toward the door by my wrist before Conall could refuse.

"But…" I protested, and stumbled.

Rhijn watched me teeter for a moment, then swept me up in his arms. *His big strong arms.* "Come on. We can't start anything, and you don't want the others to know there may be opposition to them coming back. Sounds like you have enough obstacles in your way already." He raised his eyebrows, waiting for an argument.

He was right, though. Rhijn stomped across the parking lot and set me down in the transport. I moved over so he could crawl in next to me. "You have a surprisingly high alcohol tolerance for such a small female."

"Umm, I—" I hiccupped, laughing. When I stopped, he was watching me with a mixture of agitation, confusion and an expression which was very similar to tenderness. That last part, probably the alcohol, and me seeing what I wanted to see.

"You don't actually hate me, do you, Rhijn?" I slumped into the bench seat, stretching out my legs in front of me.

Rhijn leaned forward, putting his elbows on his knees and his head in his hands. "Oh, Nayla. You really have no idea."

CHAPTER TWENTY

THE RAYS FROM the light star blazed in through the window, and their warmth crept across my bare legs.

"Ohhhh," I groaned, dragging a fluffy white pillow across my head. It felt like two drummers were beating out a war ballad on my temples.

I'd even let Rhijn carry and deposit me into my room last night. Heat flooded my cheeks, and I tried to bury myself in the bedding.

A rustling at the side of my bed caught my attention. I rolled over and leaned off the side and there was a male foot sticking out from under a blanket. The rest of his body was covered. I picked up my pillow, ignoring the aching in my head, and whacked it on the sleeping body.

"Rhijn, what are you doing in here? Get out," I demanded, noticing, thankfully, I was in the same outfit as the night before. We hadn't done anything else he would regret.

"Nayla, easy," a familiar groggy voice emanated from beneath the bedding. "It's me."

"Oh shit, Conall, sorry!"

"Yeah, enough with the pillow." He sat up and grabbed two tablets from off the table, and popped one into his mouth. He took a drink from a glass of water that was sitting next to them, swallowed, and handed the other to me. "Rhijn said these would help. Apparently that pink stuff is much stronger than wine."

"Yes, I think I'll just stick to wine or beer next time." I took the tablet from his outstretched hand and placed it on my tongue, taking the cup of water. "I guess Rhijn thought I might do something stupid if you weren't in here to babysit me?"

"He was only concerned. He didn't know if it was going to make you sick, so I told him I'd stay in here."

I patted the bed. "You didn't have to sleep on the floor. This bed is plenty big."

"Have you noticed the mess you've made with the covers? That wasn't a war zone I wanted to be a part of."

I glanced around at the bedding, which was half pulled off the bed, twisted around and on the floor, and gave him an embarrassed grin.

"Scoot over," he said, straightening out the covers. "Rhijn said the tablets will take about an hour to take effect, then we'll be as good as new."

He lay down on the bed next to me and pulled the covers over us. I propped myself up on my forearm and wiggled my fingers in front of him. "I could use these?" I reached for his forehead.

He grabbed my fingers before I started healing him. "Actually, I was thinking that you save your power, and you can portal us to the settlement later this morning? We can skip the transport ride. It will be good practice. Then we'll get back sooner, so we can go home."

I grinned. "Really? You think Vitis will approve?"

"Do we have to tell him?" Conall gave me a sly, conspiratorial smile. "I'm thinking we take the transport to the edge of the city, and find somewhere to park it where it won't be noticed, then portal. We'll be back before they know it."

I rubbed my palms together and sunk back into the bed. "I'm in."

⟡

Conall was gone when I woke up, and so was my headache. A nervous energy flitted around me as I packed my belongings into a canvas backpack for the quick trip to the settlement. I showered, not taking the time to luxuriate, dressed and threw my wet hair into a quick braid. I hoisted my backpack onto my shoulders and made my way to the landing, where the transports picked us up as planned. I saw Conall loading ours and I caught myself almost skipping toward it.

"What are you so eager for?" Asha leaned on a column under the loggia. The white gauzy dress she wore moved around her with the slightest breeze. Her cheeks were looking fuller with each day, and her bright red hair gleamed in the morning sun. She even seemed to hum with a faint energy I'd never detected before. Idia seemed to suit my friends.

"Just excited to see the settlement," I explained. "You look...." I cocked my head to the side assessing her. "Pretty," I decided.

Rhijn's eyes narrowed in my direction.

"Good morning," I called over to him.

He turned and loaded his bag into his transport. He and nineteen other Skyborne, including Leah, Rhea and two healers, were headed to the Southern settlement to deal with the creatures we'd encountered.

"Makers, are we really back to this again?" I asked, amplifying my voice, and sighed exaggeratedly. I spun around to Asha. "Where were you last night?"

She attempted to hide the sly smile twitching at the corner of her mouth. "Tired," she lied.

"*Sure you were.* Shall I consider this one of my favors repaid?" We glared at each other in jest. "I'm on to you Asha, so you might as well mark one of mine off your tally."

Chancellor Vitis came out of an alcove further down and walked over to Rhijn. The last thing I wanted to do was stick around for another scolding from him.

I hurried over to where Kelvin stood next to Conall, giving him some last-minute pointers about how to use the transport's controls. It was just going to be us, and the stewards who'd been sent a message to expect our arrival.

"Okay, let's go." I tossed my bag into the transport and climbed in, tugging at Conall's sleeve. "Come on."

Conall crawled in and Kelvin shut the door. He showed me which buttons to press, then we were off. It was a half-hour ride through the city until we found a quiet parking lot with an alley around the corner where we felt comfortable using the ember.

We tiptoed down the alley like two delinquent children. About half-way down was a deep shadow from the buildings. I pulled out the ember and touched my hand to it. The familiar dark crept up my arm to my elbow.

"Ready?" I knew my eyes had the same mischievous glint Conall's did. They always had when we went off on our adventures. It had been amazing that we'd been able to keep out of trouble as much as we had as young Skyborne. Being the realm's Chosen One and the Regent's son had its perks.

"Let's do it," he said.

I didn't hesitate. The pulsing darkness followed the path of my finger as I traced it around us on the rough-hewn stone of the alleyway floor. Then we fell.

❦

"Wow, this place is huge. There must have been a ton of people who lived here back then." Conall slowly spun in a full circle, taking in the great room of the main house.

"It's crazy that it was abandoned over a thousand years ago, and somewhere along the way the Idians started taking care of these places."

Conall had wandered off into an anteroom. "Come look at this," he called, voice echoing across the nearly empty room.

I ran my finger across the smooth wooden bench, one of which lined the large cavernous space. "Is that armor?" I asked. It was a smooth satin metal and looked like something that should have been in the museum on the Leeward Isle.

"Can you imagine wearing that? It has to be so heavy." Even in our home realm, we only reinforced our thick leather with our power. It was flexible and comparatively lightweight. I ran my finger along the smooth edge of the silver-blue metal and jumped when the suit came to life stand-ing at-the-ready. A flap popped open on the chest exposing a panel with multi-colored lights tracing patterns on a crystalline blue screen. "What in the realms?"

Lights lit up and down the lengths of the modern material and it split open on invisible hinges as if it were readying itself to be fitted to someone. It was surprisingly thin and since it was animated, maybe it wasn't so heavy after all. I made a mental note to ask Rhijn about this particular invention. Thinking of him made my stomach sink. I hoped him and the Skyborne with him would be safe.

"Do you think they wear suits like this when they go round up the creatures?" I wondered aloud. I couldn't picture Rhijn wearing such a strange piece of equipment, much less twenty Idians wearing this, but it would explain how they'd had so few casualties with the creatures. And this prototype must be an old design if it was here in this settlement propped up like a piece of décor.

"Can you imagine an army of Idians in suits like this? Our forces would be no match for them."

I scoffed. "And Emerson thought her creatures were going to be enough to take over this realm." Conall and I looked at each other then. "They would be completely immobilized if they were dusted with the creature's powder though, stuck in the metal like sitting ducks."

"Hopefully your sister can get us more of that antidote. I guess we won't know until we get back." Conall pressed his lips into a thin line. "Worrying isn't helpful. Let's keep exploring."

The suit rattled then the flap snapped shut and it sealed itself back up probably since neither of us had made any further steps to activate it. I gave the thing a wide berth as we exited the room moving into the next.

"I think I like this one better than the one south of here I went to with Asha," Conall said. "For one, it's bigger. More modern and they use more wood whereas the other one was all stone."

"You would have liked Arborvale. We use a lot of wood in the construction there because of our access to timber. More than this settlement, but this is a nice combination of materials. And everything is so tidy. The Southern settlement is definitely more rustic, but the inside of the buildings were very modern with only historical touches preserved."

"That sounds like an interesting contrast. If you had to govern one, which would it be?"

"When this is over, I'm not going to do any work for a long while.

Maybe I'll get a house on the Leeward Isle and read books in front of the sea for a while. And I'll find a dog to be my companion. What about you?"

"I think I'd govern this one. You sure you wouldn't want to stay here with me and help me govern it?"

I shook my head. "No working. That sounds like working."

"Okay, you could read books by the fire." He walked over to a window and pushed it open. The main house in the settlement, which would be the governor's residence and base of operation, was positioned high up on a hill and overlooked the land on all sides. "Look, you can still see the sea from here!"

I leaned up against the window seat next to him and enhanced my vision. "You're right. But barely," I huffed. "Besides, it's too cold. I liked the weather in Seabrook. It's like that on the Isle."

"Too sticky for me. But I guess if you were there it wouldn't be so bad."

"Come on, let's keep exploring." I ignored him, as I led him out of the large space and down the hallway the stewards told us led to the residential area.

"Wow, this must be the royal suite!" There was an enormous bed with four posts sticking up on each corner. There wasn't any bedding, but a large fluffy looking mattress sat in the middle waiting to be jumped on.

I sank in, and Conall sank right next to me. "Okay, I guess I could help if this was my room." It might have been if I'd pursued my family heritage as next in line after my mother as the true Regius of Monterra. I shivered at the unwanted thought.

Conall fixed his features into mock seriousness. "I'll see what I can do."

I gave him a half smile. That sticky, sinking feeling was creeping in again. As long as I stayed distracted, I could keep it at bay. I wrung my hands and looked toward the headboard, away from Conall.

"What is it, Nayla? Look at me." He always read me too well.

I turned my head toward him.

"You can talk to me, okay? Always." He reached over and stilled the hand that was fiddling with the end of my braid.

"Rhijn said I shouldn't say anything." I averted my guilty eyes.

"But obviously you're going to tell *me*?" he said, eyes widening. The serious, almost offended look on his face struck me.

I forced a laugh and nudged his shoulder. "Obviously."

The sudden tension in his shoulders eased. "What is it?"

"He took me back last night because I was about to throttle those males in the corner." I shrugged, pushing myself off the bed and walking to another side room. Conall followed.

"Go on. Why didn't he want you to bring it up?" I noticed the muscles in the corner of his jaw tick. He wasn't pleased with Rhijn suggesting I keep something from him, but he was trying to keep his temper in check.

"He didn't want you all to worry. When I went to the bathroom, I overheard them talking about us and ultimately not wanting us to come back. They assume we're closer to animals than Skyborne. Rhijn heard too, so he knew why I was mad."

"And your first instinct was to fight." Conall watched me.

"It would have been yours too," I said, and Conall nodded, agreeing. "Makers," I let out an exasperated breath, throwing my hands in the air. "Maybe we are an unrefined savage sect of this species. I'm terrified to tell Vitis what they will need to be prepared for when we return. Idians seem so peaceful. Those males are probably right to be afraid we'll disrupt their society in unsalvageable ways."

I dropped down onto a bench. The weight of it all was heavy on my shoulders. Conall sat down beside me and put an arm around me, pulling me into his side as the realms closed in around me.

"It's all going to work out, okay?" He looked down at me. His eyes reflected the pain of my own. We were close like that.

"You're the best, you know?" I smiled up at him.

"Obviously." His deep laugh rumbled across his broad chest to mine.

"Oooh. I have an idea!" I sat up straight and turned to him.

"We pack a dinner, then go find somewhere to take a long hike?" he suggested.

"Yes, let's do that, but that's not what I meant. We'll just tell the Idians I lost the ember and we can't go back. Then we can stay here and enjoy showers. I'll get a job at the museum or something, and—"

He frowned at me. "*You* want to work at the museum?"

"Ugh, no. I guess that means I'm going to have to tell them, huh?"

Conall stood and grabbed my hand. "Let's go find a steward who can direct us to the kitchens, then we can go walk and talk. We'll come up with a game plan, then by tomorrow, you'll feel better about it."

"Promise?" I asked.

"Promise."

CHAPTER TWENTY-ONE

W E'D BEEN IN Idia for almost three weeks, and the experience had been enlightening. Especially considering how forthcoming our hosts were in sharing information about their society and way of life. I trusted them, and it had come time to tell them what we were up against going back. Conall had convinced me of that.

Conall rocked back in his chair, the two front legs lifting off the ground as we waited for the council meeting to start. He'd drawn a map of our continent, adding the details of the terrains and boundaries of each territory. It was amazing what he'd been able to do from memory. He stretched the large paper out over the rectangular stone table in the center of the room, setting weights on each corner.

Chancellor Vitis, who was leaning over to study the map, glanced up as his son stormed into the room.

"Sorry I'm late," Rhijn announced. His hair was still wet from the shower and he wore a loose-fitting pair of linen pants and a tunic that was only half buttoned, exposing the smooth skin beneath. My fingers tingled as I remember touching it. *Focus*, I chastised myself.

"I got here as quickly as I could." His eyes flicked toward me, as if reading my thoughts, but I didn't look away.

I'd seen them when they came in this morning. Apparently, he'd used his void stone to whisk them back and forth so we could get back home sooner. They were covered in grime and cruor, but looked relatively unscathed. Rhijn had darted for his room and I had to fight this weird urge to chase after him to see if he was all right. Probably because the last time he'd fought them, I'd been there with him. Then he must have come directly here.

Rhijn stalked over to the only open chair which was across from me and took a seat, his angular frame sagging in the chair. Shifting uncomfortably, he rubbed his usually vibrant eyes, which were bloodshot and rimmed with inflamed, puffy skin. He seemed tired and I guess he also was hazy after having used so much power.

I took a steadying breath and stood. "It's time to discuss what we'll be dealing with when we return." I took a sip of my water, preparing to be speaking a lot during this meeting.

"Are you going to breeze right by the fact that you and Conall portaled to the North Settlement, then?" A wicked grin spread across Asha's face.

"You are such a pain in my ass," I growled at her.

"You did what?" Rhijn stared daggers at me, mouth ajar.

"Her and Conall ditched the transport in a parking lot near the gate. Poor Kelvin was worried sick that something had happened when he saw the tracker had stilled and not moved for several hours. He immediately stopped his very important work to rush out to make sure you guys were fine. Of course, he didn't find you. Instead, he received a message saying you'd arrived at the North Settlement earlier than expected."

Stupid tracking system.

"I thought it would be quicker to portal. And good practice. I mean, why have this power if not to use it?" I shrugged sheepishly. Rhijn's judgement crawled across my skin. "You used yours." I reminded him.

"Can we get on with this?" Rhijn slapped his hand on the table and my heart jumped into my throat. The outburst was the first I'd witnessed of any temper coming out of these even-keeled Idians and I'd be lying to myself if I didn't admit I was sorry I'd been the one to cause it.

"It's all right, Nayla. Go on." Vitis sat leaning back in his chair, hands steepled at his chest.

I spent the next hour telling them about the relationships between the six territories, with Conall and Malik interjecting as needed. I explained the alliance between Drakestone, Eastdow and Monterra, and how the late Regius Kymar had planned to use the ember to send Emerson's creatures through to block the Idians access to their power with the powdery magenta substance they produced.

Conall detailed the military force that was ready and waiting to attack the powerless Idians. I told them about the godflies and Uden, our agreement, and the deadly creatures that lived in the Swath. Finally, Seeley spoke of the allies from Arborvale, Seabrook and Sundale we'd made who didn't believe war was the path back to Idia. I'd even written out a lineage chart outlining the territories and major players to accompany Conall's maps when we'd gotten back the night before.

I rolled out several pieces of paper on the table. One I'd worked up with Conall, who's drawing skills were far superior to mine, describing the creatures which he'd only gotten a glimpse of. The result was a relatively accurate depiction of the monsters Emerson created.

Everything was out on the table.

The Idians patiently listened to our stories. When we'd finished, Vitis was quiet for a long while as he studied us. The Idians followed his lead, waiting for him to speak. His typically boisterous nature was subdued as he sat contemplative, eyes unfocused, while he processed our tale. Finally, he spoke. "While this would have been helpful to know in the preceding weeks, I understand you needed to learn to trust us before you shared it."

Makers, this male was reasonable. I had been dreading this conversation the nearer it came.

"It also would have been helpful to know that we had resistance," Conall's eyes narrowed at an auburn-haired male councilmember who I figured out was Pollux, before returning his confronting gaze to Vitis.

Vitis shot a look to Rhijn who winced. "It is true, not everyone is thrilled about your return, but we are committed to peace and are in agreement that this is the path. Isn't that right, Pollux?"

"Oh, yes. Of course, Chancellor. There are always some who oppose the path forward. That is the natural way of things. But we won't let them get in the way of what needs to be done." Pollux's voice slithered across the room into my ears as he recited his ambiguous answer. His amber eyes blinked as the room's attention focused on him.

He was a smaller male, with a quiet air about him compared to the other Skyborne on the council which was probably why I hadn't placed him when I'd heard the name. The hair at his temples was graying and fine lines were beginning to etch into his taught pale skin. He was older than Vitis by a good many years it appeared. I wondered if Vitis had been chosen over him and the slight had caused the friction between the two males. If I was right about the rift, they both were doing admirable jobs of hiding it.

I don't trust him. Malik's voice sounded in my mind.

Nor do I and I don't think Vitis does either. Must be a keep your enemies close sort of situation. I'll ask Rhijn about it... Assuming he'll speak to me. I responded to Malik, who shifted in his chair, leaning forward watching the male from the corner of his eye.

Rhijn was openly glaring between me and Conall. He'd specifically asked me not to say anything and I'd ignored his request. His demeanor must be affected by the power-induced haze because showing his emotions so openly in this setting wasn't like him.

"You are aware of what we are offering," Vitis said simply, drawing our attention back to the pressing issue. "What do you plan to do?"

We'd met in Malik and Seeley's rooms to discuss this last night and had come to a conclusion after my conversation with Conall.

"I think we need to go back, maybe bring a few Idians and start arranging for the willing, the allies, to return. Rhijn and I can portal them back to Adrina, as often as our power will allow, assuming he's willing." I gave him a pointed look, to which he kept his expression perfectly neutral. I briskly continued. "The expanding Swath and the dwindling resources will encourage others to come with us. As we relocate the Banished into the settlements, reports will spread when we return their prosperity. I believe more will choose to join us. At some rate, if those opposed to peace will not join us, then let them stay banished. Perhaps those opposed here can join them." I shot Pollux a grin that I knew didn't reach my eyes.

"You really think many will reject our offer?" Vitis tilted his head to the side, glazing past the shot I'd sent at the older council member.

"I think many fear change. They fear the unknown. They won't see you as we have grown to. It will take time before they believe you are not the evil we've been taught to fear. These beliefs are deeply ingrained and will not be shed easily. Still, we should not lose hope." My voice rose with conviction. Maybe I had been born to do this. "Most Skyborne in our realm only want their basic needs met, their youths taken care of, and an opportunity to contribute to our society. The leaders in the territories have not been able to offer them that for generations now. The system the matriarchs established after the crossover had been impressive, but that isn't the realm they are living in any longer."

"And you think we can just go back and sweep large portions of the population back without opposition?" Rhijn asked, furrowing his brows skeptically in my direction. He'd said we, so that was a good sign.

"As far as we know, Emerson and Regent Karish, Malik's father," and my own, I thought with a shiver, "have instigated no conflict. Darius, Malik's brother, will have informed them he saw us vanish from that room at the inn in Seabrook. They will realize that means we have the ember. Beyond that, we don't have any reason to suspect anything. But if that is not the case, we will do what we must. It would be prudent to have a force of Idians prepared in case we need backup. I believe our primary goal is to move and protect the innocents."

"I will see it is done," Vitis said, nodding to Kellis, who scribbled away at a notepad.

"If I were them, I would guard that inn day and night, awaiting your return. Where do you plan to land?" Kellis asked, surveying the map.

"The Swath," I said, decisively. We hadn't discussed this, and I heard intakes of breath from my companions. "My arrangement with Uden will protect us. Our enemies wouldn't dare enter the inescapable boundary. The forest's central location will be ideal in case any unanticipated events have occurred which Uden should be able to fill us in through whatever mystical channel he possesses." I still hadn't learned how exactly Uden knew so much about the activity outside the Swath.

"And if it does come to war, how will you prevent these creatures from blocking our power?" Rhijn asked, motioning to Conall's sketch.

"I'd like to go to Arborvale first, to my sisters. Balene is a healer, and she's developed an antidote. We need to determine how much she has, and figure out a way to produce more and have it distributed as a precaution in case Emerson strikes." The plan took shape in my mind as I spoke; the things we'd discussed as a group, and the answers to Chancellor Vitis's questions. It felt good to be acting, in control. And I didn't need to apologize for using my power.

"Asha will stay here and help coordinate the first groups to return." What had happened to Asha in Monterra wasn't my story to share, but I told Vitis enough when I was explaining the favor I asked for so he understood why she needed to stay safely in Idia, despite the fact that she drove me insane half of the time. She was recovering so valiantly, and she would provide an anchor to the first groups of Skyborne from our realm, not to mention a useful ally to the Chancellor. "When we find Ian, we'll let him know you're safe and cared for."

The corner of Vitis's mouth ticked up. I squinted at Asha, who seemed pleasantly surprised, though I was beginning to suspect Vitis, in whatever friendship they were developing, had already shared this tidbit with her. "It will be helpful to have one of their own here to be a liaison. My other sister Carina will want to stay until all her Skyborne are safely in Idia. When she arrives here, she would make an ideal choice to govern one of the settlements. It will be the same with Seeley's parents. My mother Renia may agree to come back with the first group, though. To aid Asha."

I finished trying to think of anything else we needed to cover.

Vitis smiled. "Very well. Sounds like the next step is to decide when you will leave." He turned to his son. "Rhijn, will one week give you enough time to recover?"

Seeley shifted uncomfortably in his seat and cleared his throat. Rhijn noticed.

"I'm recovered. We can leave as early as in the morning."

I thought of the time difference. It was night when we'd left, but only morning here. "Tonight," I urged. Relief rolled off Seeley. Rhijn could recover while we were traveling through the Swath.

"Fine," Rhijn agreed.

"Perfect," Vitis said. "Adjourned."

I made a beeline to Asha after the meeting, ushering her out into the corridor. "Why do you always have to do that? I did you a favor, and that is what I get?"

"Someone's got to call you on your bullshit." She shrugged and kept walking, expecting me to follow. When she sensed I didn't, she spun around. "Are you going to come or not?"

"Where exactly are we going?" I asked.

"I'm going to help you pack. And I have a present for your sisters. I promise they are going to love." I could hardly stay mad at the bright, toothy smile beaming back at me, as if outing me at every chance she got was no big deal. Asha shook her chest at me and wiggled her eyebrows, suggesting Carina, Balene and Jude would receive their own bralettes courtesy of Asha. A gift I'd added several more of to my collection in various designs and colors.

She looped her arm through mine and pulled me down the hall to my room. "Well, I know how much you love yours. And you'd better not take credit for my gift, either. I expect you to tell them their new best friend from Sundale was the thoughtful one."

"Uggh," I moaned. "Why do I hang out with you?"

CHAPTER TWENTY-TWO

L IGHTS TWINKLED IN the night sky across the shining city as Rhijn, Kellis, Malik, Seeley, Conall and I stood in a circle, backs together, on the terrace overlooking the city. Butterflies danced in my stomach as I touched my fingers to the ember and the familiar darkness crawled up my arm.

We'd loaded our packs with essentials, armed ourselves in case we didn't land where we expected, and said our goodbyes. We'd been gone only for a few weeks. Surely nothing horrible had happened while we were gone.

"Wish us luck," I said, and started the dark ellipse on the manicured lawn around our feet. Chancellor Vitis, Asha and Kelvin stood on a walkway under the awning, watching. I paused in front of Rhijn before I connected the circle, craning my neck up at him. We'd decided I'd create the first portal since I'd done it before and was fresh, and give Rhijn a chance to understand the unique energy signature of our realm before he made an attempt. Besides, he was exhausted from his journey to deal with the creatures. I was grateful he'd insisted we not delay on his account, aptly reading Seeley's increasing edginess.

"Ready?" I smirked at him before I connected the circle.

He nodded, solemnly.

I rolled my eyes. We were going to have to learn to get along, despite

"

what had transpired between us, for the good of the realms.] I wasn't in the mood for his angst. I stood and grabbed his and Conall's hands, squeezing them both, determined. Conall smiled, squeezing mine back. Traveling between realms was a bit more adrenaline inducing than the trip across Idia Conall and I had taken. I'd learned and I knew this was Rhijn's first experience of the sensation. I caught his eyes peeling back as the weightless feeling of falling overtook us. A tremble of laughter shook my core as we fell.

The dense canopy of the Swath protected us from the piercing rays of the light star in our banished realm. I glanced up from my crouch, assessing my companions. Kellis landed in a small puddle of water, but he indicated it was only lukewarm. I'd warned them of the scalding pools we may come across, and the other hazards in the Swath, but I was confident with Rhijn and I's healing abilities that it was worth the small risk it imposed.

"Everyone accounted for?" I asked.

"That was exciting," Kellis said, dusting himself off.

"No injuries here," Conall stated, looking around at the others. "I even landed on my feet this time."

I patted his puffed-up chest. "You landed on your feet last time too," I said under my breath.

"Yeah, but *they* don't know that," he whispered back, winking. They did though, since Asha outed us.

"Where in the Swath do you think we are?" Malik asked, sending a lick of energy out to survey the area. It was the same as the other times I'd been in the warded forest, eerily quiet, barely a breeze keeping the air from being oppressive. A trickle of moisture clung to the moss and dripped sluggishly to the moist ground below. Grasses topped with plumes and cattails grew up from the larger pools, and dead leaves scattered the ground, the decaying earthy scent of them wafting up on a gust created from our arrival.

Rhijn plucked a blade of grass and studied its alternating ochre and chartreuse bands.

"I'm not certain," I responded to Malik. It was hard to tell the position of the sun through the thick foliage above us.

Our champion returns, Uden's hollow voice echoed through the understory.

I shivered and secured the buttons on my jacket, the eerie voice creating a chill across my skin despite the tepid temperature. My companions scanned our periphery for the bearer of the voice that I knew wasn't quite like anything else they'd ever heard. It was the same for me the first time it echoed this way. That was almost a year ago when I had my first encounter with the creature I'd come to know as Uden.

Its fleshy, vaguely humanoid body approached through a thicket. Taloned feet squished through grasses and small patches of muck and briars, mud oozing between its digits.

"I brought friends—and before you ask, no, you may not eat them," I said.

A hearty chuckle rumbled the ground.

Uden approached me. Rhijn stepped ahead, his body coiled, subtly blocking Uden's direct path to me. Oddly protective of a male who's been doing his best to ignore my existence for a week now.

I placed my hand on Rhijn's forearm. "He's safe," I said under my breath, urging him to relax. He shook my arm off and frowned down at me.

I sighed, securing my temper for the good of our mission. "Uden, this is Rhijn and Kellis. They are from Idia, the realm where our kind originated."

Are you here to return us home? Uden asked, an upturned hope laced the deep current of his voice.

Carefully, I said, "Yes, we are here to return all the beings from this banished realm to their homes."

An inner lens blinked across the glowing sour fruit that was Uden's eyes, as he considered. His hands came together, steepled at his fleshy sallow chest, and an enormous grin gaped across his serrated maw. *You want to adjust the terms of our agreement then?*

"Not exactly. Traveling between realms exhausts my capacity. I will keep my promise to you, as you have to me."

"You still have a role to play in the fate of this realm," Seeley pronounced, before I could continue, stretching out his words and his hands to seem prophetic. "I have seen it," he said with finality.

I jerked my head to him, eyes narrowing. Seeley had stepped into one of the few rays of light which permeated the canopy and it made his ebony skin seem to glow making him look like a prophet if there ever was one. Knowing he'd achieved the effect he was going for he shot me a quick wink. Malik was suppressing a laugh behind him and looped an arm around his waist to whisper something in his ear.

Hmph. Uden's voice echoed, trying to understand our antics. He had no reason to doubt us, and there was more I'd explain to him when we had a chance to speak privately. *Very well. You have a friend awaiting your arrival,* he said, waving a yellow-green claw, urging us along.

I shrugged, stepping in line, glancing over my shoulder to see if my companions would follow suit. "Who is this friend?" I asked, curiously.

The wild red-headed one called Asha you brought here—he says he's her brother. They prodded him over the boundary weeks ago. I was in the area and I heard him hollering her name. Of course, we were loath to spare him, but a friend of a friend. You know how these things go. A terrifying grin crept across the creature's face, exposing rows of jagged, rotting teeth.

My companion's nervous energy hummed in the air, only lessening when Uden finally closed his mouth.

"You really liked Asha, didn't you?" I shook my head, astonished. She, like Seeley, had that effect on everyone they met. "Wait, who prodded him into the Swath?"

"One of our allies, the young Regent of Sundale, was, for all intents and purposes, executed?" Malik asked.

This wasn't good. Prodding a convicted Skyborne past the invisible boundary into the Swath had been a traditional death penalty, which was no longer used in most of the territories. And Ian was a Regent. Seemed Emerson hadn't been content to wait on our return and was doing exactly what Seeley had feared. And I knew first hand she wasn't the type who would shy away from using an archaic punishment. There wasn't much I'd put past her.

"Seeley, what was his name?" Malik continued.

"Ian. I believe Asha was the older of the two, but Ian's grandfather changed the laws there so only his sons and grandsons could take the regency." Seeley nodded.

"Yes, that was it. So, Uden, you're saying that you've been sheltering Ian for weeks?" Malik asked.

Mmmhmm, Uden replied. *It seems things have changed since you've been gone. Come, there is more to tell.*

"I never would have imagined we'd be roving through the Swath, guided by the head creature, accompanied by Idians, not to mention in possession of the ember which we just used to travel between realms. Am I the only one who's flabbergasted?" Conall asked.

"Well, now that you put it that way…" I couldn't help but give a nervous laugh as he fell into stride beside me. I knew Conall was trying to keep the tone light, so our fears wouldn't overwhelm us.

The brush opened up to a large outcropping where trees were intentionally grown into structured dwellings. It was similar to the location we'd camped before, but much more expansive. Creatures crawled and flew before us, going about their business. It was strange seeing them around their homes. Though they didn't have shops and food stalls like our kind, I saw the similarities between us and them. *Cousins,* as Uden had once said.

A tall lanky male reclined against a structure, weaving grasses into a bowl shape. A fringe of strawberry blond hair fell over his eyes, which seemed in a trance as he worked. He jerked his head up at the noise of our approach. Smiling, he jumped to his feet, abandoning the basket.

"You're the ones Asha spoke of in her letter," Ian exclaimed. His hazel eyes sparked to life. He skipped to Seeley. "I remember you! Please tell me you remember me too?" he asked, looking nervously from Seeley to Uden.

Seeley stumbled back from the force of the young Regent.

"Oh, sorry, I guess I'm just excited," the male said, waiting.

"Yes, I remember you, Ian," Seeley said.

"Thank the Makers," he exclaimed. "Where's Asha? Is she with you?" Ian scanned our group, then stilled, dread threatening his features.

"We left Asha in Idia to help prepare for our return. And trust me, she is well cared for and more than happy to keep near her current company," I explained, thinking of how close Vitis had been hovering near her the last handful of times I'd seen them together.

Rhijn stiffened at the implication, but ignored me. "Who tried to execute you?" he asked, getting to the question that was lingering on all of our minds.

"Emerson," Ian responded. "Asha's letter said she'd be home soon. When she never arrived, I started hearing rumors that the new Drakestone heir had seen you all disappear from the inn in Seabrook. Appears that one was true. Anyway, Emerson is in charge of Monterra now, and she has taken control of Sundale too. When her army arrived, we didn't know what hit us."

"No," Seeley breathed. Malik put an arm around him to steady him. "We're too late."

"We're not too late," I said firmly. *We couldn't be too late.* "Tell us what you know."

Uden gathered us around a depression in the soil, and he gurgled to some creatures around us. They scuttled over to the pit and deposited dried twigs and logs. When they were satisfied with the pile, they flicked their illuminant green gazes between us, waiting.

"They want someone to light it," I realized.

Conall's face perked up. "All you have to do is ask," he said, and extended his hand toward the wood, and glowing red and orange flames sprouted.

"You *still* don't have to do that," I teased, mimicking his flamboyant hand gesture.

"Indulge me," he laughed, scooting toward where I'd plopped down. Ever since Rhijn had backed off, things had gone back to normal between me and Conall, to my relief. I shivered, still chilly despite the temperature under the canopy, and he put a sturdy arm around my shoulders. I had a feeling his warmth was the last respite I'd have for a while, so I enjoyed every moment of it.

Rhijn was making a show of ignoring me as he and Kellis sat near Ian and Uden, the latter who he seemed completely unphased by.

"Where to begin," Ian said. "Well, I don't think Emerson has killed anyone important *yet*. It was either death, the dungeons, or the Swath. I took a gamble based on Asha's letter."

It made me cringe to think of who Ian might deem as *important*. I tried to keep an open mind as he spoke.

"That was gutsy of you," Malik complimented, the corner of his distinct mustache lifted, suggesting the impressed quirk of his lips. "What news of Seabrook, Arborvale and Eastdow?"

"This is probably the only good news I have to deliver. Ephrem passed, and Carina is now Regent. I heard Torin had aligned with Darius, but after he discovered his own son," he cleared his throat, turning to Conall, who nodded, affirming his identity. "His son had helped the traitors escape, then fled with them, causing him to reconsider. This, along with having lost the priest who'd been an advisor for years, had understandably shaken him. Again, rumors. Oh, and Carina happened to him, too. Apparently, she secured a meeting with him and convinced him to break the alliance with Drakestone."

Conall brought a hand to his mouth. Tears came to my own eyes. I wrapped both my arms around him, knowing what this must mean to him. "I told you about Carina, didn't I?!" I said. "And that shows how much your father loves you, Conall. That is great news, Ian."

"Well, that's probably where it ends. Carina and Torin have been able to hold off Emerson so far, using the threat of his might and her wit, but I'm not sure how much longer they'll last. No news on how Seabrook fares," Ian explained.

"So, considering the new information, do we go to Eastdow or Arborvale, then?" Kellis, the political strategist, asked.

"Sounds like Eastdow is the more prudent choice," Rhijn chimed in. "If your father still has his armies intact and ready, it sounds like we may need them."

"But we still need to assess the situation with the antidote. That may be a critical factor if a conflict breaks out," Malik argued.

They were both right. There was only one logical choice. "We'll separate into two groups. Conall, you, Kellis, Malik and Ian can go to visit your father. Seeley, Rhijn and I will go to Arborvale."

I sensed Conall move to protest beside me, and Rhijn glared at me across the fire.

"Please feel free to come up with a better plan," I grumbled, annoyed. No one said anything.

"She's right, considering each of our skill sets," Rhijn said, surprising me. "Uden, how far is the edge of the territories from here?"

If you started that way now, you'll be there in two days by nightfall.

"That can't be!" I jerked my head toward him.

The Swath has grown even faster since you left, Realm Walker.

I buried my head between my knees and groaned.

"Okay," I said, sitting upright. "We'll travel together to the Twin Towns, then separate from there."

Then it's settled. I will be your guide. Eat, then we will leave.

I tracked Uden as he stood and walked away from our group. I got up and followed him out of the clearing, gearing myself up for the convincing I was about to do.

⌇

We reached the traveler's inn on the Eastdow side of the river after hasty travel through the Swath exactly when Uden had predicted. Rhijn, Seeley and I had further to travel to make it to Arborvale, but Conall suggested we find a merchant willing to take us down the river by barge. I knew there was a passenger transport that ran on odd days of the week, but time had become a blur and we'd lost track of what day it would have been in our realm.

The inn only had one room by the late hour we arrived, and we made do with what we had. Chancellor Vitis had made sure we had plenty of various valuable coins, though they weren't something his citizens used, having exchanged them for paper bills. Plus, what Seeley and Conall had on them when we'd portaled from Seabrook to Idia.

At daybreak, I snuck over my sleeping companions who were littering the floor and slipped out the door of our shared room. I quickly headed out of the inn and down to the river. The dock master informed me they expected the passenger barge late tonight, and it wouldn't depart again until the following morning. Then it was almost a full day's ride on the river south. But if I didn't want to wait, she suggested I approach a burly Skyborne called Ardol.

I slipped a coin into her palm and trudged off in search of Ardol. I found him in a flat-bottom houseboat tied to the shore beyond the town. It took a full half-hour of rigorous negotiation to secure our passage.

"Don't you go anywhere," I warned him. "We'll be ready to depart within the hour."

Everyone was downstairs eating breakfast, except for Seeley and Malik when I got back. "Where are the lovebirds?" I asked. They'd become even more sickeningly romantic since their engagement.

"Saying goodbye, apparently," Conall replied.

I hated to separate them, but I wanted Seeley with me in case he had a sight. Also, I thought he and Carina needed to meet.

"Where have you been?" Conall asked.

"Securing our passage downriver," I said. "I told Ardol, the owner of a questionable houseboat, that we'd be back in an hour. That means we need to leave pretty soon."

I was eager to get to Arborvale and see my sisters, not to mention the anxiety that gripped me when I thought of Seeley and what his parents' situation could be. Femi and Alrun were the shining examples of stewards of their territory. My stomach sank every time I thought of them potentially locked in the prisons below the Seabrook keep, or whatever else Emerson might be doing with them now. Because if she had Sundale, she likely had control of Seabrook too as it was between Sundale and Drakestone. We didn't know, and that was the worst part.

I went to the bar and asked the female serving breakfast to prepare some supplies we could take with us. I ate a piece of sweet bread while she put together travel parcels.

When she'd presented them, I directed the larger of the two to Conall as Malik and Seeley emerged from upstairs. The latter's eyes rimmed in pink, and I felt a pang for them.

Conall grabbed the parcel, stuffing it in his pack, which he threw over his broad shoulders. "You sure you're going to be okay traveling with him?" he asked, nodding to Rhijn.

Not this again. Conall read my agitation perfectly.

"I'm not trying to be difficult. But I can't help but remember the state you were in after being with him for more than a few days and—"

"Conall, listen to me," I interrupted. "I appreciate your concern, but I'm fine." I jerked a hand in Rhijn's direction. "He's fine. We're fine. Everything's fine. Okay? Don't let this distract you. Go see your father and do what we need you to do. I don't have time to kick your ass right now." I gave a mock threatening stare. Rhijn shook his head, not knowing what to think of us.

"Oh, Nayla. I'll miss you, but you're right. Take care of yourself and tell the infamous Carina thank you for whatever magic she worked with my father."

"I will," I said. He pulled me into his arms, then we parted ways. I led Seeley and Rhijn down past the docks, to the rickety vessel awaiting us.

◆

"I'm going to go lie down inside," Seeley said, his deep brown skin more wan than usual. The flow of the river was gentle, I thought, but Seeley had been battling sea sickness since we'd boarded.

"Seeley, don't leave me," I whined.

He had already gotten up from the bench he, Rhijn and I had been sharing. It was the bench, or sit inside the cramped cabin.

"I won't play buffer between you two all the way to Arborvale. Not going to do it," Seeley huffed.

It tempted me to follow him into the cabin and stash myself on the floor or in a compartment. Only around eight more hours, I thought.

I leaned my head back against the cabin's exterior wall, shifting my body, trying to get comfortable. We sat there in silence while we passed leagues of open prairie and farmlands.

"Oh, look!" I exclaimed. Rhijn was doing the thing where he sat perfectly still, taking deep steady breaths. I nudged him. "Look, before you miss them."

A small herd of fallow deer grazed on the wild grasses at the edge of a desolate grainfield. Drought had hit this area hard, but the native plants were fairing the best. The deer had wandered far from the shelter of the tree line to find it.

Rhijn peeked at me out of the corner of a closed eye.

"Makers, Rhijn," I barked. "Will you quit it already and look at the damn deer?" I was fuming. "There's a fucking baby one. See its spots? Why wouldn't you want to see that?"

"Huh?" he muttered, scanning across the plain. "Oh, it is. Cute," he said, before closing his eyes again.

I groaned exaggeratedly, pulling at the roots of my hair.

"I thought this was what you wanted." He observed me from a cracked eye.

"You're impossible," I said and got up to lean against the railing. My midnight locks whipped across my face in the breeze. I pulled a ribbon from my pocket and stuck it between my teeth. I turned to the wind so it would push my hair out of my face and began braiding it.

"What?" I asked. Rhijn was staring at me as I tied the ribbon around the end of the braid. He swallowed, then stared down at his feet.

Fine. I turned back to the railing, needing to stand for a bit.

I didn't feel him move, but some time later, he fingered the bottom of the braid. I froze, not wanting to scare him off. Eventually, he let it fall to my back. It hit like a punch. I was holding my breath as he came to stand beside me, placing his veined hands on the railing. I glanced at his elegant fingers then, remembering the sensation of them hungrily raking over my skin.

I suppressed a shudder and turned around to face the back of the barge. A large hand circled my wrist, spinning me back toward the statuesque male standing before me. Slowly, I tilted my head up to him. He was so utterly male. Muscles in his jaw twitched, as if he were holding back a well of emotion. When he looked at me the way he was looking at me now, with so much intention between those clear blue eyes, my mouth went dry. I was woozy suddenly as I glanced at his supple lips. It seemed to be getting worse each time I was near him.

Control yourself.

That's what he'd said. I stiffened. Makers, I was being a simpering fool. I'd never been this reactive to a lover and it was beginning to freak me out.

He opened his mouth, gauging my reaction. "I'm sorry," he bit out. "It is unfair that I have been acting this way. Half of this is my fault too. I should have known."

"What are you talking about?" I snapped, on the defensive. "We slept together twice. It's no big deal. Skyborne do this all the time and still manage to get along afterward. You shouldn't have agreed to it if *you* couldn't handle it."

Rhijn stepped back, releasing my hand as if I'd slapped him.

I shouldn't have said any of that. He'd apologized and I knew I was being childish. It was like I couldn't get my emotions under control around him and he was right. I did need to control myself. There were bigger things at play here than whatever was going on between me and the Idian. I needed to get my shit together. And soon.

I flopped down on the bench, crossing my arms. I hated this barge.

Rhijn kneeled down, so he was eye level with me. He sat there until I finally looked at him. "You think *I'm* the one who couldn't handle it?" he drew out, his voice a low, angry grumble. "You think *I'm* impossible?"

He shook his head. "You know what? I can pretend too. If that's what would make you happy, then that's what I'll do."

I crinkled my forehead, confused. "Yes, if you would be civil to me, I would appreciate it. Others will notice we're acting strange."

"Well, we wouldn't want that." He got up and dropped onto the bench next to me. His head thudded against the wall of the cabin and his fingers splayed across his knees. "So, you were taken by Conall's father and some priest before your womanhood ceremony, and you haven't seen this Regent sister of yours since?" he asked.

I turned my head sideways to assess him. "What? We're going to play all nice now?"

"Makers, don't tell me you've changed your mind again." He exhaled, exasperated.

I giggled. I couldn't help it. If annoying Rhijn was a sport, I decided I might like to take it up. "I haven't seen her since then, but some things don't change," I said, thinking of the letter from Carina which Jude had given me.

Rhijn chuckled under his breath. "Isn't that the truth."

CHAPTER TWENTY-THREE

IT WAS LATE when we approached the modest stronghold of Arborvale which housed the Regents family, *my family*, and was the base
of operations for the territory. Unlike the weighty structures built
from various stones extracted from the ground which crowned the other
territories I'd been to, the Regent's home in Arborvale was constructed of
overlapping timber, which rose nimbly into the sky.

The town was situated in a bend of the largest river that flowed
through the territory, from the mountains to the plains and farmlands
that surrounded it. The felled trees had been easier to transport than
stone, having floated down the river from the thick forests in the foothills
that crossed the border between us and Eastdow.

"That building is where I grew up," I said, pointing to a section of
the compound with a long-pitched roof which had come into view. Little
windows with peaked awnings poked out of the second story at regular
intervals.

I recognized the aging Skyborne guard who stood at the main gate to
the residential section of the property, though I wasn't sure if he'd remember me after ten long years.

I tamped down the memories of my childhood that gurgled up as I
approached, and the male blinked as he saw me. "Nayla, is that you? We
thought you were…"

"Very much alive, Tomas! Though I have had quite the adventure. It's been a time, old friend," I said, clapping the sturdy, graying male on the shoulder not wanting to explain more. "I know it's late, but are any of my sisters around?"

Tomas shook his head as if in disbelief I'd returned after all these years and he showed us into a familiar reception area to wait while he sent for one of them.

"It's quite late to barge in here expecting to be greeted by a Regent, don't you think?" an authoritative feminine voice resonated through a corridor leading into the room. "I'm a very busy female these days."

I had been unable to anticipate my reaction as I'd thought about it these last few days. I spun toward the female who walked into the room. Carina, the Arborvale Regent, stood before me with her arms crossed over her chest, smirking. She was in a long cream nightgown with a silken robe covering it. Her feet were bare, and her dark hair was chopped bluntly at her shoulders. She was the same as I remembered, a little stiff, controlled really, with fine, discerning features. Her smokey grey eyes studied me, waiting for my response. She'd been my best friend throughout our childhood.

Glee. That's what I felt.

"Are you sure we're welcome?" Rhijn leaned down and whispered.

I bound forward and threw my arms around Carina's slim waist, picking her up and spinning her. When I set her down, we were giggling, and in tears. I tugged the ends of her stick straight locks. "I like this look. Suits you."

"Oh Nayla, we'd been told you were dead," she sobbed.

"I know, I know. Jude filled me in," I said, wiping tears off the Regent's cheeks with the hem of my sleeve.

Seeley cleared his throat behind me.

"Oh, these are my friends, Seeley, Alrun and Femi's son. And this—"

"I'm Rhijn," his deep timbre interjected. "I'm from Idia, Adrina, our capital city, specifically."

"I see," Carina said, sniffling. Suddenly, as if realizing we weren't alone and believing her behavior inappropriate for her position, she straightened, raising a regal chin. "Well, pleased to meet you both. Welcome to

Arborvale. I'm sorry you are arriving at such a tumultuous time for us. Sit," she gestured to a seating area with plush chairs surrounding a small ornate table. "We have much to discuss."

I laughed inwardly as Carina barked a few orders to an attendant who scurried out of the room. Moments later, the attendant came back in with a pitcher of coffee, four cups, and other accompaniments. I'd known the position of Regent would suit her perfectly. Carina seemed so at ease in command like she'd been born to do it.

She told us Jude was in Eastdow with Torin, working with his forces, and Balene was living day and night at the mill where she worked tirelessly with the other healers from the territory to create more of the antidote. My mother was *out in the field* using her ability to shift handling smuggling Cerisium out of Monterra. Pride welled creating a lump in my throat crowding out the fear as Carina spoke of my family. I hoped Rhijn saw how brave they were.

She handed us each a small pouch Tomas had slipped her, which she explained could be worn diagonally across our chest, or detached and placed in a pocket or on a belt. Two vials of the dark powder were inside them. "Keep those on you at all times. There is one for you and an extra dose. You can mix it with spit, then swallow. It doesn't taste great, but it's better than being blocked from your power."

"How did Balene know to make this?" I asked.

"Mother and I sent her to train with Emerson. Over the years, she'd secretly maintained correspondence with some old trusted friends in Monterra who kept her informed of the activities of the late Regius and his healer step-daughter. When she learned of what they were doing in that Cerisium mine, we decided to send her. You know Balene. She isn't really one for subterfuge, but I *encouraged* her and she understood it was her duty. And before you chastise me, she was one-hundred percent safe. Emerson loved having her as a protege. I'm sure it made the healer feel important, especially considering what a prodigy Balene is. So, when her tenure ended, she came back with these vials of red powder hidden in her luggage. It took us months to coax her into talking, but eventually, she shared the horrors she'd witnessed and became determined to create something powerful enough to combat the substance emitted by

Emerson's creatures. It only took her a few months, and she had a trial antidote ready."

"Of course, I volunteered to dose myself with that pink poison. I can still remember that feeling that crawled over my skin and under my flesh as that disgusting substance cut off the channels to my power." Carina's upper lip curled, and she twitched at the memory before continuing. "You experienced this at the ceremony in Eastdow when your identity was revealed?"

"I did," I answered. "It was awful, being blocked from my connection to the energy that surrounds us. I never realized how entrenched it is in every sensation I have until it shut me off from it."

"Yes," Carina nodded. "That's exactly it. So, after a few hours, I took her antidote. It dampened the effectiveness of the poison, but my senses didn't open to their normal levels until days later. It took several more months of experiments until we'd almost run out of the powder she'd been able to smuggle until she finally got it right."

Rhijn held up a vial. "That's quite a feat," he said. "How much of this do you have?"

"Currently, only about two hundred doses. It takes time for the healers to convert the Cerisium into this substance, and unfortunately, the only source is the mines in Monterra. Mother is working with our sources who have kept us in a steady supply, but we have lost carriers along the way. We think Emerson knows we've developed an antidote, so smuggling it out of her territory has become much more challenging."

"We'll need more," Rhijn stated.

Carina bristled. "Do you think I'm not aware of that?"

"That's not what I meant," he said. "Nayla and I can help produce it. If we use the connection to our channels the void stones give us, we should be able to increase production."

"Void stones?" Carina asked.

Rhijn and I reached into our pockets, producing the mirrored relics. Carina didn't seem impressed as she considered the pulsing objects.

"Very well," she said, yawning. "Let's get a good night's sleep, then we'll show you to the mill first thing so you can start. Seeley, I assume Nayla brought you to work with me?"

Normally effervescent, Seeley seemed like he wasn't sure what to say. I felt guilty throwing him to the wolves, but it had been my intention which Carina picked up on after she'd made her own assessment. He released a breath, "I'd be delighted."

The attendant rasped at the door and stepped into the room, rubbing his heavy eyelids.

"What is it now?" Carina barked.

"Another visitor it seems, Regent," the male mumbled, repressing a yawn.

She sighed. "Fine. Show them—"

Carina was cut short as a bright glowing presence zipped in through the cracked door, flew over and perched on the empty mug positioned right in front of me.

Meethra's pale yellow skin glowed as she beamed up at me, her pairs of translucent insect-like wings beating out her excitement. "You're alive! Oh Nayla, I was so worried about you."

I really wanted to hug the diminutive bug, but she was so small I feared I'd crush her. I held out a finger to her, and she wrapped her arms around it and pulled it to her chest in a surprisingly firm embrace.

"You've saved me twice now, my friend," I told her, thinking of how the godflies had interceded in my re-capture in Monterra.

"But you and your friends saved my entire kind from that monster. And you're going to take us home?" She asked, her already high voice, squeaking even higher.

"Yes, but how were you certain I'd be here?" I asked her.

"Conall," she said, blushing. "We'd been hiding from Emerson's creatures, but they were so close to finding us. So I went to Felicia, who told me Conall's father was now allied with your sister." Meethra spun in a circle and stopped on a slack jawed Carina. "Allied with you," she said, then turned back to me. "Felicia convinced him to offer us shelter. It was safer than the mountains. The creatures, they haven't dared come to the keep. We've been there since."

Rhijn cleared his throat and Meethra startled and spun toward him. "You—you're from Nayla's home realm, aren't you?" Her eyes widened.

Rhijn gave her an easy smile. "Yes, how can you tell?"

"It's your essence. Godflies can sense our essences," I explained. Across the table, Carina squinted, and I could see her wheels were turning.

"You can tell a lot about a person from their essence," Meethra continued.

"Indeed," Carina agreed.

"We can, like how I sensed you're Nayla's sister. And," she closed her eyes, and tapped on her mouth with her pointer finger before turning to Seeley. "You feel like the one Nayla brought to Monterra who saved my kind. The one who looks dark, but feels light."

Seeley beamed. "Malik, my partner. That must be our bond you are sensing."

"Ah, yes." Meethra confirmed, then her gaze darted between Rhijn and I. "And you two—"

"We both carry the void stones," I said, cutting her off. "Rhijn, she's seen the ember. Show her yours."

Rhijn obliged, extending his hand to show the godfly the glowing white almond shaped orb. She skittered across the table and leaned across his fingers to peer down into it, then back up at him. "Interesting, but I don't think that's it," she said, fluttering her wings.

"It's probably just different from anything you've encountered before," Rhijn said, tucking away the void stone, and getting up from the table abruptly. His formality sliding around him like a well-orchestrated façade. "Regent, it's been a long day. We are grateful for your hospitality."

A quizzical look crossed Meethra's tiny face as she scanned me and Rhijn.

"Ignore him. You know how males are. You can stay in my room tonight," I told her. "I want you to tell me everything that has happened since we left."

It was the middle of the night when attendants finally took us to our rooms and even later when I finally got to sleep, a restless energy waking me in regular intervals until the light star began its rise.

❧

Our horse drawn carriage rumbled down the bumpy road leading to the mill. Seeley and I excitedly told Carina about the transports and the power wells. I looked at Rhijn, who wore a bemused expression. "I can tell her about the settlements, right?" I asked. I figured I was allowed, but it seemed like the right thing to do to double check.

"Considering you plan to have your sister govern one, you might as well," he replied.

That perked up Carina's attention. "I'll have my pick, I assume?" she mused.

"The Northern one is the most expansive and furthest North from Adrina. I'd suggest the strongest ally govern that one. The weather is brisk there. Much like it is here," Rhijn explained.

"That is the one Conall loved, too," I said. "Maybe you and him can co-govern it."

Carina smirked across the carriage at me. "Well, I haven't met the infamous Conall yet, so we'll see."

"He's wonderful. You will love him when you meet him," Meethra chimed in from her perch on my knee. "He is strong and kind. And very handsome for a Skyborne."

"Meethra, I think you're turning pink," I said, as she giggled, hiding her face with her tiny hands.

The ride to the mill wasn't nearly long enough, and I had so much more I wanted to share with her.

We exited the carriage and Carina led us inside. It was an old wooden structure with heavy doors that hung on rickety hinges. The interior was wide open, and long tables were scattered across the expanse. Square columns which held the roof had tallies affixed to them. I studied one. It was tracking the units produced. As a female healer placed a filled vial into a crate, she added a mark to the paper.

I located Balene. She was operating a piece of equipment which appeared to crush the Cerisium into smaller parts. Her gloved hands swept the fuchsia gravel into a mortar, and she handed it to an awaiting male healer who was armed with a pestle. He took the tools over to a table and began to grind.

Balene wiped her exposed forearm across her brow and exhaled, shoulders sagging. As she looked up from her work, she saw us. A tentative grin spread across her face and she tugged the gloves off, tossing them aside.

We embraced for long moments before I pulled away to study her. "You're all grown up!" I exclaimed. Between my three sisters, Balene had been the gentler, reserved one. I hated that she'd had to endure the horrors I'd seen with my own eyes in Monterra. Balene's innocent round brown eyes blinked as we took each other in. Her long hair was pulled into a low ponytail and she wore a baggy ankle length hunter gown, which had two pockets sewn on it at her rounded hips. Her features were softer than Carina or Jude's, which gave her a more youthful appearance.

"Okay, you see each other. We can catch up once we have defeated Emerson and are safely deposited into our awaiting settlements in Idia," Carina said, interrupting our flittering conversation, all business. "Balene, this is Rhijn. He and Nayla are going to help you increase your capacity. With their power, I'd like production doubled. I'll send word to mother and see if she can have our contacts in Monterra to increase the deliveries. Meethra, Seeley, you'll both join me? We have work to do."

I couldn't tell if Carina was aware of what she was doing. The rest of us certainly were. At Carina's command, a subtle compulsion ebbed off her, probably as naturally as breathing. It was no wonder most people did what she asked. They felt like they wanted to. Carina smiled and briskly swished toward the door, expecting Seeley to follow.

"Good luck!" I told Meethra and Seeley as they hurried to catch up with her.

Once Carina left, Balene took Rhijn and I on a tour of the facility, and taught us how to develop the antidote. Fortunately, since Rhijn and I could restructure the particles relatively easily, we didn't waste too much of the precious stone. And Rhijn had been right. Once we'd gotten the hang of it, we could produce three times as much as one of the territory's healers, the void willingly giving us what we asked of it.

I was weary of sitting and focusing my energy by the time a carriage came to pick us up that evening. Both Rhijn and I had an urgency to stretch our limits, but Balene, who spent most of the time overseeing the process, suggested that to keep up our pace, we'd need plenty of food and rest between shifts.

I crawled onto the bench seat of the carriage at the end of the first day, and leaned over my knees, stretching my aching neck. A warm hand settled upon it, and a smooth healing energy radiated through my tired muscles.

When Rhijn removed his hand, I turned toward him. He was staring out the opposite window. "Thank you," I whispered, hoping this was a sign of a renewed truce.

❧

Meethra finally returned to Eastdow, and they sent daily updates via brave godflies and Bara's messenger falcons. Conall wrote that he and Torin had a shaky reunion, but were getting along better now. Both parties must have felt loss and betrayal, but had moved beyond it for the sake of their relationship. I was glad for Conall. Seeley was missing Malik desperately. The poor male was so forlorn. It was worse than the previous times they'd been separated.

Seeley reverently folded a letter I assumed was from Malik a few nights later as we lounged recuperating in the sitting room. Carina was off doing official Regent things, and Rhijn was poking the fire, claiming it was satisfying to tend the flames without using his power.

"Seeley, you look so love-sick," I told him.

"It's the bond," he confessed. "Remember when I told you to see if you noticed anything the next time you were with us?"

I nodded.

"Well, I was referring to our bond. It's a unique energy signature between partners when a certain connection is made. We don't have them here in this realm because our power is too weak. Within a few days in Idia, we realized that a channel between us had been made. I think it is why Malik proposed so suddenly. We always knew we'd wanted to be together as long as we both drew breath, so we were overjoyed once Chancellor Vitis explained to us what had happened. Considering the gravity of the situation, we kept it to ourselves for a while. I was kind of hoping you'd notice though." Seeley fidgeted with the ring Malik had given him, hurt was scrawled across his face though he tried to disguise it.

Makers, I was selfish for not seeing this huge thing that had happened with my half-brother and my dear friend. I thought back to seeing them together before we left the Twin Towns. They had seemed particularly *attuned.*

"This is what Meethra detected. So, it just happened?" I asked, realization dawning. "What if you hadn't wanted a bond? Could you remove it?"

"I wouldn't want to. I think it's even brought us closer together. From what I understand, it's not necessarily uncommon, and can be intentional or sometimes can happen between a couple accidentally without them realizing they've begun the process. Both parties must actively accept the bond for it to cement, though. Because it is permanent, more or less, I think a lot of Skyborne on Idia don't choose to bond, and are satisfied with the typical commitment ceremonies, or just living together. Apparently removing a bond is very painful."

"What if a bond happens to one and not the other?" I asked, thinking how horrifying that would be.

"Nothing, I suppose. I'm sure it's not comfortable, but I assume at some point they'd get over it or the fledgling bond falls away," Seeley speculated.

"I don't know if I would ever want anyone else to have that kind of attachment to me. I'm happy for you and Malik, because you two are obviously perfect for each other. When we get back to Idia, you should have a celebration, with vows, and food and wine. Now that sounds like something I could get on board with. I'll even help you plan!" I smiled at him, trying to make up for being a rotten friend.

Seeley shook his head at me, laughing. "Okay, I will take you up on your offer when we are established in Idia."

The fire popped, and my eyes followed the sound. Rhijn had his head on his forearm, which leaned on the mantle. His body was tense.

"Rhijn, are you okay?" I asked him.

"No," he grumbled, heading to the door.

"Is it your back?" I called after him. "I can heal it—"

The door slammed closed behind him.

"What's his problem?" I narrowed my eyes toward Seeley, who appeared all too ready to give me another lecture. I jumped to my feet and pretended to be at the edge of exhaustion. "Never mind. So tired… Good night," I said, stretching as I headed to bed.

⚘

That night I tossed and turned, unable to rest. The ember, which was sitting on my nightstand, drew my eyes toward it. I had wild dreams when I had it on my person as I slept, but at least I slept. I couldn't lie there for another hour with scattered thoughts racing through my mind or I'd go crazy.

I grabbed the ember and stuffed it into the pocket of my nightshirt and flopped back over, taking deep, steading breaths. *We can dream about whatever you want, just not him,* I directed toward the ember which vibrated in agreement, as sleep took me.

Enormous green vines the size of my midsection crawled across a craggy stone surface in front of me. I turned, noticing more interlocking hexagonal columns reaching out over the edge of my vision. I climbed up the nearest cliff, gripping the textured ridges of the vines, and dug my boots into footholds in the rock. I eased up on the flat surface of the column. There was a chasm separating the section of columns I was standing on and those beyond where I needed to go. The vines growing up the fissure and from deep cracks had been woven into a bridge spanning the distance, similar to how Uden's creatures had guided the trees in the Swath into dwellings.

I took an exploratory step on the bridge. It held. A gust of wind blew through the chasm, sending the bridge swaying violently back and forth. I gripped the living lifelines white knuckled. The swaying subsided, and I continued taking careful steps across.

A thick cluster of vines came into view and creatures like those in Uden's forest swarmed around a large central podium. A throne was made from the vines too and atop it sat Uden. No, not Uden. This creature was more grayish-green and less flabby. Its body appeared lit from within, like the eyes of the creatures from the Swath. Bones jutted from its chest, its sternum and ribs, similar in structure to ours.

What are you here for? the creature asked in the same echoing voice as Uden's. It opened its mouth, showing gleaming rows of daggers, its lips smooth and uncracked, unlike the creature I'd become familiar with. Wherever this realm was, it seemed to be gentler on these creatures than our realm had been. The creature held up a clear vessel containing a chartreuse gelatinous substance and shot a long, cupped tongue into it, lapping a scoop into its mouth.

I repressed a gag as the creature swallowed the slimy substance, and its translucent skin glimmered in a steady tempo, an obvious effect of the gelatin.

Why was I there? Then it occurred to me. "I'm here to return the creatures of the Swath to their home. To end their banishment," I announced.

The bridge moved beneath my feet. Uden was standing behind me, along with a wall of flying creatures, some hovering and others joining us on the bridge. A loud groan from the vines beneath me reverberated through the cavernous fissures.

What about him? the creature asked. *Does he belong to you?*

A cage materialized out of nowhere, made from bars of interwoven vines with no visible opening. I knew who was in the cage before I saw his face.

Rhijn.

He sat breathing like he always did, slow and controlled. But then his eyes flew open as if he sensed me. Cool blue drilled into mine, and an overwhelming sense of guilt threatened to bring me to my knees.

If you can reach him, the creatures can stay, the voice waged.

My hands shook as I moved an inch. The bridge held. A step, another groan. More creatures were crawling on it behind me with each pace.

A laugh echoed across the causeway, and the bridge gave a final groan. The vines split and I screamed as my grip on the lifelines slipped. Then I was falling.

"Wake up," a deep voice demanded.

"Makers," another softer voice joined, nudging my shoulder. "Malik told me about how vicious her dreams were. That scream. I had no idea."

I blinked, and two dark figures were standing over me in the pitch black of my room.

Rhijn ran his hand through his tousled hair, and he looked at Seeley for direction.

"Go," Seeley said. "I'll stay with her."

Rhijn reluctantly turned, leaving the room, and Seeley's weight settled on the bed beside me.

"You slept with the ember?" he asked, careful to keep judgement from his tone.

I pulled the ember from my pocket and set it on the nightstand. "I couldn't sleep," I confessed, turning to shove my face into the pillow. The dream was terrifying, but at least it had been a distraction from the ache that was gnawing at the edges of my soul.

CHAPTER TWENTY-FOUR

"HEARD YOU HAD a rough night," Carina said that evening at dinner. Seeley was gone when I'd awoken. The last thing I wanted to speak of was my dream and its meanings, and thankfully Rhijn hadn't brought it up while we'd worked on antidote all day.

After having been to Idia, I'd determined the dreams were some sort of connection to the other void stone and my subconscious, the latter of which I preferred to stay buried.

"Night terror," I said, hoping she'd drop it.

"You never had night terrors when we were children." She narrowed her eyes at me, and ladled a demure portion of pumpkin soup into a porcelain bowl, then larger helpings for me, Rhijn, and Seeley.

I raised a full spoon to my lips and blew, ignoring my prying sister.

"She doesn't want to talk about it," Rhijn pointed out.

"Rhijn," she said, turning to him, nails clicking across the table. "You have this delightful way of stating the obvious, don't you?"

I was glad he'd stepped in on my behalf, but seeing Carina spar with him amused me.

"Well, you didn't seem to pick up on it," he retorted.

"I did, in fact. It's just that as sisters, we tend to ignore these types of things. It's like an unspoken code." Carina gave him a sweet, insistent smile.

"Oh, not the female code again," I groaned thinking of Everly. "And Rhijn doesn't have siblings, so he doesn't really get it."

"I get it. Everly and I have a… I mean, we *had* a sort of sibling-like relationship."

I took another spoonful of soup, hoping he'd continue if we didn't bring so much focus to it to scare him off the topic.

Out of the corner of my eye, I saw Seeley reach a hand over and place it on Rhijn's wrist. "You haven't really spoken much about her since she died."

I set my spoon in my empty bowl and it clinked louder than I intended. "You don't have to—"

"It's okay. I know I should talk about it. After my mother left, I really relied on Everly. Though we were both really young, she helped me understand that it wasn't my fault. The life of a Chancellor's wife was just more than she wanted. You know how my father is. So driven and committed to what he believes is right. It's why he was selected for the position. And she never intended to be a mother either… I was *unplanned*."

I swallowed. It was another thing we'd had in common.

"I'd felt unwanted. Rejected by my own mother. But Everly convinced me I was loveable and that it wasn't me. I think in a way her insistence on that saved me from a lot of unneeded suffering. Anyway, I know that sounds ridiculous coming from an adult—and now you're all staring." Rhijn shifted in his chair looking like he was about to bolt. But what he'd said had made me think of his need to be needed. Wanted, even. It was like the pain rolling off him was my own and my need to protect him was overwhelming.

"So Everly really meant a lot to you." Seeley squeezed, keeping his hand in place.

Unbidden tears crept over Rhijn's lower lids. My hand moved to his face on its own accord, and I wiped a tear away with my thumb, then curled around his wrist. "I'm so sorry, Rhijn. I know what it is like to lose someone you care for." Carina and I shared a glance and I could tell she was thinking of the same thing. Of how we'd lost each other all those years ago. I hadn't thought of that before at the observatory because the pain had dulled over time, but I understood that well enough now. Only Carina and I had been reunited. Everly was gone.

The door opened and closed but none of our attention strayed away from Rhijn. The attendant coughed, walking insistently to Carina's side. "Regent, a bird came from Seabrook," he announced, urgently handing Carina a letter.

We all stood waiting as she ripped open the seal and scanned the contents.

She looked at me. "Emerson knows you're back, and she wants a meeting," she said, handing me the message.

I held it so Rhijn and Seeley could read it over my shoulder. This was terrible timing and my heart ached for Rhijn, and then Seeley as I read the message. I knew exactly when Seeley got to the worst part because his knees fell out from under him. Rhijn and I both turned to catch him and guide him over to a couch.

"She's going to kill my mother if we don't go," he muttered.

"This is all because of me," I said. "I'll go. I'll meet her and convince her to let Femi and Alrun go. They've done nothing to deserve any of this."

"What if something happens to you, Nayla?" Carina asked.

"She won't kill me. And if I'm wrong, Rhijn can take everyone back to Idia." I stormed off toward my room to gather my weapons.

"Nayla," Rhijn scolded, chasing me down the hall. "You're being rash. You can't just race halfway across the continent without a plan. We need to think about this logically."

I spun, shoving a quivering finger into his chest. "You don't get to tell me what I can or can't do. And you have no idea what I'm capable of." My voice was an angry tremor and tears were bubbling up.

"Why are you so eager to run head-long into danger?" he shouted back, wiping his own red eyes. "Whatever it is you think you're going to do isn't helping. Think of your friend in there." He motioned to the room we'd come from.

"I am thinking of him," I cried, my shoulders jerking as my sobs tore through my restraint. "I *am* thinking of him." My voice was a whisper.

Rhijn flinched, pain streaking across his features, mirroring my own. He seemed to debate something as I bawled openly before him, then grabbed my wrist, jerking me into his embrace. He pulled me over to a wall, which he leaned on, widening his feet so I could more comfortably lean into his chest. His long arms wrapped all the way around my petite form. It would be so easy to lose myself in the safety of the cocoon he'd enveloped me in, I thought as I buried myself in his chest and cried.

I was feeling shame for the decisions I'd made and self-pity that I hadn't been able to fix this yet. Makers, I was pathetic. I needed to figure out how to make Emerson stop. There wasn't a part of her hidden deep that was redeemable. I'd already exhausted that notion. But I could trick her. I'd done that before. And she had a soft spot for me. I'd use that to our advantage.

I pushed back out of Rhijn's embrace. "You're really annoying, you know that?"

His chest rumbled as he cocked his head to the side, watching me. Light blue, red rimmed eyes traced from my swollen ones, down my tear-stained cheeks, to my lips. His mouth cracked and my stomach fluttered, my lower core clenching. We'd bonded over our grief before. He brought his gaze up to meet mine, and my breath caught. The way he looked at me was hard to take, as if he could penetrate me with a glance. He grabbed my wrist and put his thumb over my pulse. It thrashed against his thumb, and he closed his eyes, throwing his head back against the chilly stones, absorbing the sensation. Damn, he was sexy, leaning against the wall like that with me in between his legs. We could get lost in this moment, carried away. I could drag him to my room and we could do things that would make us forget about the crumbling world around us like we did before. The temptation loomed.

Control yourself.

I wrestled with my wildly beating heart until it slowed to a calmer thud. Rhijn exhaled a deep breath and opened his eyes, dropping my wrist. I stepped back, and he pressed away from the wall. The tone of his look changed, warmed. As if he'd been waiting to see what I'd do and approved of my choice.

He cleared his throat, but his voice was still low when he spoke. "We should be able to create a portal from our location to Seabrook. We'll go in the morning. We can see what Emerson wants and be ready to depart before she can strike. We'll dose before we go so her creatures can't block us from our power."

I nodded.

"Good. Well, let's get some sleep and we'll talk to Seeley and Carina in the morning and come up with a precise plan. Okay?"

"Okay, sure." I let myself into my room. I paced the floor until I could see the second moon rising, every third glance was to the pile of discarded blades on the writing desk in the corner. I sighed, running my fingers through my hair. My uselessness was grating on my own nerves. Creating more antidote wasn't enough.

A lick of energy sweeping through the room caught my attention. I spun toward the opening door, and I knew a delighted glint lit my eyes.

Malik's short hair was windblown and his sharply angled brows hooded his deep-set eyes which were full of vengeance. I saw a glimpse of the male who everyone believed him to be, as his dark shadows curled around him.

He leaned against the door and crossed one foot over the other, smoothing out the black traveling jacket he wore. "Care to have an adventure?" he asked, eyebrows arching over murderous eyes.

"Thank the Makers!" I ran up to him and threw my arms around his neck. I squinted up at him when I finally released him from my hold. "Does Seeley know you're here?"

Malik gave a dark chuckle. "Not yet. I just got here, and I figured he'd demand to go, but it's too dangerous."

"But not for us?" I gave him a conspiratorial shrug as I tilted my head, frowning.

"Never." Malik winked. The male really was my brother. We had that similar thread in us that bound us together despite what had happened in Monterra.

"How did you know?" I stuttered.

"We got the same letter in Eastdow yesterday. I took the ferry this morning, then raced here as fast as I could." Malik's fingers tapped anxiously on his leg as he searched the room. "Meethra's here?"

I stopped strapping weapons to my body and I looked out the window. "Well, she was earlier. Not sure where she is at the moment."

Malik pressed his lips together. "She wasn't at Eastdow when I left. I was hoping she'd tag along. Her power would be useful with the guards. Do you have a dose?"

I patted the carrying case Carina had given us. Malik pulled out one of his own and uncorked it. "Bottom's up?"

We held each other's sly gaze as we tipped the vial of dark powder into our mouths, swishing, then swallowing. I could feel the moment it took effect, then stuffed my hand in my shirt pocket fetching the ember. I opened the cloth I carried it in and touched my finger to it, letting its power crawl up my arm.

"Since I've been to the prisons, I should be able to get us there easily."

"Going somewhere?" an ethereal voice sounded.

"You have impeccable timing, godfly," Malik said, the corner of his mouth lifting as he observed the being who'd just flown in the window. "Care to join us? We're going to instigate a prison break in Seabrook. Emerson has threatened Seeley's parents."

Meethra's tiny head darted back and forth between my half-brother and I. Her dainty shoulders rising in resignation. "I suppose you won't be able to get into too much trouble if I'm there. Let's go knock out some guards." Her wings flapped eagerly as I whipped a lasso of dark power around us.

CHAPTER TWENTY-FIVE

As soon as our boots struck the sandstone floor of the Seabrook prison, Meethra zipped toward the nearest body and dusted them. The cheep of one of Emerson's creatures bounced off the walls and the monster came into view. I locked onto its essence and did enough damage changing its makeup that it wouldn't survive, but was careful not to waste my energy. The animal thudded lifeless to the floor. In the time I'd done that, Meethra had rendered another guard unconscious and Malik had swiped the keys from his limp body.

"Off to a good start I see." I surveyed the room where we landed. It was the anteroom right outside the entrance to the prisons. "Let's make this quick."

Malik's power radiated from his body like the fog slid across the arch, slipping under the locked doorway. "There's quite a few Skyborne in there. So many I can't distinguish friend from foe," he whispered.

I held up my hand. "Meethra, stay close. Worst case I have to get us out of here really quick."

Dark shadows drew around us and Malik slipped the key into the door. The hinges whined as it swung open and the three of us slipped into the room. The scent of waste hit my nostrils and I almost gagged. I eyed Malik, who was also cringing at the conditions of the prison. "We'll just have to check each cell until we find them."

Malik nodded and we made our way, letting Meethra's light illuminate the dark corridors. Several prisoners rose, and pressed their faces against the iron of their cages. Their eyes widened as they passed, and I pressed a finger to my lips urging them to keep silent. We'd made it halfway through the prison when we came across a male standing against the bars still wearing what looked to be rumpled military regalia.

"Malik," the male hissed.

He froze and turned toward the cell the sounds had come from. Malik had been doing a good job of making his assessment with his power then moving onto the next cell, not looking at the individual inside it. I couldn't help myself though and my heart squeezed each time the flicker of hope went out as we passed by their cells. Logically, I knew we needed to focus on what we came here to do. We couldn't save all of them or we'd risk getting caught.

"They're not here," the officer whispered.

Shit. That complicated things.

"Where are they?" Malik asked in an equally hushed tone.

"I don't know where they're being held, but the rumor is they're still alive."

"You commanded the Seabrook forces, right?" Malik asked the male, who nodded in response.

My wheels were turning and Malik seemed to have come to the same conclusion I had.

"Are you strong enough to travel, fight if needed?" Malik eyed the male in a way that might intimidate the truth out of someone. My gut told me this was a bad idea.

"I am." His voice was solid, like a stone wall, as he raised to his full height showing his resilience.

Malik tried the key in the lock, but it wasn't the right one. I didn't hesitate, wrapping my hand around the lock. A few moments and shards of metal were all that was left in my palm. The commander stepped out and I offered him a blade.

"Come, I want to search the rest of the cells in case you're wrong." Meethra and I started walking forward not waiting for them to follow, but not before I caught a look of irritation from the commander.

"What's your name?" Malik whispered to the man.

"Commander Braggs, sir."

Malik must have made an acknowledgement because the male didn't speak further. We finished our sweep of the cells and as he'd suggested Femi and Alrun weren't there. I wracked my brain trying to understand where Emerson might be holding them.

"Told you," Braggs grumbled when he saw we came to his same conclusion.

"Where could they be?" I searched Malik's face which was screwed up in thought.

Meethra's light pulsed. "I could fly outside and see if I could get a sense of…" she trailed off.

"A sense of what?" Malik pushed.

"Pain. I was going to say pain, because I don't know their essence, but if I felt pain, I could find it, and that may lead to them."

We were in the deepest part of the prison. I didn't know how much longer we had before someone discovered the two slack guards and the dead monster. "I don't know, Meethra. It's too dangerous with Emerson's creatures roaming around."

I pressed the heel of my hands into my eyes and rubbed. "What do we do?"

"I have an idea. Maybe, Emerson's kept them sequestered to their rooms? We could try them, but they're a good distance from here. Could you take us there?"

"And take all six of us back?" I shook my head. "Doubtful."

"I'll subdue you if you get power crazy."

An image of the horror on Malik's face when I'd sunk my blade into his stomach flashed through my mind. "Remember what happened last time?" I gave him a pointed glance, then gestured at his abdomen.

"We have to try," he demanded. "I'll stop you; I promise."

The commander was following our conversation back and forth, clearly confused about the piece of information he was missing, and the veins in Malik's forehead and neck were protruding more prominently than before. The urgency to get to Seeley's parents was weighing on him.

I put my hand on his forearm. "I can do it. Let's do it, okay? You'll have to explain the layout and be quick. I'll get us as close as I can."

My nerves were vibrating through me and I was doing what I could to stop myself from fidgeting. Meethra moved to the center of the three of us so I could see Malik's hands as he described the wing of Seabrook's keep where Femi and Alrun resided. Searching there was a long shot, but it wasn't a bad guess. Emerson was unpredictable, and keeping them there probably fed into some delusion she had.

"Okay, got it. Let's go."

I raised my hand, but not before a thwomp sounded followed by a groan. The commander sank to his knees, and a black and crimson hilted dagger protruded from the left side of his back. Malik spun in the direction the dagger hand came from, shoving me behind him as he moved. Meethra attached herself to my shoulder, and dimed herself as much as possible, but even with Malik's deepened shadows which made us blend in with the corner he'd tucked us into, she was giving away our location.

"Did you really think we'd be stupid enough to hide them in the prisons, brother? Oh, and hello, Nayla."

The sound of metal striking a flint pierced the silence and the fire in a nearby torch sprang to life. Darius stuffed the flint back into his pocket and launched the dagger using his power enhanced speed. I only had time to dull the tip before it struck Malik square in the chest, a blow aimed to kill. The shock of it threatened to drop me. Darius was going to kill his own brother.

A second later three creatures were behind Darius. He saw me look at them and narrowed his eyes in my direction. "I wouldn't do that if I were you."

"Where are Femi and Alrun, Darius?" I asked through gritted teeth. "Or have you had your head buried so far up Emerson's skirts you hadn't noticed she was a murderous psychopath?"

Malik's hand reached behind him, grabbing ahold of my hip steadying me. "Easy," he murmured so only I could hear.

"Emerson is the only one in this realm who's had the courage to do what someone's been needing to do for a long while. I have full confidence in her ability to get us to Idia and take control of that realm too. And I'll be the one by her side."

I tapped at the mental connection between Malik and I and felt it ease open. *Keep him talking.*

"You look like a male deluding yourself. Or did you discover how to be loyal?" Malik said.

I gave him my best sneer as I slowly moved my ember shrouded hand in the shadows. I studied Darius. I was ready to kill Emerson, but the fact that he, Malik and I were related to Darius complicated things for me. Or maybe Rhijn was rubbing off on me.

Darius huffed a grimy laugh. Just looking at him made me feel like I needed to clean myself. I rolled my shoulders back at the thought as the chills worked their way down my spine.

"There isn't a force in this realm that can stop us. And soon, she'll have her and the ember." Darius's eyes moved from Malik to me. "Come, Nayla and I'll let our brother live." He nodded to the creatures flapping at his shoulder for emphasis.

Darius was too late in realizing what I'd done. The creatures were fast, but not enough to get to us before I closed the portal around us.

⁓

"Darius, is that you?" a sleepy feline voice flittered softly through the door separating Femi and Alrun's sitting room and the bedroom.

Well, that answers that question. They aren't here. I just need a few moments to gather my senses. Then I'll get us out of here. I thought it twice so both Meethra and Malik could hear and held tight to my awareness. I felt like the more I used my power, the more expansive it became and I had more time before I became power-sick from it. Tonight was definitely pushing that boundary further than I ever had before.

I gave a tight encouraging grin down to the commander who was clinging to life at our feet.

A single sconce was lit, faintly illuminating the room. For the space of a regent, it was unembellished, but comfortable looking, decorated with a simple mustard couch, a few canvas side chairs and some art of still life's on the walls. Exactly what I'd expect from the sensible ruler. The only thing it seemed Emerson had brought to the space was the cages which lined the walls.

A keening whine echoed across the room as the creatures became aware of our presence.

"Mother," a chorus of chirping erupted in the space.

This isn't good, Malik observed. *Can you distract her while I go check the other suites in this wing? She may be keeping them close.*

The door slammed open and Emerson strode through the doorway, tugging a burgundy satin robe around her. She rubbed her sable eyes with her knuckles, then covered a yawn, fanning out her claw tipped fingers, but not before Malik slipped through the door.

"No," she breathed when she caught sight of me and the expired commander at my feet and dropped her hands. Her large eyes blinked a few times and seeming to come to her senses she snapped her fingers. Seconds later, A1, her favorite pet was at her side flapping its translucent salamander wings in response. The firelight glinted off the iridescent scales along its back and its bulbous head bobbled as it waited for her command. She looked from us to the cages with eyes narrowed as if she couldn't decide her approach.

"Where's Darius?" Emerson held up a hand to still A1 who's jagged mouth was displaying eager needle-like teeth. It turned to her and made a frustrated sound jabbing the blade-like protrusions affixed to each of its appendages into the air in stabbing motions causing a grin to spread across Emerson's unpainted pink lips.

Good. She wanted to talk, which meant I wouldn't have to fight off A1 while Malik searched for Seeley's parents. "I left him in the prison. He's quite under your spell."

Emerson snorted. "Alive, I assume?"

"Where are Femi and Alrun?" I demanded.

She sighed. "I thought maybe you were coming to pay me the visit I requested. I know of your abilities, Nayla. I wasn't going to hide them somewhere you'd be able to whisk in and steal them away from me." Emerson laughed. "I'm not stupid."

"What do you want, Emerson?"

"I feel like I've been very clear about what I want. You... and the ember. My offer still stands. We could rule side-by-side. Think of what we could do—the fun we'd have. I know there is a part of you that is tempted by the idea." Emerson pulled her plump lower lip into her mouth as if it would lure me.

But I wasn't that female anymore. The accusation crawled across my skin like newly hatched spiders looking for a home. But there was no home for the idea and I wasn't tempted.

"You'll never rule Idia. I'll die before I let you and your monsters loose on that realm." My mind raced as I thought of how I could end her right here, right now. I could do it, maybe. But it would leave Malik to fend off A1 and possibly me if I lost control again. Darius was surely on his way here now. Then we'd have him to deal with. It wasn't possible. We needed to get back to Arborvale and regroup. I needed Rhijn—his power.

Emerson huffed a pout, and sauntered over to a bar cart and took the lid off a crystal decanter. She picked up the glass and swirled the brown liquid inside before pouring it between two glasses. "Drink?" she asked, holding one out, looking over her shoulder at me.

Shit. What was taking Malik so long? I glanced toward the door then back to her. "Sure." I strode forward and took the glass from her outstretched hand. Emerson leaned back against the cart raising a knee to rub the sole of her foot along her shin, which parted her robe exposing the creamy skin of her legs beneath. Before that might have worked, but I knew her now.

I walked a good distance from her and turned around taking a sip of the drink. "What do you want, Emerson?"

She ran a pointed nail down her décolletage and the burgundy satin trim of her robe. A sinful smile curled at the edge of her lips. "I think you know what I want."

"This isn't a game, Emerson," I bit back at her. My blood was heating and not in the way it had the first time I'd met her.

"I didn't say it was," she said, frowning. Emerson sighed, taking a long drink, then licking her lips as she threw the empty cup in the fireplace. It crashed and flared as the flames consumed the alcohol.

"Mother," the anxious caged creatures chimed and I felt a fearful Meethra tuck deeper into my pocket.

It was amazing that Emerson had no fear standing before me. I didn't know if she thought she could best me now, or didn't truly understand what I was capable of.

"What are you planning?" I pressed.

She tilted her head to the side, her eyes alight with her characteristic inquisitiveness. "You know you were right. Anya confessed that she'd known the entire time that Kymar wasn't going to make me his heir. I should have listened to you."

"You still can," I told her.

A dark chuckle rumbled from her throat. "So can you." A crazed look crossed her darkening gaze. "Join me or pay like Anya."

"What did you do to your mother, Emerson?" I swallowed the bile rising in my throat.

"Nothing, yet. She is very sorry though. She understands her mistake, I assure you. Just as you will. You should never have run from me. Rejected me. After everything I've done and am doing for this realm, it seems only your half-brother has any faith in me. It's really a pity."

Emerson raised her hands as she walked toward me. Her tall lithe form stood a few inches over me even with bare feet and she placed her hands on either side of my neck. I let her, confident I'd be able to shut her down, but curious to see what she'd do and needing to buy time. Energy licked through my body, enlivened by the female before me and I felt my pulse quicken. She was using her healing ability to manage the sensations of my body. I kept my ember shrouded hand behind my back, hoping Malik would return soon.

I gritted my teeth as I stared down at the enemy before me. I'd kill her once Malik got back. Emerson panted as I felt my blood warm under her ministrations, then I felt my core clench as the heat slid lower. I knew horror flashed across my eyes because it was reflected in the manic pleasure of hers. She was using her power to affect me physically and it quickly went from the warm arousal she'd intended to hot loathing.

I shot my free arm out connecting with Emerson's chest and she flew across the room, crashing into the couch, a sickening crunch sounding. She adjusted her shoulders seeming to relieve an injury from the impact and arched her back, a wicked chuckle flitting from her lips. "You're too easy. Darius and I are going to have so much fun with you," she said, wiping a trickle of blood from the corner of her mouth.

"There is something seriously wrong with you," I hissed through gritted teeth as I stormed toward the door. A1 darted toward me, but I shot a blast of power which sent it tumbling through the air in the opposite direction. Emerson sprung to her feet chasing the trajectory of her favorite creature.

We need to go, Meethra pleaded from the safety of my pocket.

I'm not leaving Malik, I thought for her, hesitating. I needed to find him. I'd fought Emerson before and we'd been too evenly matched. She fought like a snake and my power was already edging on depleted. I'd have to kill her another day. Desperately, I darted for the door. Before I got there, it crashed open and the three creatures that had been with Darius zipped in behind him. His eyes were glassy and absolutely murderous as they darted from me to Emerson. Another creature came forward with Malik in tow, a daggered appendage aimed at his throat. Tiny slices were dashed across his forehead and cheeks.

When I say, you know what to do. Malik gave a barely perceptible gesture to the creature nearest him and I nodded.

A wave of dizziness caused me to stumble, but I righted myself knowing one error could mean Malik's death. His shadows formed in a snap and created a tight wall of darkness around the creatures streaking toward me on Darius's command. It disoriented them just enough.

I threw my power out and deconstructed the creature that was nearest Malik which I'd had a lock on. *Now, Nayla.* Malik's commanding voice in my mind was like a cymbal clanging, as I felt his arms go around my waist.

I didn't hesitate. I'd never whipped the dark circle so fast. I gave one last glare toward a rage-filled Emerson, and we fell.

"I should have known you were a part of this, Malik Dsiban."

I heard Seeley's scolding voice before I saw him.

I think we're in trouble, Malik thought, winking at me even as he staggered across the room to his partner.

Seeley's throat bobbed as a look of love replaced the anger. Then concern. The creatures had managed a few extra gashes across Malik's body and he was seeping blood, but none of the injuries were life threatening.

The early morning rays of the light star were streaming in through a window in Carina's sitting room, and she had stopped her pacing. She quickly made an assessment of Malik's injuries, then me in my hazy state. "Balene's too far, I'll go get Rhijn. You deal with her," she commanded Seeley. My sister's pale blue skirts swished as she stormed from the room. She tied her cropped hair back at the base of her neck as she went.

Seeley went and picked up a vase from a side table looking from me to Malik, a question in his eye. I wasn't well, but it wasn't like before. I was less hazy than I expected, and apparently Malik had told Seeley what I'd done. Of course, he had.

"She's fine, Seeley," Malik grunted. "Right, Nayla, you're fine?"

"I'm in control," I assured them, though I had to grip onto the couch to prevent myself from tumbling backward. Seeley squinted, but lowered the vase, and ushered Malik to one of the four chairs which sat around the table we'd originally met with Carina at.

Moments later the towering Skyborne entered on her heels and they both were towing towels and rags which must have been pilfered from his room. Rhijn shot me a glare before kneeling beside Malik.

I cocked my head as I watched him work, not able to remember why I had ever been so afraid of the male. I wanted to reach down and pull the strands of unbound blond hair out of his face, but I was afraid I'd topple over on top of him. It was silly to think I'd have been drowned in waves of pleasure at his touch like in my dreams. Or that we'd form some sort of unbreakable connection. And maybe he had piqued my interest. And drawn me to him in a way I'd never exper—

Nayla, I can hear you.

I whipped my head toward Meethra who'd been hiding in my pocket, my eyes straining as they peeled back. My stomach flipped as I casually turned back to Rhijn. He was staring up at me as if my thoughts had summoned him as well. Oh Makers. Surely, he hadn't heard all that.

Just me, I think. And you should probably go lie down, Meethra commanded into my mind.

Relief replaced the rising embarrassment and I wiped my clammy hands across my pants. My real urge was to wrap my long hair around my face so I could escape behind its shadow.

As if still sensing my thoughts, Meethra was hovering in front of my face, trying to keep my attention. Her yellow hand tapped me on the nose. *Come,* she urged, *and stop thinking… please.* Her appendages covered her ears and she rattled her head.

Carina's grip on my elbow guided me over to the couch which sat in the center of the room. "Here, lie back. We'll observe you for a bit, to make sure you're okay."

Hours later strong arms picked me up and my head lulled before falling against a firm chest. The smell of sea salt and sandalwood drifted into my nostrils and I relaxed against the warm sensation that reminded me of the sun on my skin when we were on the Leeward Isle in Idia.

"*Very* impulsive," Rhijn said under his breath.

I opened my eyes and fluttered my lashes at the male carrying me. "You like it." When the corner of his mouth jerked up, my heart skipped. I buried my head into Rhijn's chest to hide my flush as he carried me the rest of the way to my room. He gently placed me on the bed, and turned to leave when he was sure I wasn't planning to disappear.

"You need to rest, and next time you decide to do something like that, please come get me." Rhijn held the door open for a moment, a reluctant crease dug into his forehead while he waited on me to acquiesce. He didn't scold though.

Don't go. I almost blurted out the words. But I said, "Okay," instead.

Rhijn closed the door and I turned and stuffed my face into the pillow, trying to shut out my emotions still swirling in the aftermath of the night.

CHAPTER TWENTY-SIX

I WAS BECOMING MORE connected to the power that surrounds us. Better at tapping into the void. This was the quickest I'd ever recovered and we were ready to make another attempt at Seeley's parents the following day, though Seeley had convinced us to use a different approach this time. And he demanded to go with us as Malik had feared.

I decided to go first again. Rhijn would hold his position, ready to protect us or whip us out of danger at a moment's notice. Apparently, he could create the portal far more quickly than he'd seen me do it, though he'd only lassoed it around creatures in Idia to return them to their homes before. And based on how many times I'd transported us the night prior, no one wanted to rely on that. I'd get us there, then Rhijn would take over.

I connected the dark circle with no fanfare. All four of us were tired and tense, afraid of what would await us once we reached Seabrook. Especially considering how we'd left things. But at least we knew they were alive.

We landed right where I'd planned, in the middle of the square, right outside the sandstone keep's outer wall. The open-air square was vacant, the vendors and musicians I'd admired my first time here absent. The Skyborne in Seabrook must have fled or been imprisoned. Hopefully that was the extent of it, I thought, scanning the expansive space for any sign of a skirmish.

A smear of dried blood was near the stairs that led to the entrance of the keep, along with several dark rust puddled stains. I imagined Emerson calmly walking up to the main entrance of the Regent's home and ordering A1 and her other creatures to slit the throat of the two guards usually stationed at the large wooden doors without a second thought. She'd had no qualms over performing experiments on children if it had meant succeeding in her work. Their lives would mean nothing to her.

There was shouting from above. My eyes traced the sound. A sentry clad in Monterra colors stood on the landing where Conall and I had danced.

A shield encapsulated us. *Rhijn's.*

There was shouting toward the interior of the building and we didn't have to wait long. She was expecting us. The click of heels resounded through the square and the svelte female I was oh too familiar with stepped across the veranda. She leaned over the edge, her pointed burgundy nails digging into the sandstone parapet which I saw with my enhanced vision. Emerson seemed to be much more stable today than she had been last night.

"Dose them," she commanded A1. The peach-colored creatures beat pairs of waxy salamander wings, eager to obey.

"Mother," A1 squeaked, then others joined him, darting toward where we stood, spear-like pincers on the ends of their appendages taking precise aim. They were unfathomably fast, even by our power enhanced standards and I checked Rhijn's slack jawed reaction at his first glimpse of them. "Mother, Mother," the creatures squealed in frustration as they jabbed against his invisible barrier protecting us. Unable to get through the boundary, they began circling above us and a dark powder fell.

It was like the translucent substance the godflies emitted, which could put other beings to sleep and alter memories. It was one of the reasons she'd use that species to interbreed creating her creatures, but instead of putting Skyborne to sleep, it would obstruct the connection all Skyborne had with the energy surrounding us.

The fine dust filtered through Rhijn's shield, the particles slipping between the vibrating air protecting us with ease. It was the first limitation of the shields we'd encountered. That and the focus they took to keep intact.

Emerson waited, smoothing the breezy skirts she wore, which I recognized as Femi's. The red streaks in her chestnut hair caught the rays from the light star high overhead. She saw me noting her attire.

"You'd look ravishing in these clothes, Nayla," she yelled across the distance, twirling so the skirts glided around her displaying the pale skin beneath.

"I do," I answered. Femi had lent me some of the attire worn by the females in Seabrook, and after I'd gotten used to it, I found I liked the feminine pieces that strategically crisscrossed and flowed over my figure. I glanced up to see one of A1's siblings ricochet off the dome protecting us.

Emerson gave a sultry laugh. "You're not as stupid as I thought you were," she said when she realized we'd taken the antidote before we'd arrived, and her creature's powder was having no effect.

"You don't think I'm stupid, Emerson. And I'm here, *again*. You need to release Femi and Alrun like you promised."

From behind her, several of her soldiers prodded two figures out on the deck.

"You've been to Idia?" she asked, eyeing Rhijn. Her voice was silken, light and hopeful like last night never happened "I was hoping we'd have more time to chat." She sighed wistfully. "But you had to leave so soon. I've punished Darius for his overreach. He won't be interrupting us today." She was speaking to me, but her eyes were glued to Rhijn.

"What do you want?" I repeated, planting my feet. I noticed my urge was to step in front of him, like he had when Uden had approached me. *Strange.*

The captive figures came into view. It was Femi and Alrun. Seeley whimpered behind me and I saw them take note of his presence. They were bound and gagged, but I didn't detect any other obvious signs of abuse.

"I told you I just want to talk. I want to know about Idia. I want to hear about your adventures. Won't you join me for another drink? I promise I'll let your other friends go free," she said sweetly, batting her lashes as if it would seduce me.

"You told me if I came, you'd release Femi," I reminded her. "I'm here."

The letter hadn't mentioned Alrun at all, but I was hopeful we'd get him back, too. Emerson just stood there with her arms crossed over her chest.

"I'll come with you if you take your army back to Monterra and leave these Skyborne alone. Evacuate Sundale too. I promise," I bartered. "That's what you want, isn't it, Emerson?" I hoped that was enough. She still held out hope she could use me, and more importantly the ember, to transport her and her creatures to Idia. I wouldn't do that, which she didn't need to know yet. But I would go with her—to save my friends. I'd made the decision last night while I tossed and turned. And while I distracted her, Rhijn could see the willing Skyborne of this realm back to Idia.

Rhijn's hand gripped my elbow as if he understood what I was planning. What I hadn't told him. I shook it off.

Emerson caught the movement. "Already on to another lover?" she seethed, perceiving what Rhijn's possessive touch meant. "You really are a slut."

Shit.

"Seeley, who do you love more?" she said, addressing the jovial male behind me. "Your *mother*—" Emerson gestured to Femi. "—or your *father*?" she crooned, running a pointed nail across Alrun's pigmentless chin.

I knew Seeley would try to remain as passive as possible, but he was terrible at shielding his emotions. They just blew off him in gusts.

"Ah, a mother's son. Very well." She gestured to the soldier to bring Femi forward. "Nayla, you've made a mistake, toying with my feelings like this. Your mistakes have consequences. But soon, you will learn," she said. "Then you will take us to Idia."

"She is *unhinged.* How did you ever?" Malik was giving me shit I supposed I deserved after what had happened in the aftermath of it all.

I groaned. "Do you have to bring that up?"

"Emerson, you said you'd let her go," Seeley cried, and fell into Malik's arms.

"I didn't specify if she'd be breathing," she hissed, grabbing Femi's bicep, digging her claws in so hard blood sprouted from the obsidian skin where the points touched.

Emerson was still for a moment. My eyes widened as I realized what she intended. Femi sagged in the soldier's grip. Alrun was thrashing, trying to free himself to reach his wife.

"No!" I screamed. "Stop it." I ran for the doors, but Rhijn pulled me back.

"You can't, Nayla," Malik chided. I struggled against Rhijn's damnable grip.

"Let me go," I demanded. "Emerson, please!"

"I thought I'd enjoy hearing my name as a plea on your lips once again. But I'm no one's scraps." Emerson's grip on Femi tightened, and she held her other hand up to the side of Femi's head. Blood trickled out of Femi's nostrils. If Rhijn hadn't touched me, my plan might have worked. But it had set Emerson off.

I had seconds before it would be too late. I shot my power out. The guard holding Femi collapsed. She fell with him, which paused Emerson momentarily.

"Shit," Rhijn said, reaching into his shirt pocket.

"She's killing her," I shouted, tossing another hand up, focusing my power. I understood why Conall did it then—it was more a visualization thing. I took out Alrun's guard then. Others replaced them, and moved behind their bodies, so my senses would become distorted by their prisoners' forms.

I whipped my gaze to Emerson, who was once again lifting her hands to Femi, teeth bared.

I focused my power on her, trying to deconstruct her very being. But she turned her own power against mine, healing herself as quickly as I tore her apart. It went on for long moments, this battle of power and wills between us. It shouldn't have been possible. *She's using the void.* It's how she'd been able to do what she did with the creatures. The revelation shook me to my core.

"Snap her neck and throw her over," Emerson screeched through gritted teeth.

In a flash, Femi's head twisted to the side, and a sickening pop echoed.

Seeley cried out as he watched his mother's limp form plummet from the second story of his home. Femi hit the ground with a thud.

Seeley tore free from Malik's embrace and ran to his mother. Arrows flew from archers I hadn't seen. I sprinted forward, catching up with Seeley, throwing a shield around us both. I was a second too late. Fire laced up my thigh, and I looked to see an arrow had made it inside the shield and was buried deep in my flesh. Malik was on our heels, shielded by Rhijn. We reached Femi, but she was gone.

Seeley draped himself over her lifeless body, sobbing. Arrows rained down, creatures smashed into the vibrating wall of air and Alrun's anguished screams echoed across the courtyard. It was pure chaos outside the shield.

We need to bring Femi's body back with us, I thought, prying at Malik and I's mental connection, hoping he'd hear me. I wrenched Seeley back so Malik could gather Femi in his arms.

"Rhijn, I've got the shield. Get us out of here," I rasped.

His shield lowered. Then a blinding light whipped around us and we were falling.

"That stupid bitch," I said, as I hobbled across the modestly decorated sitting room, which had become our base of operations in Arborvale. Carina stood wide-eyed as I dripped blood across carpets still soiled from Malik's injuries the night before.

Malik carried Femi over to the couch and laid her down gently.

"Heal her," Seeley cried, as he kneeled beside his mother. "Somebody, do something."

He darted his anxious stare up at us, confused as to why we were ignoring his desperate pleas. Then he faced Malik.

Malik shook his head, kneeling beside him, and Seeley collapsed into his partner's arms. They were distraught, but I was livid. Femi had been the one Skyborne in this Maker's forsaken realm who'd tried to do better for the citizens she was a steward of. I'd only known her for a short time, but that was all it took for her to earn my unwavering respect. Her death would hang over me like a cloud, maybe until it was my turn to expire from this realm.

Not killing Emerson was a mistake I'd never make again.

"Nayla, come, you're bleeding." Carina ushered me to a chair at the far end of the room, trying to give Malik and Seeley privacy.

The arrow still protruded from my thigh. I slumped into the chair and grabbed the fabric around the wound, tearing it away. "Will someone yank this damn thing out of my leg and heal me?" I said to no one in particular. I barely contained the rage that was boiling inside me.

Rhijn looked at Carina. "It hasn't hit anything vital that I can sense. And it's too shallow to push through without greater risk." He was ashen as he gripped the arrow's shaft. "It's a broadhead," he said, warning me.

"Trust me, I can feel what it is," I bit out, knowing exactly how much it was going to hurt when he pulled out the arrow, which was designed to shred the flesh it was embedded into. I just prayed I wouldn't pass out.

A healing energy bled into my leg and the pain lessened. He was numbing my senses. He regarded me, and I nodded.

Rhijn pulled the arrow upward in one quick and decisive stroke. I rocked back in the chair on a scream, and Carina gripped my shoulders from behind to steady me. Rhijn discarded the bloody arrow and hovered his palms over the fresh wound. I sucked in quick breaths as he worked.

Carina must have requested supplies at some point and she was dabbing the sweat from my brow with a soft cloth. Soon, there was only a pink welt where the arrow had pierced my flesh. Rhijn's healing was getting better.

I waved Rhijn off and stood, testing my leg. It was sufficient, and I didn't want Rhijn wasting any more of his energy. I still had something I needed him to do.

I walked over to Seeley and fell to my knees before him. "I am so very sorry, Seeley. I will do everything in my power to avenge your mother. She deserved so much more than this."

Seeley sniffed, putting his hands on my shoulders. "I *know* you will."

I was far from absolved. We sat with Seeley in his grief for a long time. Though everything in me wanted to fight, I knew I needed to be there for my friend. Even if there was nothing any of us could say.

Eventually, Rhijn got up and added logs to the fire and we watched Malik take such care lifting Femi. He took her from the room led by Carina. I wanted to follow, but I sensed Seeley needed a moment alone with Malik and his mother before they prepared her body.

A while later Carina stormed back into the room. "What are you going to do?" The urgency in my sister's eyes mirrored my own. Emerson had killed another Regent. Carina wanted retribution and I didn't need her compulsion to agree.

"We'll go to Eastdow. There should be enough antidote now. You need to start shipping the crates of antidote to the army immediately. Spread the word to anyone loyal in Sundale and Seabrook of Femi's death. Tell them they're to prepare to march on Emerson. I'd hoped it wouldn't come to this, but they should rally in Eastdow ready to fight. Meethra, you and the godflies stay and help Carina organize the groups of refugees. As soon as we've defeated Emerson, we'll be back ready to transport the first groups to Idia."

Meethra flitted about, nodding vigorously.

"Consider it done," Carina said. She would know how to use the news of the beloved Regent's death to garner support for our cause.

I turned to Rhijn who was watching our exchange. "You coming?"

A somber grin, almost a wince, dashed across his handsome face, and he took off toward his room.

∽

I decided it was worth testing our limits and Rhijn had agreed to portal to Eastdow. It worked. He was a little loopy, and I'd suggested he get some rest, but he promised he was fine.

Torin, the male who we'd pretended was my father for ten long years, sat across from me. We'd exchanged a few terse words, but he was trying to be civil for his son. I still couldn't understand his animosity toward me. I'd done everything they'd asked of me, though there hadn't truly been another choice.

"Seabrook is on the exact opposite side of the continent. It will take weeks or more to move an army this size," Torin argued.

"She wants to go through the Swath," Conall said, pointing to the center of the map laid out before us.

"No, no, no. That's not what she wants," Rhijn chimed in. "She wants for her and I to use our power together and sweep the entire army onto this plain right here," he slurred, jabbing a finger into an empty patch of land between the traveler's inn and the city.

"*She* is sitting right here and can speak for herself," I said.

Rhijn raised an eyebrow at me. His grin was lazy—seductive and I repressed an eye roll.

"But, yes, that last idea is what *she* is thinking," I admitted.

"Told you," Rhijn said, staring down a bristling Conall.

Sleep. Rhijn and I were exhausted, and we needed rest if we were to be effective in the coming week.

"Conall, we'll catch up tomorrow, okay? I'll show Rhijn to his room."

"I'll have an attendant do it," Conall piped up.

"It's two doors down from mine," I said, not in the mood for that nonsense. I got up and urged the towering Idian to follow.

"You just wanted to get me alone," Rhijn hummed, when we got to a dark corridor in the residential section of the keep which had been my home from eighteen to twenty-eight.

Rhijn grabbed me around the waist, pushing me against a wall, and ran his nimble fingers down my thighs, one which was still caked in my blood.

"Rhijn, what are you doing?" I breathed, already reacting to his touch. Heat blossomed in each place his hands covered my body, so unlike whatever Emerson had been trying to do to me the night before.

"Nothing we both don't want," he laughed, then grabbed my hand, dragging me further down the hallway. I directed him to the room he'd been assigned.

He pulled me in and closed the door, pressing me back against it, planting toe curling kisses along my neck and jaw as he untucked my shirt.

I grabbed his hands, stopping him. He just stared at me, confused, then leaned down, pressing his lips to mine. Instinctively, I kissed him back, and he moaned, encouraged.

"See, you *do* want. You'll always want," he said, threading his fingers through my hair as he cupped the back of my head.

I pulled away. "Rhijn, you're drunk," I said.

"No, I've had nothing to drink. Not."

Kiss.

"One."

Kiss.

"Single."

Kiss.

"Drop."

He followed that last word up with a deep languid kiss and I sighed into his mouth.

Control yourself.

It wasn't even me this time, though. He'd regret this in the morning if I allowed it to continue and I'd come to respect him enough not to permit that to happen. I mean, I respected anyone enough not to allow that to happen, so it wasn't like he was special.

I pushed him away, spinning so he couldn't grab me. He raked a hand through his pale curtain of hair. I really didn't have enough willpower for this.

"You still don't want me?" he asked. The male looked so forlorn with pent up need.

"Oh, I want you all right," I told him.

His eyes lit. "Then what's the problem?" he asked, a silly grin on his face as he came toward me once again.

I held up a hand to push him away. "*You* don't want *me*," I answered. That stopped him short. He opened his mouth to argue, but I slipped out the door.

The release I gave myself that night while I soaked in the tub in my old room wasn't enough. Just seeing that uninhibited, hungry look in Rhijn's eyes set me ablaze. A fire I couldn't seem to put out.

I huffed as I lay there in my old bed, trying to decide what to do.

⁓

The next morning, I awoke to a familiar voice calling my name through the closed door between the bedroom and the sitting area.

I flew up out of bed. "Felicia!"

She met me at the door and I threw my arms around her before she protested. Felicia, my longtime attendant, looked the same as she always did, full, rosy cheeks, and strawberry hair in a loose bun at the base of her neck. Meethra, our godfly friend, had mentioned that Felicia was still working at the keep in Eastdow. After Conall had told me she'd helped him devise a plan for Malik and I to escape before Torin could execute us, I'd worried about her safety. Conall had assured me she'd be fine.

As she squirmed in my tight embrace, I was thankful no one else had been hurt because of me. Especially Felicia.

"Okay, that's enough of that. Let's have a look at you." She stepped back and studied me. I realized this was the first time she was getting a good look at the true visage of the female who she'd taken care of all those years. She'd always seen the shift I used of Vera, the regent's deceased daughter, but had come to understand I wasn't her over the years, because she'd catch my slip ups from time to time.

"You've had quite the adventure," Felicia said.

"And it's not finished yet," I told her.

She smiled warmly and went into the bathroom, and sighed loudly at the mess I'd made the night before. My bloody clothes were in a heap beside the still full tub, and open jars of creams and scrubs littered the wooden table next to it.

"Sorry!" I sheepishly called.

By the time she'd tidied up and came into the room, I changed into the Eastdow attire I was so familiar with, which she had dropped on the bed. I had enjoyed the different clothing I'd worn with each new place I'd visited, but these utilitarian clothes felt right. Mostly because I knew I could fight in them. And I was in the mood for a fight.

"Now that you're ready, I should tell you that there is a brooding male waiting in the corridor for you."

I smiled, hopefully. "Conall?"

"No, the Idian. Do they all look like him?" she asked. A blush crept across her cheeks.

I bent over, laughing. "Oh Felicia. If only."

∾

"Hey, can I talk to you for a minute?" a hushed voice said as soon as I stepped out of my room.

"How long have you been out here?" I asked him. I raised my eyebrows, waiting.

"Not long," he said.

I sensed he was lying. "You could have knocked."

"I didn't want to disturb you."

"You didn't think lurking outside my door would disturb me, but you thought knocking would?"

"That's not what I meant."

"Rhijn, what do you want?" I asked, urging him to get to the point.

"I, umm, I guess I'm sorry. I'm embarrassed to have acted that way," he said, the muscles in his jaw flexing as he gritted out the apology. "I shouldn't have come onto you like that."

I knew it. I had known it, but it stung. This was bullshit. How dare he apologize for giving into what he was feeling—which was *me*.

I grazed my hand across his defined jaw, then brushed a thumb over his stunned mouth, thinking of what those smooth lips felt like pressed against mine. I wouldn't let him make me feel guilty for enjoying his kiss or what we'd shared before. "Nothing to forgive."

I turned and left him in the hallway.

CHAPTER TWENTY-SEVEN

"CONALL, WAIT UP!" I called, nudging my speckled blonde mare into a canter down the well-worn dirt road that led to the main training grounds and military barracks.

"Hey, there you are," he said, slowing his mount to let me catch up. "I'm going to check on the distributions of the antidote. The first batch arrived from Arborvale this morning."

It had been two weeks since we arrived in Eastdow. I was eager to move on Seabrook sooner, but Conall was right. We wouldn't stand a chance without the antidote being distributed and any stragglers willing to fight gathered.

Balene had tested the antidote and determined it would keep our channels open for over a full day before we'd need another dose. Each soldier would receive two doses. One for as soon as we sighted Emerson's creatures, and one in case this skirmish went on longer than we hoped.

"Jude is already there. She's been teaching the soldiers some new fighting techniques she's invented," Conall said.

"Of course, she is." Though the weight of what we were about to do hung heavy over me, I was happy to see my sisters in positions they were thriving in.

The barracks were long, rectangular, one-story buildings constructed from ivory hewn stone extracted from the surrounding mountains. Most of the soldiers only spent time in them for the scheduled training they did, but lived at home with their families for the rest of the year. Now they were being occupied full time, and they had thrown additional temporary tent structures up to house the overflow of soldiers.

The barracks were positioned so that the center of each grouping was a square training area. The land coming down from the old range undulated gently, so our ancestors had flattened it so the land was suitable for building this facility. Elsewhere in Eastdow, the buildings and roads were constructed more in harmony with the landscape, which made the view of the alabaster city from lower down in the valley quite breathtaking.

We came upon Jude as she flipped a disarmed female over her slight shoulder and fell upon her, bringing a knife to her throat. Jude had chopped her coal hair even shorter than the last time I'd seen it and she had it pinned back with several clips. She didn't wear a stitch of make-up and her black training garb was plastered to her petite, yet fit form. I made a mental note to get myself a set. As her long black eyelashes blinked while she instructed, I thought she looked more like a stealthy mountain cat than a female. All she needed was whiskers and a tail.

"Did you see what I did with my feet there?" she asked the soldier as she helped her up. "If you can leverage your weight and strike at the most sensitive spots, your opponent's size really doesn't matter," she instructed.

The stocky female nodded appreciatively, joining the other soldiers lined up for instruction.

Jude turned to the audience surrounding her. "Pair off, and practice what I showed you."

"Think you can beat me?" I called to her.

Jude spun around. "Nayla!" The female transformed from the sober drill leader to my still innocent younger sister. Her eyes were bright as we embraced.

"You would spar with me?" she asked, as if awed, dancing from foot to foot.

"Of course," I said. "I love a good fight, and based on the brawl you and Conall had, I'm sure you'll deliver."

And it was exactly what I needed. Everything in me was screaming for an outlet for my aggression. I suspected until Emerson was dead and we were moving Skyborne to Idia, it wouldn't be enough. Still, the exercise eased the worst of my tension. And it would be a good warmup for what was ahead of us in the coming days.

I selected two wooden long knives, and Jude picked up a small shield and a short sword. Around us, the pairs of trainees stopped to take in the spectacle of Jude and me sparing.

I couldn't help but smile. "Let's give them a show," I said to Jude and sunk into a fighting stance. The wide grin plastered across her face looked almost painful. She jostled her weapons excitedly, then lunged.

Makers, she was fast. The crowd gasped at the wooden sword which dusted off my sleeve as I jerked back before it could make solid contact. I'd not let her get that close again. She sprung forward, but I spun, cracking her in the back with my elbow. Just because she was my younger sister didn't mean I was going to go easy on her. She stumbled forward, regaining her balance a second later. Her smile had faded and a determined grimace replaced it. *Good.*

We carried on like that for a solid hour. She must have been training since the light star broke the horizon, and I could sense her energy was waning. I decided it would be fun to attempt that footwork technique she'd been training when I'd arrived, for the crowd, of course. Then I'd let her rest.

I darted forward, ducking beneath her wooden blade, and came up, hooking her shoulder with my arm and stepping in front of her. I yanked her toward my back, up and over. She thudded to the ground, giggling.

I held a hand down to her, which she took. She squeezed, then tugged me down, flipping me so I was on my back and she was straddling me with a knife she pulled from some hidden sheath pressed to my throat. I blinked up at her.

Jude, still straddling me, raised both hands to the air, pumping them. "Who's the victor now?" Her soldiers whooped from the sidelines. She crawled to her feet, wisely letting me help myself up. "Lesson?" she asked the onlookers.

"Never let your guard down," a smooth tenor answered. I turned to see Rhijn casually leaning against a barrack, clapping slowly. He was smirking in my direction.

I brushed the loose hairs out of my face and flung my braid over my shoulder, stalking over to him. "You think you could do that?" I asked him.

He nodded.

"I've not begun to tire, so please join me." I motioned to the weapons rack. My body tingled with anticipation as Rhijn prowled after me.

"You still use swords?" he mused. "*Very* primitive indeed. I think I'll pass." He waved off the rack of practice weapons and stepped up to me, crouching, ready to spring.

"You sure you don't want a weapon, Rhijn?" Conall called from the position he'd taken next to Jude amongst our ring of spectators. He stood with his arms crossed, probably hoping I'd teach Rhijn a lesson.

Rhijn turned and showed Conall his hands. Cocky bastard.

We came together, circling, waiting for the other to make the first move.

"This is getting boring," I taunted, jabbing my wooden blade in his direction. He darted back. Fine, I'd make the first move. *Again.*

I dashed forward, blocking an arm which thrust out, striking toward his exposed ribs. His other hand shot toward mine, and the butt of his palm struck my wrist, causing me to drop the weapon. Before I could blink, his hand circled my wrist, and he was spinning me toward the ground. He pinned my head to the dirt with an enormous hand, but I swung my legs up, wrapping them around his neck, flipping him. We tumbled across the training area; the crowd skipping to move out of the way.

We split apart and sprung to our feet. Despite the brisk air, sweat trickled between my cleavage, dampening the wondrous bralette I'd brought from Idia which I wore under my tunic. Rhijn wiped his own sweaty brow with a sleeve.

I held out the knife I had remaining as I waited for him to attack.

"I like how you fight," Rhijn said, barely out of breath.

"You won't when I've won," I goaded.

"Keep dreaming." He chuckled, advancing. "Oh, wait—did we do *this* in one of your dreams?" he asked, and winked.

I tried to ignore my flaming cheeks, hoping he'd take them for exertion.

We went on like that until long after the crowd departed. Jude must have pulled them away to attend to their duties. With a single sweeping movement I could barely track, Rhijn forced my other knife out of my hand, and flipped me across his body, then on the ground, rolling me so I was smashed beneath his weight.

"Okay, I'm done," I said from face down, with the heavy male lying across me on his side, pressing me into the dirt. I jerked and twisted until I was on my back, but still underneath him. His forearms were on either side of my chest, which was still heaving, and his face so close to mine we were breathing the same air. I watched his parted mouth, then his nostrils as they flexed, pulling deep breaths in.

I chanced a glance up and met his dilated eyes, which seemed to be painfully attached to my own dark stare. Things started happening in my body and warmth flooded my core as he studied my face. His weight shifted and the leg that was resting between my own brushed up against the exact wrong spot. I threw my head back into the dirt as a flicker of pleasure rippled through me.

"Careful, Rhijn," I breathed. I might have been inclined to let him take me right there, but he stiffened, and a chill chased the warmth away. In a swift motion, he pushed up off me and leaned down to offer me a hand. I scrutinized his extended palm before accepting.

Thankfully, he didn't slam me back on the ground. I'd already spent enough time there, and I wasn't sure how my traitorous body would respond to Rhijn's form pressing down against mine again. Never had I been so thoroughly beaten into the dirt. Or satiated, I thought, dusting myself off. Dirt was in my hair, my ears, and the sweaty creases of my neck. It had even snuck into my boots and was coating my toes; which was an oddly satisfying sensation.

I undid my loosened braid, and bent over shaking my hair out, searching the ground for the tie I held it together with.

"Looking for this?" Rhijn asked, holding the gold ribbon out to me, twirling it in his fingers.

"Thanks," I said, watching him. He looked more self-satisfied than a male ought to have a right to. I put the old ribbon in my teeth as I finished my braid, then wound it around the end, securing a knot. Strange, I thought I'd grabbed a new one that morning.

"That seemed *fun*," Conall said, walking up to us. "Feel better?" He massaged my shoulders for a few seconds, and I moaned, hoping he hadn't caught that last part.

"Don't stop," I whined.

He laughed. "Come on. We have a few final details to go over with my father and the council. Then we need to eat, and get a good night's rest. Tomorrow's the day."

My stomach flip-flopped, and I took a deep breath, trying to calm my nerves.

⁓

I couldn't sleep. Of course, I couldn't sleep on the night when I'd need the rest the most. I decided tossing and turning all night alone in bed was worse, so I threw on a robe and climbed the stairs that led to an unused lookout which drew me toward it.

I turned the corner at the top of the stairway and stifled a gasp. Rhijn sat there bathed in moonlight, which almost illuminated his blond hair and sun kissed skin. He showed no indication he'd heard me, but I'd made no effort to be silent either.

"What are you doing up here by yourself?" I asked him.

He cracked an eye open, looking at me. "Can't sleep," he said, resuming his breathing.

"You're doing that thing you do where you just sit and breathe," I observed.

"Yes, it's a technique I find helps me calm my mind. You'd probably benefit from it too," he said, watching me.

"What is that supposed to mean?" I asked, crossing my arms in front of my chest.

"Your urges. It might help center you. Calm them."

"What's wrong with my urges?!" I demanded, turning to storm away. Rhijn jumped up and grabbed my hand.

"Sit with me. Please?" he requested.

"So, I can calm my urges?" I glared at him.

He rolled his eyes. "Why are you always so difficult? Just sit. I'd like the company."

"Oh, okay," I said, sitting against the wall, legs stretched out before me, crossed at the ankle. Rhijn sat right next to me, mimicking my position.

"I've enjoyed getting to see where you're from. And I even think Conall is finally warming to me."

"I think he's feeling less threatened by you. He's been my best friend for over ten years now, and I think he isn't used to sharing. Probably being home helps."

We sat there quietly for a while, me thinking, him doing his breathing thing. It was pleasant, companionable.

"I look at what my life's been for over a third of it, essentially all my adult years, and I never had a choice, you know. I've done what they expected of me, from this mantel that was placed upon me by Conall and I's parents, without my consent. I think when you view my choices as urges, you are missing the fact that I haven't given into my own desires for so long, that now when I do it is almost a compulsion. I wasn't even *me* for ten years. I mean, I was, but I wasn't. Now, it's like coming to an oasis after having been lost in the desert."

"I understand," he said.

"You do? Truly?" I asked.

"In a way, we've had mirror experiences. I didn't have to be someone else, but this object has trapped me the same as you. The expectations of me, the duty I'm expected to fulfill. And not just because of the position my father holds. Maybe that is why I wanted to get to know you. To have someone to relate to."

I noticed Rhijn's hands flexing and relaxing as he spoke. He felt alone. And I'd been so awful to him when he'd just wanted someone who understood. Foolishly, he'd thought I might be that person.

An unbidden tear crept over my eyelid and crawled down my cheek. In that moment, all I wanted was to go to my room, curl up with a fluffy blanket on the chair by the fire and forget the rest of the realms existed. Maybe that's where Rhijn went when he closed his eyes.

Rhijn stilled when I reached over to grab his hand, lacing my fingers through his.

"You're not alone anymore," I said. "You'll always have a friend in me, should you like that." Tension eased from his body and I leaned my head against his shoulder. We were partners in this. So much of what would happen tomorrow would depend on us, and we were both feeling that pressure. We needed a distraction, if only for a few scant hours.

"Tell me more about what it was like growing up in Idia?" I asked him.

His eyes glinted as he looked down at him. "You want me to tell you a story?"

"Yeah." I nudged him. "Everly said you were a rambunctious youth. I still find that hard to believe."

Rhijn's chest rumbled, and he looked to the sky. I knew he was thinking of his cousin. "How about I tell you of the time Everly and I almost burned the observatory down?"

I slapped my free hand over my mouth. "You didn't?!"

"We were fifteen. And it was her birthday, so we decided to take one of the transports for a spin. The further we got from Adrina, the more empowered we became. A note from my father scrawled across the message center, 'You'd better have fun because you're both on double duty when you return.' We reprogrammed our route to the observatory town and broke in to the building you and I stayed in when we got there. No one lived in the loft then either, so we figured we'd crash there. We'd stolen a few bottles of wine from the chancellor's cellar and had started drinking an hour before we'd even arrived."

Rhijn shook his head and ran a hand over his face as he marinated in the memory.

"So, how'd you start the fire?" I pushed off the wall and turned to sit cross-legged so I could face him as he spoke. I edged up to him, unsure after I'd dropped his hand, my boldness converted into nerves. Seemingly without thinking, he reached over and wrapped his warm hand around the one I had set upon my knee. He absently played with my fingers as he continued his story.

I'd avoided him, pushed him away, practically told him I didn't want anything between us, but in that moment the thought of breathing wrong terrified me should it ruin whatever this was. What *did* I want? Sitting here with him felt so natural, at ease and this wasn't the first time I'd felt this way in his presence. The more I got to know him, the more I questioned my own reluctance.

A few strands of hair fell into his face and he reached up to push them away. "What?" he asked, as I tracked his hand.

I released a breath, trying to seem nonchalant and squeezed his hand. "I just can't wait to see how the story ends."

He laughed. "Right. Well, after we finished the first bottle, and we were well into the second, we got the bright idea to rummage around in the researchers' work. I found a half-completed experiment with a set of mirrors and lenses and easily understood what the researcher was trying to accomplish. Now mind you, we were both very drunk by now. But I made a few adjustments, and rearranged the order of the lenses. The researcher had arranged the outermost lens to funnel in starlight from the brightest star that time of year to come through. When I opened the flap which let the star's light in, I hadn't expected how amplified it would be. A line of white-hot light shot out, searing everything it touched, and left a trail of fire in its wake as I struggled to get the flap back on. The fire burned so hot I had to use the void stone's power to subdue it. Thank the Makers neither of us were injured."

"So essentially you created a weapon?" I squeezed my eyes shut trying to picture it.

"Actually, I just solved the other researcher's issue. He created it. But we don't use it of course. It was just an experiment to see what was possible. Another way to channel energy."

"And what did Vitis do when you got back?"

"Everly and I had to clean up after the cooks for three months after that, all three meals too. And that was in between our normal training. My father banned me from the laboratories during that time. I missed tinkering with the instruments so desperately that's how I knew what I wanted to do."

"You had the void stone at fifteen?"

"I think you're missing the point of the story. But yes, we knew I was connected to it. Granted I wasn't supposed to have taken it."

"And of course, that didn't stop you." I raised my incredulous eyebrows at him. And I hadn't missed the point of the story either. I was jealous that he'd found his purpose, especially as young as he had. "You've become awfully reserved in your old age." I gave him a silly grin.

He snorted. "I can still be spontaneous, adventurous even. You'll see."

Two moons of our three moons were cresting before we finally returned to our separate rooms. He shared more with me than I had expected and I'd returned the favor. I could only hope he wouldn't close back up when he rose in the morning.

CHAPTER TWENTY-EIGHT

I TOOK MY TIME to dress, lacing up a spare pair of boots left in my old closet. These were well worn, more charcoal now than black, and I loved them. I strapped on each belt and sheath with care, sliding blades into each with an almost ritualistic reverence. I'd never seen a conflict like the one I was about to witness. I didn't think any of us had.

Conall had been involved in all the small skirmishes over the years, but I'd always been deemed too valuable to be put on the front lines. So, while they'd let me fight, it was following the most violent part of the conflict. After the dust had settled, I was always allowed to go help with the clean-up efforts and to heal the injured. It had been great practice and also seeing the gore numbed me to it, to a certain extent.

A knock sounded at my door.

"Come in," I said.

Carina and Seeley slipped into the room and came to stand on either side of me, staring at my reflection in the mirror I faced. They'd come here with Balene and the last shipment of antidote.

"Want me to braid your hair?" Carina asked.

"Sure," I said and turned so she had access to my unruly locks.

She combed her fingers through them and began to braid. "Seeley, hand me a hair tie," she requested when she reached the end.

Seeley, whose eyes were slightly less hollow than they'd been the last time I'd seen him, grabbed the worn gold ribbon off the desk and handed it to her.

"No, not that one. Grab a new one from the drawer," she instructed.

"No," I said. "I want that one."

"Fine." She shrugged and used it to secure the braid. "There. Are you ready?"

"I'd be lying if I didn't admit I was nervous." I glanced between them.

Seeley leaned against the desk. "Don't worry. When you come back from defeating Emerson, Carina and I will have the first group ready to go back to Idia. We've devised a system to separate them into groups based upon who we think will be the most adaptable, to help ease the transition for those who come afterward. Renia and Kellis are organizing them as we speak, with the help of Meethra and the other godflies."

"They've been instrumental in helping us sense which Skyborne are the most receptive. I was thrilled when Conall sent them to us," Carina chimed in. "You know I still haven't gotten to meet him, but Meethra continually gushes about how fabulous the male is. I'm finding it hard to separate fact from fiction."

I made a mental note to introduce them as soon as time permitted. They were trying to distract me, I knew, and I was grateful.

"The Skyborne here couldn't be in better hands," I told them, squeezing both of their wrists. "We should probably head down there. Maybe you'll get to meet the infamous Conall."

❧

Balene was standing with Malik and Jude when we exited the keep. "Balene, you know you don't have to do this, right?" I asked her as I approached.

"I'm the best healer we have. It is my duty to use my skills for the injured. I'm going," she said, the slight tremor in her voice the only thing betraying her resolve.

"That is very brave of you," I told her.

"Well, I'll leave the bravery to the three of you," Carina said, lifting a regal chin to survey her three sisters. "This could be the last time we're all standing here together," she observed, and a single tear rolled down her stoic cheek.

"Don't talk like that, Carina," Jude chirped, bouncing on the balls of her feet. "One day, we'll all be celebrating in Idia. You'll see."

"I hope so." Carina took the time to pull each of us into an embrace. She walked back to the top of the keep's steps and stood beside Seeley as we mounted our horses and headed down through the streets of Eastdow to join the gathered forces. Carina would have to meet Conall another day.

I trotted up to Malik. "Seeley, take the goodbye, okay?" I asked him.

Malik smirked and gave me a sideways glance. "What do you think?"

"I've never really wanted to kill anyone, you know? I mean, I wanted to stab Darius a lot, but I don't think I actually wanted to kill him."

Malik grinned, waiting.

"I do now, Malik. I want to kill her. Does that make me evil?"

I nudged my horse and took off into a gallop through the white gates of the city, Malik's snickering fading behind me as I raced ahead.

The army that was gathered was an impressive sight. Torin and Conall had it organized into neat units, with different classes of troops in varying strategic positions, ready for marching when we landed. Conall had spent weeks with the different groups, training them on how to land to best protect themselves and their gear as they fell through the opening. Rhijn and I would position ourselves to connect the circle near the cavalry to swiftly heal any horses that might become injured during the fall.

After we landed, it would be a day's march on Seabrook. By then, Emerson would be aware we were coming. I rode up on Torin and his son arguing about something on the outskirts of the Army. Rhijn and Ian were on horseback, waiting for it to resolve.

"If we land where we're planned, we'll lose the element of surprise," I heard Torin argue as I approached.

"We will, but we need to give our troops the chance to get their bearings. Falling through the portal can be disorienting. And with Emerson's creatures, they may have moments where they're defenseless. Trust me, father."

I looked between them. "Not this argument again? Torin, I wish you'd let it go."

"I don't appreciate your tone, Nayla." Torin gritted his teeth as he stared at me.

"Likewise. And besides, it's not like you are the one who's in control of where we land, so I'd suggest you come around to Conall's plan, which Rhijn and I both agree with," I said, winking at Conall, and rode around to Rhijn and Ian.

"You guys ready for this?" I asked them.

"I'm ready to take Sundale back and bring my Skyborne home," Ian said.

Rhijn nodded in agreement, looking up at the light star well into its rise. "It's time."

"Positions," Conall hollered and there was a scurry of movement as males and females shifted into planned stances. Ian trotted over to the edge of a unit of foot soldiers, dismounting and gathering his mount's reins, steadying her. Rhijn and I followed Conall around to the far side opposite the calvary where we'd begin the portal. We handed off our horses to a few waiting groomsmen as planned.

I turned to Conall, who looked like he wanted to throw his arms around me, but was restraining himself trying to appear the impassive commander to his troops.

"At the ready," he yelled, voice echoing through the valley.

Rhijn and I pulled out the void stones and touched them, our forearms shrouding in contrasting colored thrumming power. We stood waiting for Conall's nod.

I'm proud of you, I mouthed to him as he nodded the go ahead, the ghost of a grin playing across my best friend's lips.

I turned to Rhijn, who'd started his half of the semicircle. A white void opened on his side, and I reached my finger into the glowing white beginnings of a portal. Conall began the countdown.

"Sixty, fifty-nine…"

Conall's voice faded in the distance. Rhijn and I figured we could pull the portal around the whole army running at full speed.

"Forty-five, forty-four…" The next stationed time keeper came and went as I pulled the portal around my half of the army. I ran and ran at breakneck speed as the power poured out of me.

My heart hammered in my chest as I approached the final counter. "Ten, nine…"

When I reached the midpoint of the cavalry, Rhijn was there waiting, standing inside his glowing white half. I ran up and jolted to a stop facing him, just inside my dark half.

"Four, three…"

Rhijn pulled his hand back on two, leaving the open end for me to make the connection.

"One." I whipped my finger forward and connected the two sides. Black and white filled in from either side and I reached over and grabbed Rhijn's vacant hand. A spotter in the center of the circle yelled, "BRACE!" and the call continued down the lines.

Rhijn and I looked at each other. "I didn't have the void stone last night," I blurted out, not really knowing why. Somehow connecting with him without it on my person meant something.

He looked at me oddly. "I didn't either."

My heart lurched and the familiar weightlessness took hold. Everything went dark, then we were falling.

CHAPTER TWENTY-NINE

I GRIPPED RHIJN'S CLAMMY palm as we landed in a crouch. I looked at him, then around at the plain we'd landed on. It was thankfully empty. "You okay?" I asked.

"Yes, you?"

"I'm good," I replied, dropping his hand and standing to recover my bearings.

"Healer!" someone cried from the distance and there was a rustling of motion in that direction. Several other cries for healers broke out, and half a dozen horses' whinnies, having become injured in the fall, their riders assessing the damage.

Rhijn and I rushed into action with the cavalry, letting the more experienced healers with full access to their power take care of the troops as planned.

"Nayla, over here." A soldier led me to the most urgent case. A chestnut stallion had a fractured cannon and completely shattered knee on one hind leg, and torn ligaments around the fetlock on both front legs. His rider was trying to soothe the beast with little success.

"You need to calm him down so I can lay my hands on him," I shouted over the commotion.

The soldier and the rider coaxed the animal to his side, the rider looking anxiously at me. His mount, clearly valuable to him, had its head pulled into his lap and the male was stroking his neck, whispering gentle words to it.

"Good," I said, and kneeled down to work, easing the pain first so the animal wouldn't jerk unexpectedly and injure one of us. I was sweating when I finished.

"Thank you," the rider exclaimed, holding back a sob.

I put my hand on his shoulder and urged him and the stallion to their feet.

Another soldier was patiently waiting to lead me to the next animal. Malik made it around to me and was monitoring my level of *power crazy*, ready to incapacitate me should I use too much and do something stupid. We figured I could use it until it was borderline spent, then I'd have a full day to rest before we saw any active conflict. Conall had arranged a wagon reserved for Rhijn and I to sleep in during the march if it came to that.

It was late in the morning when we finally finished healing the horses. Balene and the healers she led had finished with their charges an hour earlier. I stood, wiping my brow, and stumbled as I tried to step.

"Easy," Malik said, grabbing my elbow to steady me. "How are you feeling?" he asked.

"Shaky, but I promise I won't stab you or anyone else."

"The fact that you made that joke shows me the questionable mental state you're in." He raised a pointed eyebrow at me. The corner of his mouth twitched up.

There was that sly humor of his always showing up in the direst of times. I looped my arm through his and let him steady me as we went off in search of Rhijn.

We finally found him sitting on the wagon with a blonde female healer offering him a waterskin, and blushing profoundly which I completely understood. The male was objectively gorgeous and charming if I had to admit. Rhijn was chuckling at something she'd said and a slimy envious sensation slithered through me.

Malik chuckled next to me, and I glanced up at him, glaring.

What? I grumbled through our mental connection.

Someone's jealous.

How on earth would you know that? I asked.

I felt you stiffen when you saw the very attractive healer damsel blushing and the male in question laughing amiably with her.

Well, you're a poor read of people because I'm not jealous, I contradicted.

Are you afraid that he'll tire of waiting around on you and find another banished female to fancy?

Rhijn and the female healer looked up as Malik and I approached.

Malik had a sly grin plastered on his face.

"What?" Rhijn said, looking between us.

"Oh, this little liar and I were just having a very amusing side conversation. Excuse me, miss," Malik addressed the healer. "I believe Nayla is thirsty too."

"Oh, I'll go grab another water skin," she said, and started to turn away.

Malik gestured for her to hand Rhijn's skin to me. "No need. Nayla doesn't mind sharing." Malik winked at me and sauntered away, as I choked on the gulp I'd just taken.

The female gave Malik and me a suspicious look and excused herself, leaving Rhijn and I alone.

I shifted on my feet, unsure of what to do next thanks to my half-brother. "I'm going to go find Conall," I said, but Rhijn grabbed my hand and pulled me over toward the wagon, gesturing for me to sit.

"You need to rest," he said. I opened my mouth to reply, and he raised a hand to halt me. "I know. I can't tell you what to do, but you are trembling. I'm shaky too. We both need to rest."

He scooted back underneath the canopy and reclined his head on a pack, closing his eyes. I sat for several seconds, watching him. He cracked an eye and patted the spot next to him. "Come on. Lie back and relax."

I huffed, crawling back into the shade, and grabbed a pack. Tucking it beneath my head, I curled up on my side with my back facing Rhijn.

His chuckling was the last thing I remember before I drifted off.

⤦

Thudding on wood woke me, but a heavy arm was underneath my neck and gripped around my shoulder. Another was thrown over my waist and a delicious warmth pressed into my back.

"Nayla, Rhijn, wake up," Conall's familiar voice whispered. "I brought you guys breakfast. You slept all through the day and last night. We've stopped for a meal."

I tapped Rhijn's hand, and he pulled his arm out from under me.

"Sorry," he said and sat up, smoothing out his tunic.

"You guys were out cold," Conall said. "The sun shifted, and I was afraid you were going to get sunburned, so we moved you over to the wagon's shaded side."

I looked between Conall and Rhijn, glaring. "Is that how your arms ended up around me?"

Rhijn just shrugged, and Conall held up his hands. "That wasn't my doing. That was all him," he said, blaming Rhijn.

Rhijn ignored us and assessed the breakfast Conall had brought over. "I guess if the leader of the armies is personally delivering me breakfast, that must make me pretty important," he said and grabbed a flatbread, scooping up eggs and potatoes into his mouth. "This isn't bad, considering we're going to war today. Did you cook for me too, Conall?"

Makers, this wasn't going well.

They stared each other down, then Conall laughed. "Not today, but if we make it out of this, I'd gladly make you hot cakes or whipped eggs or whatever is your breakfast of choice."

I blinked, looking between them.

Rhijn extended his arm to Conall, and they clasped forearms. "I guess if you're making breakfast, then that means I'm making dinner?"

"Deal," Conall said, smiling at whatever weird cease-fire they'd struck. I guess males did weird things when encountering life and death scenarios.

"Ugh, get a room," I said, grabbing my plate. I hopped down from the wagon and went in search of less strange company. Eventually I wound my way to Jude and Balene, who were sitting cross-legged in the grass, eating off metal plates.

"So, is he your lover?" Balene asked, blushing.

I started to turn away, feeling affronted on all sides, but Jude reached out for my hand and pulled me down to sit beside her.

"So, is he?" Jude echoed Balene, giving me a toothy grin.

"He's not my lover, but there was a small dalliance. Which is over. So, we're just kind of partners in this. Because we both have the void stones," I explained in between bites.

Balene cleared her throat. "That's not what Meethra said."

"Well, I don't care what Meethra said." I gave her a pointed look. "Besides, we have way more pressing concerns than who is who's lover. Don't you both think?"

"So, what you're saying is you're waiting to make him your lover until *after* this is over?" Jude prodded.

I growled, rolling my eyes at them. They both broke out into a giggle fit, which I caved to, almost immediately.

A horn blew twice, signaling it was time to be on the move.

"Time to go," Jude said, jumping to her feet.

I stood and grabbed hold of her wrist. "Whatever happens out there today, don't try to be the hero, okay? Let's just make it out of here alive. I can't bear losing you again."

"I'll be fine, Nayla," Jude said, trying to shake free of my grip, which I tightened.

"Promise me if it gets ugly, you'll get to safety," I demanded, giving her my most serious older sister face. Of my sisters she was the one most like me. A little feisty and impulsive. I knew I couldn't control her, but that didn't stop me from trying.

"I won't do anything stupid, okay? But I'm not going to abandon my troops. I can't promise you that."

"Balene, tell her," I commanded our middle sister.

Balene shook her head. "Jude can't be told. I'm surprised you haven't figured that out by now."

"I'll be safe, Nayla. This will all turn out okay," she said, and drew me into an embrace before she turned and jogged toward the unit she was leading.

Balene stood next to me with our empty plates in hand. "I know you must feel like you weren't there to protect us when we were growing up and you want to be there now, but Jude is an adult. She knows how to lead and will do only what she must. You can't worry about her or anyone else but yourself today. Stay safe out there, Nayla."

Balene embraced me, then left to join the other healers.

I meandered through the marching soldiers, glad to have a moment to be alone with my thoughts. As the light star rose to mid-day, Seabrook proper came into view. We expected Emerson's Monterra army to be surrounding the city. Torin had convinced us we'd need to be prepared for a head-to-head confrontation, but unmanned walls stretched out in both directions and there wasn't a single soldier in sight.

My stomach started churning. Something wasn't right.

I started scanning the field in an almost panic, looking for Conall and Malik. I needed to see them before—

Blaring horns cut off my thoughts. Both the right and left flanks sounded the alarm three, four, five times.

Attack. We were under attack.

Dust kicked up from the army I hadn't noticed was being swiftly carried by the sea breeze toward us from the Drakestone border, and a force in the distance coming from Sundale was visible on the perimeter of my vision. Emerson had brought armies from both of her strongholds, anticipating our arrival. She'd had them camped, waiting. Or they had spies and anticipated our advance. That was the only way this could be happening.

I ran through the ranks, looking for Conall. I spotted him up on a large warhorse, next to Torin, both males calling out orders. Units were mobilizing, moving healers and cooks into positions of safety. I thought of Balene, and how they had planned to station the healer tents away from the battle site.

We should have known Emerson would have no regard for the rules of civil warfare. Jude was leading a unit toward the left flank, which would put her on the front line for the advancing army from Sundale which had to be Monterra troops. *Shit.*

"Nayla!" I heard Malik call. He was riding, leading my gelding to me. I grabbed the reins and threw my leg up on it, adjusting myself in the saddle. I reached up and felt the reassuring handle of the short-sword I wore across my back.

"I have to go back to my unit. Stay alive," he said, then galloped off in the direction of Drakestone. Toward his own family's armies.

The forces were finally in unimpeded view. The dusky grey of

Drakestone came from the north and the blood-red of Monterra came from the South, having been relocated to Sundale as I suspected.

I rode hard to Conall. Rhijn had done the same and rode by his side, waiting to be deployed where Conall saw fit.

"Conall," I cried, as I rounded on him.

"It's going to be fine, Nayla. We've got this." Conall turned and trotted off to issue more commands as both enemy armies crashed into the two opposing fronts, pinning us between them.

I looked at Rhijn. "What do we do?" I asked.

"We fight. You take the South front, opposite your sister's unit. I'll go North opposite Malik. If something goes wrong, get yourself out of there. We can't let them get the void stone," Rhijn said and I nodded. "Be safe, Nayla." He touched his heart once, then sped off.

Torin rode up beside me. We looked at each other for a long moment.

"What?" I finally asked him.

"You're afraid," he observed.

"I am. But I'm not afraid for myself, Torin." I felt my jaw clenching as I spoke to him.

"What do we do when we're afraid?" he asked, ignoring my response.

"I don't know. Enlighten me," I said, allowing the sarcasm to drip from my embittered voice.

"We fight, Nayla. We fight for those we are afraid for. We fight for ourselves. For our teachers. You fight like you've been trained to fight. *Do you hear me?* It's time for you to go out there on that field and save our asses."

I looked at him with my mouth agape. "That wasn't a horrible pep talk... I guess," I said when I could finally put together a string of coherent words.

"I've spent a lot of time resenting the fact that you lived and my beloved daughter died taking my wife in her grief along with her. I've treated you unfairly. I can admit where I've been wrong if that is what it takes. We might have stood a chance against Monterra, but that female wields Karish's formidable army, too. My son is out there, and if you don't figure out how to do something drastic, he will die. Do I need to make myself any more clear?"

"No," I said, looking at the watery edges of the Eastdow Regent's eyes.

"You and that light-haired male are the only things standing in the way of Emerson, and our destruction." Torin let the words sink in, then a melancholy half-smile flashed across his face. "And as crazy as it sounds, I actually believe you can do it." He started laughing under his breath and shaking his head in disbelief.

I couldn't help but surrender with him to the slightly crazed chuckle at the irony of it all. The two fronts crashed into our army and Skyborne were already dying all around us. Yet the male who'd taken me away from my family, resentfully played the role of my father, and locked me in a prison cell and sentenced me to death, was the one telling me the truths I needed to hear in this crucial time.

"You know, you really have lost it, Torin," I said to him, reining myself in, then galloped away to join the fray, not looking back.

❧

I pushed through a sea of gold, hunter, navy and ocean blue uniforms, each soldier wearing a white sash across their armored chest identifying them as one united force. Every time I saw an unmarked soldier in grey or carmine, I let my blade sing through the air cleaving through the enemy. The gelding I rode stomped over fallen bodies and bloodied trampled vegetation alike, head jerking this way and that as I urged it along. Its eyes flared with fright, as a group of Monterra soldiers moved in around me.

My animal reared back, ears shot straight to the sky and roared. I scanned the beast—a long slice ran along its left haunch. I swung a wide arch, beating back the foot soldiers before they could surround me and injure the animal further. Of all the training I'd undergone over the years, fighting from horseback was somehow overlooked. I guess they knew I wouldn't have rode into Drakestone on a mount swinging a sword to steal the ember. We were at the east edge of the melee and my animal was becoming panicked and impossible to control.

Making a split-second decision, I swung my leg around and vaulted off the horse giving it a firm slap on its unscathed haunch hoping it would flee into the open fields beyond. My boots shot out in front of my flying body and I spun in the air and cracked into the heads of two carmine clad males. Helmets and bone cracked under the impact and their bodies dropped as I hit the ground rolling behind them. I sprung to my feet, calling for a sheathed fighting knife. I kept the short sword in my left hand to block, and used my favorite weapon to advance. The remaining three soldiers were no match for my speed, and I made them regret their attempt to surround me.

A low lance under the armor at the belly for one, across the throat for another and the final male took my knife in his right eye, the left peeling back in horror before going blank. I dashed toward the front. Monterra was pushing us back, trying to squeeze us into Drakestone's force on the opposite side.

I scanned the line. Jude's unit was faring better than most and I could see the twirling maelstrom of blades around her black catsuit. She was still alive—I wouldn't allow myself to feel relieved yet, but she was fighting well. If I could hold this side, and stop letting soldiers get through we might stand a chance. A longsword ripped through the air toward me as I ran and I dropped into a sliding crouch kicking my heel out to slow me as I slid beneath it. Blood-soaked dirt squelched as my boot came to a stop and I lunged forward driving my long knife through the female's back, into her heart.

A spray of hot blood splashed across my face and a decapitated head thudded into the ground below my feet as I turned to continue forward. I wiped my sleeve across my eyes, smearing the sticky liquid, clearing my vision. My stomach lurched and I had to swallow the rising bile. *Makers*, it was the leader of one of the middle units. My eyes tracked upward following the trajectory of where the head had come from. His section of the line was caving. A riderless horse was on a wild run past me and I snatched its reins and threw myself up onto it, using my healing power to control the animal's nerves, taking that lesson from Emerson. I needed to see how the other side was fairing, then I'd go secure the line.

Conall's large form atop his even larger warhorse was racing toward the collapsing front, a group of cavalry with him. He was barking commands and taking down opponents as he went with every thrust and arc of his blade. My brother looked like some sort of warrior god of legend wielding his massive steel weapon. Conall knew how to fight and defend from a saddle. He would have the weak point shored up within a few moments and new troops installed to reinforce the barrier. We made eye contact briefly and a flicker of sorrow escaped before it was replaced with determination.

With every Skyborne I cut down, the queasiness in my gut deepened and I knew he felt the same. It wasn't the death. It was the amount. We should have been saving them, not killing them. This had to stop, but they relentlessly kept coming falsely believing we were the enemy. We were already struggling to stay afloat against the two impressive armies. I rode out to a small hill to make an assessment of the situation. Jude and Malik's units were still strong, though their numbers were weaker. Conall was riding back to the center barking commands, and I could see a pale-haired male blowing through attackers in a whirl of movement on the Drakestone front.

Back behind the lines to the North was another familiar shape.

Darius.

He sat on a horse that rivaled Conall's in size, with his arms crossed over his chest. I could see the butt of the crossbow slung over his shoulder. He was casually watching the battle rage on before him. No, he was focused on something specific. I followed his gaze.

Rhijn.

My stomach dropped and icy dread shot through my veins as he reached for the weapon. *No*, I thought and started galloping toward Rhijn, but he was almost on the opposite side of the field from me.

Darius had ridden far enough into the fray to position himself within range and a group of defenders surrounded him. He hoisted the bow, taking aim. I knew he'd released that breath and I let an involuntary cry escape as the arrow flew.

His aim was perfect. It always was, and I could feel him smiling.

Rhijn, look up, I willed.

The Idian twisted at the last minute and the arrow whizzed past, lodging in the shield of a stunned female fighting behind Rhijn. My heart was battering my insides, my breath coming in short horrified gasps.

I looked up, and Darius was seething, teeth gnashed, loading another arrow. *Shit.*

I was closer now, but still having to fight my way to him. I was determined to tell him Darius was targeting him. I cut down a male and wrenched a sword from a scabbard across his back, wielding the heavy weapon with my shorter sword, set on getting to my counterpart.

My enemy in the distance exhaled and let another bolt fly. This time Rhijn must have tracked it sooner because he plucked it out of the air with his bare hand, crushing it in his fist, which was incredibly hot. He whipped his head in the direction the second arrow had come from.

Rhijn turned toward Darius and sent blast after blast of power in his direction, mowing down soldiers, clearing the path to him. I wanted to watch. I wanted to follow him. But I couldn't. And that momentary distraction cost me.

A mace pummeled into my stomach knocking me off the horse. I landed on my back with a thud which knocked the wind out of me. I dared a look at my stomach and tiny pinpricks of blood were seeping through the tough leather. The wound was superficial.

A male outfitted in Drakestone's grey stood over me, mace poised to swing. I reached my hand out ready to unleash my power, but steel clove through the burly male's neck, and he hit his knees before tipping forward to land face first in the muck. A wicked grin lit the male's face who'd taken my attacker down. Malik, like me, was covered in blood, but considering his good spirits, I assumed none of it was his.

"Thanks," I muttered, launching to my feet. "My weapons?" I searched around, picking up the short sword I'd dropped while Malik watched my back.

"You okay?" he asked, motioning to my abdomen.

"Yeah," I grunted, considering healing myself.

The sickening flapping of fleshy wings drew our attention. I tracked the sound. In the distance, coming from Seabrook proper, Emerson approached, riding atop a white horse. Her chestnut and red-streaked hair flowed loosely behind her and an army of a hundred or more creatures flanked each side. A1 hovered at her shoulder. She halted on a high point in the plain and leaned over, saying something to A1. The creature and his siblings advanced. A company of soldiers replaced them, surrounding her protectively.

I watched in horror as Emerson's creatures assaulted the front with dizzying speed. *Save our asses.* I had to do something drastic. Torin's words rang loudly, repeating in my mind.

They were incredibly difficult to kill and there were so many of them. More than I'd seen in Monterra. Rhijn and I could use our power, but I had suspected our soldiers would struggle to take them down, but be able to do it. We knew it would be hard, but they were practically invincible to the average soldier. They were that much faster than Skyborne. I watched dumbstruck as our troops struggled to defend themselves against their aerial assaults, which gave Drakestone and Monterra soldiers openings.

The thinning of our Skyborne was happening too quickly. All these innocents. Tears followed the lump rising in my throat, but I suppressed it. Now wasn't the time, I told myself.

I darted in the direction of the healer's wagons and I found the one that was unoccupied, which Rhijn and I had slept in. I took the ember out of my pocket and touched my fingers to it. A black shadow creeped up my arm. As soon as it was in place, I whipped a circle around myself.

I caught myself in a squat right in front of the sagging inn, then darted through the invisible barrier of the Swath just beyond it. Since we'd left, the Swath had grown on this side of the continent too, which had actually brought the boundary closer to the field of battle.

As promised, hundreds of Uden's creatures were poised waiting. I stood on the edge and created a large shield that bisected the boundary, creating a tunnel from the Swath to Seabrook. The creatures hurriedly filtered out.

I knew if I'd explained this to Torin, my plan to release the creatures of the Swath on the realm, no one would have agreed. But Uden and I had spoken and altered our agreement. I just hoped I'd not mistakenly given him my trust.

CHAPTER THIRTY

RHIJN SHOT ANOTHER wave of raw shredding energy toward the male who he knew had been Nayla's former lover, *Darius.* If the crossbow wasn't the giveaway, the cowardice was. What type of male hid behind their father's army? He liked to think the Idians were better than that.

As a general rule, Rhijn didn't believe in capital punishment—it was against his principles. But this wasn't his realm. And after what Darius had tried to do to Nayla, what Conall had shared as they'd ridden out to meet the armies before sunrise a few days earlier, had made everything so much clearer. Her hesitancy and his protectiveness of her made so much more sense and it almost made his jealousy and defensiveness, two emotions which were so atypical for him, seem unfounded. *Almost.*

Darius deserved to die. He'd known males like him in Idia. *Scum.* Rhijn didn't know if he could suppress the urge for vengeance even if he wanted to. The thought of Nayla being hurt… and like that. She didn't need his protection. She'd proven that. The female was an otherworldly force, which only drew him deeper under her spell regardless of how hard he fought the incessant pull. But the thought of what Darius had done made every hair stand on end, and his vision turned red. His protective instinct went into high alert around her and he couldn't think straight, reverting to his baser instinct like he was now.

Like how he'd been when he'd told her to *control herself*, and here he was like a crazed maniac, wanting nothing more than the blood of anyone who'd ever hurt her.

Rhijn watched as Darius loaded another bolt, wrenching the string back to the latch that held it poised to fire. He'd made it within a hundred feet of the male, and paused anticipating the twang of the string's release. *Click.*

The bolt flew. Rhijn had to give him credit. Another perfect shot. Darius's eyes flared in triumph, but Rhijn twisted his shoulder so fast, he knew Darius wouldn't register the movement until it was too late.

Rhijn shot his hand out, snatching the arrow from its flight path. Capturing its momentum, he whirled, catapulting the bolt toward its origin. It flew, barely trackable, at the coward.

"Damn it," he muttered. He'd aimed for Darius's heart. It struck a few inches to the left, punching straight through and exiting on the other side. The male looked down at the gaping wound in his chest, pawing at it. Slack-jawed—astonished. He raised his gaze to Rhijn, who couldn't suppress the avenging grin. Nayla may not want him—accept him as hers, but he'd protect her, from afar if necessary. And he'd start by killing Darius.

"Get him," Darius screamed, blood bubbling from the edges of his mouth. The soldiers surrounding him advanced on Rhijn, weapons drawn. Eight swords angled toward him.

Darius sagged in the saddle over the horse and Rhijn saw him glance in the direction of Seabrook. Toward the mad healer. He couldn't let him escape.

The first soldier ran forward thrusting his shield and sword at him, and Rhijn caught the blade which disintegrated in his palm not leaving a mark. The male looked wide-eyed from the hilt of the sword missing its blade to Rhijn and took a step back.

"What are you doing you idiots? Attack him!" Darius yelled, before spinning his horse and racing off toward Emerson, using the advantage to flee.

"I really hate weapons," he growled at the reluctant soldiers. Unfortunately, they were more afraid of Darius than of him and they threw themselves at him in twos and threes. Rhijn crushed the heel of his hand into skulls, delivered knife-hand strikes to throats, and used his power to shield himself from their swinging blades. When he was finished, eight crumpled bodies lay around his feet in a circle.

He wiped his hands on his pants and tracked to where he saw Darius had made a long trek on the outskirts of the battlefield to Emerson. Rhijn scanned around for a loose horse. He'd take them both out if he had to.

Jogging across the field searching for a mount, he caught a glimpse of Conall frantically raking his eyes across the field searching for something from atop his horse. *Nayla*. He was looking for her. Somehow, he knew it.

Rhijn raced toward her brother, tracking across the distance looking for the beautiful, maddening female who had no idea of the power she wielded. A dappled smoky mare trotted by, and seizing the opportunity, he shot out a burst of energy and the red clad female rider toppled off.

"Thanks," he called back to the unconscious soldier. She would be one of the lucky ones, because when she woke up, this would all be over. Assuming she wasn't trampled to death. A shudder rattled down his spine as he mounted the horse, and sped toward Conall.

"Have you seen her?" Conall shouted over the sounds of the screeching battle.

Rhijn shook his head. "Damn it." If she was gone, surely, he'd feel it. He rode up beside Conall. "Where could she be?"

"The Swath," Conall said with finality and yanked on his horse's reins as if to charge east, in that direction.

Screaming erupted from a skirmish where an onslaught of creatures were brutally assaulting a group of soldiers with white sashes from an aerial position. They were led by their master's favorite, A1.

A gore covered battlefield healer darted in front of Conall's horse to get his attention and insistently tugged on his pant leg. "Sir, we need Nayla or Balene," the healer sobbed, "We need them." The female pointed toward the wall of soldiers protecting in a perimeter of the chaos of Skyborne and monster. Protecting whatever was in the center, despite the cost to the individual. He had a sinking feeling of which Skyborne it was.

Rhijn and Conall locked eyes in understanding. "Go get her. I'll go with the healer," Rhijn barked.

Dread sluiced down Rhijn's constricted throat pooling in his stomach as he and Conall sprinted in opposite directions.

CHAPTER THIRTY-ONE

"R EADY?" I ASKED him.

Uden gurgled to his creatures. They whined and growled in response. I turned toward them and shook my head. "Remember, only the ones in blood-red and grey, okay? And the monsters. Feel free to eat them. No white sashes. Even if they're stained with blood."

An excited cacophony of sounds erupted as I questioned what I was doing.

Gather close, Uden echoed.

They did, and I whipped a large lasso of black portal around the creatures, including myself.

Uden's clawed hand clasped over my shoulder. *I can see why they follow you, Realm Walker*, he said as darkness enveloped us.

⚶

We landed off the battle site. I wasn't gone but mere minutes and our forces were already being obliterated. "Hurry!" I cried.

Uden raced along beside me, his webbed feet crowned with pointed claws easily eating ground between where we'd landed and the field. His winged kind flew in a thick wall ahead of us, others scurrying under them, moving with preternatural speed, advancing toward the awaiting bloodshed. I nodded to Uden, knowing they'd reach the field faster than I would.

"Go on ahead," I called to him. "You know what is needed of you." Deep down, I had known they were the only match for the monsters Emerson had created and even she wouldn't fathom I would consider releasing them.

Uden made a gurgling plea, which reverberated into the distance. His creatures, as one, shot forward and left me in the empty field. I considered my hand, wondering if I could create a portal to get to the field quicker. I wasn't too unfocused, but I'd better not test my limits since there was no one here to restrain me if I lost control. I was making my way back too slowly, but I could see the impact Uden and his kind were already making.

A single rider came into view, galloping directly toward me. I recognized his form. How did Conall know this is where I disappeared off to? I heard screams that slowed my blood in the distance, both Skyborne and creature. I thought of the soldiers being confronted by the creatures of the Swath, their childhood nightmares, and scoffed. They must be terrified and I relished it.

"Nayla, come quick," Conall belted, voice desperate as he raced out to meet me. As he rode by, he lowered an arm and swung me up on his mount, turning the warhorse back to the lines of opposing forces, which had flanked the east side of the field blocking our forces in on three sides. They were pressing us toward the walls of the city. He nudged his mount into a gallop back toward the conflict.

"I knew you were going to release them," he said. "When we couldn't find you, I realized that's where you'd gone."

"You've always known me so well." The words were light, but I felt nothing but heaviness. "You shouldn't be out here though," I said, but my voice caught when I saw Rhijn hovering at the edge of the melee. Conall and I dismounted, abandoning the horse outside the skirmish to carry forward on foot.

Rhijn threw up a shield around the three of us and started shoving through the enemy line, pushing away the death and gore. Skyborne from our side jumped out of his way, but Drakestone and Monterra soldiers saw attacking the Idian as an opportunity to be a hero and threw their might at him.

His solid shield fueled by his use of the void stone, I noticed, carved a relentless path.

"Conall, what is it?" I asked, tripping to keep up with the two towering males.

Rhijn's jaw flexed as the males exchanged a look, and Conall glanced back at me, his eyes watery with the news he was about to share. Rising panic creeped up my neck, and my palms dampened, moistening the leather wraps of my knives which I sheathed at my thighs. I saw Rhijn give him a somber nod seemingly confirming the worst.

"It's Jude." Conall reached out to catch me as I stumbled at what he'd said. "She was leading the advancing center. A healer found us. She was in bad shape when I left to come get you. She kept asking for you."

I started sprinting, dread seeping through every pore, coating my insides in waves. Rhijn and Conall kept pace, keeping our path clear, and me protected. *Not Jude.* She was too alive to be lost in this pointless battle. And we hadn't had enough time. "I told her not to be a hero," I whimpered to no one in particular. "I made her promise," I sobbed. Conall grabbed my elbow as I lost my footing again and dragged me forward.

If anything happened to her, I would personally kill Emerson and Darius with my own hands. I didn't care if they surrendered. I didn't care about the Idians' modern morals. I didn't care if Rhijn thought I was primitive or was disgusted by me. They needed to die. And I would kill them.

I glanced at Rhijn. I wanted the Idian army here to obliterate them. Vitis asked us to come for them only as a last resort. He didn't want the first impression of the Idians to be as fighters, especially since they were such a peaceful society. We had agreed, and understood we were going to be up for enough of a challenge to have the Skyborne from this Realm accept help, and live alongside the Idians.

"Rhijn," I begged, my voice strained. He watched me; brows furrowed. "Please, will you go get them? Please?" I sobbed.

He knew who I was talking about. Monterra and Drakestone were just too strong. Even with Uden and his creatures unleashed, they were still holding their own.

"I will, but let me take you safely to your sister first, okay? Then I'll go," he promised. I nodded.

We raced on.

Ahead, a group of soldiers fought in a circle, obviously protecting someone in the center. It had to be her. I darted forward. Emerson's creatures, led by A1, had identified a vulnerability and were sweeping closer and closer to the surrounding fighters. We'd all dosed, so they weren't wasting the effort to emit their powder, but they could slice through skin and leather with the talons on the ends of their appendages. Many of the soldiers were trickling blood from the areas their thicker armor did not cover. If we won this, there would be days' worth of work for the healers mending the damage done by them.

I held my ember shrouded hand in their direction as I ran. A swift gust of power shot out and they were swept backward, tumbling through the air toward the back of the lines. Recognizing me, the circle parted enough for the three of us to slip through. Rhijn's shield surrounded us and the soldiers defending her. Their shoulders sagged with momentary relief. His shield was impenetrable.

A young female field healer lingered, leaning over Jude's unconscious form, shaking my vicious younger sister.

"Jude, please come back. We need you, Jude. Don't give up on us. Please," the healer cried. The healer must have known Jude personally, though her anguish was no match for my own. She was covered in Jude's blood. It pooled around her. Too much of it. *I knew.*

I stilled; breath caught in my throat. My eyes shut and I eased my energy out to scan her body. I would not fall apart, I willed myself. I could do that later.

Clenching my fists, I steeled myself. I was determined to be the leader the Skyborne needed me to be.

"She's gone," I exhaled. I'd been too late. I'd been too late for Everly, Femi, and now Jude.

My breath was coming in shallow gasps, and my vision clouded. The tight grip I had on my emotions was rapidly slipping. No, this wasn't happening. This was just another bad dream. But it wasn't. Somehow, I knew this was real.

My legs gave out and I fell to my knees, pressing my forehead into her still chest. My hands trembled as I pet her blood-soaked hair. Jude was dead.

A scream tore from my throat.

I took a breath and kept screaming. Instinctively, I had been drawing in power, like I'd done when I panicked and blasted Darius away from me in the scrublands of Sundale. I'd been drawing energy toward me from that same empty space like I'd done when we separated the particles to feed the wells in Idia. From the void. And like those flickering particles, I finally broke, split in two, and all that energy left me in an explosion.

Sheer winds of dark swirling power blasted away from me from the ends of my fingertips forming walls of vibrating current in either direction. They were an endless torrent unleashed on my scream.

"Run," I heard soldiers yell. Bodies fled in both directions. That gave me an idea. I held my hands out, reaching across the distance. They couldn't fight if they were on their knees or knocked back on their asses. Acute agony and loss fueled my fury. I tilted my head back and bellowed. The walls of flowing vibrating air became a chasm of darkness—void. Endless nothingness to mirror the vacancy in my chest.

Darkness spread across the battlefield much like Malik's shadows. Soldiers were knocked back, flattened into the ground. The wall of energy above them was so dense, they couldn't stand, only kneel or be crushed by the wind of power hurling out from my center. I gave everything I had to stopping these armies. To halting this conflict before another life could be claimed.

Rumbling shook the ground beneath me, and deafening pops resounded across the fields. I beheld the crevices in the hard ground which were spreading from the epicenter that was me. My lips clenched into a grim line as I beheld the Maker's power. Instinctively I knew that's what it was. These Skyborne would stop. This would end, or I would destroy them all.

I wasn't sure how long I was there on that field radiating power. Screaming.

Eventually, a solid hand was placed on my shoulder grounding my awareness and I turned to see a single figure above the darkened chaos.

My voice was hoarse, and a warm liquid trickled down the back of my throat. I tried to speak, but my voice wouldn't come.

"Nayla, stop," Rhijn urged. Of course, my power hadn't thrown him back. He could counter it with his own as he approached me.

I slumped against him, ceasing the onslaught and the darkness which was spread across the plain vanished drawing back toward my ember shrouded arm. Rhijn held me on my feet, and he waved for Conall to come forward. "Conall, take Jude's body to the healer's wagons."

"Wait," I said, as Conall kneeled to pick up Jude.

Rhijn let me loose, and I turned in a full circle surveying the armies, who stood completely still waiting to see what I would do next.

"Everyone stands down. This battle is over. Our realm is crumbling." I forced my vocal cords to work as I held my black arm into the sky. "Go home to your families, gather your dead, and heal your injured. Don't worry about Darius, Emerson or the other Regents. I will deal with them and I will take you home."

Rhijn caught me as I collapsed. I wrapped my arms around his neck, pressing my face into his warm skin to hide the tears welling to the surface.

CHAPTER THIRTY-TWO

S HAME COATED RHIJN'S insides as he slid his arm out from underneath Nayla. Watching her sleep, he could hardly make sense of the male he'd become during that battle. His emotions had overwhelmed him, and he'd been willing to disregard his own code of justice in favor of exacting vengeance on the sleeping female's behalf. It wasn't like him.

He shivered imagining what his father would think. Of the lives he'd taken. What he'd done was a necessary evil, but he hadn't wished to do it. He had longed to kill Darius though. That lust a thing sprung unbidden from his very core only heightened by the heat of battle. He'd lost himself and he knew it wasn't the power or the frenzied atmosphere of fighting. It was *her*. She had changed him.

Or maybe it was that he wasn't so *perfect* after all—the word she'd angrily slung at him. No different from the Banished. Perhaps it was because there hadn't been an opportunity to explore that side of himself in the now peaceful realm of Idia. There had never even been a skirmish during his lifetime.

Rhijn glanced out the window. Across the city and past the outer walls, you could make out the deep power wrought crevices and the dark ground stained by the blood of the Skyborne they were there to save. Some, who'd fought for reasons he didn't fully understand.

He ran his power over Nayla one last time to make sure she was stable, before leaving the room. Rhijn jogged through the corridors eager to find Conall. The territory leaders and healers were still scrambling to heal the injured and contain the creatures viciously searching for the mad healer. It had been confirmed that Darius had fled, gotten away, but Emerson hadn't been sighted. The way the creatures were lurking around Seabrook, indicated she must still be here.

"Rhijn, there you are." Conall's voice reverberated through the stone corridor before coming into view. "Uden thinks they've found her. I'm needed with Balene and the healers. Ian and my father are continuing to organize the survivors. Go with him and take care of her."

Rhijn knew what Conall meant. Kill Emerson. Uden would do it, and gladly. Or one of his kin. He thought about the flood of guilt he'd just experienced. It was his job, as a representative of his realm, to live up to the Idian moral standard and convince the Banished to uphold the canons of voluntary surrender which he knew would be foreign concepts to many of them. Enforcing it would fall to Kellis if he were here, but he was still in Eastdow with Nayla's sister Carina organizing the refugees.

"I'll go, but we're not killing her." Rhijn squared his jaw expecting an argument from Conall. "I'll bring her in alive. Then we'll take her to Idia and try her there."

The other male looked incredulous, running a hand across his weary forehead. It had been less than a full day since Nayla had ended the battle with the ferocious display of power and none of them had gotten more than an hour of sleep, here and there. "Nayla would want her dead," Conall said, exasperation dripping from his voice.

"It's not up to Nayla." Rhijn didn't break eye contact. He wanted Conall to know he wasn't going to budge on this.

Conall gave a hollow sigh. "Fine, go get her. We'll vote on the course of action once she is secured in the prison. That's the best I can do, Rhijn. Remember, you're still in our realm."

"The sooner you adopt Idian standards, the easier your integration will be. Starting now, with this would be prudent."

"Or create another uprising."

The two males scowled at each other. Rhijn didn't understand why

Conall was fighting him on this. Actually, he did know. Conall wanted Nayla's approval. "She'll come around, Conall. She has to and I think she knows that."

"Then you obviously don't know her like I do. On everything else, you're right. But not killing Emerson has cost her too much."

Rhijn pressed his lips into a fine line. Conall's words stung. At some point in the last week the tide between them had changed. He almost seemed resigned to the fact that Rhijn was going to be a part of Nayla's life and was treating him more or less like an ally, if not a friend. But Conall did know her better, despite the connection she shared with him. "Fine, we'll vote," he grumbled in acquiescence.

"Thank you. You'll have an opportunity to convince the council before we cast our votes. Be careful. Emerson's still dangerous."

An hour later, Rhijn was sprinting to keep up with Uden who was following one of his flying subjects through the narrow sandstone alleyways of Seabrook. They stopped outside a nondescript faded yellow door and the hovering creature's eyes went wide as it jabbed a claw at the residence. Its translucent yellow wings flapped in excitement and Uden raised a sharp digit to his maw shushing the creature, and looked to Rhijn who nodded.

The creatures not only had preternatural speed; they also had the ability to move at a crawl. Uden put his webbed hand on the doorknob and turned it so slowly its movement wouldn't be detectable unless you were staring right at it. It used the same sluggish motion to push the door open.

Soundlessly, they stepped inside what appeared to be an abandoned residence. The room they entered was dimly lit by a single sconce in the hallway to the right, which led up a wooden flight of stairs that opened into another darker corridor. Rhijn scanned the space searching through the shadows for a sign of life. It looked like the sagging furniture hadn't been sat in for weeks; a thin layer of dust covered each surface.

To his left, a doorway stood ajar which led to what must be the kitchen based on the large soot covered stone trim of a wood-fired oven visible through the opening. Flying insects were buzzing in and out and a noxious odor permeating the still air in the space floated up his nostrils as he approached.

Uden slipped silently along the wall, pausing for a moment to listen, then nodded to confirm the presence inside. Its bulbous head twisted peaking around the doorframe then turned back, impressing a wide-eyed look in Rhijn's direction. Shivering at the thought of what he was about to confront, Rhijn reached into his pocket and pulled out the void stone, allowing its bright energy to crawl up his arm. He'd seen Emerson use her power. It wasn't worth taking any chances.

His power was ready, guard raised, and Uden was at his heels. Rhijn tiptoed forward on silent feet, but couldn't suppress the gasp as he crossed the threshold into the room. The healer was sitting at a square table in one of its four wooden chairs with her back to the door. All around her, peach bodies with broken wings, missing limbs, and vacant dried-up eyes littered the floor and almost every open surface. They were her monsters who'd been killed by the creatures of the Swath—the creatures Nayla had released. She must have been sneaking out to the battlefield at night to collect their bodies and bring them here, hoping she could save them.

Emerson hadn't budged at Rhijn's startled sound, but her shoulders rose on a steady inhale. Power slipped off her, snaking across the tiled floor and up through his legs like a caress of her mind flowing alongside his blood. This must have been what Nayla was describing when she told them how Emerson would attack. *What she'd done to Femi.* Rhijn braced for the assault, for the moment Emerson would strike trying to cripple his bodily functions.

"She killed them. So many of them. They're *dead* because of her. They warned me she would do it." Emerson's voice was a low, broken thing. With a filthy hand tipped with cracked and broken nails, she gestured to the lifeless bodies that were strewn across the floor. He could understand why the healer would blame Nayla for leading to the death of her creations.

"Emerson, who's they?" Rhijn asked, narrowing his eyes.

She shook her head viciously then froze. Her stare went distant for a moment before it refocused on him. It was like she'd gone somewhere else mentally. Her behavior was erratic at best from what he understood and she seemed to shift from one persona to the next on a coin flip. He was putting the pieces together with each interaction. She wasn't just mad, she was sick.

"You need to come with us." He had every intention of taking her back to the prison beneath Seabrook alive. In Idia they didn't kill people like Emerson, they healed them. His gut told him Nayla would hate the idea, maybe even despise him for it, but it would be the right thing to do. The Dar Kepler had offered their enemies a chance to right their wrongs after that final battle when the rest of the Sol Ros had been banished. They could have killed them, but they didn't, and Idia's productive society was proof of their effort. He knew it was the right course of action, despite how crazy it sounded.

Emerson shifted in her chair to face him, running her eyes up and down the length of him. The heart-stopping sight of Uden should have been what drew her attention, but she was focused on Rhijn. "You're not going to kill me then?"

There was no *try* in her sentence. She regarded his hand as if she knew he could. That she would be powerless to stop him.

"Emerson, you've lost. If you come with us, we can help you."

She scoffed. "You think I'm redeemable?"

"I think you have an opportunity to salvage your life. *If* you accept what I am offering."

Emerson frowned, and pressed herself up from the chair. "And what makes you think I want to be salvaged? That I need some shining hero to save me from myself. Is that what you think? That I'm weak like Nayla? That I'll succumb to your Idian ways? Your *allure*? She's quite impulsive, isn't she? She'll tire of you soon enough. Seems to be a trend with her." Emerson batted her lashes like there wasn't a layer of grime coating her skin, or the gooey blood-like substance from her monsters splashed across her face and coating her fingers.

"Look around you. You're sitting in a room full of dead things." His voice was sharper than he'd intended. Hearing the enemy call his—no, *Nayla*. Calling *Nayla* impulsive grated on him. He regretted ever throwing the term at her. Especially after she'd explained what things had been like for her. And little did Emerson know he'd already been discarded, so the joke was on her.

"Oh, did I offend your precarious male ego?" A sly smile crossed her lips and a seductive glint lit her eye. "Tell you a truth you weren't pre-pared to hear?"

Rhijn clenched his teeth.

Are you sure we can't rid you of her? Uden echoed.

Rhijn replayed how he'd rebuffed the Idian's saviors complex and half-heartedly thought about giving her to the creatures of the Swath.

You're considering it? Uden observed.

Emerson regarded Uden then, and sneered in disapproval before addressing Rhijn. "Don't forget I'm not the one who released them when it all goes terribly wrong. And you think I'm the crazy one…" She huffed a sigh. "Fine, I'll go with you." She turned and headed for the door; chin high as she waited for one of them to open it for her.

Uden splayed his clawed hand across the outer door and pushed it open. *As if you're any better.* His voice was a soft echo that would have been under his breath if it weren't for the resonating sound.

Rhijn caught the quaver of her shoulders as she dashed past the crea-ture's towering form and out into the street.

CHAPTER THIRTY-THREE

I WOKE UP IN a comfortable bed sometime after that. I surveyed my body. Someone had cleaned the ichor from my skin and had changed me into a stiff cotton sleeping gown. I tried to sit up, but dizziness overtook me and I slumped back into the covers.

"Easy," that familiar timber said.

I tried to speak, but my voice came out as a croak. Rhijn stepped forward and placed his hand on my bare throat. I groaned as a steady, healing energy eased the pain.

"Your nerves are frayed from all that power you used. I've been healing you every few hours for two days now."

Did it work? I thought. I pushed at Rhijn's mind like I had done to open Malik and I's connection. *Rhijn,* I pleaded. He jerked back, removing that pleasant hand from my neck.

Nayla? he thought back, raising his eyebrows at me.

I exposed my throat to him, beckoning for him to return his hand. He did.

Did it work? I demanded again.

"Yes, but you almost killed yourself in the process. Emerson and Darius tried to keep the armies in line, but even the officer level soldiers left. I couldn't believe it. Malik explained that the Skyborne here have always been taught that a Chosen One would one day arrive, and that the rumor is that it was you. When you unleashed that power, it convinced them."

But I'm not—

"I know you're not. But if that is what it took to stop the bloodshed…" he replied.

What about Uden? I asked. I could tell I was fading.

"He's here in the keep. That's where we are. Seabrook. He's been checking on you, asking about when you can fulfill your part of your bargain."

That made me smile. Then I thought of Jude and tears began streaming down my cheeks. My heart cracking in two.

"You need to rest," he said.

But how can I rest when my chest is aching like this? I asked him, my body convulsing in a sob.

"Scoot over," he said. I obeyed, and he pulled me into his arms. I lay my head on his chest and absorbed the healing energy he gave me.

"She's fine," I heard Rhijn whisper some undetermined amount of time later. He was still with me and I was tangled around his lean, muscled form. He slid his arm out from under me, trying to undo the knots I'd made of our limbs.

Don't go, I thought.

He inspected me, brushing a stray hair from my forehead. "I've been here all night. I'm hungry and I need to attend to my other needs," he said. My mind immediately went to the pretty healer who'd given him water before the battle and panic rose anew.

I stared at Rhijn, who was speaking to Conall. It seemed the truce those two had come to was sticking this time, to my relief. Rhijn walked toward the door Conall held open for him. I panicked and tried to speak. Still a rasp.

"Can't," I eked out. It still wouldn't come. And it hurt. Bad.

I can't speak to him this way. I was afraid of being awake and not being able to communicate.

Conall looked between us, confused.

"She is unable to speak until her voice is healed. All her screaming created some hemorrhaging in her vocal cords. I've been slowly working on them, along with the rest of her. This sensitive healing is best not rushed. Balene has been alternating with me."

I sat up, pulling the sleeping gown down over my knees. I must have pulled it up around my hips in my attempt to be closer to Rhijn. He hadn't seemed to mind, though we certainly weren't sleeping like friends would have, even though he'd been comforting me. The last thing I wanted was for me to do something and for him to pull away again. And possibly toward another female. The closeness between us was the only thing keeping me from dissolving into a pit of grief I wasn't sure I'd ever recover from.

What we'd been able to do moving that army together was nothing short of incredible. And it had felt right to work with him that way. To share power like that.

Rhijn? I wasn't sure what I was asking.

"Conall brought you food. I'll be back, okay? Try to eat."

I nodded. I felt awful for being helpless like this, but I tried not to guilt myself about it. Despite that I wanted to curl into myself and pretend my youngest sister wasn't gone, that there wasn't a gaping hole in my chest, I knew I needed to be there for the survivors. Conall was here, Balene, Malik and Seeley. I had so many others who loved me, who I needed to show up for. Conall's eyes were locked in a permanent wince as he watched me. He deserved my best. I had to try for them. No matter how much it hurt.

Conall set a platter down on the nightstand. Makers, my bladder was full. I should drink the clear broth he set before me, but I couldn't. This was so embarrassing.

"Eat, Nayla," Conall gently urged me.

I pointed to the bathroom.

"Oh," he said, seemingly relieved that was all it was and knowing him, probably glad to be useful. "All right, let's get you up."

He helped me swing my legs off the bed, and walked me into the toilet chamber. When he was satisfied I wouldn't topple into it, he left to give me privacy. My muscles were still incredibly weak. It wasn't like when I felt drunk, when I'd used too much power. Or maybe I had already slept that part off. Now I just felt a soul level exhaustion, and every step was like running miles. And the tears wouldn't stop. They crawled over my lower lids like lava with no end in sight.

When I finished, I pushed myself up to a standing position and eased my way over to the door, leaning against the wall for support. I pulled on the handle. Conall, seeing the movement, opened the door and put his arm around my waist, helping me back to bed.

"When you collapsed and Rhijn picked you up, I thought that was it," he confessed. I opened my mouth. I wasn't sure what I was planning to do. It's not like I could say anything. "Just listen and eat," he commanded.

When I picked up the spoon, he continued. "That was maybe the scariest moment of my life. I'm glad he was there to catch you."

I picked up a cracker and threw it at him, glaring. It wasn't fair to make me cry when I wasn't able to speak and already a mess over Jude. And it seemed after not shedding a single tear for ten years, everything set me off these days.

"I know, I know. You want to tell me how much I mean to you, I'm your best friend and the greatest brother ever, and that you weren't going to let me off the hook that easily by dying on me. Don't worry, I know we still have plenty of adventures to go on."

I nodded. He's said the same words to me when he'd injured his leg and I thought I might lose him. Hearing them back filled me with a warmth that radiated from my aching heart.

"So, since you have been able to stay awake for more than five minutes, I figure I should fill you in on what's been going on. We have Emerson imprisoned. Darius went missing after the armies scattered. When Rhijn hasn't been in here with you, he and Uden have been helping round up Emerson's creatures, who've been lingering around the keep. They sense she is still here."

I made a face to show I didn't understand, and a knife across the throat gesture.

"Oh, Rhijn didn't want to kill them. He said it wasn't really their fault they were monsters. He thought if we caught them, we could release them once we'd cleared everyone from this Realm so they'd have a home. Let's see, what else? Oh, Malik and Seeley have been checking on you as much as I have. You've had a few brief conversations with Malik, though you probably don't remember.

My eyes went wide.

"Yes, he told me about the mental connection you have. And yes, I demanded that he teach me how to do it. No luck so far. You can probably do it with Malik because he's your half-brother. I assume that is what you've been doing with Rhijn too. The connection between you because of the stones."

I nodded.

"Yeah, that is what I figured. Alrun is free, though he was in pretty bad shape when we pulled him from the prison. He's recovering, though. We've decided to use Seabrook as the base of operations for now on this side of the Swath. Carina, who I still haven't formally met, is making preparations with Torin, Malik and Kellis to organize how they are going to bring the first groups of Skyborne back. We're getting a bird from her and your mother daily."

I yawned, and winced.

"You okay?" he asked.

I pointed at my throat.

There was a knock at the door, and Rhijn slipped back in. He was freshly bathed and had a clean set of clothes on.

I didn't think they'd bathed me yet. Probably only a warm rag washdown. I smelled myself and cringed.

"She ate?" Rhijn asked Conall as if I wasn't there.

Yes, she ate. And she'd really like a bath, too. My eyelids drooped, betraying me.

"I'll arrange for you to have a bath next time you wake up, okay?" Rhijn said, walking over and placing a hand on my throat. The burning sensation lessened and he moved, hovering his hands over my body. Conall slipped out of the room, and I slipped from consciousness.

⁓

I opened my eyes to a gaping maw and two large nostrils that were scenting me. Honestly, I figured it was a dream at first, so I didn't have the urge to yell.

Uden leaned up. *The hero has awoken*, his voice echoed in the small chamber. I scanned the room. Malik was seated in the corner, thank the Makers.

Tell him I remember my promise, I thought to Malik.

Exactly how many creatures do you owe favors to? Malik teased, before he complied and assured Uden not to worry. I stuck my tongue out at him.

We spoke through our minds, catching up, as Uden sat patiently waiting. I made a point to congratulate him on his and Seeley's bond, and promised to help with planning their commitment ceremony when we were safely back in Idia. He'd been taken aback by my power display, probably bringing up old memories, so I was working hard to stay in his good graces. At least he was still joking with me.

Have I ever told you about the realm of my kind? Uden asked.

I shook my head.

You will need to have knowledge about it to return us there, will you not?

I raised my shoulders to Malik, who also shrugged. I wasn't sure how Rhijn did it with the creatures that had landed in Idia. He didn't learn about their realms, so I assumed the answer was no. To transport that many creatures, though, Rhijn and I would likely have to travel with them, so I was curious what his realm was like. Besides, it would be a welcome distraction from the ache in my chest because of the loss of my youngest sister.

I must have fallen asleep during Uden's stories about his realm. I think I may have even dreamed of them as if he'd kept talking while I slept. I awoke in a cold sweat as the dream became too similar to the one I'd had before in Arborvale.

I sat up, looking around the vacant room. I got out of bed, determined to have that bath that had been promised to me. Passing the window on limbs steadier than they'd been in days, something caught my eye. A crater had formed in the distance beyond the wall of Seabrook proper and webbed veins of collapsed earth crawled in every direction.

"It's impressive, isn't it?" Rhijn asked, stepping in the door.

"That's what I did?" I knew the answer, but I supposed I asked, whispering to try out my voice. It still hurt, but at least I recognized it as mine.

"You should probably keep speaking to me with your mind if you can. Keep resting it. You'll probably feel like speaking more in the morning," Rhijn instructed.

He saw me look longingly at the bathroom.

"I still owe you a bath. Let me go find an attendant," he said, turning to leave.

I don't want an attendant, Rhijn, I thought. *Can't you help me?*

There was nothing sexual about the request, but he stiffened all the same.

I don't know the Skyborne here, and I'd rather have someone I am comfortable with to make *sure I don't fall asleep in the tub. And I can wash myself, so I'm not asking that. Please just sit with me?*

"I can go find Conall or Malik," he protested.

But I want it to be you.

Rhijn didn't say anything as he stomped into the bathroom seemingly resigned and plunged his hand into the water, heating it.

I dug some salts out of a drawer and sprinkled them into the water. As they dissolved, the scent of musk and oranges floated up into the air. I grabbed a few more bottles I'd learned the purpose of from an attendant called May the first time I was here. I'd inquired after her, but I'd learned that when Emerson had attacked, many fled, and she was believed to be among them. Others stayed and fell under her rule, with little other option. Of course, she'd brought her own cooks and personal attendants with her. She wasn't stupid.

By the time I had towels and clothes sitting beside the tub, Rhijn had the water warmed. I unlaced the nightgown, and Rhijn turned away as I let it slip off my shoulders and fall to the floor in a crumpled mess. I stepped into the tub, sighing at the hot water. It was perfect, pricking my skin and soothing my aching body.

When I was submerged fully in the cloudy water, I told Rhijn he could turn around. He walked over to a smaller window instead, looking out as I took my time soaking.

How will you know if I drown if you can't see me?

"I figure you'll make a plunk or some other unflattering sound," he scoffed.

After I'd soaked my fill, I lathered my hair and took a final dunk to rinse the suds. Sighing, I wrenched myself from the tub. Rhijn kept his back turned as I toweled my hair off and rubbed creams into my dry skin. I stuck my hand in front of his face. "Doesn't this smell wonderful?"

"Your fingers are shriveled up prunes. I didn't think you were ever going to get out of there."

I picked up the bottle of cream. "This one is pear and honeysuckle. Do you like it?"

"Yes, it's fine." He scratched the back of his neck and shifted on the stool he'd brought into the bathroom when he'd gotten tired of standing.

I wrapped the towel tight around my torso and walked over to the bed, picking up a piece of cheese from a platter that was delivered.

This is tasty. You should try it, I thought to him.

"I *should* go back to my room." He watched me plop a piece of fruit into my mouth, sucking the juice off my finger. "Makers, why do you have to make everything like that?"

Stay with me. It was clear this towel and my wet hair were doing things to the male side of him, and I found I enjoyed that. Wanted it even. Horrible things had happened, yet I still found myself wanting. Maybe he'd been right, and I'd always want when I was around him.

I huffed, setting the platter on the bed as a gesture of good faith, and got up. Digging through my pack that had been deposited in this room, I pulled out something to throw on and went to the bathroom.

He was sitting on the bed snacking when I came out. I walked over and plopped on the opposite side, reaching for another piece of cheese.

"As if that's any better." Rhijn eyed the loose white undershirt I had on.

I'm certainly not putting that frumpy smock of a nightgown back on, besides the fact it's filthy and smells.

And it made me think of the prison frock I'd been forced to wear during the weeks I'd spend in the Eastdow prison as I awaited my fate, though I wasn't going to tell Rhijn that. I shivered at the memory.

"You don't have any pants on." His gaze darted from my short hem-line to the floor.

And you have seen me in far less.

"How are you feeling?" he asked, changing the subject.

Seems like the longer I'm awake, the stronger I feel.

"I'm glad. Another good night's sleep and you should be nearly back to normal." He set the plate off to the side of the bed and crawled under the covers. "What are you waiting on? Climb in."

I didn't hesitate to curl up under the arm he offered.

I woke up with one of the moons flooding in through the window. I had been sleeping hard. Groggily, I tugged on Rhijn's shirt, waking him up.

"What?" he asked.

"Off," I whispered, my voice notably stronger.

"What?" he asked.

"Take this off. It's scratchy," I said.

He sat up and surveyed me. "Makers, Nayla, where's your shirt?"

"Floor," I grumbled, still tugging at his shirt. I flipped the thin strap of the bralette I still wore. "This is fine. This—" I pointed to his tunic. "—itchy."

He groaned exaggeratedly and pulled the tunic over his head, his defined torso deliciously flexing as he did.

"Thank you." I pulled myself toward him, absorbing the comfort of our skin touching. I ran my hand up over his chest, to his shoulder, then down his firm bicep.

"Nayla," he scolded, his voice deepening, "you need to sleep."

"Oh, Rhijn," I whined, "you're no fun."

His chest rumbled beneath my head, and he wrapped his arm around me, pulling me closer. "If only you understood."

CHAPTER THIRTY-FOUR

I OBSERVED RHIJN AS he awoke. He seemed so peaceful when he slept. And him being here had helped me cope with the loss of my sister. It still hurt, and there were moments when I'd be taken to my knees from the pain, but it was becoming manageable thanks to my friends and him. I wanted to reach over and touch his beautiful mouth, but I figured he wouldn't appreciate the gesture.

His icy eyes fluttered open and narrowed on me. "What are you doing?" he asked in a low, gravelly voice.

"Watching you," I said.

"Why?" he sounded out slowly, hopefully maybe?

"I enjoy looking at you," I said, which was apparently the wrong thing to say.

He got up from the bed, pulling away from me more aggressively than he had the morning before. I could almost see the walls going back up now that he'd sensed I was healed.

"I don't know why you act like that when we're both consenting adults."

"Nothing I do around you is consensual, Nayla."

I froze. "What does that even mean? You're not making any sense," I eyed him as he tugged the tunic over his head.

"I *love* that you still don't get it," he bit back.

"Get what?" I threw my hands into the air.

"Look, I think you've healed enough to take breakfast with everyone else. I'm going to my room to freshen up. I don't think you'll need my healing again, so I'll plan to sleep in my own room tonight."

"I'm sorry, I didn't realize I was such a burden to you," I said, strutting across the room in the bralette and underwear I'd slept in.

His gaze tracked me, unfazed, cold. "There are still injured who need to be healed."

"There are still injured who need healing?" I asked him, incredulous. "Really?"

He nodded. If that was true, I did seem selfish, expecting so much of his time. Had I been aware, I'd probably offered to help, though I was still healing myself.

"Only a few," he confessed.

"And the healers can't help them?"

"They can, but I want to."

He enjoyed it. Rhijn enjoyed using this power to help others in the most direct way possible, healing. And it made him feel needed. Makers, he was the worst, and too perfect at the same time.

"Well, let them deal with it because there is something else we need to do," I said, storming into the bathroom, determined to uphold my promise as soon as I was strong enough.

Whispers erupted when I entered the central meeting hall where I'd first met Seeley, Femi and Alrun, which they'd converted into an infirmary. The first thing I wanted to do upon leaving my room was see those who were still injured.

I spent all morning walking down the rows of cots, stopping to thank the brave Skyborne who'd fought for us, for themselves, really. I saw Rhijn come in after lunch and hurriedly make his way across the room. He stopped at a cot across the expanse and leaned over the male lying on it. I watched him move his hands over the male, and smile at the result he sensed. He glanced up, making eye contact with me briefly across the rows of cots before returning his focus. My heart stuttered unexpectedly.

"Nayla," a small hand grabbed my wrist, interrupting my racing thoughts.

I looked down at the female, whose quiet voice had beckoned me. The unique honey hew of her hair was familiar to me. I studied her pale face and plain features, trying to remember where I recognized her from.

"I'm so sorry I couldn't save her." Fresh tears welled up and trickled down the healer's cheeks, one which was marred with a nasty scar.

Recognition glimmered at the edge of my mind. She was the field healer who'd been with Jude when she died.

"May I sit?" I steeled myself and gestured to a stool sitting next to her cot. She nodded eagerly. "What's your name?"

"Becca. I'm from Sundale. I came to Eastdow when Balene put out the call for healers to join the army. She said I was good, so she put me with the field healers. But I couldn't do enough." Red blotches bloomed across her face and she rubbed the sleeve of her gown across her eyes.

"What happened to you, Becca?" I studied her hands, taking them in my own. "May I?" I gestured to her sleeve.

"Okay," she whimpered.

I pushed up the garment and ran my finger across the crisscrossing scars that ran up her forearm.

"Emerson's creatures," she sniffed. "Almost all of the battlefield healers have them. So do most of the soldiers… who survived. The other healers believe we will be left with these scars. We had to heal the most life-threatening wounds first. It took days. These cuts have healed over themselves by our body's natural processes and the salves we've put on them. We only used our power to heal the ones that were too deep. To remove the scarring, the old wounds would need to be reopened." Becca clenched and unclenched her fist.

"Healers are in cots every so often you'll see." She pointed to a few cots where Skyborne in similar gowns as hers were sleeping. "We are alternating rest breaks until we feel rejuvenated enough to keep going. I should probably get ready for my next shift." She swung her legs off the bed so our knees were nearly touching.

"Becca," I stopped her. "Would you let me try to remove one of your scars? Just to see if it can be done?" My throat tightened as I waited for her response.

She studied my eyes, bringing her hand to the long scar that ran from the corner of her eye to her jaw protectively. "Not this one, not yet. But you can try on the others." She rolled her sleeve back up, thrusting her forearm toward me. The muscles ticked in her jaw as if she was bracing for more pain.

I held her hand in my left as I thumbed across a particularly jagged scar, closing my eyes. "It won't hurt." Her grip loosened. I sensed the damaged and misaligned units. It differed from when I healed a fresh wound, but I thought I could do it. I focused on the unmarred skin around the mangled flesh and restructured it until it felt smooth and ordered. I exhaled, opening my eyes.

Becca and I studied her forearm where fresh skin had replaced the twisted red line that had been there before.

"Oh," she said, running the pads of her fingers across it. "It worked. I didn't think it would work... I should go."

"Okay. Please tell the other healers, if they would like help with their scars, I'm happy to remove them."

"Yeah, okay. Thanks, Nayla." Becca stood and scurried away to check on her patients. I sat on the stool, stunned by her reaction. I supposed we were all a little traumatized and in need of the therapies from the specialized healers who mended the mind. Shrugging, I got up and went to find Conall to see if he needed my help with anything.

Loud boots stomped down the hallway, heading away from me. Whoever they belonged to must have charged out of a room nearby and sped off in the opposite direction, piquing my interest. I raced to catch up with whoever it was.

"What do you mean Emerson isn't in her cell?" Conall's voice boomed.

When I caught up with them, he and Malik were moving swiftly toward the prison in the lower section of the keep.

"She was just gone. The lock looks tinkered with, but none of the other prisoners are talking. We still haven't rounded up A1. We have most of the ones that haven't fled back to Monterra. But A1 must have sensed her and picked the lock."

"Damn it. Still no sign of Darius either?"

"Nothing," Malik answered.

"I thought Nayla said he and Emerson were involved. You don't think he came to try to rescue her?" Conall asked.

"Not his style. He's a coward at heart," Malik answered.

I thought of the last I'd seen of Darius hanging back behind the lines, aiming his crossbow at Rhijn, who'd been relentlessly charging toward him. It's how he'd been able to slip away, by lingering on the fringes.

Emerson, on the other hand, had accidentally caged herself between us and the great wall surrounding Seabrook, so Uden had no trouble sniffing her out and bringing her in.

"We found her." An excited guard brushed past me into the hall. Conall and Malik spun to meet him.

"Jax, where was she?" Conall grabbed the young male by the shoulders. It was amazing how he remembered every single one of their names.

"Well, sir, she's still there. On the parapet. Follow me." He took off hurriedly in the direction he'd come from.

Conall noticed me. "Nayla, you're up."

I fell into line with them. "I told you, you should have just killed her and been done with it."

"Rhijn convinced us otherwise." Conall gave me a pointed look.

"He is having a little too much influence on you these days, don't you think?" I returned the gesture.

Malik shook his head. "I'm with Nayla. I don't see what the point of keeping her alive is."

"Malik, even my father agreed with Rhijn's logic. To integrate with the Idian society, we're going to have to start adopting some of their ways, so why not start now?" Conall asked.

"We should have started right after you let me kill Emerson." I said, pursing my lips at him. "You *still could?*"

Conall stopped, grabbing my arm. "We voted Nayla. And even if we took your vote to execute her into account, you lost. End of story."

Jax cleared his throat, and we all turned to him. "She's up there." He pointed up a stairwell. "We had her cornered on the balcony, but she climbed on the wall," he explained, leading us up the stairs which opened directly on the terrace Conall and I had once danced upon. The same one where Emerson had taken Femi's life a month earlier.

Across the expanse, several guards were standing around her, but at a distance. She was sitting on the wall, feet dangling over the edge, humming.

"She said if we got any closer, she'd jump, so I went to find you since you said she was to be kept alive until her trial, sir."

"Thank you, Jax. You did the right thing." Conall turned to me. "What do we do now?" His voice was hushed so the guards wouldn't hear.

I rolled my eyes. "Let me handle this."

I walked across the terrace and Emerson startled at the sound of approaching boots. She stiffened and turned, mouth open, ready to yell more threats, but she froze when she saw me. Then a feline grin spread across her face.

"Can I come sit with you?" I asked her, my voice monotone.

She nodded, and I crawled up on the wall, dangling my feet off like her. I sat far enough away that I was just out of reach, in case she tried something.

"They told me you were alive, but healing. I asked for you." She batted her lashes as if her actions hadn't led to the death of hundreds a few days earlier.

"What are you doing, Emerson?" I let out a long breath and cocked my head to the side, watching her.

"None of this would have happened if you weren't such a traitorous bitch," she said, crossing her arms, looking away.

"Where is A1?" I asked, not taking her bait.

"Haven't seen him. He's probably abandoned me like everyone else." Emerson sighed, and a tear trickled down her dirt smudged cheek. She reached into her pocket and pulled out a hairpin, showed it to me, and tossed it over the edge.

I shot a glance back at Conall for the oversight.

Emerson was finger combing her hair when I glanced back at her. "What are they going to do with me now? I'm told they won't kill me. Something to do with your new lover and the laws of the Idians."

"*I* would kill you, if that makes you feel any better," I said, giving her a smile that I knew didn't reach my eyes.

She chuckled grimly, the normal spark in her eyes dimmed under heavy eyelids. "I'd probably let you. At least I wouldn't have to hear them anymore…" Emerson muttered that last part under her breath and I narrowed my eyes in her direction trying to understand what she was talking about. She reached toward me across the wall and scooted close enough to touch the hand I was leaning on. "Do you think I'm that unredeemable?" Her pretty face was pinched into an uncomfortable-looking squint.

"We both know you are, but the leadership here doesn't seem to agree. So, prove me wrong and let them take you back into custody."

She winced at my words, but nodded. "Fine."

I gestured for the soldiers to approach. "*Slowly,*" I mouthed.

Out of the corner of my eye, I caught movement darting forward from a pillar a few steps behind the approaching guards. Alrun stepped out of the shadow and pushed through the guards, using power to enhance his speed.

"Hey! What are you doing?" a guard shouted. "Oof!"

"Stop!" I cried, but it happened so fast. My eyes darted to the colorless male standing behind Emerson, then to his hands, which were white knuckled around the handle of the broadsword he'd lifted off the guard. The male was now writhing around on the ground, clutching his groin.

Emerson dropped my gaze to peer down at the tip of the blade protruding from her chest. In a few seconds Alrun had stolen the guard's sword, impaled Emerson from behind, and none of us had caught what he was doing quick enough to stop him. My hand cramped as Emerson squeezed it, and she gave me a crazed smile, teeth gritted through the pain. "You're right," she bit out. Her tone transformed into another one of the identities who lived inside Emerson, which I was only now starting to piece together. "I really wouldn't have been redeemable." Blood trickled down the edge of her mouth, and she scrutinized the tip of the blade, running her finger along its edge, cutting it.

I watched as the cut healed in a flash. Alrun must have seen it too, because he forced the blade to the hilt, and gave a shove. Emerson tipped forward, jagged nails grabbing for purchase at the ledge and my wrist.

I grabbed her sleeve, but it ripped as she slipped from the edge. She didn't scream. Only thudded when she hit the stone street below.

Alrun moved forward to lean over the edge to view the mangled female and the pool of blood growing around her. He looked at me with glassy amber eyes.

I shrugged. "Let me guess, you were another one of the no votes?"

The corner of Alrun's full mouth ticked up and I winked in response.

Malik approached beside me and leaned over the edge, looking at the gore that was Emerson. *You probably could have saved her if you'd not let her fall.*

I tried.

You are still a terrible liar, Nayla.

I studied the claw marks on my wrist where she'd tried to keep hold of me, the last lifeline she had.

Conall turned his head to the sky, raking his hands through his ash brown hair. "What a mess. Jax, send someone to go get that, *her*, cleaned up. Nayla—"

"I'm going to go take a nap," I said, hopping down off the wall.

"Nayla," Conall pleaded, but I held my hand up as I walked past, silencing him, and I escaped through the corridor which led to the guest suites.

⤜

A few hours later, there was a light tap at the door. "Can I come in?"

Rhijn slipped his head in the door.

I gestured over my shoulder to his spot on the bed and turned back over to face the window, feeling his weight settle upon the bed a moment later.

He leaned over me and grabbed my marred wrist. "What happened to you?"

"Emerson," I said, rolling on my back.

"I heard." Concern filled his eyes. "Did you eat dinner?"

"I'm not hungry. What are they gonna do with Alrun?"

"Torin convinced us all to sweep it under the rug. Truthfully, nobody faults him after what happened to his wife. I probably would have done the same if I'd seen her execute my own wife."

"You would have taken vengeance?" I asked, unconvinced.

"Yes." His jaw clenched as he studied my face, like he wanted to touch it or he was wrestling a thought. "Are you okay?"

"I'm tired, Rhijn." I buried my face in the pillow.

Rhijn stroked his firm hand up and down my back. "I know you tried to do the right thing, but you couldn't save her."

I jerked up and turned to face him. His face was the perfect combination of angles and smooth planes, I thought as the moonlight streamed in through the window, highlighting it. I had the weirdest feeling of saudade as I looked at him. I shook it off before it overwhelmed me.

"I didn't try to do the right thing, Rhijn. I chose to let her fall. To let Alrun finish it. I probably could have saved her or helped her heal herself from that sword wound, but I swore I'd never let her hurt anyone I loved again. You all voted, but eventually I would have killed her. And I wouldn't have been sorry. I'm glad Alrun got to do it though."

I was shaking as I turned to face the wall. I lifted my unsteady fingers to the scratches on my wrist and healed them so they were no longer even pink. I couldn't bear to see the judgement in his painfully beautiful eyes. But I couldn't lie to him either.

His body shifted, and his weight rose off the bed. The door closed quietly. I was alone again with my thoughts.

Some time later, the bed moved as Rhijn sat on it and crawled under the covers. He didn't put his arms around me, and after a few moments, I detected slow, rhythmic breathing that told me he was asleep. I looked behind me. Rhijn was facing the opposite wall. His broad shoulders were drawn up to his ears and the muscles in his back appeared stiff, like he was flexing. He seemed so tense.

I held my hand a measure away from his lower back and released my healing energy. His body notably relaxed, and he shifted on his stomach.

I turned back to the window and watched the second and third moons come up, knowing eventually I'd never see them again.

CHAPTER THIRTY-FIVE

RHIJN WAS GONE when I awoke. I reached my hand across the now cool side of the bed he'd been occupying for days now. I couldn't figure out what had shifted between us—on my side, anyway. He seemed to oscillate between a light camaraderie, then exasperation. Last night it was disappointment.

My grief over Jude was still raw and palpable, but the gnawing at my very being had lessened somehow. And he and Conall had been jovial, friendly even.

For the first day in a while, I was excited to be up. Maybe Becca shared my success removing her scar with the other healers, and I could do some good. I washed up, got dressed and headed down to breakfast, already smelling the cooking sausages wafting through the air as I walked across the courtyard to the kitchens.

Seeley, who Malik had convinced Rhijn to portal back to Eastdow to fetch, stood by a griddle being heated by the hot stone slab beneath it, scrambling eggs and laughing at something another cook said.

"Can I help?" I asked.

He turned and gave me a Seeley smile. Handing his spatula off to another Skyborne, he grabbed a bowl and started filling it with delicious-looking breakfast selections. Seeley shoved it into my hands, eyeing me pointedly. "Yes, by eating this."

Seeley shooed me out the door, and my shoulders slumped. No one needed my help. I took my dish and roamed the tables, looking for a friendly face, feeling rather useless. My mouth watered, so I took a bite off a piece of a water-fowl sausage link as I scanned the crowd.

"Becca!" I called out, jogging over to meet the healer, who was carrying a bowl of eggs and grits to a nearby table. "Can I join you?"

"Hi Nayla." Becca smiled with a lighter air about her than I'd noted before and set her steaming bowl on the table. Days were becoming easier to bear. "Sure," she said and motioned to the space on the bench next to where she'd sat.

"Did you tell the other healers I could heal their scars? None of them have come to me yet." I glanced between her and the other Skyborne, who I assumed were healers, already sitting at her table.

"I apologize for eavesdropping, but Becca did tell us. She said you could remove them, and were eager to do it," a young male healer with ruddy brown hair interjected.

"And none of you want my help? You want to keep your scars?" I scanned the table, slowly shaking my head.

The healers fidgeted with their forks and moved their food around their bowls, avoiding eye contact with me.

"What is it you're not saying?" I asked, setting my own fork down with a clang. "Speak freely, please."

The ruddy haired one lifted a freckled face toward me. "We want your help, Nayla."

"Good. Okay, then—"

"We need your help to bring us *home*," he cut me off. "You have more important things you should use your power for than healing superficial scars. Besides, a lot of us healers consider them badges of honor or they remind us of those we've lost."

I looked at Becca's cheek, understanding dawning.

"Has anyone told you the Swath has already moved past the traveler's inn? The healers will be among the last groups transported, because our skills may be needed here until the end. We are ready to go to Idia."

"And you're ready for me to get to work making that happen?" I asked, pausing so he'd offer his name.

"Peetr. And yes. Please." The rest of the healers paused, darting their stares between their daring representative and their realm's Chosen One.

A sheepish grin spread across my face, and I felt more than a little guilty. "You're right. There's just one thing I need to do first." I got up from the table, abandoning my half-eaten bowl, and trudged down a side street which led out of the city.

⸎

"Rhijn, it's time," I called out.

He was directing cleanup out on the battlefield. It had been an argument between Torin and Conall, whether the enemies' dead would be buried or left to decay under the heat of the light star which radiated year-round down on Seabrook. Rhijn had sided with Conall, so here they were, digging graves for dead Skyborne in slate grey and blood red.

He pulled a cloth from his back pocket and wiped it across his brow. "Makers, this place is a furnace. Why are you running?"

I grabbed his sleeve, tugging him back toward the keep. "Come on," I huffed between breaths.

"Can't you tell I'm busy?"

"You groaning every time you see me is getting old, you know. I have a promise to keep, and I need your help to do it."

He stilled, studying my eyes.

I nodded knowing he understood. "Today. We do it today." We had to before I lost the nerve. If I were being honest with myself, the prospect of what we needed to do first was terrifying. There was an entire realm of them. I shuddered at the thought.

Rhijn stuffed the cloth back into his pocket, and jogged off to the nearest Skyborne, who seemed to agree with whatever Rhijn was saying to him.

When he returned to my side, a familiar power licked across my skin and slipped beneath, searching. I got chills at the knowledge that power was Rhijn's, running through my body scanning my energy. "You're ready?"

"I am. I mean, I *did* receive a nudge in the right direction from an overly blunt healer, but he was right. I'm ready. They're fine without us now. Let's go."

"Fine." Rhijn successfully repressed the smile trying to escape his lips, but I caught the subtle twinkle in his eye before he took off jogging for the keep, not waiting on me. I shook my head, laughing, and sprinted to catch up.

◆

A few hours later we found Conall in the hallway, and led him down to the kitchens, where we filled our packs with rations.

"So, I can see you two are going somewhere?" Conall asked, glancing between us.

"You keep making sure I'm aware that you know her so well, you practically know what she's going to do before she even does." Rhijn gave Conall a teasing nudge on the shoulder to which I couldn't help but roll my eyes at.

"It's true," Conall said, with a jokingly antagonistic gleam in his eye.

"Then you understand where we're going," Rhijn replied.

"Makers, how long will you be gone?" Conall asked. His features had dropped into a concerned grimace.

"We only plan to be there overnight, or long enough to revive our power. Transporting that many creatures over such a great distance will be a substantial drain, so it will take some rest before we attempt our return."

"Knowing you Rhijn, I suspect you've already worked this out. How can it be safe with creatures like Uden inhabiting the place?" Conall asked.

I cleared my throat. "Are you suggesting I've not thought far enough ahead to be cautious?"

Conall raised his eyebrows. "That's not what I'm saying, though that's not a strong point for you these days."

"Uden told me they don't feed off animals there, but drink a substance produced from the plants that blanket their realm." I thought of the gelatinous substance I'd seen the creature lap up from the goblet in my nightmare. "He said that is their evolved diet. They actually tried to drink the sap from the trees in the Swath at first, but it made them sick. After experimenting, they found they could eat the animals here for sustenance, including Skyborne, though it wasn't nearly as nourishing for them. Also, he said they will watch over us." I mounted my fists on my hips in defiance.

| 297 |

"I see," Conall said, "and you'll come back here to Seabrook?"

"Yes, but if it takes longer, I don't want you to worry, okay?" I pressed.

He nodded. A stable hand walked into the kitchen and startled at our presence.

"You busy, Colt?" Conall asked the young male.

"No, sir. I was going to grab something to eat and brush down the horses, but I can do it later." Colt waited for Conall's instruction, his bulging eyes flicking between Rhijn and I.

"Good. Grab whatever you were headed for, then go find the creature, Uden. Have him gather his kind at the traveler's inn immediately. Then meet us at the stables. I'm going to have you escort these two to the Swath so you can bring their horses back."

Colt gulped down a bite he'd taken. "Yes, sir." He hurried from the room.

Conall turned to us. "Well, where next?"

Conall helped us load our packs on two horses and we were saying our goodbyes when Malik and Seeley rounded the corner.

"You weren't going to tell us goodbye?" Seeley had his arms crossed and was looking aloofly over his shoulder. "What if you never come back? And to think the last words we would have spoken were about a supply of salted cod!"

"Oh Seeley, you are too dramatic." I pulled him into a tight embrace and he had to wriggle his crossed arms out from between us to return the hug. "I'm trying to do this before I lose the nerve."

Rhijn squeezed my shoulder. "She'll be fine. You have my word."

Malik grabbed me and pulled me into him. *I'm proud you're my sister.*

Does this mean you have officially forgiven me for stabbing you? I thought.

I suppose it does. And now we will definitely win any brother-sister argument comparisons, because I doubt many sibling pairs have stabbed each other.

I laughed into his chest.

Why did you get on board with me so easily? I thought, looking up at him. *It's not my fault you had some preconceived expectation of me to be this shining hero. That's a lot of pressure.*

Malik smiled and brushed a lock of hair out of my face as he looked down at me. *I guess I saw you as who I wanted you to be. The hope I wanted to believe in.*

I blinked a few times to keep the tears at bay. *That is awfully sentimental coming from you.*

"Be safe, Nayla," Malik said aloud, giving me a final squeeze.

"I will, brother. I won't let you down again." I stuck my foot into the stirrup when a big hand closed around my bicep and I was pulled into a beefy chest.

"Makers, Conall." I shifted in his embrace so I could look up at him. Two fat tears dripped from each of his eyes. I pulled my hands free and wiped them away with my thumbs. "What's wrong?"

He wiped a third that had spilled over the edge and replaced his arm back around my waist. "It's always been me and you, you know? I can't wait until you can get rid of the ember and it goes back to that, because I feel like I'm losing you," he whispered so the others wouldn't hear him.

I think my heart cracked a little. I wanted to comfort him, but I was afraid nothing I could say would. Something irrevocable had happened, broken over a tipping point, and not even I had the power to stop it now. "I love you, Conall."

He sniffed and gave me a sheepish grin. "I know you do. I love you too."

"I'll be back, okay?"

Leaning down, he kissed my forehead. "Okay. Well, I guess I'd better let you go."

I nodded, patting his chest. I walked over to my horse and took the reins from Malik. Launching myself up into the saddle, I gave them a last glance before nudging the animal into a gallop in the direction of the Swath.

CHAPTER THIRTY-SIX

I FELT BAD FOR how hard I was riding the black mare, but she had a strong heart and seemed to be enjoying the sprint as much as I was. After we'd gotten out of the city and a distance across the plain, I let Rhijn catch up. I'd needed the ride. To feel the wind blowing my hair back and no one to witness the tears that were streaming down my cheeks. I knew Conall was hurting, but I had to go.

"What was that about?" Rhijn asked, cautiously trotting up beside me.

"Oh, just my life being one giant pain in my ass." I turned toward him, exposing my tear-stained face. I could tell if I didn't get it together soon, I'd be full ugly crying in front of him.

"Do you love him?" Rhijn appeared to be holding his breath.

"Of course, I love him. He's my brother. What type of dumb question is that?!" I shook my head and pressed forward.

"Oh, I see." He looked like he wanted to reach out to me.

"Perfect," I growled. "If you see everything so well, please enlighten me then."

Before Rhijn could speak we caught sight of Uden, who Conall had sent ahead to ready the creatures. They were perched on and around the now abandoned traveler's inn.

You are truly here to take us home? Uden asked, tapping his claws across his cracked lips, as if I might be here to restructure our arrangement again.

"Truly," I said. "Are you ready?"

A tremor ran across the creature's face. An odd sort of melancholy washed over me knowing after Rhijn and I deposited him in his realm, that would be the last time I'd see his terrifying, yet familiar, face.

Rhijn and I dismounted and gave our horses to Colt, who'd finally caught up to us. He gave me a strange look and took the horses, moving away from the inn and back toward Seabrook in a slow trot.

Uden gurgled commands to his creatures, and they responded, gathering around him. I tried to imagine what he must be feeling, thinking of the similar experience I'd had a few months earlier when I'd led my friends from this realm to Idia.

Rhijn took my hand in his, threading our fingers together and brought it to his cheek so that the back of my hand was touching his skin. "I'm sorry. I didn't mean to assume I understood how you feel. Are you going to be okay?" he asked, kissing my palm. It was the tenderest gesture, and my heart melted a bit.

I nodded, wondering what I'd have to do to make him want to kiss me again.

Uden cleared his throat. *We're ready.*

I watched Rhijn. He released my hand and gave me a defrosted smile.

"I'm going to be just fine," I answered him. I walked over to Uden. "You nervous?" I asked him.

Nervous? he echoed.

"Yeah, you know. Jittery, afraid of what we'll find when we arrive there," I clarified.

No, I am not nervous. I am... Uden hesitated for a long moment, considering. *I am at peace.*

"Good," I said, "because it's time."

We took the stones from our pockets, touched them and waited.

When our arms were ready, we drew the circle around the creatures of the Swath. I didn't know exactly how getting them to their home realm was going to work, but I couldn't help but sense there was something else at play as I moved around them. I made it around to Rhijn and his white half of the portal. I pulled my hand up, stopping mine.

"Go ahead." I pointed at the edge, urging him to complete the circle this time. He did, and the dark and light began to draw together. We stood inside the circle, and I grabbed his hand. He stared down at me with such clarity in his cool blue eyes.

"I think we're getting pretty good at this," I said, and winked up at him, before everything went dark.

EPILOGUE

A S DARKNESS OVERTOOK them, a thousand thoughts raced through Rhijn's mind. But all of them led back to the captivating female gripping his hand like it was her only connection to life.

His stomach twisted at the sensation of weightlessness, and the thought of what the new world called Uden, which had evolved such curious creatures as those traveling between realms with them, would be like. Or maybe it was fluttering because of the way her eyes glinted as she looked up at him when they'd connected the portal.

He'd accidentally let her back in—because she'd almost gotten herself killed. But he knew what she wanted from him. *Nothing.* She'd made it clear she didn't want what was brewing between them for any more than a passing romance, if that. Once they got back to Idia, he'd have to remember to re-establish the distance between them before the inevitable happened and his heart was the one to pay the price.

The creature called A1 flapped its peach fleshy wings furiously, hovering over the pile of bodies which still weren't buried in the graves the survivors in Seabrook had been tirelessly digging. Something below was causing two decaying corpses to stir. A1 zeroed in on the slight movement. Its bulbous head teetered back and forth as it zipped circles around the shifting bodies. Sniffing the air, it locked onto what it had been searching for.

There were no other ears in the vicinity to hear the creature screak, "Mother!"

AUTHOR'S NOTE

Thank you for taking the time to read Realm of the Skyborne. I had a blast writing this book as I got to know the characters on a deeper level, and introduce some new ones—particularly a certain blue eyed someone from Nayla's dreams. I can't wait for you to see what's next in their journey for the final book of the series.

If you enjoyed the second installment in Nayla's story, even a little, I would be honored if you jumped on Amazon or goodreads and left Realm of the Skyborne a review. I know leaving a review can be time consuming, but it helps us indie authors more than you know and may help other readers become exposed to our work.

And again, thank you!!

Find me on Instagram @j.m.waldrop and my website www.jennifermwaldrop.com for:

Character Mood Reels

Name Pronunciation Guide

Updates on my current WIP

Giveaways

and More

ACKNOWLEDGEMENTS

Writing a book is a hell of a journey full of up and downs. Cathartic joy and moments of crippling self-doubt. I am lucky enough to have the support of an amazing family and friend group around me, who read my books, order copies, share it, get it in their local libraries, and listen to me ramble on relentlessly about plot problems, character dilemmas, give writing critiques, and share in my overall excitement. These lovely people include the best husband a girl could ask for, Max, my consistently positive and encouraging sister, Kristen, my enthusiastic mother, Karen, and my super supportive friends, Becky, Chris, Shona, and Angelica.

A group of beta readers have made an undeniable positive impact on Realm of the Skyborne. Their feedback was spot on and this book is far better due to the feedback from the following people: Megan K. Hill (@_megan_kat), Anakha Ashok (@iawkwardturtle), Jennifer Becker (@dreaminfiction), Brittney Green (@our.bookish.reads), Mari Gallmeyer, Karen Heid, and Jacob Flowers-Olnowich.

Finally, I am grateful to have worked with an outstanding editor, Roxana Coumans of Roth Notions and proofreader, Belle Manuel.

ABOUT THE AUTHOR

Jennifer is an artist, small business owner and author of the new novel Realm of the Banished. She holds a Bachelor of Fine Arts with a minor in Art History from the University of Central Oklahoma. Jennifer enjoys creating and paints with that same imaginative stroke throughout her writing.

When she's not writing, you might find her whipping together her favorite dark chocolate mousse, power walking a beach in a tropical destination, or lost in the minutia of one of her excel spreadsheets. Jennifer lives with her husband and two dog children in Oklahoma City.